I've broken every promise I ever made to Hannah Grace Whittaker. But this time, the one I make might be the one that saves her life.

Seven years ago, I told her I'd marry her someday. Instead, I left her behind with a shattered heart—and walked away with a broken one of my own. Now, she's in danger, and I'm the only one who can protect her. She doesn't want me here, doesn't want the memories, the pain, or the past we buried.

But I'll take the hit if it means keeping her safe.

She draws a line between then and now, between protection and anything more. But with every glance, every accidental touch, the need to shield her is battling the deeper ache to have her again—to hold her like she still belongs to me.

I promised I'd never hurt her again.

Now I just need to prove I'm still the man who can keep that promise.

But if I can keep her safe… will she let me fight for her heart, too?

BODYGUARD FOR THE BEAUTY QUEEN

SAFE HAVEN SECURITY
BOOK TWO

BREANNA LYNN

ISBN: 978-1-955359-56-6 (ebook)

ISBN: 978-1-955359-57-3 (paperback)

Cover Design by: Najla Amber, Amber Designs
Photographer: CJC Photography
Model: Joseph McGee

Edited by: Happily Editing Anns

Printed in United States of America

https://breannalynnauthor.com

For Vicki...
For being my sanity 40+ hours a week, my cheerleader, and partner in
crime
Thank you for loving almost all of my characters
(And I won't mention the name of the one you don't)

PROLOGUE

COLE

7 YEARS AGO

"*W*hat's the matter, Honey Girl?" I glance away from the windshield to spy my girlfriend curled up on the opposite side of the truck seat, clutching the door handle and looking like third runner-up in the Miss Mistletoe Creek County Fair Pageant.

But even me using a nickname for her that ordinarily makes her smile only creates a sigh.

Fuck.

I flip on the radio, tuning in to our favorite station as we wind the back roads through the foothills of the Smokies that surround our hometown of Mistletoe Creek, Tennessee. The reception is spotty the farther up we drive, but it fills the silence as I rack my brain and try to figure out how to make our last night together a happy memory rather than a sad one.

I'm going to need that memory to keep me going until I can see her again. Hopefully ten weeks from now when I'm finishing

1

up basic. That's if she can make it out to South Carolina for my graduation.

She's still waiting on the information on when her freshmen move-in date is. I'm so fucking proud of my girl for getting into Vanderbilt.

"I'm fine," she says.

But the normal lyrical cadence to her voice is flat. Robotic.

"Sweetheart, it's been a long time since you weren't snuggled against my side. And the last time you were this quiet was the time you lost your voice at the football game we won against Devil Falls."

I find the turn that's little more than a gap between two of the trees. The path is clear, but only barely fits my old truck. Between the bumps and the trees I've skimmed with my fingers when my window is down, I can't watch for her response.

The trees finally spread out more until they're in my rearview and all that's left in front of us is a vista of Mistletoe Creek. The high school is on the edge of town, quiet now that school is out for the summer, and the rest of the little town nestles around it. It's idyllic and it's charming, but it's too small for what I want in my life. I've grown up here, but I'm not willing to just settle down and be a Volunteer before coming back to work in Dad's distillery. That plan might make sense for Justin and Jared, but I am not like my older brothers.

It's what makes the military so exciting—because it wasn't planned out for me.

I put the truck in park and reach for Hannah Grace's hand to tug her toward me.

"Han."

"Don't."

Fuck. Her voice is thick with tears, and proof of one drops on my hands.

"Sweetheart."

I pull her against my chest, rubbing my hand along her back while she sobs into the cotton of my T-shirt.

The scent of her citrus shampoo tickles my nose, and I take a deep breath.

"It's our last night together, baby. I don't want you to cry."

I don't want this memory.

Already the guilt is enough to have me second-guessing my choice.

"I don't want you to go," she mumbles, the words hard to understand through the tears and hiccuping breaths.

"I know." I drop my lips to her hair and keep the steady rhythm of my hand on her back.

She leans up, those cornflower-blue eyes shiny with tears.

"It didn't feel real before, Cole. I want this to be a dream. To wake up tomorrow and not have to say goodbye." Her lower lip trembles, and she sinks her teeth into it to stop the vibration.

I lift my hand and glide my thumb along the swollen flesh.

"It's not forever," I tell her.

More tears slide under my palm that rests against her cheek.

"I can call you...and write. And it's only ten weeks until graduation."

"It's not the same. I've seen you every day for as long as I can remember. I won't be able to do this"—she runs her hands up my chest— "when you're four hours away."

I try to ignore my body's natural reaction to her touch, but my dick jumps. And since she's almost on top of me, I can't hide it.

"Fuck, Hannah Grace, I'm sorry. I didn't bring you up here for this." I groan and lean my head back against the seat.

Even though *this* is something I've thought about since I hit puberty.

"I know. You've never..."

"No."

I respected Hannah Grace too much to push her to do something she wasn't ready for. I respected my own mama's hand upside the back of my head too. I didn't need any other reason to make her want to use it. Between five kids, she has plenty of her own reasons.

Her expression shifts, the tears only salty trails on her cheeks, while mischief tilts her lips.

"What's that look, Hannah Grace Whittaker?"

It's one that's never boded well for me.

In fact it normally results in one or both of us getting grounded.

It's not like Mom can ground me, since I'm leaving tomorrow morning.

It's an accurate statement, but I'm still hesitant to go along with anything involved in that particular expression on Hannah's face.

The last time had resulted in us launching over a thousand bouncy balls in the high school's auditorium during the county's beauty pageant that Hannah hadn't wanted to participate in. Turns out, it didn't stop the pageant. However, it did end up getting back to both our mamas.

Being grounded and voluntold into helping with the high school's locker clean-out day was a consequence I never wanted to live again. Several lockers hadn't been cleaned out all year—and the lunch bag/science experiments inside had proven it.

"Why did you bring me up here?"

"This is our spot, sweetheart. I couldn't imagine our last date happening anywhere else. My favorite view in this world is this view with you in it."

Reaching forward, I grab my phone off the dash and shake it toward her.

"Come with me," I tell her and open my door.

"No pictures. I'm a mess. I'm all splotchy." She tries to stay in the car, but our connected hands make it easy to tug her out.

"You're not splotchy; you'll always be beautiful to me," I murmur and brush a kiss on the tip of her nose.

Her hands come up and rest against my biceps, her fingers skimming the underside of my arms and coming close to my ticklish spot.

I shy away.

"No, you don't."

"It pays to have known you forever," she tells me and sneaks past my defenses to run her fingers up my side.

I giggle and clear my throat as I wrap my arms around her and hold her to my chest with her hands trapped between us.

"Gotcha," I say.

She moves to her tiptoes and puckers her lips in my direction, and I oblige by covering her mouth with mine.

"Would you please take a picture with me?" My lips tease hers with my question. "I want to have one with me that's recent. That's us. Not made-up for prom. But the real us."

"How do you always know what to say that makes me want to say yes?"

Her question is innocent enough, but I hope there's more truth to it since I have another question to ask her. One more important than to take a picture with me.

I position us so that she's still wrapped in one arm, the vista behind us, and lift the camera to capture one selfie of the two of us smiling.

"How about one with a kiss?" she suggests.

"Hannah Grace!" I hold my phone against my chest, pretending an affront that the older generation in our town has down pat.

Something I will never say to the leaders of that generation—Fern, Fawn, and Merry. Although deep down, I think they enjoy watching young couples in love.

"Stop pretending like you don't want to kiss me, Cole Strickland." She smacks my chest playfully.

I oblige her request for a kiss and lift my camera at just the right time to capture the two of us locked together. I manage to separate us before my hormones take over then pocket my phone.

My fingers brush the velvet box in my pocket, and I suck in a deep breath as Hannah turns in my arms to focus on the view at our feet.

I clear my throat again, swallowing the lump of nerves that wants to take up residence on my vocal cords.

"I'm going to miss you, sweetheart," I whisper.

She rotates in my arms and squeezes her arms around me.

"I'm going to miss you too."

"I love you."

It's not the first time I've said the words, but this is the moment when they take on the most meaning they've ever had.

"I love you," she murmurs and presses her lips against my heart.

"Hannah Grace, I've loved you for forever, and I'm going to love you for the rest of my life. Maybe even longer."

"Cole?" She looks up, her brows furrowed as she studies my expression.

I take advantage and drop my lips to hers again. She's where I find my strength and my peace. And I doubt she even realizes it.

"I've known I was going to marry you from the time I was ten years old. You walked into the community center Christmas dance in that red party dress with white lace—the one you told me you hated—and all I could think about was how soft it looked. And how nice you were to wear it because your mama wanted you to match the dress she had."

"What are you saying, Cole?"

"I won't ask you to marry me now, Hannah Grace. Partly because I haven't talked to your daddy for his permission, but mostly because I want to see you finish school, sweetheart. I'm so fucking proud of you for getting into Vanderbilt. And I refuse to let you give that up to follow me. You're going to be something, baby. And I'm going to be cheering you on. But until then, I won't ask you the question I really want and instead, I want to make you a promise. Someday, Hannah Grace, someday I'm going to ask you to marry me. With your daddy's blessing and when we're ready. Nothing is going to stop me." I pull the box from my pocket and flip up the lid. "It's not a ring, not yet. I want you to have one—the one you deserve—but I also wanted you to have something that sealed my promise."

I lift out the chain where a key rests next to a small heart with the initials C and H engraved in it.

"What I'm asking is if you'll accept my promise? If you'll let me love you forever and wait for me, for us, for the right time. To someday be my wife."

She nods furiously, throwing her arms around me as soon as I'm done with the speech I've rehearsed a thousand times.

"Yes!"

My arms tighten around her and I hold her to me, burying my head in her neck and breathing in her sweet citrus scent.

She said yes.

Her lips find mine, and she bounces in my arms until we break the kiss with a laugh.

"Put it on me, please?"

She spins again, and I lift the necklace over her head and wait for her to move her hair out of the way.

"There." Closing the clasp, I kiss the back of her neck and relish the shiver that works its way down her spine.

"Cold, sweetheart?" I ask, already knowing that even in the mountains, our June weather is hard to be cold in.

"Can we get back in the truck?" Her question catches me off guard.

"Sure. Sorry. I didn't think. It is colder up here…" I boost her into the truck and climb in behind her.

The door snicks shut and she straddles me, her mouth

claiming mine while her hands grip the hem of my T-shirt and tug. My dick hardens in a rush, pushing against the zipper of my shorts.

"Whoa, whoa, whoa, what's all this?" I ask, pulling away and holding her at arm's length when she appears ready to dive back in again.

"I want to, Cole. I—"

"I didn't make my promise for anything like this from you, Hannah Grace. We can wait."

"*I* can't wait. I want you. Right now."

She grinds her pelvis against my dick, and I can't hold back the moan that works its way out of my throat. Every part of my self-control is focused on being a gentleman even though she's telling me that's not what she wants.

Her lips find the pulse point in my neck and her tongue laves the spot, pleasure overwhelming every other conscious thought.

"Please. We just have tonight."

Apparently done fighting my shirt, she sits up and lifts hers over her head, displaying a perfect pair of tits clad in a light-pink lace bra.

I squeeze my eyes shut and fist my hands into the cotton of her shorts. She wiggles some more before grabbing my hands and lifting them to her now bare chest, and my eyes fly open to find my traitorous palms grazing the soft skin of her breasts, her nipples poking into the center of my palms.

"*Please.*"

Any chance I had of fighting against her temptation evaporates. With more strength than I think I have, I lift one hand and cup her nape to bring her lips back to mine and give in to the fire that burns us both until all that's left is the two of us...no longer two, but one.

CHAPTER 1

HANNAH GRACE

I roll over, my hands brushing the plush fabric of my warm, soft comforter.

It's only been a few hours since I went to bed. Ugh, why am I awake?

You're not. Stop thinking and get back to your dream.

Blue lights up my bedroom as lightning arcs across the sky and thunder rumbles, rattling the window.

That's what it is. The storm must have woken me.

How many nights have I fallen asleep to the sound of rain outside my window? But this storm isn't the gentle noise that will lull me to sleep. The lightning flashes in dramatic sweeps of blue through my room.

"Sleep, Hannah Grace."

If only it were that easy. My students won't care if I don't sleep tonight. But they require all my energy, and I try to will myself to sleep.

Only my brain starts to think about parent-teacher conferences next week. And the special holiday project I'll be starting with the kids in the next few weeks.

Another flash, followed by the echo of thunder. I keep my

eyes closed, breathing deeply and trying to pretend that the rumbles are just leftover white noise from that phone app I use sometimes.

"Fine." I'll read for a while.

It wouldn't be the first time I fell asleep while losing myself in a book.

Only a glance at my phone tells me that we've lost power, and I don't want to risk my phone running down and not having my alarm wake me up.

After yesterday's field trip, I'm tired. I *should* be asleep right now.

Leaning against my headboard, I snuggle into my pillow and smooth the covers over me, letting my fingers drift against the soft material, and keep my gaze fastened to the window.

Another flash.

One-Mississippi. Two-Mississippi. Three—

Thunder vibrates the windowpane, and I take a deep breath and blow it out.

I repeat the steps for every lightning flash and echoing sound until the storm grows more faint, becoming only a distant memory. The gentle patter of rain taps against the house and my eyelids grow heavy. My fingers stop their pattern on the comforter and I take another deep breath, blowing it out, as my lids flutter shut.

The rain loses momentum as I drift, wishing that I had opened my window so I could smell the rain-soaked yard, have the light breeze blow through.

I'm going to get up and do that.

Right after this next breath.

Hours later, the noise from my alarm on my phone wakes me earlier than I'm ready after my midnight storm. I toss back the covers and sit on the edge of the bed, turning to look at the window where the light gray of the pre-dawn filters through the blinds.

"Time to wake up, Hannah Grace." My mumble echoes around the room.

I stand and head for the bathroom, flipping on the radio to fill the silence as I get ready for the day. But my day spent with twenty five-year-olds is a lot different for wardrobe choices than my days spent as Miss Tennessee. I love the fact that my job involves comfortable shoes decorated with cartoon dogs as opposed to the three-inch heels I don't miss wearing.

Ignoring all those boxes in the closet, I grab a pair of light pink pants and a black-and-white polka-dotted shirt then grab my denim jacket that hangs on the hook just inside my closet door. I shrug it on just in case the morning is cool after the storm and tug my long blonde ponytail out from the collar.

My mirror shows someone who is poised, ready to take on the challenge of keeping twenty small children focused on a variety of tasks for the day. By the time I make it back to my bedroom, the sun is shining around the blinds, and I walk over and spin the rod to let more of it in. A few flicks of my wrist and my bed is remade and I'm ready to head out for the day. Five more minutes and I need to leave if I want to be at school on time.

As I walk by my dresser, my foot lands on the squeaky floorboard I keep meaning to google how to fix, and something sparkly that peeks out from under my dresser catches my attention. I squat down and snag the small travel bottle of my perfume wedged under the narrow opening between my dresser and the floor.

"Why is my purse perfume in here?"

I always keep it in my purse. I even painted a little pink circle on the bottom of it in nail polish so I knew I liked this one more than the other one that is also in my bag. It must have rolled out of my bag when I switched out my purses last week.

"Hannah Grace, if your head wasn't attached..." I may be

saying the words, but it's Mom's voice that echoes through my memories.

How often had I heard those words as a kid?

I spin the perfume through my fingers, dropping it into my purse once I'm in the kitchen where my bags are. My gaze snags on the time on the clock on the stove as it flashes and I groan. I forgot about the power going out. Tapping on my phone, my body freezes as I realize that somewhere in getting ready, I've lost those five minutes I needed to be to school on time plus another five.

"Shit."

I wrench open the fridge and grab my lunch—thank God I packed it last night—and then shoulder my purse and school bag off the table, rushing toward the detached garage and my little crossover SUV I bought myself when I won Miss Tennessee. The universe cuts me a break with a light commute, and I screech into the lot of the elementary school ten minutes later—earning several glares from parents waiting in front of the school with their kids.

I attempt to ignore the curious looks, hunching my shoulders and ducking my head as I scan my ID and slide through the doors as soon as they're wide enough to let me. I come up short, my shoulder bag strap catching on the door handle and yanking me back. My lunch bag goes flying into the lobby while I struggle with the tangled strap.

"Of course."

"Morning, HG. Rough one?" Zach Nolan steps out of the gym wearing athletic shorts and a hoodie, a whistle hanging off his lanyard that is centered across his broad chest.

Zach replaced the gym teacher who retired here my second year of teaching. He's one of the few teachers at Meadow Ridge Elementary that is close to my age, and he and I bonded over being the younger generation with mostly seasoned peers who continued to retire year after year.

"You have no idea," I say, pulling my strap free of the door.

Freaking finally.

I start down the early primary hallway, and Zach falls into step beside me.

"You're usually here earlier than I am." He looks over and shoots me a smile.

Not for the first time, I wish I could be attracted to Zach. He's cute—blond hair, blue eyes, boy-next-door good looks—but no matter how hard I've tried, I can't create something out of nothing.

It isn't fair to me. Or to him. He's made it clear plenty of times he'd be interested in more. And I've ignored every subtle and not-so-subtle hint.

"I like getting here early." I push him and he chuckles but doesn't budge.

Rude.

"You've told me that before."

My classroom is the second in the hallway and I walk in, my eyes landing on a cup of coffee steaming on my desk.

"Oh my God, have I told you lately how much I love you?" I ask, dropping my bags and grabbing the coffee.

Seriously, fall in love with him already!

If only it was that easy.

He smirks.

"Last week when I ordered lunch in when you forgot yours," he reminds me.

Neither of us will risk the cafeteria food unless we absolutely have to. I had planned to order something, but there hadn't been time. I had resigned myself to the cafeteria special that day when Zach popped into my classroom with two takeout bags in his hand.

"It'll be my treat next time."

"Yeah. We'll see." He hands me my lunch box.

"I will."

He lifts his hands with a laugh.

"Okay, okay. So why are you skating in here"—he looks at the clock above my door—"fifteen minutes before school starts? Hot date?"

I hide my grimace behind my mug as I take another drink.

Dating and I don't mix. And I'm done trying after the last two first dates I went on ended up in disaster. Both of which I relayed to Zach over the phone when I got home after each date.

"I swore off dating, remember? No, I...I have to tell you something."

"What? What's up?" He leans against my bookcase and crosses his ankles.

He really is athletic. Even I can admit he's good-looking. But sparks? Nope. None.

Darn it.

"Did it storm at your house last night?" I ask.

"Yeah. Briefly. Did it hit your house too?"

I nod.

"It woke me up."

"Okay?" Zach gestures for me to keep going.

"Storms don't normally wake me up. But, that's not the weirdest thing that happened."

"What?"

I move closer, dropping my voice to a whisper.

"Zach, something weird happened."

"Weird with you can mean any number of things, HG."

I roll my eyes but don't argue the point. Because there's too much truth in it to argue.

"This is going to sound stupid."

"Try me."

He lifts his eyebrows and crosses his arms, waiting.

I take a deep breath and let it out in a sigh before I take another drink of my coffee.

"My purse perfume was under the dresser in my room."

"Huh?" His brow is furrowed and he studies me like I just told him I'm quitting my job to go back into pageants. "HG, how are these two related?"

I shrug. "I'm not sure, but it's creepy, right? Like what if someone was there and that's what woke me up?"

"I won't repeat myself about the true crime before bed—"

"So what are you doing now?" I ask.

"I'm sure it was weird but—"

"This"—I reach in and grab the little bottle and shake it in his direction—"was under my dresser this morning."

"But that's your purse perfume."

"I know!"

"How did it get in your room?"

"I don't know."

"Didn't you tell me last week about the window you accidentally left open? The one you thought you closed?" he asks.

My purse perfume was just the latest in a lot of recent abnormal circumstances.

"You're right. I forgot about that."

"Did you ever remember for sure?" he asks.

I shake my head.

"No, I just figured I was going crazy and left the window open when I woke up that morning."

But I never did that.

So why had my bedroom window been open?

"HG, I tease you a lot about watching true crime before bed, but…" He smiles, a dimple popping to the right of his mouth.

"But I haven't been. Not for the last two weeks."

His smile fades.

"I think maybe you ought to have someone check your locks and windows. I could come take a look if you want. After school?"

"You don't need a reason to come hang out. But sure, if it makes you feel better."

"It would make me feel better if you called the cops to tell them about all this."

"They wouldn't take me seriously."

"They won't unless you try."

"And tell them what, my purse perfume was under my dresser and I may or may not have forgotten about leaving my bedroom window open?" I scoff. "There's no proof."

He opens his mouth, but I cut him off.

"If you want, come over and check my windows and doors. I'll make dinner and we can hang out. I'll even call the pageant people. They helped me before."

Right after I won Miss Tennessee, I'd gotten a ton of fan mail and responded to every letter personally. Most from little girls who wanted to know what it felt like to wear a real crown. But one had stood out. The original letter from Eric was a congratulations followed by a request for advice on how to build confidence. We'd written back and forth half a dozen times before the tone of his letters changed. From sweet and thoughtful to full-on love letters filled with flowery prose. I'd ignored the confession and tried to keep up the platonic nature of our original letters. But then the confessions turned to graphic details of what he wanted to do with me. To me. The last one was the most explicit of all and included a picture of me while I was out one day running errands.

When I called the pageant people, I turned all the letters over to them and they stopped.

I had shared everything with Zach before, and he nods at the reminder.

"That's a good idea. Hopefully they can help again. Do you want me to plan on crashing on your couch for a few days?"

I smile, picturing Zach's tall frame crammed on my tiny couch the one time he fell asleep over here after a late move night.

"No. It'll be okay. But I would appreciate the lock and door check."

"It's the least I can do."

The bell rings and I follow him to the door of my classroom.

"The kids have music this morning, so I'll reach out to the pageant people then."

"Promise?"

I lift my hand and cross my index finger over my heart.

The herd of kids heads our direction and I nod.

"Promise."

CHAPTER 2

COLE

*I*t's a perfect day.

Or at least as perfect as the big city gets in November. But it's days like today—low seventies, perfect blue sky still visible despite all the smog—that makes living in Los Angeles worth it. I step into the stairwell of the converted building Sawyer bought for SAFE Haven Security and admire the woodwork on the banister as I climb to the second story offices.

My whistle rendition of Morgan Wallen's "Spin You Around" echoes down as I climb. Even though it's been six months since Sawyer opened the offices, it's still hard to believe that SAFE Haven has grown from our team of three to a significantly larger organization. Although most of the employees report over to Featherlight Studios where our main contract is located.

"God, do you have to be so loud?" Sydney walks up behind me, grimacing and clutching a travel coffee cup like her life depends on it.

"Oh my God, I didn't think vampires could come into buildings without being invited in." I lift my messenger bag in front of me.

It's not the first time I've teased her about her line of work being more related to the mythical creatures that suck blood and only come out at night. But it never fails to get a rise out of her.

She doesn't disappoint me this morning either.

"Ass." Her shoulder bumps mine as she continues forward. "It's too early."

Sydney's wizardry with a computer and an Internet connection knows no bounds, but her work—and that of her small team —is limited to remote work.

"What has you gracing us with your presence, youngster?"

"Sawyer texted. He wants to meet with me this morning."

"I want to meet with both of you." Sawyer steps out of his office. "Five minutes."

"Well, that's…cryptic," I say and study my boss and friend as he walks to the coffee pot with a cup.

And unusual.

Sawyer generally gives me a heads-up when he needs to meet with me.

"Any idea what it's about?" I ask Sydney as we walk side by side to our offices.

I'm so preoccupied by Sawyer's lack of communication, I don't even give Sydney the usual ration of shit about why she needs an office in our building when she only uses it once in a blue moon.

"No idea."

She disappears into the cave of her office and I step into mine, hanging up my bag and the sport coat I put on this morning to stave off some of the chill in the early morning air.

I knew I wouldn't need it for long.

Grabbing my laptop and a pad of paper and pen, I head into the main office area and note a few lights flipped on in other offices. I stop for my own coffee and balance everything as I step into Sawyer's office.

"What's up, King?" I ask and situate myself in one of the two chairs across from his desk.

"Let's wait for Sydney. It's easier to tell you both at once."

"She's always late," I remind him. "If she even shows up at all."

"I resent that remark," Sydney says, stepping into the office and closing the door.

"You resemble that remark," I mumble behind the safety of my coffee mug.

Sawyer rolls his eyes.

"This is why I hate in-person meetings. I do not have the energy to deal with the two of you bickering like teenagers."

"Ooooo, hear that, Cole? We've been upgraded from toddlers to teenagers."

I lift my hand and she slaps it as Sawyer groans.

"Let's get this over with."

Sydney opens her laptop, fingers poised.

"I had a phone call this morning from Tracy Chabert—"

"Who is Tracy Chabert?" Sydney asks.

"Tracy Smith Chabert. She's the head of the board of directors for the Tennessee pageant." The words are out of my mouth before I can even process them.

"How the hell do you know that?" Sydney's gaze swings to me.

Even Sawyer's eyes narrow as he studies me, lifting his fingers to steeple in front of his mouth.

"What? Tennessee is small. You guys always talk about my pageant info—"

Sawyer clears his throat, and my explanation dies on my lips.

"As I was saying, the *recently* elected board of directors called me this morning." His eyebrows lift as if daring me to call him out on the word he emphasizes.

Nope, not going to say a word.

"Tennessee? How do they know about us?" Sydney asks, voicing the same question pinging around my head.

"Who else would have given them our number? Tom," Sawyer explains.

The facility operations manager with Featherlight is well-connected, and this isn't the first time we've gotten a job because of him.

"That man has his finger on the pulse more than I do," Sydney says.

"To get more connected you'd have to disconnect yourself from your computer," I tell her.

"No, thanks. Resistance is futile, Strickland. Come to the dark side. We have cookies."

"You're mixing your metaphors, Syd. *Star Trek* and *Star Wars* are different universes. And neither have cookies." The corners of Sawyer's lips twitch.

The sun glints off his wedding ring, and happiness for my friend filters through my blood. He and his wife, Evie, had a hell of a time getting to the finish line. But they've now enjoyed their fairy tale for two years, and their wedding six months ago was one even I shed a tear at.

"Let's talk about the kid's lack of sci-fi education later. What kind of job do they have for us?" I ask.

"One of their former winners contacted them. Right after she won, she had some creepy fan mail that they sent me to take a look at."

"How long ago was this? You said a former winner, right? Not the current Miss?"

"Yeah." Sawyer picks up his notebook and looks at it, even though he doesn't need to.

He's slow-rolling this information.

Why?

But there's something niggling at me that tells me I *know* why, and I'm doing everything I can to ignore that sensation.

"Around four years ago. Winner's name was—"

"Hannah Grace Whittaker." I say the name at the same time Sawyer does.

He doesn't seem surprised. He shouldn't. I mentioned Hannah Grace's name enough times when we were deployed together that it should be just as burned into his brain as it still is in mine.

My grip tightens on the pen in my hand, the plastic squeaking in protest. Sawyer's gaze flicks to my fist and back up, eyebrows raised.

Taking a deep breath, I focus on inhaling and exhaling, relaxing each finger one by one until my pen rests casually against my palm.

Sydney's gaze moves between the two of us.

"Am I missing something?" Her green eyes narrow as she focuses on me. "You. What am I missing?"

"Why me?"

"Because you said the name at the same time Sawyer did. Who is Hayley Grace?"

"Hannah Grace," I correct.

My Honey Girl.

Or at least, once upon a time.

"Who is she?"

"She's from Mistletoe Creek." The words are said with way more calm than I actually feel, but I don't want to get into the details with Sydney right now. Instead I want to know what's going on.

Why is Hannah Grace calling the pageant people? What creepy fan mail? Mom hadn't mentioned anything to me about that, and it was over three fucking years ago.

"You have an ex? Someone actually liked you enough to date you?" Sydney ribs.

"She was going to marry me," I tell her, like I've just told her the sky is blue.

Until I fucked it up.

"What?! How am I just hearing about this now? This isn't anywhere on your socials—"

And I made sure to scrub all my social media right after I broke up with her. I didn't need the reminder of how badly I fucked up my life.

"What's happening now?" I ask, some of my anger punching through.

Sawyer only lifts an eyebrow.

"Nothing."

Record scratch. That wasn't what I was expecting him to say.

"Nothing? What do you mean nothing?"

"Per Ms. Smith Chabert, Hannah only had hunches that something weird was happening. Her window being left open in her house when she remembers closing it. Something she keeps in her bag being under her dresser. She was concerned enough that she wanted to reach out. She doesn't think there's enough to go to the cops, but she wanted it checked out."

"She's right. There isn't enough to go to the cops," Sydney says, still side-eyeing me.

"Are we taking the job?" I ask.

"Would it matter if I said yes or no?" Sawyer asks me.

I shake my head.

"If we aren't, I'm requesting vacation time."

"We're taking the job. I want you on the first flight to Nashville."

"Nashville?"

"Question?" Sawyer asks.

"I...uh...I assumed Hannah Grace lived in Mistletoe Creek."

Sawyer's gaze sharpens as I stumble over the words.

"Guess you don't know everything. Hannah Grace stayed in Nashville after college. She currently works at Meadow Ridge Elementary as a kindergarten teacher." Sydney's focus is on her computer screen.

"How the fuck do you know that?"

"Duh." She gestures to her computer.

Goddamnit, Hannah Grace. She was always too trusting, and it looks like that hasn't changed.

"Fuck. Lock down her socials," I tell Sydney.

"What's the magic word?" she asks me.

I growl.

"Sydney, stop giving Cole a hard time. Please do as he asked." Sawyer's ability to referee is the true testament to his level of patience.

"I'm already on it. I was just giving him a hard time. Sheesh. Calm down."

"Anything else?" I ask, standing.

My mind is already on grabbing my go bag and getting to the airport as fast as possible.

"Not right now. Are you sure?" Sawyer stands as well, his too astute gaze locking with mine.

"If this were Evie, what would you do?"

The right corner of his mouth lifts and he nods.

"Same thing you're going to do."

A grin stretches across my face. This is why he and I are friends.

"Let's touch base once you connect with Hannah Grace. See what we're working with," he tells me.

"Do the pageant people have those letters from before?" I ask.

"You think you need them?"

I shrug.

"Maybe. Maybe not. Better to have them and not need them than need them and not have them."

"I have scans I requested earlier. I'll email them to you. They're…"

He doesn't finish his sentence and that alone leaves a rock in my stomach. We've both seen way more shit in this life than we should have.

"They're what?"

"They're not love letters, Cole. That's all I'm going to say."

But there's more that he's not saying. And that alone lights a bigger fire under my ass.

"I'll call you when I land," I say.

My long stride eats up the space between Sawyer's office and mine, and I'm back outside in under five minutes, practically sprinting to my car.

Whether she wants it or not, Hannah Grace needs me. I try not to think about what it means that I need her safe as desperately as I do.

It's the only thing I'm going to allow myself to focus on.

Her safety.

There was a definite warning in Sawyer's voice when he told me about the fan mail. I should have listened. Instead, I'm tempted to rip open the emergency exit and toss my laptop into the sky after reading through some of them.

They don't start off bad. The first one was all about how the writer struggled with confidence issues and enjoyed watching Hannah Grace on several of the news programs she had been on. He'd even been in the audience when she was crowned Miss Tennessee.

It's hard to ignore the slash of guilt.

He was there.

And I wasn't.

There aren't copies of Hannah Grace's responses, but I can almost write her response myself. Humility, empathy, and all the sunshine that made her who she was. There are a lot of letters which tells me that they corresponded a lot.

I skim through some of those and don't notice anything weird until the letter after the love confession.

You didn't answer my last letter, Hannah Grace, and that's not like you. You always answer. What if I came and told you in person how in love with you I am? How much I want to be with you? How I know we'll be together forever?

Another letter where Hannah Grace did apparently respond.

I don't want to scare you. I want to be with you. Even if you don't feel the same, I know you'll grow to love me too. I'll wait for you. Forever.

The other letters grow more graphic in content, and a red haze still covers my vision whenever I think about the disturbed, explicit things the author wrote her. How scared she must have been to read that shit.

Fuck that.

But the pageant people had shared with Sawyer—who passed it to me with the letters—that once Hannah Grace had reached out to them the letters had stopped. And since they stopped, they felt there was no need to track down this Eric that had written these letters to her.

If it were up to me, I would have.

And now she was in trouble again. Or thought she was. But she didn't imagine things easily.

You knew her a long time ago.

Nobody changes that much.

"Ladies and gentlemen, we are making our final descent into Nashville International Airport. Local time is 5:30 PM and weather is sitting in the midfifties with a breeze coming from the west."

The pilot's disembodied voice comes over the speakers, and I sigh and gaze out the window at the darkened sky and the lights of Nashville.

When was the last time I was home?

Before I broke up with Hannah Grace. I didn't want to run into her after. I didn't think I was that strong.

But I'm not going home. Although I wouldn't mind a trip to Mistletoe Creek for a homemade meal from Mama.

First things first. It was time I faced my past.

And hope that she doesn't slam the door in my face.

CHAPTER 3

HANNAH GRACE

"*I* checked all the windows from the outside. They're all locked up," Zach says, walking through the back door into the kitchen.

"I really do think I left the window open the other day. It was a nice night and I just wanted some fresh air to help me fall asleep," I tell him and pass him a beer from the fridge.

"You shouldn't be sleeping with your window open. You live in a one-story house. Anyone—"

"I live in a nice neighborhood. Nothing bad ever happens here." I take my own beer and head to the living room to wait for the pizza I ordered when Zach first got here.

"It only takes once, HG."

"It's never happened in Mistletoe Creek."

My small hometown is about three hours from Nashville, but it might as well be on a different planet. Nothing ever happens there—unless three older women living in the town and match-making the younger generations counts. There's a reason I didn't move home after college despite the many requests from my parents and younger sister, Laura Leigh.

"You don't live there anymore. This is the big city. No more opening your windows at night."

My hackles rise with the directive.

"Zach, thank you for caring and for checking things out. But you of all people ought to realize that no one tells me what to do. If I want to sleep with my window open, that's a risk that I'm willing to take."

"But—"

"Now, let's pick a movie and wait for the pizza," I say, changing the subject.

I like Zach. As my friend. But every once in a while he gets too bossy and forgets that no one tells me what to do anymore.

He opens his mouth before he closes it again and shakes his head with a sigh.

"What do you want to watch?" he asks.

I shoot him a smile for going along with my change of subject.

"I picked last time. You pick."

"I'm not picking anything on Hallmark," he warns.

I laugh and a smile curves his lips upward.

"I didn't figure you would. That's my go-to."

"Exactly."

We settle onto the couch and I take a sip of my beer while he scrolls through my streaming services and finds the movie he wants.

"*Scream?*" I ask and my fingers go numb around my bottle.

I hate horror movies. My overactive imagination works triple time after watching one. Forget sleeping with the window open or not; tonight I'll be sleeping with every light in my house on.

"This one's not so bad. Unless you want to watch *The Conjuring* or *Annabelle?*"

"No!" The sound is louder in my little living room than I planned and I wince.

I've seen previews for both of them and given that Mama still collects porcelain dolls, *Annabelle* is out.

He hits the button to play the movie and I resign myself to curl into the corner of my couch and hide behind my hands when necessary. Zach chuckles and scoots into the middle of the couch, allowing me to dig my toes under his thigh.

"I'll hold your hand at the scary parts," he promises.

"Just be prepared to hold it the entire time," I mumble.

He reaches over, palm up, and I grip his hand like a lifeline.

"The more you watch these, the less scared you'll be," he says.

"So you keep saying. But if watching all four of the first ones didn't desensitize me, I don't think anything will."

The words are out of my mouth faster than the memory can surface.

I had watched all four of them—or pieces of them anyway.

Maybe it would have helped if we had watched versus making out off and on for the eight plus hours of movies.

"You never told me that." He pauses the movie to study me.

I shrug and attempt to ignore the memory that wants to pull me deeper under. It's been a long time since I thought of Cole Strickland. I wasn't going to let myself start now.

"It was a long time ago."

"With whom?"

"Nobody important," I say and stand up. "Do you want another beer?"

He lifts his bottle from the table and drains the rest of it before handing me the empty.

"Sure."

"You can unpause it," I tell him.

I don't mind missing any of the scary movie.

"You'll miss something if I do," he calls after me.

I open the two bottles and walk back into the living room where the movie is still paused on the opening scene.

"Here." I hand him his beer and flop down onto the couch, being careful not to spill my own.

He unpauses the movie and I keep my focus on the screen,

using the horror unfolding to push out the memories now that the lid to that Pandora's box has been opened.

This is what happens. Over the last four years since we broke up, it's become a familiar pattern. Something random will remind me of Cole—in this case, a horror movie—and I'll spend the next few weeks with him more on my mind until he fades back into my past.

My second beer sits untouched on the coffee table, and despite my inner turmoil, I'm into the movie enough to hide my face against Zach's shirt during the gorier parts. Definitely will be sleeping with all the lights on tonight.

We're maybe thirty minutes in—and it's one of those parts—when there's a knock on my door. Grabbing my remote, I pause the movie and release the breath I've been holding.

"Pizza's here!" I crow and jump up from the couch.

"Saved by the knock?" he jokes.

I'm still giggling when I open the door.

Only it's not the delivery person standing there holding my pizza. Not unless my ex-boyfriend became a pizza delivery person in the last four years.

"Hello, Hannah Grace." His voice still holds that same smooth cadence I used to love.

Without a word, I slam the door, turning around to lean against the thick wood.

"Who was that?" Zach asks, standing up from the couch.

A knock sounds on the door, reverberating behind my ear.

"Nobody."

"Was Nobody holding our pizza?"

Shit. Damn. Fuck.

I forgot to grab the pizza out of his hands.

Spinning, I wrench open the door and snatch the box and try to shove the door closed again. Only it doesn't work since he wedges himself inside before I can close the door.

"Who the fuck are you?" Zach's fists clench and he moves closer to me.

"Who the fuck are you?" Cole repeats and only arches an eyebrow.

His voice maintains the calm cadence. It's irritating how peaceful he is right now. Meanwhile I'm a train wreck of sensations—anger, sadness, frustration, curiosity, regret. They all circle my brain vying for the prime spot now that my ex has resurfaced after all this time.

Why?

"Get out, Cole." My words are quiet, but given how silent the room is, he can hear them.

"You know this guy?" Zach jumps in, crossing his arms over his chest and standing straight.

Cole's natural posture doesn't change.

"I can't." He ignores Zach's question and keeps his focus on me.

"This is my ex. One who isn't welcome here," I tell Zach.

If I wasn't studying Cole so closely I would have missed the flash of hurt on his face. But he has no reason to hurt. He's the one who broke up with me and fell off the face of the earth. Not the other way around.

"You heard her. You need to leave. Or do you need help with that?"

Cole spares Zach a fleeting look before refocusing that warm, brown gaze on me.

"Aren't you even curious why I'm here?"

No. The word is on the tip of my tongue, but something holds it back.

Because it would be a lie.

I *am* curious why he's deciding to reemerge after all this time. But I won't give him the satisfaction of telling him that.

"I'm going to take my pizza into the kitchen, and I want you gone by the time I come back," I say.

It's nearly impossible to walk away without a second glance. To catalog all the differences the years have made since I saw him last—a month before he deployed for the last time. But I manage to not turn around.

Setting the pizza on the counter, I'm no longer hungry. Instead, I move to the window above the kitchen sink and stare into the dark backyard.

"Hannah Grace, I need to talk to you."

He's backlit by the lights in the living room, only the shadow of a reflection. And even though the ten-foot width of the room separates us, my body remembers him.

"I have nothing to say to you." I spin around, taking a deep breath and holding on to the edge of the sink to keep myself from running toward him.

Movement catches my attention behind Cole, where Zach stands directly behind him.

"I told you she didn't want to talk to you."

"Look, I can appreciate you sticking up for Hannah Grace, but this is between her and me." He cranes his head over his shoulder to look at Zach before turning his attention back to me. "Five minutes. The pageant people sent me."

Well, fuck.

Just like that, all my adrenaline rushes out like the breath I exhale.

"The pageant people sent *you*?"

The universe has a twisted sense of humor.

"Can I talk to you alone?" He moves closer.

I attempt to retreat, but am blocked by the solid mass of my kitchen counter.

"We can talk in front of Zach."

A witness will be good. Especially one with as much hostility as Zach is leveling Cole's direction.

He sighs and scrubs a hand down his face, highlighting the

scruff of a five o'clock shadow. He'd been clean-shaven the last time I saw him.

He's dressed in jeans and a button-down shirt, his leather jacket beat up and scarred from years of wear.

When did he get that?

It's an odd realization. His life has moved on just like mine has. A small part of me thought of him as frozen in time, getting into the truck that last time for his brother to take him back to Knoxville to the airport before his last deployment. Before we broke up.

But he's no more the same twenty-one-year-old kid than I am. We're both older.

Wiser.

"Well?" The word comes out snarkier than I intend.

Good.

"Why don't we go sit down?"

Southern manners kick in before I can stop them. "Are you hungry? Thirsty?"

His stomach growls in response, and the right side of his mouth quirks in a smile full of self-deprecation.

"I'd appreciate something to eat. That little snack pack on the plane didn't do much."

I grab three plates and put pizza on all three before turning to hand both him and Zach a plate.

"Beer?" I ask.

"I'll take water."

"Zach?"

"I still have my beer," he mumbles and walks back to the living room.

I follow Cole and we all sit down, me next to Zach on the sofa and Cole in the chair closest to me.

"*Scream?*" Cole asks, gesturing toward the TV with his pizza.

"Yeah." Leaning forward, I snag my beer and take a drink to clear the frog sitting on my vocal cords.

"You hate scary movies," he tells me.

He's making assumptions based on the person he used to know.

"I used to. You have no idea who I am anymore." The words are out before I can stop them.

Well, shit, why did I say that?

Because he needs to stop trying to act like we're friends. We're not even acquaintances anymore. He's a stranger.

Cole clears his throat and takes a bite of pizza, chewing and swallowing before he speaks again.

"The company I work for, SAFE Haven Security, got a phone call from Tracy Smith Chabert."

"I just called Ms. Smith Chabert this morning."

"My boss, Sawyer, got the call from her shortly after you called her. Luckily, she's taking the situation seriously. Unfortunately, whoever was in her role before didn't take the fan mail you got with more gravity."

"That happened a long time ago," I tell him.

"It could still be related."

I'm glad I no longer have those letters—having sent the originals to the pageant people at the time—but the memory of their content creates a shiver of ice that skates down my spine.

"Tell me about what's been going on."

It comes slowly, awkwardly. In some ways, sitting with Cole, eating pizza, is a surreal moment. It wasn't one I ever let myself imagine. But eventually I manage to tell him the whole story.

"I checked all the windows and doors from the outside. Her house is secure." Zach speaks up after observing the two of us silently.

"What about the locks?" Cole asks.

"What about them?" My nose wrinkles in confusion.

Zach just said the house is secure.

"Have they been changed?"

"No. Not since right after I bought the house. Why?"

"It is possible that somebody has a spare key. You don't keep one under the doormat, do you?"

"No, *Dad*, I don't. I have a key, my parents have a key, Laura Leigh, and Zach."

"You have a key?" Cole asks Zach.

"Yeah. Since I live closer to her than her parents, if she locks herself out."

"Are you guys…" He gestures between the two of us.

"That's none of your business, Cole." I reach over and squeeze Zach's hand with mine.

I shouldn't lead him on like this. I know that. But it's more important that I get Cole to leave.

Zach smiles, a mix of hope and something else—the tension that exists with Cole in the house.

I don't blame him.

Cole's attention is centered on where my hand connects to Zach's when I turn my head back in his direction.

"I want to do my own look. Tomorrow. But for tonight, we should get some sleep."

"You're coming back tomorrow?" I can't quite keep the dread out of my voice.

"You're not getting rid of me that easily, Hannah Grace. I want to look more into all of this before I head back to LA."

"Can't you send someone else? Isn't this"—I gesture between the two of us— "a conflict of interest?"

He shrugs. "I doubt Sawyer would care. And, no, no one else is coming. I need to make sure you're safe myself."

"I don't get home from school until after four," I tell him and stand, walking toward the front door to show him out.

"I'm staying here. I don't like the idea of you being left here alone."

"You're not staying here," I tell him and prop my hands on my hips.

"I am."

"You're not." My voice is growing louder.

What is it with these two men in particular who seem to think I'm a weak female that needs their protection? First Zach and now Cole both make assumptions that they're going to stay with me.

"Someone is trying to scare you," he tells me, and I steel my spine against the shiver that wants to shake free.

"Maybe. We don't know that for sure. If I need someone to stay, Zach will be here. It wouldn't be the first time." I look back at Zach who nods.

"Hannah Grace." I hate the way my name sounds on his lips.

No, you don't.

Fine. I *want* to hate how it sounds. But the walk down memory lane needs to close for the night. I need a good night's sleep for work tomorrow. And I won't sleep at all if Cole is in the next room.

"Cole, you had your five minutes. And then some. I'm willing to accept your help, but I'm not willing to have you stay here. I'm not some damsel in distress for you to rescue. We can talk more tomorrow, but for now, I think you need to go find a hotel."

"I don't think it's a good idea for you to be here alone."

"That's no longer your concern."

I can see him gearing up for a fight, his wheels already spinning and looking for whatever way he can to win the argument.

"Please," I whisper.

His eyes lock with mine, and the fight is replaced with exhaustion.

After several heartbeats in tense silence, he nods.

"Fine. But I am coming back tomorrow."

Digging into his back pocket, he grabs his wallet and drops a business card on the table.

I stand my ground, not bothering to pick up the card, and open the door. With a sigh, he grabs his jacket off the back of the chair. Relief grows with every step he takes toward the door. But so does my body's awareness of his as he closes the distance between us.

"Good night, Hannah Grace. I *will* see you tomorrow." His eyes search mine.

My lips tingle, remembering all the good night kisses we've shared in the past. But that was a long time ago.

"Good night."

He steps into the light on the porch and reaches back, his fingers brushing mine where they're wrapped around the doorknob.

"You've always been my concern. I've never stopped caring for you."

Another soft skim of his fingertips against my hand and he's walking toward the rental car parked on the street.

"I can stay on the couch," Zach asks.

I jump, having completely forgotten he was even here.

I shake my head.

"No, it's okay."

"I don't like him, but I have to admit he's right. You need someone to keep an eye on you."

I focus on him, and the hatred he feels is clear. I've never seen that look on his face. But given everything I've shared about Cole with Zach, I can understand it. Even more so since Zach has made it obvious to me that he'd be interested in being more than friends.

"I don't need to have someone 'keep an eye' on me. I'm perfectly okay on my own. I'll make sure the doors and windows are locked, but I really just want to be alone right now."

His nostrils flare and for a split second he opens his mouth, the argument clear on his face. But just as fast, he closes his mouth and stands up.

"Fine. You're right. I'll get going too then. But call me if you need me."

"I will."

"I'll see you tomorrow, HG." He squeezes my shoulders in a quick hug.

"Okay. Good night."

I follow him to the door and wait until he gets into his truck in the driveway before closing the door and locking the deadbolt. On autopilot, I clean up the pizza plates, bottles, and glass and head to my room. I leave the card exactly where Cole dropped it on my table.

Alone in bed, with the covers pulled up, I lift my hand and stare at the skin on the back of my hand. Along my fingers. But no matter how hard I study the area, there's nothing, no visible mark.

But Cole's impact on me has never been a tangible thing.

CHAPTER 4

COLE

*I*f Hannah Grace thinks I'm leaving for long, she's out of her goddamn mind.

I pull down the street and turn off the lights, waiting for her boyfriend to leave.

What if he doesn't?

I flip the bird to the insecurity that voices that question. I have no right to Hannah Grace. I gave up any and all claim on her emotions when I broke up with her.

Why do I care if he's there?

But it didn't sit right. She didn't act like he was anyone to her.

It might have had something to do with you showing back up in her life after four years of no contact.

But I'd used my gut more times than I could count to tell me things. To keep me safe.

And my gut was telling me that there wasn't anything between them.

Fortunately, I don't have to keep trying to convince myself of their relationship status when Lover Boy's truck pulls past where I'm parked. I wait several beats, putting enough distance between us in the neighborhood to not appear suspicious, then blending into the other cars once we hit the main roads. Forty-five minutes later, he pulls into an apartment complex, and I circle the block and pull in, finding his truck parked in front of one of the buildings.

He's already climbing the stairs to his unit, and I make a note to look up the address and find out who he is. Had I not been so focused on Hannah Grace, I may have gotten his name. He's close to her, so I want to know who the fuck he is.

I don't need a pic of his license plate since I grabbed one as I was walking up Hannah Grace's driveway.

I wait until he's in his apartment before pulling back out of the lot and retracing my route back to Hannah Grace's house. The lights are all off, and I recline the driver's seat and try to stretch out in the little compact they gave me. I hate small cars for the size, but I love them for how well they blend into the world around them.

I opt not to go check around the house since I'd rather not deal with the local cops if a neighbor sees me poking around. The neighborhood is quiet, and all the lights are off except for the front porch lights that wink at each other across the wide street. In some ways, this place reminds me of home.

Is that why Hannah Grace moved here? Close enough to home for the good feelings and far enough away to avoid the bad memories? Hell, more power to her. Los Angeles, California couldn't be any more different from Mistletoe Creek, Tennessee if it tried. Which meant little chance of memories of Hannah Grace sneaking in, even though they did every once in a while.

The sneaky bastards would come out of the blue, the guilt riding the wake like a skilled surfboarder to pull me into a riptide of second-guessing the decision I had made.

The only one I could.

My gaze flicks from window to darkened window. The living room windows are easy to pick out, but does Hannah Grace's bedroom face the street? Or off to the side? Her bedroom in high school had been a mix of her mama's floral wallpaper, remnants of her tomboy stage in a mix of college football and concert tickets pinned to a bulletin board, and her own style of posters tacked to the wall.

Not that I was allowed in her bedroom much when we transitioned from friends to dating.

What is her bedroom like now?

Danger, danger, Will Robinson.

The alarm blares in my head, and I blink before continuing to scan the quiet neighborhood. There's nothing. Leaning my head back, I marvel at the fact that no cars go down the street—this one or the one visible running perpendicular at the end of the block. No alarms, no animals, no rustling of wind through leaves.

It's the sound of silence.

And not one I'm familiar with anymore.

It's peaceful.

Retracing my pattern, there's still nothing, and I lean my head back against the headrest. I'll just rest here for a few minutes and then I'll keep my vigil.

A dog barking wakes me just as the sun is changing the color from light blue to peach-tinted pink. I'm parked in the perfect spot that the shaft of sunlight hits me square in the face.

"Christ," I groan and attempt to stretch.

My phone pings and I lift it and note the time. Shit. I need to leave soon or risk Hannah Grace seeing me camping out in front of her house.

SAWYER

Just checking in.

How's it going?

It's going.

She's not super happy I showed up.

43

SYDNEY

She has good taste.

SAWYER

Sydney.

Did you tell her?

SYDNEY

Her who? Her me?

SAWYER

No.

SYDNEY

What don't I know that you two do?

If I'm doing my job, I need the details.

SAWYER

This detail didn't matter.

SYDNEY

It might.

SAWYER

I don't think so.

It's fine.

Hannah Grace is my ex.

SYDNEY

What?!

How did I not know this?

You were married?

I sigh and shake my head at Sydney's rapid-fire questions.

Not married.

Not quite. Not even engaged. The memory of my clasping the necklace around her neck the day before I left for boot camp swims to the surface, and I clear my throat and glance up to clear the memory with the presence of reality.

SYDNEY

So why does your ex-girlfriend care that you showed up?

Shouldn't she be happy you're there to help?

It's complicated.

Not important.

SAWYER

Was she able to share anything more than what the pageant people gave us?

Negative.

I do have a plate and address check I need Sydney to run.

Boyfriend.

The word is harder to type than it should be.

SYDNEY

Awkward.

SAWYER

Focus, Sydney.

SYDNEY

Ugh. Fine.

I can multitask.

SAWYER

Multitask later.

Focus now.

> I need to go soon. Gotta go find a hotel.

SYDNEY

Why? What'd you do? Stay in your car in her driveway like a creeper?

> Not exactly.

I refuse to admit she's almost right on the nose.

> Just run this plate info and address please without commentary.

> Also a full background on whoever the owner is.

SYDNEY

Me digging up dirt on your ex's new boyfriend doesn't sound related to the case.

Fuck. Leave it to Sydney to create a migraine where none existed before. Reaching up, I rub the bridge of my nose and pray for sanity.

> I'm not asking for that.

> I want to know if he's a suspect.

SYDNEY

You want to know if he's a suspect or you want him to be the suspect?

God, grant me the serenity to accept the things I cannot change and the reminder that if I murder Sydney, Sawyer will have to hire a new hacker. Fortunately, he steps in before I have to.

SAWYER

Sydney.

> Please pull the background check Cole is
> asking for.

SYDNEY

> You never let me have any fun.

SAWYER

> Elevating Cole's blood pressure is not fun I'm
> going to allow.

SYDNEY

> Spoilsport.

Normally, I have more patience to deal with Sydney. But today, I'm running out of time as the eastern sky continues to brighten.

> Did you pull one on Hannah Grace when the
> pageant people called?

SYDNEY

> Contrary to both your opinions, I know what I'm
> doing.

> I already emailed that to you after I ran it last
> night. It's in your encrypted files.

This is why we put up with Sydney despite being on the verge of strangling her on an almost daily basis. She's fucking amazing at her job and anticipates whatever we could ask for—and it's been that way since it was just Sawyer, her, and me, to now with how large the company has grown.

> Thanks.

A door across the street opens and closes with an early morning commuter heading to their car.

I need to find a hotel close by and clean up.

You'll send me the info once you have it?

SYDNEY

Don't I always?

And here we go.

SAWYER

I want those files as well. I'll do a review and see if anything stands out to me.

Sawyer's instincts are more honed than mine, and I'll take all the help I can get. The sooner I can help Hannah Grace the sooner I can go back to attempting to forget her.

Thanks.

SAWYER

Let us know if there's anything else you need.

Will do.

Another car pulls past me in the street, the driver moving slow enough to do a thorough inspection as they pass.

Time to go.

Despite the burning need to drop my shit and turn back around for Hannah Grace's house, I take my time and force myself to lie down. I'm not going to be any good to her if I'm falling asleep—literally—on the job.

Years of training from the military and the need to sleep when I could allow me to catch a few more hours of sleep. I wake up still stiff thanks to the plane ride and sleeping in the car this morning, but it's not as bad as I've had before.

Stretching, I stand and stagger my way to the in-room coffee maker and brew a cup.

It's late morning edging into lunchtime, and I want to make it back over to Hannah Grace's before she gets home from school. As the coffee brews, I grab my laptop and boot up to log into the server Sydney set up for our encrypted files. For once she hasn't named the file something to fuck with me.

"I wonder if Sawyer had her rename it," I mumble aloud.

Since it's later than I anticipated, there's a higher likelihood of that than of Sydney not taking an opportunity to bust my balls. Ignoring the documents with HW—Hannah Grace Whittaker—in the title, I click on the others. The first is a background check for Zachary Nolan. He rents the apartment I tailed him to last night and the car is registered in his name. He must own it outright since there's no loan on it.

The apartment history goes back a few years as does his employment history.

Fuck.

He works at Hannah Grace's school.

Jealousy sits like an unwelcome rock in my stomach, but I continue to scroll instead of slamming the lid of my laptop closed like I want to.

There are no credit cards in his name, and there's a note next to the education info Sydney pulled.

This was harder to find than normal.

Next up are his socials. I click on one of the links and it's picture after picture of him and Hannah Grace. Hiking, bowling, hanging out in different locations. Granted, the profile is locked down pretty well, but it doesn't change the way my gut churns.

But is it personal? Or is this professional?

Don't kid yourself, Strickland. With Hannah Grace, it will always *be personal.*

"No," I tell the empty room.

Pushing the voice away that wants to argue, I key in a note to Sydney.

What do you see on his socials?

Sydney's ability to dive below the normal locks put into place by the apps means she can see more. And I need that insight right now. Something is niggling at me. I don't like that his history is so spotty and almost nonexistent before he came into Hannah Grace's life.

You don't like it or the green-eyed monster doesn't?

I reach the end of his report and shut it down, sliding the mouse to hover over Hannah Grace's file. A part of me doesn't want to open it. Doesn't want to read through everything I've missed over the last few years.

Had I not broken up with her, I could have lived it with her firsthand.

In a different life. A different universe.

One where I didn't break her heart and mine in the process.

"Fuck," I grit out and lift a fist to my chest, rubbing at the pain where my heart thumps with a pitiful, limping beat.

Quit being a pussy and click the fucking button.

It's like the voice takes control of my body, depressing my finger until the arrow spins in a circle before opening to the same type of report I just read. There are pictures and the information on her winning Miss Tennessee at the top, and I find myself studying the picture. Tracing the way her curls wave around her face to tease her arms. My hands have tangled in the softness of those curls. I've breathed in the citrus and coconut scent of the strands as they wrapped themselves around us. My fingers and then my lips have memorized that smile.

But it's not one hundred percent. There's something missing from her smile.

Something very few people would notice.

The smile doesn't create the crinkle next to her eyes that I'm used to. There's a spark missing. I'm not conceited enough to think it's because the pageant was shortly after we broke up, but the guilt eats at my stomach.

Swallowing, I continue to scroll, skimming over her graduation from Vanderbilt. Getting the job at the elementary school where she teaches kindergarten.

The grade she always wanted to teach.

It looks like she and her parents cosigned for the house, but she's the only one listed on her car. I keep scrolling and find her socials. These are more open than I wish they were, and I make a note to ask Sydney what the status of locking down Hannah Grace's accounts is. But not before I glance at her relationship status like the masochist I am.

Single.

Not in a relationship with Lover Boy.

Zach.

Whatever. Like I care what his name is. It doesn't change what I already figured out—I could read him like a book. There may not be anything between them, but not for lack of desire on his part. He wants something more. Who wouldn't?

You, remember, asshole? You broke up with her.

Not because I wanted to.

I had to.

She didn't deserve who I had become. Everything that had shaped me when I was deployed. I wasn't the same man who left her when I joined the army. The same one who promised her forever.

And she deserved more.

There was another note from Sydney under the socials that I skim over.

Lots of acquaintances but more from her pageant life than anything else. Lots of people from Mistletoe Creek and Vanderbilt. A few other pageant contestants. Some seriously hot guys...she dated you? P.S. Ask Hannah Grace about the other apps she subscribes to. Dating apps, find friends apps, etc.

Thanks, Sydney. Way to make a guy feel good and be cryptic all in one. Two for the price of one. A part of me wants to dive further into her friends list, but I don't have time. I also want to grill Sydney about the cryptic comment. But again, time. I need to stop my hike down memory lane and focus on the task at hand. And not the one where I demand Sydney tell me what the hell she meant. I was going to make sure Hannah Grace got the life she deserved. The one I broke my heart to give her.

Glancing at my watch, I have a few hours before she's set to be done with school. More than enough time to check out the house without nosy neighbors calling the cops like some Neighborhood Watch on steroids.

It doesn't take me long to shower, and the only other thing I do before I leave is brush my teeth, leaving the two days' growth covering my cheeks. I hate shaving. I pack up my laptop and drop it in my bag before swinging the worn leather of the messenger bag over my shoulder. I don't leave my laptop anywhere. Something Sydney taught me after she hacked into my locked laptop in less than five minutes and changed all my systems settings.

It took Sawyer threatening to fire her before she finally put the original settings back.

My keys are the last thing I slide into my pocket before leaving the room.

I take a different route back to Hannah Grace's, memorizing the secondary route just in case I need it. It's not as direct, but the secondary path doesn't need to be.

The sky is a brilliant blue, and I lift the aviator sunglasses to my face to avoid squinting into the brightness when I exit the car.

The chill in the air reminds me that the holidays aren't far off, and I pull the collar of my jacket up around my neck, wishing for the warm California weather about now.

I scan each house in my line of sight before moving away from the car. Her neighbors across the street still have curtains closed over the main window, and a late model Jeep I didn't see last night is parked in the driveway.

"May work nights," I murmur and move to the next house.

There's nothing different in the neighboring houses, and I close my car door and take the walkway to the front door. Flower beds border the path, and I can't help but imagine the weathered concrete surrounded by bright pops of color next to soft green grass even though the beds are currently empty.

Because that's what there would be. Those bright pops of fragrant color.

So Hannah Grace that it creates a lump in my throat.

Coughing to clear the ball of emotion, I reach the porch and check under the doormat and breathe a sigh of relief when I don't find the key. The Hannah Grace I remember was too trusting and would have left a key in plain sight. There's also no sign of any hiding rocks or planters.

"That's good, Honey Girl."

The nickname slips from my lips easily, and I'm relieved no one is around to call me out on my slip.

I try the front door, relieved when I can tell both the regular lock and the deadbolt are engaged. The curtains are open, but the blinds are closed enough that I can't see in when I try to peer in the window that doesn't move when I try to push it open.

I don't like the lack of security system, but I'll talk to her about that later.

The side of the house looks into an empty dining room since the blinds are open wider here.

The backyard is fenced in, but it's easy enough to hop since the gate must be on the other side. The back of the house holds the kitchen and a door that leads out here to the detached garage. On the other side of the door is her bedroom. The blinds and curtains are both wide open.

"Fuck."

The room is feminine, decorated in hues of soft pastels and completely vulnerable to anyone who could get back here.

"Because I'm guessing the gate isn't locked," I say, already heading to the other side of the house.

I hate that I'm right.

Doubling back, I walk by what I'm assuming is the bathroom window when something on the ground catches my attention.

If the day were any more gray, I might not catch it, but the sun glinting off a coin catches my attention where it lies innocently between two deep footprints. They line up perfectly with the angle into the window that can also see into the bedroom, and I snap a pic with my phone and text it to Sawyer.

> Looks like Hannah Grace had a reason to be concerned.

SAWYER

> I'm going to reach out to the NPD.

There's nothing more and I pocket my phone, searching along the ground for any other signs that someone has been watching her. It doesn't take me long to find one now that I'm searching for it. In front of one of her bedroom windows are two more areas where a print could have been but instead there are rocks that seem to be pressed deeper into the ground. Someone stood here for a while. Looking directly at her bed.

The hair on the back of my neck stands on end and I spin, half expecting someone behind me.

But there's nothing except the sound of the dog barking against the fence from the house behind hers.

I don't like my body's reaction to the indentations.

It's telling me there's danger.

And Hannah Grace is in the crosshairs.

The need to see her, to confirm she's safe, overwhelms me.

Forget later.

Right the fuck now.

CHAPTER 5

HANNAH GRACE

I sleep a deep, dreamless sleep. When my alarm goes off it's as though I've only blinked since I went to bed.

There were no dreams of Cole like I was afraid would happen. Instead, there was nothing.

And I'm not sure if I should be relieved or concerned.

I haven't slept this well in seven years.

But I decide not to examine that too closely as I get ready for school and leave the house.

I pull into the parking lot of the elementary school at the same time as Zach and bound over to his car.

"Good morning, Mr. Nolan, isn't it a beautiful day?" I greet as soon as he opens the door.

He grimaces, but can't hide the smile that takes over.

"Has anyone ever said you're too much of a morning person?" he teases and I laugh.

"You. Almost every day."

"Good. Just making sure I've said it out loud." He leans into his car and grabs his bag and a travel mug of coffee.

"Don't you ever have one of those nights where you sleep so well you wake up as rested as after summer vacation?"

"Ummm…no."

"It's because you play video games until all hours of the night."

Zach's let it slip on more than one occasion that he'll stay up most of the night online playing games with friends.

Crazy.

I'm in bed by ten at the absolute latest.

"Got to have my fun somehow since you don't ever want to go out on a school night."

"Well, we can't all have cushy PE teacher jobs where your first class doesn't come in until partway through the morning. I've got twenty blinking sets of eyes on me at 8:15 sharp."

"Awww, poor HG. Your kids love you."

"They do," I agree. "But I love them just as much. They're so sweet at this age."

He badges into the door and holds it open for me before following. The school is mostly dark, the administration still thirty minutes from getting here. It's just Zach, me, and Mrs. Wilkes, one of the lunch ladies that preps breakfast every day for students who arrive early.

"Your class is pretty sweet. Maybe we should do the balloon exercise this week."

"That's my favorite!" I tell him, bouncing in place.

"Does that mean you'll stick around through class?" he asks.

"Duh! I wouldn't miss it."

We stop in the teachers' lounge and drop off my lunch bag.

"Did you forget lunch?"

He groans. "At home on my counter. What's on the menu for today?"

The crestfallen look he gives me is pathetic.

"Poor baby. I'll share mine with you today," I offer. "Leftovers."

"You're the best."

"What are friends for?" I ask. "Besides, you rescued me when I forgot mine last time."

"It's a deal. See you at lunch?"

"It's a date," I say.

Only it's not a date. Because you don't like him. Why can't you like Zach? He's a nice guy. Local. He's a teacher. No plans on leaving.

Unlike—no. There's no use in comparing him to anyone else. Regardless, I don't like Zach. Not like that. He's my friend. My best friend.

"I like your shoes by the way," he says, rescuing me from my awkwardness.

I glance past my floral dress and jean jacket to the pink slip-on shoes I put on this morning.

"Thanks. These are the ones I picked up last weekend at the mall."

"I remember."

"Are those the new ones you got?" I ask.

"No. Those didn't fit right after all. I just cleaned my old ones."

"You're pretty handy. Maybe I'll bring you my shoes next," I tease him and start to walk down the hall.

"HG?"

I spin around, my bag bumping against my hip.

"Yeah?"

"Any word from your ex?" Zach asks.

"Cole?"

"Yeah." He may appear nonchalant, but there's a tension that wasn't there before.

"No. Not a peep. He probably thinks I'm crazy too," I say.

Zach's posture relaxes.

"Just curious."

So am I, but I won't admit it out loud. Will Cole stick around?

"See you at lunch?" I ask. "I need to go check my lesson plan for the holiday projects that start today."

"See you later." He salutes and turns to head to the gym.

But when I walk the kids down to the lunchroom, there's no sign of him just inside the cafeteria like normal. Instead, I drop the kids off with the monitors for the day and walk to the gym. It's dark except for the office.

"Zach?" I ask, poking my head into the room.

The woman behind the desk looks up from the book she's reading.

"Sorry?"

"My fault. I was looking for Mr. Nolan?"

She shrugs. "I'm not sure. I got a call earlier saying they needed a sub for PE today."

"Oh. Okay. Thanks."

I leave the gym and grab my lunch bag from the lounge before walking the rest of the way back to my classroom since I forgot my phone. Sure enough there's a text from him.

ZACH

Sorry, HG, went home with a migraine.

Rain check on the lunch?

It's not the first time he's suffered from those stupid migraines, and I frown as I key in my response.

Of course! Hope you feel better soon!

Do you need anything?

There's no response from him by the time I finish eating, and I hope he's sleeping it off.

Hope you're getting some sleep. I'll stop by with dinner and drop it off for you after school.

The rest of the afternoon feels like it drags until the end of the school day, but finally, the bell rings and I walk my class out to meet their parents.

"Bye, Miss Whittaker."

"Bye! Hey, Mom…"

"Bye, Miss W, see you tomorrow!"

I smile and wave as each student departs before going back to my classroom to gather my bags. I stop at a local restaurant for things he can eat when he's recovering—things that won't trigger another migraine—and head to his apartment.

I need to remind him to schedule something with his doctor. He told me he was going to last time he ended up with a migraine that lasted a week, but I doubt he has.

His apartment complex is clean and well-lit, but older than some of the nearby complexes. At least the insides all look nicer than the faded exteriors.

Adjusting the bag to not spill the soup, I walk the stairs to his apartment and knock on the door.

And wait.

"Zach?" I call through the door and knock again. "It's me. Hannah Grace. I brought food."

He knows who you are, dummy.

I knock again.

"Are you home?"

Wouldn't he have answered the door if he was? Is he still sleeping?

I shift my weight from foot to foot in front of his door.

This has never happened before.

I've never been to his apartment where he hasn't answered. Come to think of it, it's rare we're here at all. It's more likely he'll come hang out with me at my place.

My stomach churns with a mix of worry for him and disappointment, and I bend over and leave the bag in front of his door. His car is in the parking lot when I walk back down and I groan.

"I hope this isn't another week-long migraine."

I miss him when he's not at school. Not around to hang out and talk to. Once I'm seated back in my car, I find his contact in my phone, and my finger hovers over the call button.

"No, I shouldn't call him if he has a migraine."

I shake my head and switch to our text thread.

> Hope you're feeling better.

> I dropped off dinner on your porch.

My drive home is a mix of worry about Zach and serious consideration about Cole's reappearance in my life. Speaking of, I'm surprised that I haven't heard from him all day. Does that mean he's waiting for me now?

My foot comes off the accelerator with the question.

Do I want him to be waiting for me? Or would I rather pretend that him showing up last night was a figment of my imagination?

"Ugh. Get out of my head, Cole Strickland." I hit the steering wheel with my command.

There's no sign of his car anywhere on my street, and I breathe a sigh of relief. The second relief comes as my phone pings with a text. I wait until I'm in the garage to look at my phone.

ZACH

Sorry. I just woke up.

Thanks for dinner.

> Are you feeling better?

ZACH

Yeah, finally.

See you tomorrow?

> Okay. Want me to grab a coffee on the way to school? Something with extra caffeine and sugar?

ZACH

Who needs sugar when I have you?

I groan and send a GIF of a person hiding their face.

That's terrible.

ZACH

Made you smile though.

I shake my head at his text, but he's right. I am smiling.

You did. But save your strength.

And don't forget balloon day.

ZACH

Never.

See you tomorrow.

ZACH

Night, HG.

I'm relieved that I finally heard from him and he's feeling better.

I'm still smiling when I walk into my kitchen and drop my lunch bag on the counter and my big bag for school on the chair at the table. I'm still smiling when I walk into my room to change into a pair of sweatpants and a T-shirt.

Only my smile fades as my gaze lands on the crimson-red flower petals that are all over my bed. On the dozen roses that are a mix of living and dead resting against my pillow. No, not just a dozen. Two.

My phone is still in the kitchen as fear pounds through my veins with every pulse of my heart. At least it's still beating. The scream I want to echo is lodged in my throat.

Run!

Spinning on my heel, I race back into the kitchen and try to grab my phone that slides out of reach and crashes to the floor with my clumsy fingers grasping air.

I crawl under the table, grabbing my phone as the doorbell

rings. My head jerks against the underside of the solid wood, and stars dot my vision.

"Ow, fuck, dammit."

I rub my head with one hand while gripping my phone with the other. But I stay crouched next to my table, paralyzed by the choice to answer the door or run from my house.

"Hannah Grace?"

I'd recognize that voice anywhere.

Relief floods my body so quickly, my vision dims, and I grip the chair as dizziness swims through my body.

The doorbell rings again with an accompanying knock.

"Hannah Grace?"

The second use of my name unlocks my body and I rush to the door, slamming it open as I jump against Cole, who catches me.

"Honey Girl, what is it? What's happened?"

His arms lock around me, his hands spanning my back, and the cold terror of fear since I walked into my bedroom begins to dissolve.

My fingers grip his shirt and I bury my nose against his chest, breathing in the warm, spicy scent of his cologne. It's a far cry from the Coolwater he wore in high school, but the warm scent is familiar. It's quintessential Cole.

"Hannah Grace, you're scaring me, sweetheart. What's going on?"

I take another deep breath, the icy fist releasing from around my heart.

"My b-b-bedroom."

He walks us back inside, and I shudder as the door closes behind us.

"It's okay, I'm right here."

His hand rubs up and down my back in a soothing motion. Only then do I realize I'm shaking.

"I'll go check it out," he tells me, and extricates himself from my grip.

"Don't leave."

"I'm not going anywhere, sweetheart. But I need to see what's happened. I need to make sure you're safe."

He pulls a gun from behind his back and I shiver.

"Stay here," he commands.

"No."

He opens his mouth to argue before snapping it shut, then readjusts his grip on the gun.

"Stay close then. And behind me."

I nod and crowd against his back as he leads the way to my bedroom.

"What the actual fuck?" he growls.

I squeeze my eyes shut, not wanting to see the bed again.

"I-it was like this when I came h-home."

"Fuck. It wasn't like this earlier. Is anyone here?"

Maybe it's stupid, but I hadn't even considered that.

"I-I-I—"

"It's okay, I can check."

"We—"

"I'm putting my foot down on this one, Honey Girl." He leads the way to my bathroom, and once he's convinced it's only us, he pulls me out from behind him. "Stay here. Lock the door. I'll come get you when I make sure it's safe."

Warm, brown eyes lock on mine with a seriousness I can't argue with.

There's a familiarity in those depths. One I've trusted for the majority of my life.

But there's also a stranger, one with a determination that didn't exist the last time I saw him.

He's Cole. But he's not.

"Hannah Grace?" he murmurs my name.

I nod. "Okay."

He steps through the doorway.

"Lock it. I'll be back soon."

I nod again and close the door, twisting the lock in place. Leaning against the solid wood, I press my ear against it and strain to hear anything.

But the only things audible are my shallow breathing and the way my heart beats in my ears. Is someone else in the house with us? Will Cole be okay?

I breathe out a sigh with that question.

How many times have I asked myself that question? How many times had I prayed for him to be safe while he was overseas? He's no longer anything to me other than my past, but I don't want anything bad to happen to him either.

Especially not because of me.

I pace the length of the bathroom, wrapping my arms around myself.

My house isn't that big. It shouldn't take him this long to search the house.

Maybe he left.

No. He wouldn't have.

He did before.

"That was different," I whisper and move back to the door again.

He wouldn't leave. Not right now. Not like this.

"Cole, where are you?"

The only answer is my own voice echoing back at me.

I lift my hand to the door, flicking the lock but changing my mind at the last second. I reengage the lock and spin, grabbing my hairspray off the counter before turning back around and unlocking the door. Throwing it open, I scream and depress the button. Only my aim is off and all I manage to do is douse Cole's shirt with the megahold hairspray.

He grimaces and reaches for the hairspray that thankfully I

already stopped spraying, but not soon enough based on the large spot on his light-blue shirt.

"Sorry," I mumble as he recaps the spray and reaches around me to deposit it back on the counter.

"I thought I told you to stay in the bathroom until I came back."

"I was worried about you."

The corners of his lips twitch with his smile, but he doesn't let it stretch across his face.

"Sweetheart, I can take care of myself. And you."

I sigh and move to the linen cupboard in my bathroom to grab a washcloth for him. Our fingers brush as I pass him the small terrycloth square, and I try to ignore the little electric zing that travels from my fingertips through my body.

"Thanks." He dampens the cloth in the sink and unbuttons several buttons on his shirt to swipe it across the hairspray that has transferred from his shirt to his skin.

Holy muscles on muscles. Even with his shirt still on, the definition of his chest is clearly evident.

I force my attention to his face in the mirror, relieved that he hasn't caught me ogling him.

"Did you find anything?" I ask.

His gaze meets mine in the reflection, and the disappointment is obvious.

"No. There's no sign of forced entry, and nothing else has been disturbed—I think. Just your room. When did you last change your locks?"

"Right after I bought the house. My dad..."

Cole knows how protective Dad is over both my sister and me. He's the one who bought the locks and showed up on my front porch the weekend after I closed to change them.

"Did anyone have a key? Do you have a hide-a-key anywhere? I looked earlier—"

His statement reminds me about what he said.

"You were here earlier?"

He nods.

"Around lunchtime. I wanted to check out the house without having a nosy neighbor call the cops."

"Most of my neighbors work during the day. Except for Braeden who bartends at night."

"Across the street?" he asks.

"Yeah."

"Did you come in through the back door?" he asks, changing the subject.

"Yeah, I always do."

"And the door was locked when you got home?" He buttons his shirt and swipes at the material with the washcloth.

"I-I'm not sure. I wasn't paying attention when I got home. But…"

His hand freezes and his gaze lifts back to mine again.

"But what?"

"I've been meaning to call my dad, but I noticed that the lock is getting loose. If you shake the door hard enough it unlocks. I locked myself out and figured that out trying to get back in and—"

"Fuck. Hannah Grace! How long?"

I shrug.

"I noticed it a few weeks ago. That's when I locked myself out."

He closes his eyes and his lips move but there's no sound. It takes me a minute, but I realize he's counting to ten. His eyes reopen with a blaze of anger, but it's banked behind the serious facade he's perfected.

Would anyone who knows him less recognize the tension beneath the surface?

"I'm here to keep you safe," he tells me.

"I know."

Because regardless of what's happened between us, I can say that.

"Until I find whoever did that"—he motions toward my bedroom— "it's not safe for you to be alone."

I'm not so trusting that I don't believe him, but I also don't want to give up my independence. I also know what it means if I do.

"I've lived alone all this time without anything happening."

A muscle tics in his jaw.

"And you've never had something like this happen before."

He tugs me into the room where the roses are still a garish display. I can't stop the shudder that works its way down my spine to sit in a ball of anxiety and fear in my stomach.

"It's not safe," he tells me.

"So what? I run home to Mom and Dad's? I have a job, Cole. I have a life. One that I can't just run away from."

He sucks in a breath.

That was below the belt, Hannah Grace.

But I don't take it back. I can't.

"I'm not saying to run away."

"What are you saying?" I ask.

"Well, for starters, we're going to call the police and file an official report."

"That sounds reasonable," I tell him.

But I should know better.

"Second, you can't stay here alone. You have two options."

Something tells me I'm not going to like either option.

"What?" I ask.

"I can stay here with you. Or you can come to my hotel with me."

Called it.

"What's it going to be, Hannah Grace?"

CHAPTER 6

HANNAH GRACE

*T*he door hasn't even fully shut before Cole is tossing my suitcase on the second bed and turning back around.

"Let's go," he says.

"Go? Go where?"

Haven't we gone enough? I'm exhausted and just want to unpack and crawl into bed and forget today ever happened. After Cole finished cleaning hairspray off his shirt, we had to wait for the police to come take a statement and Cole wanted to go buy a new lock for the back door. He'd installed it while I grabbed a trash bag and removed any trace of the flowers from my bed after the two officers had taken their pictures. They'd even taken a few samples, although Cole didn't think that was worth anything.

"We both could use something to eat, and I don't know about you, but I could use a beer."

I open my mouth to argue, to tell him I'm not hungry, but my stomach betrays me, growling loudly into the room. The corners of Cole's lips twitch and he arches an eyebrow as he waits for my response.

"Ugh. Fine. I'm starving."

He makes me wait until he opens the door first, but I follow him out and down the elevator to the bar in the lobby. It's almost empty, the drone of a TV the only noise on a weeknight after eight.

The bartender takes our food and drink orders, and my lips are on the glass the bartender drops off before Cole speaks again.

"I want to ask you some questions."

I set the glass down and shift my stool to face him.

He's already facing me, his arm resting casually on the back of the chair, legs spread wide. For anyone looking, it would look like a relaxed posture. Only I can see the tension in how he holds himself. His poised body ready to spring into action if need be.

"Why?"

"We need to figure out who would want to scare you. Or I at least need to give Sydney some ideas of where to look."

"There's nobody that I can—"

"Why not let me be the judge of that?" he asks.

"Aren't you a little close to the situation to be objective?"

Does it bother him as much as it bothers me that we're forced together like this? If so, he doesn't act like it. Meanwhile, my stomach churns and my palms are clammy.

"I know how to be professional."

I wouldn't know, would I? The Cole I knew was a teenager going off to join the army. And in some ways, he's stayed that way in my mind. But the proof that he didn't freeze in a time capsule is evidenced by the man sitting in front of me.

Rolling my eyes, I reach for my glass. "Fine. Ask your questions."

"Tell me about your dating history."

The question—can I even call it that?—has me choking on the drink I've just taken.

"Excuse me?" I manage to croak out between coughs.

For his part, his expression hasn't changed. So either he really is asking from a professional standpoint or his poker face has gotten way better in the last seven years.

"Stalkers usually have some sort of romantic connection—either current or past—with their victims."

"I'm not with anyone!" I shout and immediately lower my voice as the bartender glances away from the TV they're watching at the other end of the bar.

"What about Zach?"

"I knew you were going to ask about him. Tell me again how this is going to help Sydney."

I knew it. I fucking *knew* it. Cole isn't asking me these questions for my case. He's asking for himself.

"Look, I don't give a shit if you and Zach are together or not," he says, but a twitch in his jaw tells me he's lying now. "What I care about is if I should be looking at anyone else."

"It's not Zach. He's my best friend." I cross my arms over my chest and fume.

"Then tell me who else to look at. For example, who's he?" He lifts his phone, swiping until he finds what he's looking for and showing me a picture.

I recognize it from one of the preliminary events during the Miss Tennessee pageant I won. I'm dressed in an evening gown with my arms wrapped around the former college football player.

"Brody?"

"Is that his name?"

"Yes, that's Brody. He's my sorority sister Casey's husband. Although I guess then he was her boyfriend. She's the one taking the picture by the way. They came to Miss Tennessee to support me during the competition."

Something I had needed even if I never uttered the words out loud. I may have been smiling on the outside, but inside I was still reeling from the Dear Jane letter Cole had sent me to break up with me.

He swallows slowly and glances away, setting his phone down

and reaching for his own glass for a drink. The bartender drops off our food, and it sits untouched in front of both of us.

"Any other questions?" I ask and finally reach for a fry that came as a side to my burger.

"Sydney told me to ask you about the other apps you subscribe to. Ones with a social setting."

"Huh?" I ask, grabbing my burger finally.

"You know. Friend apps, ones that give you ideas for what's going on for the week or weekend like activities, dating apps." He says the words so fast, I almost miss them.

But like a double take, my attention focuses on them.

"Dating apps?"

"She didn't specify outside of social apps. Just wanted me to ask you. What do you subscribe to?"

"Nothing. Not anymore anyway."

"Not anymore?"

Shit. I'm not sure whether to appreciate the fact that Sydney didn't tell him or be pissed at the fact that I'm left to explain. But these were my decisions, and I don't owe anything to either one of them. The guilt currently pricking at my stomach and the two bites of burger I've had can go right to hell.

"I used to pay for a few dating apps."

Because supposedly those were more reputable.

"A few?" The short phrase sounds strangled as he chokes on the words.

I shrug and grab another fry.

"It's not like one for hookups or anything. These are more serious than that. For people who want relationships instead of the casual thing."

Or at least that's what they touted. There were still plenty of men on those apps only looking for hookups too.

"Anyone we should look into?"

"I…don't think so? I went on a few first dates. Two second dates. But…"

How do I explain that neither of the guys that made it to the second date stage created the chemistry that existed with Cole? Even now, my body is tuned to his like we're on the same frequency—no matter how hard I try to pretend otherwise.

"But?"

I shrug. "It just didn't work out."

There's more nonchalance than I feel, but I'm good at faking it until I make it.

Hence the pageant title.

He grunts and takes a bite of his sandwich, chewing for a minute as I take a deep breath.

"Anybody else?"

"Like whom?"

He sighs.

"I don't know, Hannah Grace. Was there anyone who showed interest in you while you were at Vanderbilt? Guys that hit on you? Anything like that?"

"Worried I cheated on you while you were gone?" The words are out of my mouth before I can stop them.

Shit. Shit. Shit.

I focus on the remaining fries on my plate, rolling them around the glossy surface.

"You were never that person," he murmurs.

The words melt my insides into a large pile of goo.

"No," I whisper.

Because he was the only one I thought of when I was in school. Even after we broke up and I was still there.

"Anybody not want to take no for an answer when you shot them down?"

"Not really—wait. The grocery store guy." I look up as the memory of the creepy produce guy surfaces.

"Grocery store guy?" he asks.

"I used to go the store closest to my house. And would see the same guy in the produce aisle—like he always got there right when I did and started his shopping. He asked me once about picking out watermelon and we started talking. Michael. That was his name."

"Did you tell him yours?"

I shoot him the *duh* look. "Of course. What else do you do when someone introduces themselves to you?"

"You make up a fake name," he mutters.

"He seemed harmless enough."

"But?"

"He asked me out the second or third time I saw him there. Offered to make me dinner."

"What did you say?"

"I may be naïve, Cole, but I'm not that stupid. I know better than to go to a strange man's house. So he asked me for drinks instead."

"Did you go?"

Cole looks at me expectantly, waiting for my answer much the same way that Michael had all those years ago.

"No," I start and his entire body deflates. "There was just something in my gut that told me I shouldn't. I told him I had plans and switched my shopping day so I wouldn't risk running into him again. Only he was there when I did that. And he asked me out again. I told him no, thanks and he told me that he knew I was lying because he followed me home after the last time and I didn't leave my house. That was when Zach came to stay with me for a few weeks and I switched grocery stores."

"How long ago did this happen?"

"I don't know. Maybe a year ago or so?"

"Do you know his last name? What he drove? Anything like that?"

I shake my head. "No. Why? You think it's him? Now?"

"Fuck, Hannah Grace, I don't know." He blows out a breath. "It could be. But I have a whole lot more could bes than anything definitive right now. Switching gears, what about the pageant?"

"What about it?"

"Are you still involved with it? Alumni lunches, anything like that?"

"I was more so during that first year, but I've only gone to two of their events over the last couple of years."

"Any of the girls pissed at you about something? Any drama?"

"There was a reason *Miss Congeniality* was such a hit, Cole. There's always drama," I say.

"Anybody willing to scare you like this? The runner-up maybe?"

"Josie? She's the sweetest. And funnily enough, she was our Miss Congeniality."

"Organizers? Employees? Rumors? Anything like that?"

"I mean one of the girls accused me of sleeping with one of the judges. Actually, that wasn't the only rumor about him. In my year or anyone else's."

"Name?"

"You want me to remember his name? Cole, that was four years ago. He was just a perv who liked to surprise the girls backstage. Wait, that's it. Pervy Pete."

"Jesus Christ, Hannah Grace." He drops his head in his hands, and his thumbs dig into his temples.

"What? What did I say?"

"You've literally given me a minimum of seven different suspects in the span of thirty minutes. And you're telling me no one has checked on any of these guys?"

"I don't see why you're getting upset with me. None of them ever seemed connected."

"Until we find out who the fuck decided to leave you a present, just assume that everything is connected. And tell me everything."

"What if I don't—"

"Everything," he repeats, locking eyes with me.

The snarky comment I want to make—the one about him not being the boss of me—dies on my lips.

"Okay. I will."

Cole pays the bill, and we both head upstairs where he follows me into my room.

"Hello, privacy. I'm not sharing a room with you," I say.

"I'm through there." He points at the connecting door.

Of course he has a logical, professional reason for coming in. Especially given the connection between the two rooms.

"Oh."

The corners of his lips twitch but he doesn't smile. Good. I'd probably slap it off his face with the way I'm feeling right now.

"I'm going to review a few files and pass on the information you shared with me to Sydney and Sawyer. Let me know if you need me."

"Does Sydney need any of my passwords?"

Cole huffs a laugh.

"If she does, she'd never tell me. But more than likely not. She won Sawyer's hacking contest when she was seventeen. She can get in anywhere. But I'm sure she'd appreciate your permission."

"Of course. If I can answer anything for her, you can have her reach out directly. You don't have to keep playing the middleman."

"Sydney is…a lot for people to handle. It's better I buffer you from her full antisocial personality."

"Just because she's a strong woman doesn't make her too much to handle," I tell him.

"How did you—"

"She'd have to be incredibly strong to be successful in a male-dominated world like IT. Also, she has to put up with you."

A surprised laugh escapes him and he lifts his hand.

"I'm sorry I said anything. I'll pass on your contact info."

"Thank you."

"Anything else?"

"No. I think I'm going to unpack and watch some TV."

"Let me know if you need me."

"You said that already," I point out.

"I mean it."

I'm sure he does.

But it doesn't mean I'm any more likely to ask for help.

Especially from Cole Strickland.

He finally leaves, and I let out the breath I've been holding.

"Okay, Hannah Grace, let's get moving."

Because maybe if I move, I won't think about the fact that my ex-boyfriend still sets off sparks in me. I move from the dresser to the bed, unpacking my clothes as I attempt to ignore the male presence through the connecting door. It *should* be easy given that he's out of sight. But his cologne still lingers in the air which means he might as well be in the same room.

It doesn't take me long before my suitcase is empty, and I hang one of the dresses I brought in the closet. I try not to crane my neck into Cole's room, but I can't help but see him hunched over his desk, switching his attention between his phone, his laptop, and a notebook that he scribbles furiously in.

Keep your distance, girl. That boy is trouble.

Only he never was. Even when we were younger he almost never broke the rules, and I was always looking for the loopholes. With a sigh, I sit next to the suitcase on the bed and reach for my own phone.

It might be late, but it's not like I'm sleeping anytime soon.

Between the "gift" on my bed, my conversation with Cole at the bar, and just his reappearance in my life, I'm tired, but not sleepy.

The TV is set on some sitcom rerun, the volume low. But the show doesn't hold my attention. Instead, I pull up my social media and start scrolling until my sister's latest post pops up.

Laura Leigh is a senior at the University of Tennessee in Knoxville which is a little closer to home than I chose. She and her sorority had done some volunteer work, and she's posed with several of her sisters holding a puppy.

"I'm sure Mom and Dad had a hard time telling Laura Leigh no on the dog," I murmur.

"What was that?"

Cole's voice from the door startles me and I drop my phone.

"Sorry," he says and moves close enough to pick up my phone where it skittered away and hands it to me.

"Laura Leigh"—I show him the picture—"and her sorority sisters did a volunteer event with a shelter in Knoxville. I'm sure she wanted to adopt the puppy she's holding, and I'm wondering if Mom and Dad were able to tell her no."

"Fuck. She's all grown up, isn't she?" he asks and sits on the end of the other bed.

It takes me a minute to figure out when the last time was that he saw her.

"Well, the last time you saw her was what...when she was what? Thirteen? Fourteen?"

He reaches behind him, squeezing the back of his neck, and for a heartbeat his face is full of...regret.

"Yeah, I guess so."

A part of me wants to reach over, to comfort him for the regret that's written so clearly in the way his body hunches in on itself. How often had I offered comfort over a bad grade or a lost football game when we were younger? Or tried to comfort him when we would talk while he was deployed when something had gone wrong and he'd lost friends? And where had that led?

Me getting my heart broken.

This isn't a happy reunion with a fun-filled walk down memory lane.

"What did you think? That she was forever going to be twelve? Things change, Cole. It's been seven years since you saw her last. Just because you forgot about us doesn't mean we stayed frozen in some time capsule."

I surge from the bed and pace to my empty suitcase, zipping it up with angry motions.

"I know," he says the words quietly.

Almost a whisper.

They might as well be shouted with how clearly they resonate.

How they pierce my heart and make me want to forget. To forgive.

But I can't.

I walk the suitcase to the closet and toss it in. I don't turn around. I can't. I don't want to lose my anger in my sympathy toward him.

My traitor of a body can sense him though. I *know* when he stands from the bed with a sigh. Out of the corner of my eye, I can barely make out his steady movement to the door that connects the two of our rooms. I turn, with every intention of shutting the door after him and locking him out, but he pauses between the two rooms. His fingers grip the cheap wood, but he doesn't turn back. Just stays where he is, facing forward.

"For what it's worth, Hannah Grace, I'm sorry."

"You've said that before." My voice is hoarse and I clear the lump from my throat.

"I meant it."

"Saying you're sorry doesn't change anything, Cole. You still…"

You still broke my heart.

I don't say the words, but I don't need to.

His knuckles whiten for a beat before he takes a deep breath and releases it, letting go of the wood.

"I know."

"Then why are you here? Why did you come back?"

His shoulders drop, but he still won't look back.

"What time do we need to head for your school?" he asks, changing the subject.

A scream bubbles inside me, but I tamp it down and stalk toward the door.

"Early."

I close the door, pushing him the rest of the way into his room as I lock it.

"Good night, Hannah Grace." His words come clearly through the door as if nothing is between us.

But there is.

Four years of heartbreak and a whole lifetime of memories.

And karma, bitch that she is, replays every stupid memory on a repeat loop from hell.

Riding bikes in the summer through town before we got ice cream from Scoops, the ice cream parlor on the main street, to eat in the town square. Elementary field trips and middle school lockers. Boy-girl parties when it started to mean something. Him asking me out to our first date and that first kiss. Nights spent at football games or pretending to do homework at each other's houses until everyone left us alone to make out. That first time in his old pickup truck.

Seeing him when he graduated from basic. I'd ridden with Cole's older brothers, Justin and Jared, when his parents had to stay home with his sisters who both had gotten sick just before we were all due to leave for North Carolina. Instead, his brothers and I had a road trip and then they disappeared and left us their hotel room for the night.

Cole had looked so different. His normal unruly hair had been short, his back ramrod straight. He'd carried himself with a different kind of confidence than he had in high school. But the night we had in the hotel room—and the morning—is more vivid than a memory, and I wake up hot and bothered. There's an ache between my thighs that begs me to finish what the dream started. My fingers are already breaching the edge of my sleep shorts before I recognize what I'm about to do.

"I don't think so."

I fling my arm to the side before shrugging out of the covers.

Touching myself to thoughts of Cole? To the few memories like that I had with him?

That was something I did before he broke my heart.

Since then, it was only thoughts of Justin Hartley or Ryan Reynolds that occupied my private time.

Liar, liar, pants on fire.

"Not for long," I say out loud and head for the bathroom.

Cranking the handle, I don't wait for the water to warm up before I'm shedding my clothes and stepping into the cool spray. I gasp as the cold tingles along my skin and stand in the frigid stream for several agonizing heartbeats. Finally, when I'm ready to jump from the ice-filled shower, I lift my frozen fingers to the knob and shift the water to a more palatable temperature. My limbs relax, and I grab my shampoo to squeeze into my palm.

"He's not even that good-looking," I grumble as I scrub my scalp.

Yeah, because the scruffy, sexy Hemsworth look-alike doesn't do it for you?

"It's not about the looks."

It's not not *about the looks.*

"I—" Snapping my mouth shut, I focus on rinsing the suds from my hair and grab my body wash.

I'm not going to argue with myself. Is he good-looking? Yes. He always has been. And the softer teenage-heartthrob features have faded to strong lines covered in an intriguing looking scruff. He's better looking now than he was when I was in love with him.

But that doesn't change the last four years of history between us.

"Why did he have to show up?"

The shower head doesn't answer my question, and eventually I have to get out and finish getting ready. Before Cole had shown up at my front door night before last, I hadn't given him more than five minutes of thought in over a year.

Apparently that was not okay with the universe.

And now he was here, sharing a wall with me, for however long until he figured out who was behind the flowers on my bed.

"That sounds ridiculous," I murmur as I rub the towel over my skin.

Ridiculous as it may sound though, it still creates gooseflesh that ripples down my arms at the memory of the roses.

The letters before had been one thing. Eventually whoever had sent them stopped. I could even sort of ignore the perfume being out of my purse. But I couldn't ignore the loud warning bells clanging that *someone* had broken into my house and left a mix of fresh and dried roses and rose petals all over my bed.

A shiver skates down my spine and I hurry to my room, flipping on all the lights before I reach the dresser and grab the white sweater and light purple pants I packed. It's one of my favorite outfits—the sweater is soft and warm and the pants just make me happy.

A glance at the clock tells me I'm up even earlier than normal. I'd rather not be alone with my thoughts so the key is to stay busy. So even though I normally do minimal hair and cosmetics, I spend a solid forty-five minutes between blow-drying my hair and doing my makeup.

And anytime Cole tries to intrude on my self-made zen?

I start humming Duo Lipa's "New Rules" as loud as I can—a firm reminder.

But once I'm done, I have no choice but to remind myself that Cole exists.

84

I trudge to the connecting doors like a death row inmate standing at the door to my execution.

"Don't be so dramatic," I tell the door and unlock my door before opening it.

I expect for Cole's door to be closed too.

But it's not.

"Cole?" I ask, stepping into the dark room.

The lights in my room cast everything in shadow, but there's enough light that I confirm the bed is empty at the same time my brain registers the sound of a shower from his bathroom.

The polite thing to do—the safe thing for me to do—would be to go back to my room and wait for Cole. But my attention snags on a stack of papers and file folders strewn across the other half of the used bed, and my curiosity gets the better of me.

Closing the distance, I lean over the bed and read the first file label.

Whittaker.

Directly beneath the manila card stock of the folder is the notebook with Cole's neat scrawl.

You have handwriting that's prettier than mine.

I take my time, Honey Girl. With everything.

The breath of Cole's murmured words from a conversation we had in high school tickles my neck and I glance up, half expecting him to be next to me. But I'm alone with the memory and the subsequent one where he had proven how he liked to take his time by kissing every spot on my neck and discovering where I liked his lips best.

Shaking my head, I clear the memory and focus on the words that appear to be a summary of what's in the file as well as a summary of what I had shared with Cole. Finally come the questions.

WHO IS "PERVY PETE?" HOW IS HE AFFILIATED WITH PAGEANT BOARD?

MICHAEL? WHICH GROCERY STORE? SECURITY FOOTAGE?
HAVE SYDNEY CHECK DATING APPS. BACKGROUND CHECKS ON
EVERYONE.
WHO IS ZACH TO HANNAH?

That question is different from the rest. I've already explained to Cole that there's nothing between Zach and me other than him being my best friend. Why is this still a question?

"What are you doing?" Cole's question startles me and I whirl around, dropping the notebook.

Busted.

But that word scatters as I take in Cole as he stands highlighted by the bathroom light. His dark hair is still damp, moisture clinging to every line and ridge of muscles that sculpt toned shoulders to a well-defined chest with the smattering of chest hair. My eyes betray me and continue their perusal south to the faint outline of washboard abs that disappear along with the twin dimples on either side of his waist below the low-slung towel.

Oh. My. God.

Every ounce of saliva that existed—that even had the chance to exist—dries in an instant as desire pools in my belly. His spicy scent reaches out, wrapping around me and tempting me like the Pied Piper.

The groan he lets out sounds pained, and he clenches his hands at his side.

"Honey Girl."

How many times had he whispered that nickname to me? And every time without fail, it had the same effect on the strength of my knees.

Even now.

"Hmm?"

It's like I'm under some spell that the sight and smell of him has created—paralyzed, waiting.

Wanting.

"My eyes are up here."

His words are a bucket of ice water on my libido, and I scramble to lift my gaze back into a safe spot instead of centered on the towel knotted at his waist. Once my gaze finds his, the amused smirk kills any lingering desire.

Asshole.

"See something you like?" he asks.

"Nope." I pop the *p* and give him a wide berth as I make my way back to the connecting room.

Holding my breath like that will help me ignore that damn mesmerizing cologne that clings to him and mixes into the room. At the threshold, I release the breath, finally in the clear.

"Hannah Grace."

"What?" I snap and spin back around.

He tilts his head in my direction.

"Can I have my notebook back?"

I glance down, surprised to see my fingers still gripping the yellow paper. Embarrassment overwhelms me—a combination of being caught snooping and ogling and anger for feeling anything more than indifference toward the man who broke my heart when he broke his promise.

"Here." I toss it at him.

He leans forward, stretching all those delicious looking muscles and scooping up the flying pad with ease.

"You can ask me, you know," he tells me quietly.

"Ask you what?"

"About your case. My notes. Anything you want."

Is it as obvious to him as it is to me that he didn't add anything about our past to his list? Opening my mouth, I almost ask him about it. About why he did what he did. Maybe then I could finally move on if I knew the answer and get closure.

But having an answer wouldn't change the past. And I am over him. Momentary lapse of sanity just now notwithstanding.

"Hannah Grace?"

Cole's question snaps me from my internal debate.

"Let me know when you're ready to go," I say and step through the door, closing it behind me.

Cole better figure this out soon.

It's been one day. Less than a day. More like twelve hours. But my sanity—and my heart—can't take this proximity for much longer.

CHAPTER 7

COLE

*I*t's for the best that Hannah Grace hides back in her room. That she hates me.

Yeah, keep telling yourself that, Strickland.

I'd stayed awake for hours last night, poring over the information I had. Reading and rereading her file until I had most of the information memorized. Until I'd passed out. Even then Hannah Grace wasn't far since she decided to star in my dreams.

If we had the same relationship we had seven years ago, I'd ask her if she was tired from running through my dreams last night. But dream Hannah had let me catch her. Real-life Hannah was an enigma. She looked at me like she wanted to kiss me in one breath and like she was ready to strangle me in the next.

Can you blame her?

"No," I say with a sigh.

I toss the notebook toward the bed and walk to the dresser to grab my clothes and get dressed now that the cold registers. Funny, I hadn't been cold when Hannah Grace was in the room. Neither had she based on the heat in her expression.

Even now my dick twitches at the memory.

"Knock it off," I mumble and dress quickly before tossing the towel back in the bathroom.

It doesn't take me long to finish getting ready even after I decide to shave, and twenty minutes—and one serious lecture in the mirror—later, I'm knocking on the now-locked door that separates my room from Hannah Grace's.

"Hannah Grace?" I call through the door and wait.

After several heartbeats, I'm still waiting and I try again.

"Hannah Grace?" I knock louder in case she didn't hear me the first time.

This time, I don't have to wait.

"What?" Her voice is muffled by the door, but still full of suspicion.

"Are you going to open the door?"

"Are you dressed?"

Her quick question has my lips twitching.

"Why? Worried you won't be able to control yourself?"

The door flies open and her hand snaps out, her index finger digging into my chest.

"You don't need to concern yourself with that, you egotistical asshole. You're not that attractive."

I can't help the flare of amusement and continue to push her buttons.

"Not *that* attractive means you think I'm at least a little attractive."

"I'm not going to argue with you or deny anything. In theory? Sure. I have no doubt that you have plenty of women who are more than happy to tell you how attractive you are."

Not as many as she thinks there are. Or were.

But none of them are you.

Fuck. The amusement fades and suddenly I want out of this conversation as fast as I jumped into it. This isn't my girlfriend who I used to joke around with. She isn't even my friend. Not anymore.

Hannah Grace is a client. And I need to act like a professional. But I can't stop the question before it pops out.

"What about you?"

She sighs and closes her eyes. Taking a step back, when those dark lashes flutter back open, her blue eyes have a mask in place that I hate. I don't want her to hide what she feels.

Maybe it's for the best.

"It doesn't matter what I think, Cole. The only thing that matters is getting through this and..."

She trails off, but the resignation of what she hasn't said is written in her expression.

"Moving on with your life," I supply for her.

She nods.

It's true.

That should be all that matters.

So why does that create a hollow ache where my heart beats in my chest?

"Can we go to school now?" she asks.

"Let me just grab my bag."

I'm already at my desk when she speaks again.

"I want to drive myself."

Last night, I'd followed her to the hotel. My plan had been to use her car if we needed it for a distraction, but the separation will do us some good.

"Okay. Just don't lose me."

"You know where I work," she grumbles and turns into her room.

I'm smiling again before I realize it.

"And wipe that grin off your face," she says louder, calling me out.

It's probably a good thing I don't have to hide my smile on our way to the school since it's almost impossible to completely wipe away my grin—although I do manage to bite it back when I'm with her in the hotel elevator and walking toward her car. I only let her climb in once I've done a sweep of the outside and don't notice anything different from when she parked it last night.

She gets in without another word, but does wait for me to back out behind her. I keep a healthy distance between my car and hers as we drive toward her school and allow her to park where she normally does while I grab a spot in the back of the lot, backing in so I can keep an eye on the school from my car if the administrators don't want me inside. Not that I plan to stay inside much. Once school starts for Hannah Grace, I'm going to head back to her place—with her permission—to see if I can find anything at her house. She was too upset for me to spend much time there checking things once the police left and I'd taken my own photographs. Once the lock was changed and the flowers were cleaned up, we had soon left for the hotel.

I had sent the photographs to Sawyer and Sydney late last night in hopes that they would see something the police and I missed.

Hannah Grace's friend Zach is already in the parking lot, and I have a front row seat to the way she smiles at him. Fuck.

I rub at my chest as jealousy and something else creates a physical pang.

I give myself the moment before leaving my car to join them.

"Zach, right? Good morning." I extend my hand even though I'd rather deck the man on the receiving end of Hannah Grace's smile.

"Morning…"

"Cole," I remind him.

"Cole." He nods once, gripping my hand before releasing it.

I don't like you either, dude.

But for Hannah Grace's sake, I'll deal with him. He's her friend.

"Cole's going to come see my classroom this morning," she explains, leaving out the part that we're staying at a hotel.

It was something I told her last night—keep it to herself.

"How's Principal Green going to feel about that?" Zach asks, leading her toward the school.

My molars grind together as his arm wraps behind her. Almost touching, but not quite.

"I'll introduce myself to him when he gets in," I speak up from behind them.

I don't like that Hannah Grace is here almost by herself in the morning. But I'll bring that up with her later. And maybe a conversation with Zach too. About how close he is to her.

Yeah, because that won't piss off Hannah Grace.

Pissed off or not, I need someone looking out for her. Even if it means entrusting her to Zach.

"Where's your lunch, HG?" Zach asks her.

"Oh…um…shoot. I must have forgotten it," she says.

I want to groan because Hannah Grace is a terrible liar. Same as she always was.

Even Zach sees right through her.

"Why you gonna try to lie to your best friend?"

He bumps her shoulder with his and she shoots me a look over her shoulder.

No. I mouth the word and shake my head just in case she can't read my lips.

"HG?" Zach asks again.

"I-I'm in a hotel right now."

Zach stops and spins in my direction.

"What?"

"Hannah Grace!"

Goddammit. I asked her to keep that quiet.

"He's my best friend and he already knows everything," she tells me, perching her hands on her hips.

"Not everything," I remind her.

"What? What don't I know?" Zach turns his attention back to Hannah Grace.

"Someone—"

"Not out here at least," I say and usher them both toward the door.

"No one's here anyway," Hannah protests but still swipes her ID at the door to go in.

"Where's your classroom?" I ask.

It's Zach who leads the way. The fact that he knows and I don't irritates the hell out of me.

It should be fine. They both work here—of course he knows where her classroom is. But my gut wants to throw a fit. Wants to insist that he stay here and I'll walk Hannah Grace to her classroom.

But instead I bite my tongue and follow the two of them. We're barely past the doorway when Zach stops again.

"Okay, what am I missing?"

I close the door and nod at Hannah Grace to tell the story.

"Someone was in my house," she says without any lead-in.

"You saw them?" he asks.

She shakes her head.

"No. But they left s-something for me. Roses. All over my bed."

"Living and dead," I add.

"Hannah Grace, it's not safe to stay there right now. Not alone."

"That's what Cole said. So we're staying at a hotel for right now. Until Cole can figure out what's happening and who's behind it."

"You need to call the cops!" His tone says he holds little faith in my efforts.

"We already did," I growl.

"Any leads?" Zach looks to me.

"Nothing yet. I have my team working on it too."

"Have the police figured anything out yet?"

I shake my head.

"No. They were going to canvas the neighborhood to see if anybody saw anything, but they weren't holding out much hope."

"You think it was creepy grocery store guy?" he asks Hannah Grace.

"It's been a year since that happened," she says.

"Maybe he saw you again." He turns to me. "He drives a Dodge Ram and I have part of his license plate in my phone."

I pull out my phone and open the text thread to Sydney and Sawyer.

"What's the number?" I ask.

It takes him a minute but eventually he finds the number and rattles it off to me, and I key in the partial plate. I only get the thumbs-up emoji from Sydney and nothing from Sawyer, so I repocket my phone.

"So now you know everything," Hannah Grace says.

"Except for what's next," Zach responds, crossing his arms and looking first at me before looking back to Hannah Grace.

"What's next is my meeting Principal Green. Hannah Grace won't be left alone from now until I find the son of a bitch who's scaring her."

"Oh goody," she mumbles and I shoot a glare in her direction.

"Is your principal here yet?" I ask.

She glances at the clock above her door.

"He should be. Come on. We'll go meet him."

Zach walks with us in the direction of the office, but stops at the gym. Principal Green is in, and after explaining the situation and assuring him that his staff and students are safe, he agrees to letting me stay as a visitor with Hannah Grace. It helps that Sawyer reached out to him yesterday while I was sleeping to brief him about what was going on.

Thanks for sharing the info, boss.

"School starts soon," Hannah Grace says as we walk out of the office.

"I'll be back in a little while."

I want to take the time while she's at school to go to her house again.

"Where are you going?"

"Your house. I just want to go check things out again. Want me to bring lunch when I come back?" I ask.

"Unless you want to eat cafeteria food. I thought you said you weren't going to leave me alone until you found the person doing this," she says.

On the surface she may appear calm, but I can see the hint of fear she tries to keep hidden. I move closer, reaching out and squeezing her hand.

I try to ignore the frisson of awareness that travels from her skin to mine.

"You're safe here. It's a public place. And Zach's here too. I *will* be back by lunch. I promise."

"You better be. I don't want to eat cafeteria food."

I bark out a laugh at her comment.

"Yes, ma'am."

She turns toward her hallway and takes enough steps so my hand loses connection with hers.

"Be good at school," I call after her.

She stops and shoots me a smile over her shoulder that takes my breath away.

"Be careful," she murmurs.

It's still loud enough for me to catch and I nod.

"I will."

She's counting on me.

CHAPTER 8

COLE

*A*s soon as I'm back in my car, I hit the button for Sawyer's number and turn on speaker phone.

"King."

"Heard you had a convo with the principal," I say in lieu of a greeting.

"Figured you were going to get to it sooner rather than later. Also thought it wouldn't hurt to give Ms. Whittaker's workplace a heads-up that you would be hanging around."

"I appreciate it."

"How'd it go?"

"He wanted some assurances about the safety of his staff and students. Since whoever it is seems to be targeting Hannah Grace, I see no reason to be concerned that anyone else is in jeopardy. With or without me at school."

Whoever it was, they wanted to scare Hannah Grace. But I had no idea why.

"You sound like you're driving."

"I am. Heading back to Hannah Grace's to see if I can figure anything out about who was in her place."

"Have you thought about installing a camera?" Sydney pipes up from the background.

"What the hell? Did you bug Sawyer's phone and join in for fun?" I ask.

It's six in the morning in LA.

"I asked Sydney to come in and show me what she did for Featherlight's security on their servers."

"And the best time to do that was six?"

"It helps from a bandwidth perspective. And no one else is at work yet. We wrote it into their contract that the latest they want me running anything is no later than seven," Sydney explains. "Now what about the camera?"

"Awww, Syd, look at you sounding all adult and rational. I figured you might have a suggestion or two for one I can pick up that can be monitored and recorded remotely."

"Oh my God, is know-it-all Cole asking *me* for recommendations?" Every word drips with her signature sarcasm.

"Don't let it go to your head. You have more time than I do to track down that kind of stuff."

"Who needs to track it down? I already have a list of what I recommend. Let me see if they have what I'm thinking of local and you can pick it up. Otherwise we'll have to ship it and that could take a few days."

I bite back the groan.

A few days in close quarters with Hannah Grace is not what I need. Even if it might be what my body craves.

"Find something local." I bite the words out.

"Sir, yes, sir," she snarks and I can picture her saluting.

"Sydney, put your arm down," Sawyer tells her.

Called it.

"Do either of you have any suggestions for a full security system?" I ask, changing the subject.

I have no doubt Sawyer does.

"I have a couple of concepts I can send you. What are you thinking? Windows? Doors? Motion sensors?" Sawyer asks.

"I—"

"Does Hannah Grace want a security system?" Sydney asks.

"I haven't talked to her about it."

If it keeps her safe, of course she'll want it.

"Since it's her house and she's going to have to pay for it, don't you think you should ask?"

"I'm trying to keep her safe. You should recognize that. Your apartment is like a maximum security prison."

"Part of that was at Jax's insistence. He's pretty protective of Jessie."

Sydney lives with her college roommate, Jessie Bryant, whose older brother is a famous musician. But the few times I've been to their place, I've been impressed by the amount of security for the two of them.

"And," Sydney continues, "there's a difference in that I control the security of my house, Cole. I don't have some overprotective Neanderthal shoving it on me with an 'ask forgiveness' mentality. You need to see what Hannah Grace wants."

"What she wants doesn't matter. What matters is keeping her safe." I'm all but yelling at the dash.

Why can't Sydney understand that protecting Hannah Grace is the most important thing? She is the client.

Yeah, because you'd argue like this for anyone.

"Why don't you talk to Ms. Whittaker and get her thoughts on a security system?" Sawyer breaks into the conversation.

But I'm not giving this up.

"I still—"

"I'll send you the specs. But don't do anything until she approves."

I turn into Hannah Grace's neighborhood and relax my grip on the steering wheel.

"Did you see my notes I sent you on the names I got from

Hannah Grace and on Zach's socials?" I ask, attempting to lower my blood pressure by choosing something else to talk about.

"I did. I've already managed to track down three of the five on the dating app—God, remind me I will never be that desperate. Do you know how many dick pics Hannah Grace had in her deleted messages? Gag."

Her comment is not helping my blood pressure.

"Fuck, Sydney, I don't want to hear about that."

"What? It's the truth. It makes me feel a little better that none of those guys got a response in return. The five she scheduled dates with were all aboveboard from what I can see. One with a second date ended up messaging her after on their lack of chemistry, so I've already eliminated him. The second wasn't as nice, so I'm diving a little deeper. Seems our boy struck out with a bunch of women he met for dates."

Red hazes my vision and I take several deep breaths for it to clear.

"What about the partial plate?"

"You just fucking sent that! How about asking me about something I've had a little time to look into. Like the socials."

My molars click together.

"Fine," I grit out. "Tell me."

"Say please."

I'm going to need some serious dental work after this.

"Sydney," Sawyer warns before I can say anything.

"You guys seriously are no fun. It's perfectly fine to give me shit, but neither of you can take it as well as you can dish it out."

"Sydney," Sawyer repeats her name.

She sighs.

"Fine. I'm running a couple of different programs both on the current social media and seeing if anything else exists with his info. So far, all I can tell is your boy has a serious hard-on for your ex-girlfriend."

Will she ever learn to sugarcoat anything?

"Sydney." This time Sawyer's use of her name is more like an invocation.

Probably for patience.

"What? It's true. You've seen it too."

The silence on Sawyer's part is all the confirmation I need.

Tell me something I don't know.

Zach wants more with Hannah Grace. Whether she does is not as clear.

"He's her friend," I tell the two of them.

"Does he have any ideas? Has he seen anybody outside the school or around them when they're together?"

"The grocery store guy. He's the one who gave me the partial plate."

"Does he know about the dating apps?" Sawyer asks.

"Not that I'm aware of."

"You didn't ask him?" The surprise is clear in Sawyer's question.

"The dating apps are none of his business," I growl.

"If my best friend were on a dating app, she would tell me. There's safety in phoning a friend on a bad date," Sydney says.

"He wants more. I'm sure her sharing that with him would be awkward."

"Does she know that he wants more?" Sawyer asks.

"I have no fucking idea. This is only my second full day here. I've been a little busy talking to the police, getting Hannah Grace settled at the hotel, and cleaning up fucking flowers."

"Do I need to come out there? I can tell Evie—"

"No. This is my assignment."

And no one is going to replace me. Even if it's my boss.

"What if it's an order?" The question is quiet, but steady. Exactly like Sawyer himself.

"What would you do if it was Evie?" I fire back.

I already have the answer. Sawyer had almost gotten himself killed protecting his now wife when her ex-label rep found out where she was hiding. Granted, he found out from Sawyer, but neither of us expected the asshole to brain Sawyer with a rock that could have killed him.

"Fine. But if you get too close, I will replace you."

"Not going to happen. She hates me."

It didn't change how I felt about her. How I had always felt about her.

I pass Hannah Grace's house and turn onto the adjoining street before I park. I don't want the neighbors to question my car's presence if any of them happen to be home, and I'm less conspicuous on foot.

"I'm at Hannah Grace's now. I'll circle back with you if I find anything. Syd, keep me posted."

"Will do."

We may irritate the shit out of each other, but I know I can trust her. Just like she knows she can trust me too. The phone beeps and I pocket it only to have it vibrate with a text. Sawyer's name is on the screen when I pull it back out.

SAWYER

She may hate you, but that doesn't mean you don't still have feelings for her.

Didn't ask about the police. Anything?

Nothing yet. They told me they'd call with updates.

Got assigned a detective. Murphy O'Connell.

SAWYER

Keep me up to date.

SAWYER

And be careful.

Something tells me Sawyer isn't just talking about my physical safety. But I can keep myself in check. I will find who's terrorizing Hannah Grace so that she can move on with her life. It's the least I can do.

Much like every other time I've been on Hannah Grace's street, it's quiet. A dog barks on the next street over but no cars and no people on her street.

The late model Jeep is in the driveway again. Pulling out my phone, I snap a pic and text it to Sydney. This time her response is the middle finger emoji which for her is the same as a thumbs-up.

"Can I help you?" The voice is smooth as velvet, a southern drawl coloring the tone, but the steel is unmistakable.

It's not often I'm caught off guard, but I didn't see anyone come up behind me. Whirling around, I reach for the gun tucked against my back. My hand closes around the handle, but I keep it there given that he appears unarmed.

"Who the fuck are you?" I ask the man standing in front of me.

"Who the fuck are you?" he repeats.

"I asked you first."

Because that's a strong argument.

"Well, given that you're taking a picture of my fucking Jeep, I'd say I get to know who you are first."

"This is yours?" I gesture to the SUV.

He crosses muscular arms across his chest.

"That's what I said. Now who the fuck are you?"

"I'm a friend of Hannah Grace's."

"She's not home," he says.

If anything, I'm sure the stone-cold glare he's giving me is meant to send me on my way. Too bad I don't scare easy.

"Who are you?" I repeat.

"You think I'm just going to buy the fact that you're a friend of Hannah Grace's and you don't know her schedule? You're not the first asshole I've sent packing. Probably won't be the last."

"Goddammit. I am friends with her. My company sent me to

protect her. I know she's fucking at school. I have a key to her house." I lift the key from my pocket.

He huffs a laugh.

"That could be your key for all I know. Prove you're her friend."

Fuck. How do I do that? Especially since we're not really friends and she's instead just putting up with my presence here.

"My name is Cole Strickland—"

"You're Cole?" he asks, relaxing his stance slightly.

"She's mentioned me?"

"A time or two. Is that really her key?"

"Yes. You can text or call her if you want but she's probably got about twenty five-year-olds running around her right now."

He nods slowly, his bright green eyes losing their wary expression. He shifts closer, extending a hand that I reluctantly shake.

"Braeden Medina. I'm Hannah Grace's neighbor."

"Cole Strickland."

One corner of his lips quirks.

"I take it whatever you've heard hasn't been the best?"

"You could say that. I haven't heard much. But one night she came to the bar I work at to hang out. She ended up having one too many and your name was on repeat for the rest of the evening. And before you ask, no, I didn't send her home by herself. I brought her home and made sure she was all set before going back to my own house."

"How did you know I would ask?"

He lifts a shoulder and lets it drop.

"It's the next question I would have if I was in your shoes. Especially with her. Your girl gets quite a bit of attention."

I don't bother to correct him.

"You lived here long?" I ask.

"I moved in about six months before Hannah Grace. It's a quiet neighborhood, but better to be safe than sorry, you know?

We've gotten to know each other pretty well over the last few years. I'm just looking out for her the same as I would want someone to do with my sisters."

"Appreciate it. You said you've seen other guys around here?"

"A couple. I didn't catch any names, and since I didn't see them back again, figured they got the hint." The smirk he gives me reminds me a lot of myself.

"Anyone recent?"

"Last one was a couple of months ago. Why?" His wariness is back as he eyes me.

"I'm not really able to say right now. But there's a reason I'm here. And I'm not going anywhere."

He nods. "Good to hear it."

"You'll let me know if you see anything I should be aware of?"

"Absolutely. If you need me, Hannah Grace has my number. Or you can find me at Duke's. That's where I bartend most nights."

He reaches over and we shake hands again.

"Now, if you'll excuse me, I'm going to head to bed. I was moving in that direction when I saw you staring at my Jeep."

He leaves and I'm left alone outside Hannah Grace's. I'm glad she seems to have found a community to keep an eye on her.

Are you?

Does Braeden have feelings for Hannah Grace? If so, I didn't get that vibe. But I don't need to add to her list of admirers, even if he is a suspect until proven otherwise.

"Okay, Strickland, this isn't getting anything done. You didn't find anything outside yesterday. But whoever was here was in the house."

Which means maybe they left a clue. Pulling the key from my pocket, I unlock the front door and let myself into the dimly lit living room.

Thank God Hannah Grace didn't fight me when I asked to hang on to it last night.

The air is a mix of cinnamon and vanilla, the room as clean as it was last night when we left. Several candles crowd the mantel next to a picture of Hannah Grace and Laura Leigh in front of the gazebo in Mistletoe Creek's town square. The sundresses and Laura Leigh's age in the photo tell me it was taken within the last several years. Laura Leigh's graduation maybe? Hannah Grace and I took a similar picture after our high school graduation in that same spot. Does she still have that picture? Mine is tucked in an envelope in a box I refuse to open. Clearing my throat, I yank myself out of memory lane and back to my task at hand.

The light layer of dust is undisturbed, and I turn for the hallway to her bedroom, moving slowly as I look for any sign of whoever visited here yesterday. There's an errant flower petal—a semi fresh one—that I pick up and pocket from where it rests against the closed door to a combination guest room and office.

The brass door handle to Hannah Grace's bedroom is shiny, wiped clean of any evidence. I asked her about it last night and the way the color drained from her face, it was clear that whoever left the flowers had also wiped the handle clean. We kept the door open when we left, and the curtains are pulled across the windows, casting a dim light through the room. I open them carefully, looking along the ground for any sign that someone may have left. But whoever was here is good.

Too good.

There's absolutely no sign of anyone but Hannah Grace in this room. Even under the bed when I drop to my hands and knees and lift the bed skirt.

"What the fuck?" I mutter to myself and stand.

For any sign of someone being here, they might as well be a ghost. Except ghosts don't leave tangible "gifts" on my ex-girl-friend's bed.

No prints, no wrappers from pockets, no nothing, and I'm back at square one wondering who the hell is harassing her and if I can figure it out before I lose my sanity.

Frustrated at the lack of anything, I lock up the house and head back to my car. Sydney has texted that she ordered the cameras she wanted from the local electronics store so I pick them up, stopping back by the house and installing one at the back door and one at the front. There are still too many entrances that I can't cover with the cameras, but the others are all windows that are locked tightly—confirmed all three times that I check them before locking the house back up again.

With nothing else to do at the house, I stop by and pick up lunch for Hannah Grace and me and head back to the school.

I meet her in the lobby of the school, her face brightening when our eyes connect.

"Happy to see me?" I tease.

"I had just reconciled to eating cafeteria food. What'd you bring?" She nods toward the plastic bag clutched in my hand.

"It's a surprise."

She steps closer and studies the bag, but there's no label on it, so I don't try to hide it from her.

"What'd you bring me?"

A corner of my mouth kicks up in a soft smile. Her question transports me back to a simpler time when I would show up at Silver Screens, the movie theater in Mistletoe Creek where Hannah Grace worked in high school, with dinner for her. She had always loved breakfast for dinner so I took a chance with breakfast for lunch.

"Want to go to your classroom to eat? I want to talk to you about a few things."

She gives me an odd look, confusion and curiosity painted in the arch of her eyebrows before she nods.

"Okay."

The silence that engulfs us on the short walk to her classroom isn't awkward, but companionable.

Is she thinking about all those times I'd swing by when she was working and we'd share whatever plates Mama had packed?

She always seemed to recognize that I was going to eat again and inevitably packed a plate for Hannah Grace and a second one for me.

My mouth waters for the Sunday roast that was my favorite, and I make a note to visit my parents after this job is over and sweet-talk Mama into a good, old-fashioned Sunday dinner.

"When was the last time you were home?" I ask as we step into her classroom.

The smell of crayons and glue permeates the air as Hannah Grace moves gracefully to fold herself on the carpet at the front of the room. I eye the desk, but join her on the floor where she starts to unpack two takeout containers I grabbed from the diner.

"I usually go back in the summer, but I taught summer school this year. Last Christmas was my last trip back. You know Mom and Dad."

The words are almost silent, even in the quiet classroom.

She's right. I do. They both play Santa and Mrs. Claus every year for breakfast with Santa for the entire town on Christmas Eve. Mistletoe Creek is home and is one of my favorite places in the world, but it shines the brightest at Christmas.

"Not even a weekend here or there?" I ask, picking up the Styrofoam container marked with my name.

She sinks her teeth into her lush lower lip, her focus moving to the container in her lap before she shakes her head.

"It's...hard," she finally says.

Maybe she doesn't go home because it's just as hard for her as it is for you.

Guilt eats at my stomach and I drop my gaze to the alphabet pattern on the dark blue rug. She loves Mistletoe Creek.

Doesn't sound like it anymore.

"You brought me biscuits and gravy?" she asks, and I blink at the Styrofoam container still clutched in my grip before I lift my gaze to where she's opened hers.

"You still like breakfast for dinner?"

"Pfft. I like breakfast anytime. Especially the b&g goodness."

"There's bacon too." I point at the pile in the container and attempt to ignore my body's reaction to the moan that hums from her lips.

I open my own box and start eating the scramble I ordered for myself.

"What'd you order?" She leans over and makes a face. "Ew."

"Still don't like eggs?" I ask around my fork.

"Deviled only."

"Good, that means I don't have to share." I focus on my food, polishing it off quickly while she works on hers.

"I forgot how fast you eat," she mumbles as I reach over and throw my container in her trash can.

"There isn't always extra time for food. Eat when you can."

Her expression is full of mischief that morphs to a look full of fire.

"There's always time to savor." Her lips wrap around the words as she draws out the last syllable, her tongue sliding along her lips before her expression morphs back to one of amusement.

"I never said I didn't have time to savor." I fight her fire with one of my own.

She clears her throat and centers her attention on her fork as she drags it through the leftover gravy.

"You said you wanted to talk to me about a few things. What's up?" she asks, but keeps her gaze averted.

Moment over.

It's for the best. But if that's the case, why do I want to reach over and lift her chin with my fingers?

I take a deep breath and blow it out.

"I went to the house to check things out. Nothing new since last night." I don't bother to hide my disappointment.

"I didn't think you missed anything." There's no censure in her voice, none of the distrust that normally colors every word with bad memories.

Instead, she seems…understanding.

"I was hoping I would have seen something. Maybe if they come back the cameras will catch them."

She chokes on the drink of water she's taking, coughing and sputtering until she can speak.

"Cameras?"

"I also want your opinion on the security system we're going to install at your house."

She drops her fork, her spine straightening as her eyes narrow.

"Excuse me?"

Danger, danger, abort.

I ignore the alarm.

"You need something for the house. Something that can help protect you."

"I've lived alone for almost four years. I think I'm the one qualified to make that decision about *my* house. I don't want a security system."

"If you're worried about the cost, I—"

"First, I'm not worried about the cost. I can pay for myself. Second, read my lips. I. Do. Not. Want. A. Security. System." She ticks a finger up for every word she spits in my direction.

"I want—need—you safe, Hannah Grace. I couldn't stand if something happened to you."

"Why do you care all of a sudden? You didn't care for the last four years."

"That's not true. I've always cared about you."

She scoffs.

"Yeah, right. You have a great way of showing it."

"I stayed away from you because I care. Because you deserve more than the life I could have given you."

She stands and throws her trash into the can by her desk.

"Why don't you want a security system?" I ask.

I've never had someone argue against one so adamantly. But she hasn't told me why.

"I'm not getting into this with you. I've managed to look after myself for years. I take a self-defense class every year with Zach. I'm not putting a security system at my house. That's final."

Trying to argue with her when she's shutting down like this is a lost cause.

"Okay, fine. Just tell me why. If you give me a good reason, I'll let it go."

She sighs but doesn't say anything. That's fine. I can bide my time and wait for her to respond.

"Because if I get one it admits that it's real. That someone really did break into my house."

The words are whispered against her whiteboard, but each one pierces my heart.

I close the distance, lifting my hands to rub up and down her arms.

"It's real regardless. I just want you to be safe. And I promised not to push, so I won't."

She steps out of the circle of my arms and moves closer to her desk.

"Thank you."

"I only promised on the security system. And only for right now. I reserve the right to change my mind if something else happens. But would you agree to cameras?"

She blows out a breath and sets a strand of blonde hair waving next to her cheek. I have to clench my fists at my side to fight the temptation to shift the hair behind her ear.

"Where?" she asks.

"The front and back doors. There's an app we can monitor, and it notifies you when there's motion at each door."

"If I let you install the cameras, does that mean I can go home?"

I fidget uncomfortably, not admitting that I've already installed them.

"I still don't think it's safe to stay there by yourself."

"Well...I do have a guest room. Maybe...I want to go home, Cole."

"So you'd be willing to let me stay in your guest room?"

Am I insane even considering this idea? The hotel is bad enough. But her house? Surrounded by everything Hannah Grace all the time?

"Yeah."

"If I say yes, will you not yell at me for already installing the cameras?"

"You already installed them?!"

"If it means you can go back home?"

She closes her eyes, her lips moving as she mutters numbers under her breath.

"Fine," she grits out. "If it means I can go home, you're forgiven."

There's still an edge to her voice, but I'll take it.

"You want to see?" I ask, pulling my phone out and opening the app the cameras feed to.

Our fingers brush as I pass her the phone, the electric current zinging up my arm. I lock my jaw, fighting my body's reaction. And failing.

"And they're only staying until we find out whoever's doing this."

"Let's talk about that later. I'm going to try to convince you to keep them. To add everything, Hannah Grace. Someone has been in your house at least once, probably more times than that. And who knows if they've ever decided to come in while you're there. You may not want them, but please just think about it."

She opens her mouth—I'm sure to argue with me—before snapping it shut.

"If you really don't want them, I'll pull them down once this is done," I promise her.

It's the only promise I can keep with her.

"Can I have this app?" She holds up my phone.

I nod. "Of course. Where's your phone?"

She bends behind her desk, and I try not to zero in on the curves of her ass under the light purple fabric of her pants. My dick has no problems with focusing on the way the fabric outlines her body, and my hands flex with a mind of their own.

Thank God for the rough denim of my jeans that hides my semi.

"Here." She hands me the unlocked phone without touching me.

I find the app and install it, logging her in.

"The password is Mistletoe Creek and your birthday," I tell her, passing her back the phone.

The alarm starts to sound on her phone.

"I have to go pick up the kids from lunch."

"What are you going to tell them about me?" We probably should have spent some of the lunch period coming up with that plan.

She shrugs.

"You're a friend from home visiting and wanted to meet the kids. They're five. They're just excited when someone new is here."

She's right. Once the kids are back from lunch, she calls them to the carpet and introduces them to me, and we play a round of favorite things courtesy of the thousand and one questions they all want to ask. But once that's done, the rest of the afternoon passes in a blur of activity, questions, and watching Hannah Grace in her element. She's a natural with the kids, and by the time we're walking them to the front door, I'm in awe of her and her ability to connect with her students. It leads me to imagine a different path I could have taken with my life. To watching Hannah Grace be the mother to our children.

Not that I can ever tell her that.

"Bye, Ms. W. Bye, Cole!" Adam, one of Hannah Grace's students who was my shadow all day, waves and runs off to a woman standing with another student.

It's chaos in front of the school for a few minutes as kids leave until only a few teachers remain.

"Now what?" Hannah Grace asks.

"You tell me. What do you do after school?"

She shrugs.

"A little classroom pick up and home."

"So does that mean you want to go home tonight?"

She nods excitedly.

"So back to the hotel for our stuff?" I ask.

"Yes, please. I just need my bags and I'm ready to go."

"I thought you said clean up too? Do you need some help?"

She shakes her head.

"It won't take me long. Ten minutes?"

Ten minutes Hannah Grace-free before being immersed in her world. I'll take that break. Gladly.

Anything for my sanity that already hangs by a thread.

She reaches over, throwing her arms around me in a quick hug.

"I'll be right back."

She skips down the hallway, and I can't fight the smile that tugs at my lips.

"You guys seem to be getting along better," Zach says, walking out of the gym and closing the door.

I shrug, but don't say anything.

"She never could stay mad at anyone for long," he adds.

His words hit a nerve, despite his conversational tone.

"Sounds like you know her really well."

"Better than anyone."

That fucking taps my nerve like a damn woodpecker in a tree, but I don't let my irritation show.

"Glad you guys are such good friends." It takes everything I have not to stress the last word, but I manage not to.

Barely.

This time he grunts in response.

"Tell HG I'll call her later," he says after several moments of awkward silence.

"Have a good night."

He waves and the door slams shut behind him, leaving me alone in the lobby. But it isn't long before Hannah Grace is back, her bags bumping along her hips with how quickly she's moving.

"Ready?"

Fuck. To see her smile like this? I'd do anything to keep it in place.

Including giving up my sanity.

"Lead the way."

CHAPTER 9

COLE

I'm in hell.

Not the seventh circle or anything like that, but my own personal one.

Does it make me a masochist that I never want to leave?

Sharing Hannah Grace's thirteen hundred square foot house is a torture of want. Of the near-constant awareness of my fraying self-control. I am immersed in a world that smells of citrus and vanilla, of soft pastels, and my beautiful ex-girlfriend whose inner beauty far exceeds her outer beauty. A world where her soft voice hums songs from the radio and her favorite movie soundtracks. It's being transported back in time to the days when I could reach out and snag her wrist to pull her in for a kiss. Of nights spent wrapped in each other.

But that's not my reality anymore.

Instead, I'm relegated back to my life as a teenage boy in my parents' house, cold showers when necessary or longer, warmer showers when I can't stand it anymore and stand under the stream of water to let my memories of Hannah Grace take over as I seek some relief in the form of my hand.

I'd been driven from my bed—from Hannah Grace's guest bed—

after a dream so real I'd run for the bathroom. Now, thirty minutes later, my thoughts are my own and I can get dressed for school.

I open the door, surprising Hannah Grace who is still mussed from sleep.

Her hair still holds a small portion of a messy bun, but most of it has slithered out in her sleep. She's dressed in a white spaghetti-strapped tank top, the thin material doing nothing to conceal her pert nipples from my attention, and my dick twitches behind my towel.

Fuuuuuck.

I avert my eyes, attempting to find somewhere safe for my attention to land—difficult between her nipple-pebbled tank and the smooth skin of her thighs exposed in her tiny sleep shorts.

The last thirty minutes of my life never happened and my dick is rock hard beneath the towel.

"Ohhh."

Her hand still hangs between us, raised to knock. It's like there's some invisible force between her fingers and my chest, and gooseflesh ripples across my exposed chest despite the humid heat of the bathroom at my back.

What is it about us meeting with me in a towel?

"I—sorry. I was...you're usually not..." She sputters off, a pretty pink flushing her collarbone and climbing her neck.

My fingers twitch with the urge to trace that color from its start, to cup her cheeks before I lower my lips to hers, dipping my tongue in to enjoy the sweetness that would await me.

"Couldn't sleep." My voice is barely audible but contains a roughness I blame on lack of sleep.

Not my physical reaction to her proximity. To all the things I want to do to her inspired by said proximity. I could excuse myself, run away to my bedroom to get ready for the last day of school before the Thanksgiving break.

What the hell am I going to do without twenty five-year-olds to distract me from my overwhelming attraction that still burns for this woman?

"Why not?"

"You don't really want to ask me that, Honey Girl." The endearment slips out before I can stop it, but she doesn't bristle like she used to.

"I don't?" Her pupils dilate and her tongue peeks out to slick along her lips.

"Not unless you want the answer," I murmur and close the distance until her fingers graze my chest.

"What if I do?"

I open my mouth to tell her or to kiss her—I'm not sure which—when the ringer sounds on the phone in my room. Just like that, whatever magic had been weaving between us dissipates, and she takes several steps back.

"You should grab that. It's early. It might be important."

I step out of the bathroom and she retreats inside, closing the door behind her.

I'm not sure whether to be irritated or relieved that my phone is ringing this early.

By the time I make it to the phone plugged in next to my pillow, it has stopped and started again.

"What?" I bark into the phone.

"Hello to you too." Sydney's voice sounds far too awake right now.

"Why are you up at"—I do the math in my head— "three in the morning?"

"Haven't been to bed yet." She slurps whatever drink she has on her end. "That's why they make Monsters."

"You should try water every once in a while. I'm sure your bloodstream is primarily caffeine."

"Don't forget the alcohol," she adds.

I bark out a laugh.

"I'm sure you didn't call me just to shoot the shit at this time of day. What's up?"

"Sawyer asked me to check in. Let you know what the programs have pulled. Which is a big fat nothing." The disgust is clear in her voice.

"Nothing?"

"I did a full social dive on Zach Nolan—who is boring as hell, by the way—and there's nothing beyond the initial pull."

"Nothing?" The hair on the nape of my neck stands up.

"Nope." She pops the *p*.

"Why do I feel like that's not all of it?"

"Because it's not. Pageant friends are all clear but I am trying to dig up records of Pervy Pete. There's no record of him online, but it would help if I had a last name or even a real first name."

"Have you reached out to the pageant board director who contacted us?"

"Duh. Ms. Chabert is currently on vacation and doesn't have cell phone service on the cruise she's on."

"When does she get back?"

"Two weeks from now."

Shit. Damn. Fuck.

"Any luck with the guys from the dating app?"

"Two of them with first dates were clear. One recently got married and the other is in a committed relationship with a woman he was talking to at the same time he was talking to Hannah Grace."

"And?"

"And what?"

She's stalling. And it's not something she does.

"What about the other guys? There's one left each, right? One with a first date and one that had two dates?"

"Yeah."

"Sydney, if you don't stop slow-rolling, I'm going to reach through this fucking phone and smash your computer to bits."

She sighs.

"One with a second date popped on one of my background check services. He had an assault charge six months ago and was a person of interest in a stalking case three months ago."

My stomach twists as I process the information.

"Shit."

"I've requested the files, but the courthouse doesn't open for a few more hours."

"Thanks, Syd."

She's already doing all she can. But it doesn't stop this feeling of failure that throbs painfully through my body.

"I'm still tracking down the guy that pushed back when she tried to sever the connection."

"What do you mean, track him down?"

"Well, Hannah Grace reported him after he messaged her and wouldn't stop. So the company banned him and canceled his account. But it wasn't set up with any accurate information anyway, so that was a dead end."

"Jesus Christ."

"Tell me about it. No dating apps, ever. Not for me. Although I wouldn't mind thirty minutes with Hannah Grace's sexy neighbor."

"Braeden?"

"Hell yes. That boy has those plump, kissable lips. I wouldn't mind a taste or twelve."

And just like that all my goodwill is evaporating.

"TMI," I groan.

She laughs.

"Sorry, not sorry. But he's good to go too. Older brother, three younger sisters, has bartended at one place the whole time he's lived in Nashville. Family lives in North Carolina."

"I didn't think you were the settling down type."

"Pfft. I'm not. But I don't need to settle down to enjoy myself."

"Alright, enough about your love life. Is there anything else you have an update on for me right now?"

"Nothing yet. I'll let you know if I find anything."

I hate the helpless sensation that claws at my throat. I fucking despise waiting.

A headache is building between my eyes, and I squeeze the bridge of my nose to ward it off.

"What about the cameras? They're working, right? Anything?" she asks.

"They're working. But nothing. I've managed to see notifications of the mailman, the neighborhood cat, and four solicitors, but no more visits from our gift giver. So I'm still at fucking square one."

"You think the cameras and you being there have scared them off again?"

I blow out a breath and shift my hand to the back of my neck, squeezing the tight muscles.

"Maybe. But I doubt it. Regardless, what happens if I pull the cameras down and leave without figuring out who's doing this? They come back."

"Leave the cameras up." The *duh* is super clear in her suggestion.

"She doesn't want them."

"What about a self-defense class?"

"Supposedly she takes one every year with Zach." His name tastes bitter in my mouth.

Jealous. Who's jealous? Not me.

Liar, liar, pants on fire.

They would be. If I were wearing any.

Sydney snorts.

"What the hell does she see in that stick-in-the-mud?"

"He's her friend."

"Why?"

I've asked myself that same question, but I don't have an

answer.

"I wish I knew. Just…check on the pageant thing, okay?"

"What do you want me to tell Sawyer?"

"Nothing. I'll call him later. See if he has any ideas."

"I'll tell him you'll call him. Later."

"Bye."

The phone beeps in my ear and I toss it back on the bed.

That was not the news I wanted.

I needed something to show up soon. Before the sliver of a thread I still had on my control broke completely.

"You want to do what?" Hannah Grace asks me as we leave her classroom and head for the exit.

"Let's go bowling. It'll be fun."

Based on Zach's social media posts, it's something she still does, but she hesitates now.

"Why?"

So I don't kiss you as soon as we cross the threshold to your house.

I can't tell her that though.

"It's Friday night. We can do the cosmic style thing. It's been forever since I bowled. Come on, it'll be fun."

And maybe help fortify my control a little bit.

Because it won't remind you of the dates you used to take her on as a teenager? Ones that ended up with you two fogging up the windows in your truck when you brought her home?

Well, fuck.

That hadn't crossed my mind until now, but it's too late since the invitation is already out there.

"You sure that's what you want to do?"

"Why not?"

Her teeth sink into her lip as she considers the invitation.

"What if I invited my friends? Casey and Brody live here

and it's been a while since I've seen them. Oh, I can invite Braeden too. That'll give you the chance to get to know everyone."

"Everyone, huh?" I love her enthusiasm and the way she practically vibrates with it. "Whoever you want, Hannah Grace," I say.

When am I going to learn to watch what I say?

"We have to invite Zach. He loves to bowl."

Of course he does.

I want to come up with any reason not to invite him, but she's already ducking into the gym, bounding over to him like a brand-new puppy running to her favorite person.

Is he that person for her?

That's question to explore never.

"Zach, it's Friday! You want to hit up cosmic bowling at Pinheadz?"

"Pinheadz?" He finishes tossing balls into a basket and turns his full attention on her like she is the center of his universe.

How the hell does she not see that he has feelings for her?

A blind mouse could see it. It's plain as day to me. But she seems oblivious.

His gaze lands on me and his face falls.

"Yeah. It's been ages since we went. Your birthday in July and that was cut short by league night."

Nope. Not jealous at all that she's discussing memories she's made with him.

"I don't know. I'm kind of—"

Whatever he was about to finish that sentence with is cut off by her bounding forward and clutching his forearm with her hands.

"*Please?* It'll be fun. I promise. I'm going to invite Casey and Brody. You and Brody hit it off last time we hung out. And Braeden. You can ask him about that concert that Duke's is going to host next month."

I widen my stance and cross my arms as his gaze once more

flickers to me. I'm curious if he's able to deny her. God knows I never was. Not when she was like that.

His attention focuses back on her, his face softening.

"Fine. Because you said please. And you're springing for the loaded fries this time."

"Absolutely. We didn't get them the last time. It's tradition too."

Does she remember our tradition that I got a kiss for every strike?

Mind out of memory lane, Strickland.

Somebody needs to rip up the road that leads down that direction.

I end up standing at the edge of the gym while Hannah Grace and Zach finish the little bit of cleanup in the gym.

"You ready?" she asks, joining me as we wait for Zach to grab his bag from his office.

"Ready as a runner-up for the crown." The words fly out of my mouth faster than I can catch them.

She freezes, her mouth open as she studies me for several long moments.

"You'll catch flies, Hannah Grace." Reaching over, I lift her chin, closing her plump lips.

"You still use that?" Her voice is a whisper, like what I just said was something scandalous.

Maybe to her, our past is scandalous. Or at least something to tiptoe around. Not jump feetfirst in it like I just did.

I lift a shoulder and let it drop.

"Sometimes."

Watching her compete in pageants was a big part of my childhood and even some of my preteen and teenage years. When I first started coming up with phrases that related to everything, it was to get her to smile. Not the fake one that graced her lips when she was on stage. But the real one. The one that lit her up from the inside out.

The one I got to see when we were anywhere but a pageant.

"Y'all ready?" Zach walks up and the spell that surrounded us is broken.

"Y-yeah. Let's go." Hannah Grace heads for the door first with Zach hot on her heels.

I take the rear and roll my eyes.

"This was your idea, dumbass," I mutter to myself.

It's a phrase I have to repeat in my head once we get to the bowling alley. Hannah Grace's friend Casey and her husband, Brody, end up not being able to come since they already had plans. But Braeden is planning on meeting us here.

Just walking in the door, everyone who works at the alley recognizes Zach and Hannah Grace and wave hello while multitasking to give me the curious eye as I tag along behind the two of them. It isn't too busy yet, and I go to stand in line when Hannah Grace calls my name after she and Zach head for the little bar attached to the lanes.

"Not yet," she tells me.

"Not yet?"

She shakes her head, sending her ponytail flying.

"Cosmic bowling starts in an hour. Long enough to grab our fries and a drink. We always wait for the cosmic bowling to start. Come on. I'm starving and Braeden's probably waiting for us in the bar."

She grabs my arm and yanks me toward the bar.

"What if all the lanes are taken?" I gesture toward the counter where the employee is waiting to ring up a lane.

"It never gets that busy this early."

Braeden is leaning against the bar as we walk up, his face brightening when he spots us.

"Braeden!" Hannah Grace rushes over, wrapping her arms around him.

He returns the embrace, lifting her off her feet until she

squeals. I glance at Zach, and the thundercloud expression he's currently sporting is exactly how I feel.

But Braeden doesn't have the look of a puppy dog begging at Hannah Grace's feet, so is there anything to worry about?

I hate that I can't answer that.

We grab an open booth and Zach squeezes in right after Hannah Grace on one side of the booth, leaving me and Braeden to cram ourselves into the other side. He eyes the size of the booth and flips a neighboring chair around at the edge of our table, leaving me the bench. It faces outward so I can keep an eye on the lanes behind Hannah Grace and Zach, but my attention is zeroed in on the casual affection that exists between the two of them.

Not your job.

Hannah Grace glances up from where she's been studying the beers on tap on the table menu with Zach.

"I'm so glad you could come out tonight, Brae. You haven't been able to for the longest time."

"Gotta pay the bills there, Gracie Lou."

"Gracie Lou?" I ask.

Braeden shifts his attention to me.

"Yeah, you know, like *Miss Congeniality?*"

"I know the movie," I tell him.

"When he found out I won Miss Tennessee, he started teasing me about the movie and Grace...Gracie Lou." Hannah Grace lifts a shoulder and lets it drop.

"I get it."

Do you remember my nickname for you, Honey Girl?

I shift my attention from the group, scanning the crowd and noticing the shirts, wrist braces, and custom shoes of the league crowd. The background music in the bar mixes with the echoes of balls striking the pins and cheers that filter into the bar.

"Cole, you ready?" Hannah Grace's question draws my attention back, and I glance up to see a server next to our table.

"What can I get you to drink, hon?"

"I'll take a root beer."

"Anything to eat?"

I shift my attention to Hannah Grace.

"We ordered the loaded fries. There's plenty to share," she offers.

I nod.

"I'll do that then."

The corners of Zach's lips turn down.

Back at you, pal. I don't like you being here anymore than you don't like me here.

If it were up to me, it would be just Hannah Grace and me.

"Root beer?" Hannah Grace asks. "They have a pretty good selection on tap."

"I'm good with the soda." I don't give any additional explanation.

Normally, if I were in LA, I might grab a beer. But I'm on a job, in public, with Hannah Grace and the man who wishes he was in a relationship with my ex-girlfriend and another one I can't get a read on.

Actually, a beer sounds like heaven in this circumstance.

But I won't.

The server brings our drinks—my soda, beers for both Hannah Grace and Zach, and another soda for Braeden. Looks like I'm not the only one not drinking.

"Since when do you drink beer?" I ask Hannah Grace.

She always hated it in high school.

"It's peach cider." Zach's words are muffled by his own drink but still audible.

Hannah Grace finishes her sip and sets down her glass.

"I do like a couple of lighter beers. But this is my favorite. The pear cider is good too."

"Nothing like the beer we drank in high school," I say.

She grimaces, her skin turning a pale shade of green, and laughter bubbles up.

"Thank God."

"You never really did regain your taste for it after Jenna's birthday party our senior year," I tease her.

"That's what a two-day hangover and being grounded for a week will do to you," she groans. "Besides, you can't tell me you ever want vodka again after Dan's party our junior year."

Just the thought of the hard alcohol turns my stomach.

"Hard pass."

I take a drink of the root beer, my eyes locking with Hannah Grace who is also trying to contain her laughter.

I wag my finger at her.

"Those in glass houses. You had a two-day hangover. I was sick for a damn week after that party."

The laughter that she's been struggling to contain bursts free, and I try to hold back a smile at the infectious sound.

"I'm not laughing at you," she manages to get out.

"I'm not laughing," I tell her while attempting to keep a straight face.

"You're smiling." She points at my face.

I cover my mouth with my hand.

"Just drink your cider," I tell her.

"Why? Trying to get me drunk?" she challenges.

"Oh, Honey Girl, you ought to have learned by now, I much prefer you sober." The words are low, meant only for her ears, and her quick intake of breath tells me she understood them.

Zach clears his throat, and my attention flicks to him as he lifts his glass and drains a large portion of his drink.

Sorry, not sorry, dude.

"Who's ready for fries?"

The server is back bearing a large platter of fries covered in sausage gravy and cheddar cheese.

Braeden's phone buzzes and he glances at it before groaning.

"Fuck, I knew a Friday night off was too good to be true." He stands and tosses a twenty on the table. "Sorry, guys, the new guy didn't show up tonight and my boss needs me to close."

"We could come hang out with you?" Hannah Grace offers.

Braeden shakes his head. "Tonight's college night. No way do you need to be anywhere near that madness, Gracie Lou."

He reaches out and taps his index finger against the tip of her nose.

"Have fun tonight."

"It would be more fun with you here," she pouts.

"Next time," he says.

"Promise?"

"Promise."

With a wave he's gone.

And then there were three.

CHAPTER 10

HANNAH GRACE

*F*alling back into the routine of teasing—of that push, pull banter that made up my relationship with Cole —is easy. Too easy.

And no matter how many warnings I give myself, it's as effortless as breathing.

"These are loaded fries?" Cole asks and lifts a fry covered in the thick white gravy.

Pinheadz has two types of the delicious appetizer. One is the more traditional version with cheese, sour cream, bacon, and jalapeños. But they also have the second variety that is my favorite.

I lift a fry as well.

"Loaded Elvis fries," I explain.

I can already predict he'll love them even if he's never had them. Zach and I discovered them our first time here a couple of years ago.

"You okay?" I lean against Zach, who has been silent during most of our time at the bowling alley.

Not surprising given how shy he is, and it's my fault for excluding him from the conversation.

"Yeah." He leans forward and snags a couple of fries with a pile of shredded cheese and pops them into his mouth.

He gestures to the fries as he chews, and I take the hint and snag another piece of one of the reasons that keeps us coming back here.

The burst of the gravy and sharpness of the cheddar cheese is one of my favorite combinations.

"Mmm," I moan, closing my eyes to savor the goodness.

When I open them again, there's a deep burn in Cole's brown eyes that turns the color to an amber hue that makes swallowing suddenly difficult.

"W-what do you think? About the fries." I clarify my question quickly.

"I think I haven't had Elvis fries in years. These are pretty good." He snags a few fries and swipes them through the gravy before shoveling the mass into his mouth.

Between Zach and Cole, I have to hold my own for my share of the fries, and most of our conversation dies down in lieu of working through the plate of fries. Before long, the plate and our glasses are empty.

"Ready to bowl?" I ask the guys.

Zach nods.

"Let's do it," Cole says.

Like I had told Cole, it still isn't too busy and we get a lane right away. Cosmic bowling is now well under way, the black light creating a neon glow to the colors as music thumps through the speakers. After switching our shoes, we each find a ball we like and start. After the first few frames, I have the strong desire to bow out as both Zach and Cole are evenly matched and do far better than I do.

Zach sits next to me and bumps my shoulder with his now that his turn is done and Cole is up.

"You're doing pretty good."

I snort a laugh.

"Yeah, I handle third place well."

He laughs.

"No gutter ball frames though. That's a personal best for you."

I stick out my tongue just as the sound of the ball hitting all the pins reverberates down our lane. The screen above our lane plays a cartoon that ends with a giant X on the screen as Cole saunters back in our direction.

His eyes lock with mine across the lane, and the memory of our last trip to the lanes in Devil Falls swims to the surface.

A kiss for every strike.

Time slows as he closes the distance, and I slick my tongue along my dry lips. Maybe I should order a water.

"You ready, Hannah Grace?" he asks and my breathing shallows.

I stand on legs that have the consistency of Jell-O.

"R-ready?"

"It's your turn." He nods toward the end of the lane where the pins all stand at attention once more.

"Oh."

Why am I suddenly disappointed that that's what he meant?

"Nice strike, man," Zach says, reaching out a fist for Cole to bump.

I should be happy that Zach and Cole are hanging out.

I shouldn't be thinking about what it would be like to kiss Cole Strickland again.

Giving Cole—and my own traitorous body—a wide berth, I grab my ball and line up my shot only to witness my ball immediately find the gutter.

"You got this, HG!"

I take a deep breath and release it as I wait at our ball return for the bright pink ball to come back.

"Don't forget to line up on the dots," Zach says from behind me as I pick up my ball, startling me.

I spin around, nearly dropping the ball at our feet.

"Whoa." Zach moves closer, grasping the ball and holding it in place with one hand.

"Sorry."

"You got this. Remember how I taught you to line up on the dots back here so you can aim on the arrows when you get ready to release."

After a few times of bowling with me, Zach had taken it upon himself to teach me the game. I was better, but nowhere near his or Cole's level.

I nod.

"Yeah."

"Show me what you got." He winks.

Squaring my shoulders, I shift the ball and turn toward the lane.

"Don't forget the dots."

I stop and look down at my feet, lining up where Zach had taught me before. Feet in place, I take a deep breath, closing my eyes and picturing the lane in front of me.

Be one with the ball.

Is bowling meditation a thing? Maybe it should be.

Focus!

I release the breath I've been holding and open my eyes before I count off my steps to the line.

"One...two...three."

My fingers loosen their grip and the ball rolls forward. I freeze, too afraid to move and break my concentration that is just as much guiding the ball toward that center pin as the aim when I released it. The ball continues to roll in slow motion, closing the distance in a wobbly path forward.

"Come on, come on, come on," I murmur, my muscles tightening as I wait until the ball connects, and like dominoes, the pins fall one at a time until nothing else remains.

"Wooo! Go, HG!" Zach rushes up behind me, wrapping his arms around me as he spins me on the slick wooden floor.

"Zach, put me down!" I laugh, thrilled to have the little slash that tells me I got a spare.

Our neighboring bowler smiles at us as Zach carts me down into the waiting area before releasing me.

"Good job." The words are quiet, but cut through the noise as Cole holds out a fist just like Zach did earlier.

His dark brown gaze locks with mine, and the heat is still there from earlier, but there's something else. Anger? Jealousy? Maybe a mix of both as his attention shifts to Zach—and where his hand still rests on my waist—for a heartbeat before coming back to me.

A shiver works its way down my spine as my fist connects to Cole's.

"Are you cold?" Zach asks, moving closer to me.

"A little." I chafe my hands up and down my arms to rub away the gooseflesh that has rippled across them.

But not from cold. From an awareness of the man standing in front of me.

"Here." Cole shrugs out of the lightweight jacket he's wearing and offers it to me.

"I'm okay," I start to protest.

Cole shakes his finger, waving the jacket closer to me. The spicy scent of whatever cologne he wears clings to the fabric, and suddenly my denial dies on my lips.

I reach out, gripping the soft fabric and shrugging into it.

"Thanks," I say and take my seat back on the hard plastic chair.

"You're up," Cole reminds Zach with a nod toward the screen.

"Show me how it's done, Nolan," I tease Zach.

He smiles at my teasing, and the awkward moment that just happened starts to fade slightly.

"I think maybe the student has become the master, grasshopper," he fires back before turning toward the lane.

The atmosphere shifts as Cole and I trade remarks and Zach

and I tease each other through the rest of the first game and most of the second. Cole even congratulates Zach when he wins the first game which gives me hope that they'll become friends too. Or at least make it less awkward.

I'd settle for that at least.

Zach grabs the soda he ordered at the beginning of the second game and slurps the dregs through the straw.

"Having fun?" I ask him.

"Yeah," he says, nodding.

"You sound surprised."

Cole rolls his first ball, and six of the pins tumble to the shiny wooden floor.

"I didn't think this would be as much fun having your body-guard tag along. But he seems okay."

"Yeah," I say and reach for my own soda to avoid saying anything else.

Because Cole is *okay*. Once upon a time he was my best friend before he was my boyfriend. And we seem to have fallen back into that same rhythm as friends.

I just wish he didn't still have the impact he does on me. If he was attractive before, he's lethal now. His body looks like it's been carved from granite without him being some muscle-bound gym bro. He carries himself with a confidence and an awareness that didn't used to be there, and the five o'clock shadow he always has no matter what time of day it is makes my palms itch to feel the whiskers against my skin.

And that isn't the only part of me that tingles with that need.

Mind out of the gutter, girl.

I wasn't going to act on any of these tingles. Cole had broken my heart once before, and I was well aware of how to finish the statement that involved fooling me twice.

"I'm gonna run to the restroom." Zach's words bring me back to the present, and I release the straw that has sat empty in my mouth for the last several moments.

"Okay."

He squeezes my shoulder as he passes me. Stifling a yawn—look at party animal me out until almost eight—I shift my attention back to Cole who has just released his second ball.

The four pins never stood a chance.

He spins, that lopsided grin I remember so well curving his lips as he swaggers toward me.

"Nice job," I tell him as he gets closer.

"Thanks. You're up."

I glance at the screen for our scores. With Cole's last frame he has Zach edged slightly out, and my seventy-three points are a pittance in comparison to the two.

I sigh. "Okay. Let's get this over with."

"It's not the electric chair. It's supposed to be fun," he reminds me.

"It's probably more fun if you get a strike every once in a while." I gesture to the screen, my own natural competitiveness coming to the surface when faced with several of the x's for both Cole and Zach.

"Do you want my advice?"

I shrug. "It can't make me worse, right?"

He barks out a laugh. "I doubt it."

"Then sure."

"You're not releasing the ball at the right time so you're losing your momentum."

"Huh?"

"Walking from where you set up to releasing the ball should be one fluid motion. You're stopping when you reach the line and then swinging your arm."

"Isn't that what you're supposed to do?"

I've bowled enough that I'm familiar with the basics of the game, but based on his words, he might as well be speaking Greek.

"Not quite."

"Ugh. I thought you said you were going to help me?"

I throw up my arms and head for the ball holder, grabbing my glowing pink ball. Finding the finger holes, I lift the ball and back up, running into the solid wall of muscle.

"I am trying to help you," he says, his hands gripping my arms lightly.

"I don't understand what you're talking about." Glancing up over my shoulder, I crane my neck to look up at him.

Even this close, his eyes are cast in shadow with the black light set up the way that it is.

"I'll show you."

He guides us to the two dots I've been lining up with, closing the distance between us until we're pressed together with my back to his front. The tingles have now broken out along my whole body, and I have to resist the urge to rock my hips against him.

One of his hands grips my waist, and his fingertips brush my skin along the top of my pants, while the other helps lift my ball into place in front of me.

"Are you ready?" His lips brush my ear as he murmurs the words against it to be heard over the music that still thumps through the speakers.

My breathing shallows as desire unfurls in my stomach.

"O-okay."

"I'll count us off and then let me guide you."

I nod and attempt to focus on the lane in front of us and not the heat of the man pressed against me.

"1...2...3."

He counts off and moves us forward, guiding my arm back as he pushes his thigh against mine to take the three steps from the dots to the beginning of the lane. We're not even completely stopped, when my hand comes forward and my fingers release their grip on the holes of the ball.

It glides along the lane with a single-minded purpose, moving faster than normal as it speeds toward its destination. Once it connects, the pins topple over all at once, all ten lying down in surrender.

It happened. I finally got a strike. Spinning, I throw my arms around Cole's neck, jumping up as I celebrate.

"I did it!"

One of his arms bands around my waist, holding me in place.

"You sure the fuck did!"

My gaze locks with his as the lights shimmer around us. The brown is eclipsed but the heat that greets me is clearly written in the pulse of the muscle in his jaw and the way his arm tightens around my waist.

"You...can put me down now," I tell him, fighting the need to test the softness of his lips with mine.

He looks different, but does he still kiss the way I remember?

With a grunt, he loosens his arm, and I slide down the hard planes of his body, aware of every inch of pressure between the two of us.

He doesn't step back and neither do I as we continue to stare at each other.

A kiss for every strike.

It was a rule we had in high school. One I want to demand he fulfill right now.

Friends don't bowl with those kinds of rules. You don't have that rule with Zach.

But even that little voice doesn't completely erase the desire that simmers in my stomach. And based on the serious attention he's giving my lips, he remembers our rule from before.

I want to kiss him. But I also don't trust him. Not completely. Not with my heart.

His gaze flicks to mine and he lifts a hand, one finger sliding along the piece of hair that has slithered loose from my ponytail to rest against my cheek. His calloused finger brushes my cheek as he traces the strand to the end and glides it back along my jaw to tuck it behind my ear.

"Congratulations, Honey Girl." The way his lips form the words is more visible than they are audible above the noise around us and the rush of blood in my ears as my breathing speeds up.

I want to lean against his hand that hasn't moved.

I want to step away.

But before I can make a decision, he makes it for us, stepping away and dropping his hand.

It's the smart choice.

The only one we should make.

So why am I disappointed?

CHAPTER 11

HANNAH GRACE

"$\mathcal{J}$ could have sworn I had it in my hand when I came to bed," I tell myself, flipping the covers over and back and moving the pillows in case it fell under them when I was changing into my pajamas.

It wouldn't be the first time my phone has ended up under my pillows or under my bed when I walked in and tossed it down on my way to change my clothes.

But no luck.

Which means my plan to avoid Cole for the rest of the night isn't going to work either. We'd finished the second game and I begged off, wanting to end on a high note with my strike. I was refusing to acknowledge my last frame of two gutter balls.

At least to Cole and Zach. Even if the way Cole studied me told me he didn't believe a word I was saying.

But even though he was right, I wasn't going to admit it.

The truth was, I was avoiding how badly I had wanted him to kiss me. How much I had wanted to rise to my tiptoes and let my lips refamiliarize themselves with his. I have no idea how I stopped myself, but by some small miracle I had.

I couldn't trust myself without some distance, and I needed

more than the length of the drive home in separate cars. Once we had gotten home, I had said good night as fast as possible while not all-out sprinting for my room.

I was proud of my restraint.

But now I had no choice but to go out and search for my phone so I could read on it and try to relax a little, fall asleep, and *not* think about the fact that Cole was in my guest bedroom.

Creeping to my bedroom door, I open it, searching for any sign of the man I'm trying to avoid.

"Cole?" I keep my voice at a whisper to avoid calling him if he's not within earshot.

Light filters below the door of the guest room, but the sound of the shower is what moves me from my hiding spot behind my bedroom door. If he's in the shower, I have no idea how long I have and I'd rather not have another encounter of him in a towel.

He looks good in a towel.

"Which is why I don't need that temptation right now," I mutter to myself.

My phone is exactly where I left it—on the kitchen counter next to my bags—and I grab it and scurry back toward my room. Fingers wrapped around my doorknob, I'm almost there when a hollow thud echoes from the bathroom.

"He's fine," I say to myself.

The words are meant to be an assurance, but I also can't help but picture something bad happening. Especially with the low moan that reaches me next.

Spinning on my heel, I don't bother to knock. Instead, my mad dash to make sure he's okay is frozen in place by the scene in front of me as the sandalwood-scented steam teases my nostrils and wraps around me to hold me in place. Like I'm going anywhere.

The clear glass shower door provides more of a highlight than any sort of privacy, and the bathroom lights highlight the way water sluices over toned muscle. His dark hair is almost black from the water, his eyes closed as he leans against the shower wall. His breathing is a ragged in and out and alternates with the muscle tic when his mouth closes on another moan.

My eyes have a mind of their own, gobbling up the broad shoulders and smattering of hair on a chest that I've imagined touching more than once. It tapers down toward his abs, and the muscles tighten and flex under my perusal, highlighting the lines that bracket his hips. But it's what comes next that has heat flooding my core and my panties dampening.

His dick is rock hard, gripped tightly in his hand as it moves up and down the shaft. His forearm muscles stand in relief as he drags his hand down before moving immediately back up, his speed increasing in a hypnotic beat that is tied to the way my pussy clenches.

I should leave. I shouldn't be here, watching this like some sort of Peeping Tom. But I can't look away.

"Fuck, *Hannah Grace.*"

My attention flies to his face as heat that has nothing to do with desire fills my cheeks. But his eyes are still closed, his hand speeding up again.

"Yes," he hisses the word. "Fuck, yes, Honey Girl."

Oh my God. Am I what he's imagining right now? Is that why he's in the shower like this with my name on his lips?

Desire drives out all other rational thought, my own hands inching along the waistband of my sleep shorts the more I witness. I squeeze my thighs together to seek relief, but find none despite the pressure. The hand not still holding my phone dips below my shorts and panties, and my fingers zero in on the spot that aches the most. My knees almost buckle at the first pass of my fingers against my clit, and I bite my lip, a low whimper escaping.

His hand drops and his eyes fly open and drop to where my hand disappears below my sleep shorts. His nostrils flare, his dick bobbing in my direction like it's been programmed to find me.

Maybe it has.

"Oh God."

I yank my hand from my shorts, humiliation burning along my collarbone and cheeks as I straighten my shorts and sleep tank.

"I-I'm sorry. I heard...I'm sorry." I don't bother to try to explain any more.

Get out, get out, get out.

The door is still open from when I burst in here before. I need to get out of here. I need to go to my bedroom and attempt to forget what just happened. Otherwise how am I going to look him in the face?

Guess you should have thought of that before...

Time to go. I race toward my escape, intent on disappearing into my bedroom and locked door. A wet hand reaches above my head and slams the door shut, another one spinning me back around against damp, hard muscles. And something else that's hard that isn't a muscle.

The fire he's managed to keep controlled the few times I've caught it in his gaze is an inferno. There's no pretense, no walls, nothing to shield me from the intensity that burns in front of me, that travels through my blood to center in my core.

"What are you doing in here?" His voice is full of gravel as he backs me against the door.

"Y-you're naked."

Way to state the obvious, Hannah Grace.

One corner of his mouth lifts.

"I normally am when I take a shower."

"I heard a thud and you moaned..."

Suddenly it hits me. The thud was probably him leaning against the shower wall. And the moan, well...I witnessed first-hand where that came from.

"You were worried about me?" His question is innocent enough, but the drag of his fingers against the sensitive skin of my stomach where his hand grips my hip is scrambling my brain.

His expression softens slightly, but if anything, it only makes the fire banked in his eyes burn brighter.

"Of course I was!" I grip his biceps, my fingernails pricking into the skin along the back of his arm.

Too many nights I had lain awake, worrying about him when he was deployed. Wondering if he would be okay, praying he would come home to me. It wasn't something I could turn off even if I was able to push him to the back of my mind when he decided he couldn't come home to me.

"Why?" His thumb sweeps my hipbone in a maddening pattern of nonsense that makes me want to strip as naked as he is and demand he really touch me.

I shake my head, unable to voice the answer to that question. I don't want to think about that right now. All I want to do is allow myself this temporary insanity and loosen the tight grip I have on the lust he inspires. Dragging one hand down his still-damp chest, I use my index finger to bisect his breastbone and abs until I can drag it along his waist. His breath is a hiss of sound as his fingers flex into the fabric of my shorts.

"I got a strike tonight," I murmur and continue to drag my hand lower.

"You did." The timbre of his voice is rough and connected via a superhighway to whatever is feeding this craziness between us.

"Do you remember our deal?" I graze his thigh with my fingertips and he shudders.

A muscle tics in his jaw and he drops his nose, dragging it along my cheek until his lips brush the sensitive skin of my earlobe.

"A kiss for every strike," he whispers.

A giddy rush of warmth travels from my heart to war with the desire that reigns supreme. He remembers. As if to prove his point, his lips pucker to place a chaste kiss against my hairline.

"Do you want me to kiss you, Honey Girl?"

I don't answer. At least not with words. Turning my head, my lips find the corner of his while my fingers wrap around his hard length.

I unleash a beast. His mouth slams against mine, our tongues tangling for supremacy of the kiss as sensations from right now in this tiny bathroom mix with memories from the past. His hand that had been pressed to the door above my head drops to my hip while the other drags a line back, palming my ass and squeezing.

I moan, but he doesn't let the sound escape the fusion of our mouths. My phone falls from my fingers, freeing my other hand, and I use it to pull him closer. He deepens the kiss, his second hand joining the first as he boosts me up and I wrap my legs around his waist. My hands tangle in his hair and his dick rubs the center seam of my shorts, creating a delicious friction.

But it's not enough.

My lungs scream for oxygen but I refuse to break the kiss first, relishing the minty fresh flavor of his toothpaste mixed with something that is uniquely him. His fingertips brush my folds and I whimper, ready for the next step, my lungs screaming at me, while everything about this moment is centered on the man kissing me brainless against the bathroom door.

He breaks the kiss, and I gulp in the sweet relief of air while he presses hot open-mouthed kisses down my neck before tonguing the pulse point at the base of my throat.

Too much, too soon, too...tempting.

I silence the voice that tries to warn me from jumping off the deep end. As if I had any other choice once I saw him again.

I hold him in place, not like he seems to want to go anywhere from his focus on my neck and collarbone as he traces the line from one side to the other and back up to my jaw.

Leaning my head back against the door, I squirm against his

grip, desperate for his fingers to move a little more south from where they barely brush me.

"*Cole.*"

"Do you know how many times I've heard you say my name like that in my dreams, Honey Girl? How desperate I was to feel you. To savor you." He licks along my jaw before nipping at my earlobe.

I cry out, tilting my head to give him better access, and he takes it, fitting his mouth against my neck in a combination of lips, tongue, and teeth that has me ready to combust on the spot.

"I've never forgotten, Honey Girl. Nothing. Not the taste of you. Not the sounds you make when I do this." He lowers his head, nipping at the tendon between my neck and shoulder.

I cry out, pushing myself as close to him as I can with the position we're in.

He chuckles, the sound vibrating against me.

"You're so fucking hot. I couldn't stop thinking about you earlier. I couldn't fight you anymore." The words are murmured against my skin followed by a groan.

"I...didn't think you'd be...doing that...when I walked in," I manage to pant as I struggle to form a coherent thought as his lips continue to move.

"I couldn't stop myself. And opening my eyes to see you with your hand in your panties. My good girl has a naughty side to her."

Reaching between us, I trust him to hold my weight as I wrap my hand around his dick and run my thumb over the head.

"Fuuuck, Hannah Grace." His muscles lock, tendons standing in relief on his neck as he leans his head back and pushes me farther into the door.

We stand like that as my heartbeat trips faster, my pussy begging for relief as I continue to drag my hand up and down his cock. Pre-cum leaks from the tip and I run it along his length.

"I'm going to fucking come." The words rip from his lips like he's fighting a losing battle.

"Isn't that the idea?" I ask and moan as his tongue pushes past my lips in response.

My nipples tighten against my shirt, and the layer of fabric between us is beyond frustrating at this point.

"Maybe we should take this to my room," I say, breaking the kiss and trailing my lips back to his ear.

There's a sensitive part just below the lobe that still causes him to shiver.

"Oh yeah?" His growl is one of the sexiest sounds and ratchets the steam between us.

"Mmm. I want you. I need you to fuck me." I rim his ear with my tongue after my statement.

He freezes, his eyes popping open.

"Fuck you?" He pulls back far enough that he can bring me back into focus.

I nod.

"Yes."

"Is that what this is to you?" The fire dims in his gaze and he steps back, lowering me to the floor until my feet are once more beneath me.

"Isn't that what this is?" I ask in return.

I'm confused. One second he'd been kissing me like I was the only method of his survival, and now he's studying me like I'm a stranger.

"Is that what you think?" He adds additional space between us and reaches for a towel to wrap around himself.

What the hell?

Disappointment, sexual frustration, and anger war with a weird combination of relief and humiliation. He was just as into this as I was, but maybe we both shouldn't have been. Or maybe I was the only one who wanted things to continue.

"We're not in a relationship, but that doesn't mean we can't have sex." We're both consenting, interested adults.

Or we both were until thirty seconds ago.

"It's never going to be just sex between us."

"It's never going to be anything more than sex again."

"I can't do that." He drags a hand through his hair, and it bounces back into the crazy hairstyle created by my fingers.

Why does it feel like he's suddenly rejecting me all over again? The back of my nose burns, but I refuse to give in to the sensation regardless if the tears are ones of anger, disappointment, or something else I don't want to put a name to.

"Why not? We were both on board with the idea a few minutes ago."

"It's never going to be just sex. Not for me. I still have feelings for you, Hannah Grace. I never stopped."

I still have feelings for you.

Those six words may be small on the surface, but each one is like a roller coaster drop for my stomach.

"You don't have to tell me things you don't mean to sleep with me, Cole. I already told you I was okay with just sex."

Please let him be lying. Let me be able to call his bluff.

He closes the distance, his brown eyes searching mine, the glimmer of hope buried deep within them.

"You had to feel it in how I kissed you, Honey Girl. It's not something I can hide. Not from you. Not once you kissed me."

I try to retreat and slam into the door at my back.

"Stop."

"Hannah G—"

"No! Stop!" I cover my ears with my hands.

While it will do nothing to truly block the words if he wants to say them, the action is enough that he pauses.

"No," I repeat, lowering my hands and taking a deep breath. "You broke up with me, Cole. Not the other way around. You can't do something like that. You can't tell me you love me, promise to marry me someday, break my heart, and then walk back in four years later and tell me you never stopped."

My hand fumbles for the knob at my hip and I twist it, wrenching the door open. Cool air rushes into the room, removing all traces of the steam. In more ways than one.

"Hannah Grace," he whispers, and it's another cut to my heart.

My already bruised and scarred heart.

"Good night, Cole."

Rushing from the bathroom, I don't stop until I'm leaning against my closed and locked bedroom door.

That was too close. I should be grateful things didn't go further. Even if I now have the worst case of blue bean ever.

It's worth it to avoid that level of heartbreak again.

CHAPTER 12

COLE

*I*s it any wonder I sleep like shit since the vision of Hannah Grace walking away from my admission haunts me every time I close my eyes?

My dick was absolutely on board with sex, no matter what stipulations she wanted to add.

But my heart was too locked up with her to not have emotion involved.

Wasn't hers?

I snort and flop to my other side, punching the pillow under my head several times for good measure.

Apparently not.

Light is beginning to filter in around the blinds and I sigh, tossing the covers back and giving up on any semblance of sleep. Frustration has my body wound into knots, and my normal release—running until I'm too exhausted to see straight—isn't feasible given that Hannah Grace is in danger. Early or not, I'm not putting her in jeopardy.

Instead I change into a tank and athletic shorts and drop to the floor, doing push-ups until my biceps burn and sweat rolls down my temple, pooling at the tip of my nose, before dripping onto the floor beneath me.

I keep my rhythm, pushing long past the burn until my arms grow numb, until thoughts of Hannah Grace don't cause my dick to stir because my entire being is too focused on the limp noodles that shake with every move.

Only then do I flip onto my back, rolling to tuck my feet under the bed, and start the same punishing pace with sit-ups, pouring the mix of emotions that have plagued me all night into every contraction.

Regret that I put a stop to kissing Hannah Grace.

Disappointment that she didn't want to respond to my declaration.

Sadness that she obviously isn't interested in my heart...just my body.

That's a bad thing?

Yes, that's a fucking bad thing. If I can't have her—all of her—I won't settle for anything less. Even if just the reminder of her pressed between me and the door has my dick stirring in my shorts.

Fuck, this isn't working. Normally, I can run to clear my head, a combination of endorphins and fresh air helping me work shit out. But this? This is punishment. This is torture.

This isn't fucking working.

Grunting, I flip back onto my hands and knees, jumping up before immediately crouching into a squat. My arms still shake, my abs are as sensitive as if I've taken multiple punches to them, and now my legs are calling me seven kinds of motherfucker as I fold as low as I can and hold it until it takes all my concentration to lift back up.

The physical exhaustion doesn't stop my mind from its endless pursuit of answers when it comes to how to get through to Hannah Grace. Maybe caffeine will help.

The coffee maker is already sounding off in the kitchen, cluing me in that the object of my thoughts is awake, and I swallow the lump that now sits on my vocal cords like a damn boulder. Clearing my throat, I step all the way into the kitchen and pray for sanity.

The black yoga pants cup her ass the way my hands itch to, the turquoise tank top drawing my attention to the strip of skin between the skintight pants and the soft top. She leans against the counter in front of the machine.

"Good morning," I say, giving her a wide berth to grab my own cup.

She stiffens.

"Good would have involved an orgasm that wasn't self-delivered," she mutters.

I almost swallow my tongue.

"What?"

She rounds on me as the coffee sputters to a stop, the kind of fire I'm not hoping to see dancing in those deep-blue eyes.

"You heard me. And I wanted you to."

"You…"

The image of her with her legs spread, hand between her thighs, takes away any ability to speak.

Holy fuck.

"It wasn't the first time. It won't be the last. At least your hot and cold behavior is good for something."

Barb thrown, she spins back around, adding creamer to her coffee before slamming the bottle back into the refrigerator.

Leaning against the counter, I study her, her movements a mix of grace of the beauty queen she was and physical frustration I just tried to torture out of my body. I struggle with whether to be amused or not, but the corners of my lips twitch at how obvious it is that she's pissed at me. I open my mouth to say something—anything—but she beats me to the punch.

"You know, Cole, I had higher expectations of you. Guess my fantasies were better than reality."

Oh, no, she fucking didn't.

Closing the distance, I grab the cup from her fingers and crowd her against the counter. She always knew exactly which combination of buttons to hit to drive me crazy. Maybe I need to return the favor.

"What's the matter, Honey Girl? What are you more mad about? That I left your sweet pussy aching for me or that I won't just use your body like it doesn't mean something to me…like *you don't* mean everything to me."

Her breathing comes in shallow pants between her kissable lips, the fire morphing to a mix of anger and a desire so strong it's nuclear. My free hand rests against her hip, the heat practically singeing me through the material, and all I want is to say fuck it. To claim what's mine. What has always been mine.

"You're forgetting something," she says, swiping her cup back from my fingers and taking a drink.

"What's that?"

"I may have wanted you last night, Cole. But that was last night. Your present declarations don't match your past actions. Which you already proved to me when you promised me forever. Funny how that changed to a Dear Jane letter after I slept with you, you fucking coward."

"You seem to be forgetting there were several years between us sleeping together and me sending you that letter. I—"

She pushes against my chest and I release her. Another push and she's outside my reach.

"What's worse than anything though? The fact that I loved you so much that I made myself sick worrying about you every goddamn day you were gone. I ate up every single one of those letters you sent, every phone call where I could hear your voice for the few minutes we got, for what? To be dumped in a letter like I meant nothing to you. Like what we had meant less than zero."

"I broke up with you because I loved you. Because I thought you deserved better than me," I argue.

"Well, there, I'll agree with you. I do deserve better."

The sting of her comment is a direct hit to my chest and makes it hard to breathe. I want to apologize. I want to be sorry. For everything. But I still think I made the right choice—both four years ago and last night. Even if she doesn't agree.

The one thing I need to do now is clear this awkwardness between us. Her safety is going to depend on her trusting me. And right now, that's the last emotion between her and me.

"Hannah Grace?" Even her name doesn't roll as smoothly off my tongue.

She pauses in the doorway and turns so slowly, I almost don't think she's going to look at me.

Because all the walls I thought I had ripped down are stacked and reinforced.

Fuck. Fuck. Fuck.

"What?" She cocks a hip to the side and drums her fingers along her thigh.

"We need to talk about last night." I have to force my voice not to crack, and I'm grateful for the little bit of control over my body I still have.

She takes a sip of her coffee, and I try not to stare at the way her lips wrap around the edge of the mug or the way the sheen of coffee begs me to close the distance.

Yeah, because that worked well last night.

"There's nothing left to say."

"Bullshit."

What the fuck?

She shrugs and takes another drink of her coffee.

"We kissed. You caught me in the shower and started—"

"I don't need the replay." She slings her mug wide and her coffee comes close to going everywhere.

"We need to talk about that kiss," I argue.

"There's nothing to talk about. What we had to say we said last night."

To hell with this.

I take two steps toward her.

"We're having a conversation about the past, so wrap your head around it now if you need to, but it's happening," I promise.

She retreats and holds her coffee cup in front of her like a shield.

"You can't make me talk to you."

"Maybe you'll want to when you hear what I have to say."

"There's nothing you can say that's going to change my mind. The only thing between us is our past, Cole. There's no future."

"What about last night?"

"Last night was a momentary lapse in judgment. A weakness. It won't happen again."

Fuck, I hate that I can't pull her in for a hug based on the forlorn note to her voice. She's not alone in this swirl of emotions. Even if she doesn't want to hear it.

"I can accept that. But we do need to talk about everything, Hannah Grace. It's time to clear the air. I'll let you decide when. You just need to say the word."

Her entire body relaxes as relief takes over her features. Is she really that willing to avoid the conversation four years in the making?

"But I'll only wait so long. My patience only goes so far."

She doesn't say anything else, but turns for the living room and curls up in the overstuffed armchair by the window. The way the sun filters through the window and creates a halo of gold in her hair, I wish this tension between us was gone. I wish everything could be different.

Turning back to the coffee, I make a promise to the both of us.

I will fix this. No amount of walls she can throw between us will stop it from happening.

Two days later, my patience is wearing thin. She's made it a point to invite Zach over every day and the two of them hang out all day. Making cookies and a pie for Zach's family Thanksgiving or watching Christmas movies on TV. And not just any Christmas movies. A mix of lovey-dovey Hallmark Christmas movies and nostalgic movies from when we grew up.

That's okay, Honey Girl, throw up whatever obstacle you think is going to keep us from this conversation. It won't work.

The two of them stay sprawled on the couch with a giant bowl of popcorn between them most of every day and leave the chair for me. But there are only so many conversations they can have that I have no idea what they're talking about before I've had enough.

Time for reinforcements.

> I fucked up.

SYDNEY

Surprised it took you this long.

SAWYER

What do you mean you fucked up?

My fingers hesitate on the screen.

This is worse than telling Dad about the time that I accidentally hit the back of his brand-new car with my old pickup pulling into the driveway.

And I'm not sure how much I actually want to admit to.

SAWYER

Cole.

Fuck, time's up.

> I pissed off Hannah Grace again.

SYDNEY

Who didn't see that coming?

SAWYER

Sydney.

Why do I always feel like I'm the parent talking to two bickering children?

I thought you guys were getting along.

> We were.

SAWYER

So how did you manage to piss her off again?

SYDNEY

I bet the list on what he didn't do to piss her off is shorter.

Sorry, I'll stop.

But I had to take that one.

> We went bowling Friday night.

SAWYER

It's Monday.

> I was hoping she'd get over it.

SAWYER

Over what?

Fuck, fuck, fuck.

> I admitted I still had feelings for her.

There's multiple dots from Sydney and Sawyer, but nothing pops up on the screen so I keep typing.

> She doesn't want to go down that path again.

SYDNEY

When did you admit you still had feelings for her?

> Why does that matter?

SYDNEY

You're such a guy.

It matters.

SAWYER

We don't need to know that.

What I'm concerned about is your ability to still keep things professional. I'll ask again, do you want someone else to come replace you?

> What was my first response to that?

SAWYER

You asked what I would do if it were Evie.

> And?

SAWYER

I'm trusting you to tell me when you hit that point.

You won't do you or Hannah Grace any favors if you get too involved.

> I know.

SAWYER

Also, it sounds like you have a big apology you're going to have to make.

> To who?

SYDNEY

Now I feel like that parent.

To Hannah Grace, dumbass.

> Why do I need to apologize? I didn't do anything wrong.

It wasn't wrong to kiss Hannah Grace. It was everything right. It was the universe coming back into alignment for the first time in years.

SYDNEY

::facepalm emoji::

Sawyer, help.

SAWYER

Without knowing the details, you told her you have feelings for her at a time when she didn't believe you.

> I don't think that's the issue.

> She believes me.

SYDNEY

So maybe she doesn't return your feelings.

SAWYER

Have you talked to her about why you broke up with her before?

SYDNEY

Why did you break up with her?

> No.

> I tried, but she didn't want to hear it.

SAWYER

You're going to have to figure it out.

She needs to know.

SYDNEY

I want to know!

Let's just say I was an idiot.

SYDNEY

Not hard for you.

SAWYER

Apologize. Talk to her about before.

What if she doesn't want to listen?

SAWYER

Then that's her decision.

That's what I'm afraid of.

That her decision will be to not listen.

But even worse, what if she listens before walking away again?

Pocketing my phone, I leave the guest room to find Zach on the couch, Hannah Grace next to him on the phone.

"No, Mama, it's okay. Mm-hmm."

I pass through the living room into the kitchen and grab a bottle of water before sitting on the open chair.

"If Laura Leigh wants y'all to come to the Thanksgiving at her sorority house I think that'll be fun. I can grab something. There are restaurants open in Nashville for the holiday." She sighs and rolls her eyes. "Yes, someday I'll need to learn how to make the turkey. But why would I make a whole turkey for myself? No, Zach is going to visit his family for Thanksgiving. No, I'm not going to invite myself to his family celebration."

Zach sits up, his expression lighting up as if he just figured out he *could* invite her to Thanksgiving dinner.

Nice try, pal, but where she goes, I go.

And I doubt he wants to explain my presence to his family.

There's a long pause and Hannah Grace sighs again.

"Yes, ma'am. Okay. Mama, I can hear Daddy telling you it's time for you guys to go. Why don't you call me later?" She mouths something that I don't quite catch. "Love you too. Okay. Bye."

She tosses her phone on the couch and grabs for the soda on the table to take a long drink.

"Mama Beth?" Zach asks.

I bristle. Who is this jackass to refer to Hannah Grace's mom that way? Even growing up in the same town and seeing her through my childhood, she was still Mrs. Whittaker or Mrs. Claus, depending on where she was and what time of year it was.

But she doesn't react. Are they that close? Has he met her parents and sister? Has he walked our town? Did she take him to our spot? The questions are still spinning when she nods.

"Yeah. Laura Leigh invited them to the Thanksgiving they're hosting at the Iota Delta Kappa house and they want to go. It's an event that she planned so they want to support her."

"So no Mistletoe Creek for Thanksgiving?" Zach asks.

How would we have handled that? I wasn't going to let her out of my sight in a different town and the three-hour drive it took to get there. Probably a good thing it wasn't happening.

"Nope. Which means I get to lie around on the couch in my pjs and watch the Thanksgiving Day parade and football I want to instead of being locked in the kitchen with my mom."

"She's adamant about you learning how to do the whole meal, huh?" he asks her.

She shoots me a look and I focus on my phone, pretending to read through something that means I'm more focused on that than on the edge of my seat eating up every word she says. I must be pretty convincing since she turns back to Zach, turning in her seat to face him head-on.

"I would have thought she would have learned after last year when I nearly dropped the turkey on the floor. I'm a sous chef only. I don't want all that responsibility."

He laughs and I have to suck my lips into my mouth to avoid showing a reaction. I can picture her in her parents' kitchen in one of her mama's aprons and bobbling the turkey.

"You can watch football with me. Come for Thanksgiving. I'm leaving tomorrow evening and coming back Saturday. You can come to a Nolan family Thanksgiving in Ohio."

Another blue-eyed glance my direction coupled with a sigh.

"I don't want to crash your Thanksgiving plans."

Her look my direction says something else—she would have said yes if I wasn't here.

"You wouldn't. I'm inviting you. Mom and Dave won't care. They've heard enough about you, so they'd finally have the chance to meet you."

Why does it give me a sense of satisfaction that while he's familiar with her family, she's never met his?

"Next time," she promises.

The little bit of relief deflates faster than a popped balloon.

Because there will be a next time. He's a permanent fixture in her life, and I'm only here temporarily. With no sign of anything since I put the cameras up, I'm beginning to think that was enough to scare that person away.

So why am I still here?

"I'm going to hold you to that," he says and reaches over, holding out a pinky.

She hooks hers through his.

"Promise."

"Good, now what movie are we watching next?" He settles back against the couch and hands her the remote.

"*Die Hard?*"

"Thank you for agreeing with me that it's a Christmas movie," he tells her.

The only reason she thinks it's a Christmas movie is because I convinced her in high school that it was.

I keep that comment to myself and push harder on my phone screen to scroll the page I'm pretending to read.

"It's one of my favorites."

Mine too, Honey Girl.

"Ready?"

"Let's do it."

I take another drink from my water bottle and try not to grind my teeth together.

Apologize. Explain.

Only I can't do that while Lover Boy is still in my way.

CHAPTER 13

COLE

*a*fter days of hanging on to my patience by a thread, I have a plan. Today is the day.

Without the buffer of Zach, I'm going to talk to Hannah Grace about what happened. He left yesterday for Ohio for his family Thanksgiving, and there's nothing else for Hannah Grace to use as a distraction.

Like a kid on Christmas Eve, I've been awake most of the night, formulating a plan. And a backup plan if the first one doesn't work.

My goal? To take a drive with Hannah Grace.

The one spot she can't refuse to hear me.

Our spot.

Three hours away.

Details.

The plan is simple. Let her wake up on her own timing and convince her that we should go buy groceries for tomorrow. I'll tell her that I'll cook—it's not exactly a lie; I have cooked a turkey before—but I want her to come along and help pick out the side dishes.

Hannah Grace's early natural alarm clock wakes her while I'm finishing my first cup of coffee, and I sit in the chair reviewing security camera footage from the night before on my laptop. Or attempting to. It's hard to concentrate on the lack of activity when I want to just pick her up and toss her in the car, plan be damned.

Cup of coffee in hand, she sits on the couch and picks up the remote for her TV.

"I was thinking about making dinner tomorrow night."

She pauses, her hand in midair before she lowers it.

"You're going to make dinner?" She stumbles over the words, like she can't believe them.

"I've made a turkey before."

Once.

Well, a turkey breast.

But I'm not going to go into the details.

"Why?"

I shrug, trying to play it cool.

"Why not? It's been a while since I've had a home-cooked Thanksgiving dinner. I've worked the last few so was looking forward to a home-cooked meal this year."

"Were you going to cook if you were in LA?"

The thought of making a meal all by myself for myself was too sad to dwell on and I shake my head.

"I'd have ended up at Sawyer's maybe. He hosts the orphans."

"Orphans?"

"Those of us with no family in LA. His sister hosted the last time I was in LA for the holiday though. I tagged along. Lots of people and noise. Reminded me a lot of Mistletoe Creek holidays. Like the open house at The Glass Slipper."

The long-standing bed and breakfast hosted an open house all day on Thanksgiving, and even those with families and their own dinners stopped by at some point to visit with each other.

"I went a few years ago. It's not the same without Mr. and Mrs. Thompson. Elle tries, but…it's just not the same."

"What happened to Mr. Thompson?"

The last time I had seen the owner of The Glass Slipper had been on a rare trip home after I enlisted before I deployed.

"You don't know?"

"What?"

A pit settles in my stomach and her guarded expression turns to one of pity.

"He...passed away. A car accident."

"Fuck." Memories of my teenage years and childhood filter through. And Mr. Thompson is in most of them, even if it's just peripheral. He should still be there.

"I'm sorry. I thought you had heard," she says.

I shake my head.

"I don't ask too many questions about home when I talk to my family."

If I do, I risk news about Hannah Grace. Like she's dating. Engaged. Married to someone who isn't me. It was safer for my heart not to ask questions.

We fall into an awkward silence, and she takes a drink of her coffee and lifts the remote again.

"Would you go?" I ask.

"Go?" She lowers the remote again, dropping it to the couch next to her.

"With me. To the grocery store."

Form coherent words. They shouldn't be hard since you've been thinking about this all night.

"For what?"

"Maybe you could help me pick out the side dishes."

"You know what I like."

I deserve credit for the Herculean effort it takes not to fire back with a response more suitable to a twelve-year-old.

"Please?"

I'm not above begging.

"So you're going to cook the turkey, but I need to go to the grocery store with you?"

"Yes?"

Fuck, that sounds believable. Not.

"Is that a question or a statement?"

Busted.

"Would you please go with me? I'd appreciate the help in picking things out. I'll even spring for breakfast." At a gas station on the way to our destination.

Her eyes narrow, brow furrowing as she studies me for so long I'm sure she's going to say no. Plan B is nowhere as good as Plan A, and details for why else I would need her in the car try to take shape.

"Can I finish my coffee first?" she asks.

The relief that floods me is instantaneous.

"Absolutely. No rush."

Well, a small one given that it's a three-hour drive there and back, but it's still early enough that it doesn't bring us back too much past sundown.

She lifts her cup to her lips but stops and holds up a finger.

"One stipulation."

"And what's that?"

"We don't talk about the other night." She freezes as she waits for my answer.

My poker face may be decent enough, but fuck my life.

"Deal." Reaching across the table, I hold my palm out, relishing the sensation of hers sliding into mine and that zing that travels along my body from the brief contact. "But if you bring it up first, it's fair game."

She snorts into her cup.

"I'm already pretending it didn't happen."

Keep pretending, Honey Girl. I'm here to remind you.

"Same."

How I'm not struck by lightning as the lie crosses my lips I have no idea. Maybe it's a holiday miracle. I refuse to pretend it didn't happen. I *wanted* to kiss her again. And as for the conversation, she could have the other night. Because it's time to talk about four years ago.

It doesn't take long for either of us to get ready, and we're in the rental pulling away from her driveway in less than ninety minutes.

"The grocery store—"

"I called to see who had turkeys left while you were in the shower. I figured a lot of places would be sold out since Thanksgiving is tomorrow. But one said they had a few left on the other side of the school," I tell her.

"Oh."

"Worried we'll run into the guy from before? Michael?"

"Yeah."

I nearly slam my foot on the brake at the stop sign.

"Yeah? As in that's the one you met him at?" If so, I may have to rethink my plans and hit the grocery store before we head to the destination I have in mind.

"No. That was his name. I've only gone to the store you're talking about once."

"You don't sound happy about us heading there," I say and fight the smile that wants to curl my lips.

"It's fine." Her words are more of a sigh than a response.

"You don't mind being in the car with me, do you?"

She turns her head to look out the window, her hands tucked under her thighs.

"It's only a few extra minutes."

I grunt and make several turns before she speaks up again.

"Where are we going? The school is that direction." She points to the left.

"Car accident. I'm avoiding traffic." The radio has been on since we got in the car, even if she is too distracted to actually hear it.

"I didn't hear about any car accident."

"Really? They just did the traffic report a few minutes ago."

A pretty pink steals into her cheeks. One I want to trace the heat of with my fingers.

"Oh."

"Just relax. If I can drive in LA, I can navigate Nashville traffic." After that nightmare, I can probably handle traffic anywhere.

Although I'm looking forward to the lack of anyone as we get closer to Mistletoe Creek.

She settles back into her seat and pulls up an app on her phone, and I breathe a sigh of relief when I glance over and can make out the words of the reading app she has open. One thing about Hannah Grace is that she could always lose herself in a book. And I'm counting on that now as I stop the pretense of staying in town and head for the highway.

The universe is on my side because it takes almost an hour before she glances up.

"Where are we?" Her phone clicks off as she sits up to take in the lack of city around us.

"Don't get mad." Probably not the best way to start this conversation, but the words are out. No turning back.

"Cole, where the fuck are you taking me?"

"Somewhere you wouldn't go if I asked you."

"This is not okay! You said we were going to the grocery store. This is…this is kidnapping. I can call the police." She shakes her phone in my peripheral vision.

"You could."

"Take me home." Her tone reminds me of a toddler minus the foot stomping, but I keep that comment to myself.

"I will."

"Right now."

This time the foot stomp hits the floor of the car, and I have to bite my lip to keep from smiling.

"This is not funny. Take me home right now, Cole Matthew Strickland."

"Triple naming me doesn't scare me, Hannah Grace Whittaker. I heard it too often as a kid for it to mean much."

Unless it was coming from Mom with a specific tone. Then all bets were off.

"Why are you doing this?" she groans and leans her head back against her seat with a thud.

The answer to her question isn't easy, so I settle for the simplest answer I can think of.

"It's important. I want to have a conversation with you—not about the other night unless you bring it up—but I need to explain why. Why I did what I did. This was the only thing I could think of."

"We couldn't have this conversation at my house? Or anywhere close to my house? Why Mistletoe Creek?"

I shoot her a look of surprise before focusing back on the road again.

"Yes, I figured out where we're going. I've done this trip enough to recognize where we are. We're either going there or Devil Falls so it was a fifty-fifty shot."

"You're right," I confirm.

"And we have to be there for this?"

"You have to admit you've made it difficult for me to talk to you the last few days. I thought you and Zach were going to become attached at the hip."

She's silent and I glance over at her again, noting her deep blush, and bark out a laugh.

"I figured," I say.

"It wasn't the only reason," she defends.

"But it certainly didn't hurt, did it?"

"No." The word is more grumble than anything and a smile stretches my cheeks.

"You can wipe that smile off your face, Cole. I'm still pissed at you for lying to me."

"If I would have asked you to come with me, would you have said yes?"

"Maybe."

I snort. "Try again, Hannah Grace. You don't lie that well."

"Probably not."

"That's what I thought."

Several miles go by without either of us saying anything.

"Didn't you promise me breakfast?" she asks.

"I did."

"So how did you think you were going to meet that promise?"

"How does a package of Pop-Tarts sound?"

"Like breakfast for one of my students. And like you should probably think of something else."

"Ouch." I lift a hand to my chest. "Okay, got it. Your tastes are not as discerning as they once were. I'll think of something else."

"That's what I'm afraid of," she mutters.

Breakfast is more of a brunch in the form of sandwiches we grab from a general store just past the halfway mark. Between the sandwiches, bag of chips, and a couple of sodas, it's like we're traveling for a picnic in the colorful foliage, instead of a conversation four years overdue.

Hannah Grace doesn't have much to say during our drive, but it's not like I do much to keep the conversation going—nerves starting to tie my tongue as I sort through everything I want to tell her and what her reaction will be.

I haven't been this nervous around her since our first date. And even then it hadn't been because of how she was going to react, but how I should *act*.

Mistletoe Creek, 10 miles.

I slow down, looking for the turnoff that I've taken hundreds of times before. It's more overgrown than it was, barely noticeable. The broken tree branch that used to be my clue is nothing more than a memory since the entire tree it belonged to is long gone.

Hannah Grace squeaks as I make the turn, the rental car bumping way worse than my old pickup ever did. Maybe I should have gotten the rental insurance.

But eventually the deep divots that rock us back and forth shallow until they disappear and we coast to a stop. Putting the car in park, I can't help but stare. The vista in front of me is the same, the area around us more overgrown—like Hannah Grace and I were the only two to ever discover it—but it's the view that tells me I'm home. That and the woman beside me.

The high school still rests at the edge of town, and wisps of smoke drift in the bright blue sky from the homes scattered through the small town. The large house built by the town founder that now houses the town government and other miscellaneous meeting rooms sits on the opposite end of the high school and gleams a bright white in the wintry sunlight.

"It hasn't changed, has it?" I whisper the question.

"No idea."

I turn in her direction, hating that sunglasses cover most of her expression. It's impossible to tell what's behind her statement.

"I thought you still came home for Christmas at least?"

"I do. But that's home." She points toward the town in front of the windshield. "The last time I was here was with you."

Nine words have the power to cripple me.

"Fuck, don't tell me that, Hannah Grace," I groan and lean my head back against the headrest.

"Why?"

Tilting my head, I open my eyes. I could lose myself in the way she studies me. In the mix of wariness and genuine

173

curiosity that turn her bright eyes to a turbulent blue. Or maybe it's not about losing myself, but about finding myself again.

"Because it makes me want to hope. It makes me want something I shouldn't."

"What?"

"You," I whisper the word.

She sucks in a breath, her lips parting, and it takes everything I have not to close the distance. But I want more than the physical release that kissing her would bring.

"Why shouldn't you want me?" Her voice is small, quiet, like she's afraid of the answer.

When I'm the one who should be scared.

"You ask a lot of why questions."

A corner of her lips lifts in a small smile.

"Habit of who I hang out with Monday through Friday."

A laugh rumbles from my chest. That question *had* come up more times than I could count when I was at school with her.

"You didn't answer my question," she reminds me.

"I already told you. I want more. And based on what you said, you aren't interested in anything more than physical. Because part of me hopes that what I have to tell you will help you understand why I broke up with you. But the bigger part of me is afraid that it will only make you hate me more."

"I don't hate you, Cole. I used to; I'm not going to lie. Or maybe I was lying to myself when I said I hated you."

She reaches out, her hand resting against my thigh, and I cover it with mine and lace our fingers together.

"I'm sorry." The words warble and I clear my throat, but I don't break eye contact, needing her to recognize how sorry I am.

"I know."

"I...I didn't think I was good enough for you anymore."

"Wasn't that my choice to make?"

Fuck. This woman has never hesitated to call me on my bull-shit. I don't know why now would be any different.

"Not then. Because I'm pretty sure you would have tried to love me through it all. And I wasn't safe to love. Not even to be around. I'm surprised Sawyer stuck."

It probably helped that he had gone through similar events. Losing friends—brothers—who should have had the chance to grow old. Losing the woman he loved. Losing the innocent outlook on the world.

For the kid from Mistletoe Creek, Tennessee, that had been the rudest awakening. That the world wasn't always goodness and light. But that belief still wrapped around Hannah Grace in a bright aura that drew me to her.

"I don't understand. You never said anything. Your letters didn't change. Not until…"

"Not until the last one," I finish for her.

It's obvious by the hurt etched between the furrow in her eyebrows.

"I…thought I had done something wrong. Even though the letter said it was you. How cliché is that? It's not you, it's me. Why would you want to come home after you had seen the world—"

"It's because of what I had seen of the world, Honey Girl. Men who would befriend you only to lead you into a trap. Men too focused on power and the things they do to grab it. Kids who should have been in school instead strapped to a gun they had no idea how to shoot." The memories burst through the gate I've locked them behind, hammering me with the strength of a physical blow.

"Do you remember that kid I told you about?" Already a bitter tang coats my tongue and I struggle to swallow.

She's silent for a heartbeat.

"The one I sent you the candy for?"

"Hakeem. Yeah. He was ten when we got there. And came up

to us speaking clear English, fascinated with all things associated with America and the soldiers who he saw every day. We'd get candy bars on the base and take them out with us when we would go into town. And no matter where we went, Hakeem would find us. It got to a point where I was saving multiple bars just for him. And then I would load my pockets down with the other candy you sent me."

"The way you talked about him, it made me think of him as a little brother."

"I think we all felt that way about him. His dad had been killed a few years earlier so he, his mom, and his little sister lived with his grandparents. He always promised he would take some of the candy home for her to try and would come back with stories about what she thought."

I don't have to try too hard before an image of Hakeem swims to the surface, his bright eyes and smile as he chatted almost nonstop anytime he found us. My stomach cramps and I close my eyes and take a deep breath, trying to dispel the image.

"We'd already had some missions. People were getting hurt. Dying. I...I shot people, Hannah Grace. Men who would have killed me or my friends if I didn't. And it was getting harder to live with the constant echoes of fighting that filtered to the base, constant awareness that we weren't safe. Not truly. But we were surviving."

"And those times I would get to talk to you, I could picture you on the other side of the world. You were enjoying college. Pledging your sorority. Meeting friends. Planning your future. When I wasn't even sure I'd have one."

"I didn't mean to—"

"Honey Girl, you did nothing wrong." I lift a hand to her cheek, running my thumb along her jawline and appreciating the warmth of her smooth skin.

"I needed that normalcy in a way I didn't understand. It was a drug to cope with the fucked-up world I was living in. You and Hakeem kept me sane."

"What happened?" There's a hesitation in her question.

A natural reaction of anyone to protect themselves from answers they don't want. I don't blame her.

"We went into town on patrol one afternoon. It had been a quiet week and maybe that had something to do with it. I don't know. But not many people were out on the streets we were assigned to. It was eerie looking back at it. Like everyone knew to avoid it. Everyone except us. Geoff was twenty-four. Just got married before being deployed and he was in the front of the group. When he turned the corner, it took a minute for all of us to realize the echo we heard before he fell was a gunshot. Two other guys were hit as we all scrambled to find some protection. We were familiar with the streets, and I knew there was a different way to the street where the gunfire was coming from so I managed to double back and came from the opposite direction. I...I didn't want to believe what I saw when I got there. It wasn't a man holding the gun. It was fucking bigger than he was. Hakeem was always a skinny little shit despite all the candy."

That black strap around his shoulders had looked out of place. Evil wrapped around a good kid.

"I must have said his name. I don't fucking remember, but he spun around and pointed the gun in my direction. His eyes were filled with so much hatred, I wondered how we hadn't seen it. Were we all really that blind? Or had something happened? His second hand gripped the front of the rifle, and I didn't think. I just reacted. I... he died because of me, Hannah Grace. Because I killed him. He was fucking ten years old and I ended his life."

The confession rips from my lips, bile rising in my throat. Her fingers squeeze mine and I try to release her hand but she grips me tighter. I'd rather remember Hakeem with the bright eyes and quick smile.

Not the one lying on the ground with evil wrapped around his body.

"Cole—"

"We didn't have another mission before coming home. Geoff was gone. Max and Colin were recovering from gunshot wounds, and I was a fucking mess. We got closer to coming home and I knew I couldn't be around you. I couldn't be around anyone."

"So you sent me the letter."

I nod, the burn of tears in my throat making speaking impossible.

"Then what happened?"

"What do you mean, what happened?"

"You didn't come home."

I shake my head.

"No. I didn't think I needed to be around anyone who knew me. I needed to disappear. I didn't have a plan, and Sawyer told me he was heading to LA. He had a friend who worked in security who was going to give him a job. He understood the need to disappear."

"So you did."

"Yeah. I'm not going to lie. Those first few months back stateside were rough. I drank—a lot—until Sawyer gave me the choice to find someone to talk to or he was going to cut ties. I found a support group of other men who had served and had the same demons I did."

"Is that why you didn't drink the other night?" she asks.

"No. I don't have the issues with alcohol now. I don't drink on duty."

"Was that what the other night was? A job?"

"Honey Girl, nothing about protecting you feels like a job. If I had to pay someone to be here, I would. Being here with you? It's like the universe finally realized what was wrong and fixed it. For the first time in four years, I don't feel like a stranger in my own life. You're my home. You always have been, even though I don't deserve you. Even if the only thing I can do is keep you safe and let you walk away to the life you deserve."

Saying those words out loud makes it hard to breathe, my chest constricting to the point of pain. I don't give her the chance to respond, unbuckling my seat belt and opening the car door. I move to the front of the car, leaning against the hood as I drag several deep breaths of fresh air in through my nose.

For the first time in four years, the guilt that has plagued me —over Hakeem, over Hannah Grace—releases its clench on my heart. The relief is like a limb that's been asleep is suddenly waking up, tingling through my blood, and the tension ebbs from my body.

Just one more breath. One more moment of this peace.

Besides Hannah Grace, it's the only thing I need.

CHAPTER 14

HANNAH GRACE

*M*y heart breaks for Cole. For everything he just shared about his deployment, about Hakeem. *Wait a damn minute.*

He just dropped that massive heartbreaking bomb but then made the decision that I couldn't help him with that.

Slamming open the car door, I stalk toward him.

"What the hell, Cole?"

He whips around, his face a mix of surprise and confusion.

"Excuse me?"

"No, I will not 'excuse you.' Who were you to decide my future for me? To determine that I couldn't handle what you had gone through. That I couldn't help you just the way you had always helped me. You told me I was home to you, but your actions speak louder than your words. Instead of leaning on me, letting me be there for you while you worked your shit out, you made the decision that I couldn't handle it."

I poke him once with my finger, the motion somewhat satisfying, and repeat it several more times until he lifts his hand and captures mine from a fourth drill into his solid chest.

"You're right. I...you...I..."

"You forgot about me."

That's probably what hurts the most. That he could just walk away without a second glance.

"Never." His other hand comes up to grip my bicep. "I thought about you all the time, Hannah Grace."

I snort.

"Yeah, right. So that's why you never came back? Never tried to call once you did talk to someone."

"I thought you hated me. That there would be nothing if I tried to come back—"

"But you're back now. Why? Did you want to be the one to come back and rescue me? To be able to ride in on a white horse and rescue the damsel in distress before you turned around and rode back out?"

"You don't—"

"You don't get to tell me what I do and don't need. Or what I can and can't handle. I don't need anyone to rescue me. I can rescue my—"

My words are cut off as Cole yanks me forward, crushing his lips to mine. He catches me by surprise, but it doesn't take me long to catch up, our tongues tangling together as I drag my fingers up his chest, circling his neck.

I pour every ounce of frustration, of heartbreak, of sadness, and memory into the way I kiss him, into the way my fingers tunnel through his hair and hold him to me. But for every ounce of heartbreak I give, desire is returned one hundredfold.

He spins us, lifting me up to the hood of the car and stepping between my spread legs without breaking contact with my mouth. His thumbs sweep along my hipbones, singeing me through the fabric of the leggings I tossed on this morning when I thought we were only running to the grocery store.

I lean back, trying to pull him with me and better align our lower bodies to allow the delicious friction where I need it the most, but he resists. I whimper and my fingers claw at his arms as

I attempt to quell the ache in my breasts. His lips release mine and trail along my jaw to my ear, before moving south down the column of my throat.

One kiss should not have the power it does over me. It shouldn't create the ache between my thighs and the desperate need that claws through my body. But I learned a long time ago that "shouldn't" with this man didn't exist.

"I'm trying to be good," he murmurs against the pulse point of my throat before closing his lips against the skin.

"Don't."

He leans back, breaking the connection, and my legs lock around his waist to keep him next to me.

"What are you doing?"

And why isn't he still kissing me?

"You said don't."

"I meant don't try to be good. I don't need that. I need you to kiss me again."

Closing his eyes, he groans, and the sound has a direct connection to my pussy that spasms. My legs tighten around his waist and his eyes pop back open, burning into me, nostrils flaring. A muscle tics in his jaw, tempting me, and my lips tingle with the need to taste that skin.

"Nothing has changed since the other night, Honey Girl. This" —his hand flexes against my hip and I struggle to stay focused on what he's saying and not my body's reaction— "isn't just physical for me. Not with you. Especially not here."

It hits me. This is where we lost our virginity.

He was trying to be good then too.

Slicking my tongue over my lips, I meet his gaze, needing him to see the truth I'm afraid to admit.

"I know what I said. About it only being physical. I...I was lying to myself. And to you. If we have sex, I won't be able to turn off my feelings, Cole. Even if I wanted to say that the other night because blue bean fucking sucks."

He barks out a laugh.

"Blue bean?"

I nod.

"It's my equivalent to blue balls. When you kissed me the other night, when I walked in on you, I was so turned on it—"

"I was too."

"Yeah, but I bet you didn't need a not-so-quick session with your battery-operated boyfriend to calm down enough to go to sleep."

That not-so-quick session had involved me, BOB, and a handful of orgasms that still didn't satisfy the ache. Only one person could do that. And he's standing in front of me. His mouth pops open, his eyes narrowing on me, and I'm dead center of the raging inferno there.

"You shouldn't tell me things like that, Honey Girl."

His voice is all gravel, sending delicious shivers down my spine.

"Why?"

"It's hard to be good when that's all I can picture right now."

"I can help you picture something else."

"We need to stop." He says the words reluctantly and tries to step out of the circle of my legs.

When I don't release my legs, he groans.

"Hannah Grace."

He could easily push outside the circle I've created. But he doesn't want to. Just like he doesn't want to be good. Criss-crossing my arms, I wrap my fingers in the hem of my light-weight hoodie.

"Or," I say, fingering the fabric at my waist and whipping off the sweatshirt before I can think twice. "We can keep going."

I toss the shirt next to me on the car, gooseflesh rippling down my skin in the cool fall air. My nipples tighten against the plain white cotton of my bra, and his attention drops to my chest.

"What are you doing?"

"Showing you what I want."

"Fuck. We should think about this. Not get caught up in the moment."

"We're not. I am thinking about this. And this." Reaching behind me, I twist the clasp on my bra and shrug the material down my shoulders to pool at my waist.

My nipples tighten even further, almost to the point of pain.

"I don't want you to hold back, Cole. I want you. I want to be with you."

His fingers tremble as he lifts his hand to my cheek and brushes his thumb over the heat pooled there. The moment stretches between us as his eyes search mine.

"You're sure?" he asks.

"Any surer and I'd be naked on the hood of this car." Reaching up, I grab his hand and tug it down to wrap our joined hands around my breast. "Touch me."

The words still vibrate on my lips as his hand contracts, his mouth claiming mine in a move so fast I'm not expecting it, despite how desperate I am for it. His tongue licks along the seam of my lips, requesting entry that I've already given him. He leans me back, following me as my back comes in contact with the cool metal of the car.

It's not completely cold with the residual heat of the engine but not warm either, and I break the kiss on a hiss as I settle farther against it. I'm a mix of contrasts with the heat inside warring with the cool outside. Cole is even warmer where he surrounds me, his mouth now trailing hot, open-mouthed kisses down my collarbone to the valley between my breasts.

My hands tunnel through his hair as I try to direct him where my body begs for his touch. But he won't be sped to his direction, taking his time as he traces a path of kisses up the slope of my breast before orbiting my nipple, teasing caresses that only serve to drive my need for him even higher. His hard dick is a ridge in his jeans that rubs against the center seam of my leggings and panties as he pulses his hips against mine.

"Please," I beg.

"Please what? Please this?" His thumb coasts over my nipple and my breath breaks. "Please this?" His finger joins with his thumb, and the light pinch has me arching into him, into it. "Please this?"

His mouth replaces his fingers, his tongue sparring with the hard peak of my nipple, and fireworks explode behind my eyelids.

"*Yes.*"

He switches sides, the cool air rushing over the wetness until his hand covers my breast, his fingers plucking and tugging at the distended tip while he lavishes attention from his mouth on the other.

He closes his teeth around my nipple, and the sensation resonates in my core, my legs tightening around his waist as my nails scrape his scalp.

"Again," he murmurs and repeats the caress.

I cry out and he chuckles before claiming my mouth with his. Digging my nails into the fabric on his shoulders, I squirm between him and the car hood, trying to gain friction where I need it the most.

"Hold still, baby. Otherwise this will be over before it even gets started."

"I need you...more...please."

That fire from the other night is back, reminding me that it never went away.

He groans, the sound vibrating against my skin.

"This car isn't as big as my truck was."

Leaning up, I find his ear with my lips.

"Who said we need the car?"

He rears back, his face morphing from surprise at my words to a panty-melting smirk.

"How is it that what comes out of your mouth still surprises me?"

"What comes out of it or what I can do with it?" I close my teeth over his lobe and tug slightly.

He hisses out a breath.

"Both. Fuck. Definitely both."

"So maybe find a different way to occupy it."

His eyes flare with the challenge and his hands grip my hips, lifting me effortlessly until I slide down his body to stand on my own two feet.

"All you have to do is ask."

His hands are warm on my back, running up and pressing between my shoulder blades until my breasts press against his chest.

"No fair," I murmur.

"What?"

"You have more clothes on than I do."

"Another thing that's easily remedied."

Holding one arm around me, he reaches back with the other, tugging his collar up and over until his shirt can drop to the ground.

"Better?" he asks, tugging me back against his chest.

I gasp as my sensitive nipples rub over the dusting of hair across his rock-hard chest.

He doesn't give me the chance to respond, claiming the echo of my gasp between our mouths as he fuses the two of them together. Gripping his biceps, I toe off first one boot and then the other.

Thank God for UGGs.

Free of my shoes, I move to the waist of my leggings, dipping below the band and taking them and my panties down my thighs until I can kick free of them to stand naked in front of Cole. His lips leave mine, and he looks down at the fabric of my pants and panties on the ground at our feet.

"You don't understand what fire you're playing with, Honey Girl."

"I do," I argue. "The same one that burns in me."

His hands slide down, gripping my ass until he can boost me and lift me back to the hood of the car. I squeal as my bare ass slides along the cool metal.

"Cold."

"I'll heat you up, Honey Girl." A gleam in his eyes promises pure carnal wickedness as he says the words.

His hands grip both of my knees, splaying them open as he leans me back against the hood. There's no room for second-guessing, for embarrassment at how I'm exposed to the whole world or anyone who wanders by.

It's me and Cole. It's our spot. And all I can focus on is the hunger in his gaze as he zeroes in on where I crave him most.

"You're so fucking sexy." His words are barely discernible, his voice more gravel and growl than anything else.

He steps between my spread legs, feathering his fingers along the inside of my thighs. The sensation verges on ticklish to teasing, and I squirm against the hood.

"Do you know how many nights I imagined this? You and me back here. Just like this."

Kneeling down, he presses his lips first to one side of my knee before switching to the other.

"How many?"

"I lost count. All the ways I wanted to kiss you. To hear my name on your lips. I feel like I've waited a lifetime for this."

"Cole."

"I want to savor, Hannah Grace. I want to take my time. But I'm not sure you're going to make that possible." His thumbs skirt the line between my thigh and my pussy and I whimper.

"Savor later. Right now, I need you too damn much to go slowly."

"Just a taste then," he murmurs.

Before I can process the words, his tongue drags through my folds, back to front.

Crying out, I thread my fingers through his hair and hang on for dear life as he continues to focus his attention on the bundle of nerves that seems made for him.

Lightning arcs from that pleasure point into my toes and fingers as he taps my clit, sliding his hands under my ass to lift me closer to his mouth.

"*Cole.*"

He hums, too intent on his current activities to say anything. The vibration adds another layer of pleasure and the orgasm builds in my toes, curling them into the metal of the hood. Keeping one hand under my ass, he shifts his other until one finger presses inside me knuckle deep. My pussy spasms, gripping at the digit as he continues to draw circles around my clit with his tongue before tapping the hard bundle in different tempos to keep me balanced on a razor's edge of pleasure.

Why didn't we do this before?

I want to ask, but the only thing I'm capable of forming with my mouth is gasping breaths interspersed with Cole's name and God's.

A second finger joins the first and he curls them inside, rubbing along a spot that has stars dancing in my vision.

"Oh fuck," I moan and my hands tighten in his hair. "Don't stop. Please. I'm so close."

He takes my words to heart, doubling down and sucking my clit into his mouth while his tongue continues to work.

The orgasm picks up speed, locking my legs as they tighten against Cole's shoulders. It hovers at the edge, ready to crest, while the promise of pleasure shimmers like the warm sunlight behind my eyelids.

"Fuck, Cole. *Please.*"

I'm not sure what exactly I'm asking for, other than that little something extra to push me over the edge.

He sucks hard, hollowing his cheeks as his teeth close softly around the bundle, and his fingers press a particular spot and I detonate.

White-hot pleasure shoots through my body as the sunlight glows brighter as I fly apart, flying into the flashes as the orgasm goes on and on until I'm convinced that one blurs into a second, and still Cole seems content to keep doing what he's doing. Finally, the orgasm ebbs and he crawls up my body.

"Fuck, that was the sexiest thing I've ever witnessed. And I fucking love my name on your lips," he says.

My hands are still threaded through his hair, and I use the leverage and pull him down to my mouth, pushing my tongue past his lips. My nipples drag against his chest, his denim-encased cock brushing through my sensitive folds, and I shiver.

He tastes like Cole, but something more. Me.

"Now, please. I want you inside me," I tell him, breaking the kiss to trace his jaw with my lips and tongue.

He groans.

"I-I don't have anything with me."

I'm not sure whether to be flattered. Or disappointed.

"I have us covered. I'm on birth control. There…haven't been many since—"

He presses a chaste kiss against my lips.

"I had a full physical a few months ago and haven't been with anyone since then. But I've always used protection before."

"Then what are you waiting for?" I ask.

"Are you sure?"

The fact that he needs me to confirm only makes me want him more.

I nod.

"Words, Honey Girl."

"Yes." My hands move to his belt, attempting to unbuckle it between us.

One more kiss and he stands, unbuckling his belt and undoing his fly in a blur of fingers until he's able to pull his jeans down enough so that his hard cock pops free. My pussy clenches and my mouth waters, but before I can reach out and wrap a hand around him, Cole is doing it himself, dragging his hand down his dick.

"Cole." I crook a finger and wiggle it in his direction.

He shifts us until I'm at the edge of the car and lines up at my center, pressing forward inch by inch as he stretches me.

"*Oh my God.*" Another orgasm is ready to detonate, and I clench my muscles to hold it off.

"Fuck, Honey Girl. I'm not going to last," he grits out as his pelvis bumps mine.

"Me…neither." My hands slip along his biceps until I dig my fingernails in.

He retreats, almost withdrawing completely before snapping his hips forward again.

"*Ohhh.*" My eyes close and my other senses heighten.

The grip of his fingers against my hips, the spicy smell of his cologne mixing with the fresh air outside, the sound of his breathing as he starts to move, pistoning his hips. His pelvis slaps against mine, the friction rubbing on my overly sensitive clit, driving the orgasm one more step higher.

"Are you close, Honey Girl?" he asks, his lips finding the pulse point in my throat.

"Mm-hmm."

"I'm so goddamn close. But I'm not going to. Not until you do again."

"I'm close." I moan the words and try to focus the orgasm into existence.

He leans up, one of his hands leaving my hip for his thumb to find my clit while he continues to rock into me.

"Oh God. *Cole.*"

"That's right, baby. I'm here. And I'm about to come so I need you to fucking let go. I need you to come now. Right the fuck now. Come all over my cock."

His words, the fullness of his cock, coupled with the brush of his thumb over my clit is enough to shoot me into the heavens again, the entire world collapsing around me except for the man finding his own release above me.

His rhythm falters as he speeds up, the muscles in his neck and shoulders standing in relief as his release overtakes him and he pulses inside me.

"Fuck. *Hannah Grace.*"

He's right. My name groaned on his lips as he works through his orgasm may be the sexiest thing I've ever heard. Spent, he collapses on top of me, his lips pressing kisses along my collarbone while his cheek is pillowed on my breasts.

Our breathing slows and my heart rate returns to normal as we lie there, my hands roaming his back while his breath tickles my skin.

"That was…" He looks up, at a loss for words.

"Yeah," I say.

Because what can I say after *that*?

CHAPTER 15

COLE

*I*f I live to be a hundred, I'll never forget today. Every other memory might leave my head, including the knowledge of my own name, but I will always remember what Hannah Grace felt like with nothing between us. What she tasted like. What a vision she made against the hood of the car in the late fall sunshine.

The breeze kicks against my bare ass and causes me to shiver. Since I'm still inside her, she moans and my dick immediately starts to harden.

Take a break, dude. Next time needs to be on a bed...or a couch...or even just inside.

In my defense, I hadn't planned on this happening—hence the lack of condom.

A harder breeze rushes across my ass and I groan.

"Fuck, that's getting colder. We should probably get dressed."

I lean back, keeping a steadying hand on her hip as I separate us. She sits up, her breasts swaying, and my mouth waters for another sample. Instead, I dip my head and press another kiss to her lips and pull my jeans and boxers back up my legs.

By the time I've reached down and snagged my shirt and her leggings and panties, she's put her bra and sweatshirt back on.

"I didn't plan this," I tell her as I hand her the leggings and panties.

"I know. Neither did I." She separates her leggings and panties, flipping the leggings right-side out and sliding them over her feet.

Wobbling as she stands, she uses her panties to clean up, wiping the combination of us off her thighs in moves I can only describe as mesmerizing.

Why else do I stop what I'm doing?

"I'll tell you something else," she says, focused on her task and not on my lack of movement. "I don't regret it either."

With that statement she looks up. The relief her words bring is something I didn't realize I needed until she said them. With so much history between us, she very well could have.

"What?" She tugs her leggings into place, balling her underwear up in her hand.

Closing the small bit of distance between us, I reach for her panties and tuck them into my pocket.

"You're so goddamn sexy." I growl the words, resting my hand against her hip before moving it backward to squeeze her ass.

I now have firsthand knowledge that she is bare underneath her leggings.

Fuck, the car ride home just got longer.

"I'm a bad influence," she teases and throws me an exaggerated wink, moaning as my hand clenches against her ass.

"You're the best kind of influence, Honey Girl. One I don't regret either," I tell her.

Her smile morphs from a teasing one to genuine happiness, stretching her cheeks as it reaches her eyes.

She needed those words too.

"In fact, I wouldn't mind a round two." I pull her against me, evidence of how much I'm ready for round two hardening in my jeans.

Her expressive eyes widen, her mouth forming an O.

"But I wasn't kidding when I said I had plans to take it slow. Which requires a bed…or at least being inside out of this wind."

She giggles and leans her head against my chest.

"Agreed." She squeezes her arms around my waist. "We're going home, right? I'm not dressed to go wandering around Mistletoe Creek right now."

I swear I can feel the heat of her panties in my pocket. No, I'd rather not wander through our hometown answering a myriad of questions from friends and neighbors while carrying my girl-friend's panties in my pocket as she goes commando.

Is she your girlfriend?

It's a question we need to figure out before we run into anyone we know. Especially Flora, Fawn, and Merry. Those blue-haired ladies are like three of the Golden Girls mixed with the good fairies from *Sleeping Beauty*. And despite being elderly, they are sharp-eyed matchmakers on the hunt for their next happily ever after.

"Yeah."

We finish straightening ourselves up and I open her door for her, lingering in the open door as she settles into her seat.

"You're staring," she grumbles and runs her hands through her hair self-consciously.

"Can you blame me? You're beautiful."

"Crazy. I wish I had a brush." She winces as her fingers catch a snarl.

I squat next to her, brushing a kiss on her cheek.

"Your beauty has nothing to do with what's on the outside, Honey Girl. It never has been."

I unfold and shut the door softly before moving around the hood, only now noticing the prints all over the side where we were.

"The car is going to need a wash." I nod toward the hood as I sit in the driver's seat.

"We should probably be glad that's all it needs."

Barking out a laugh, I focus on turning around in the opening, heading back down the path while navigating the divots.

"Remind me next time we come back I need to switch the car for an SUV. Or a truck." The words are out of my mouth before I can think about them.

Yeah, way to make assumptions that there will be a next time.

I tighten my fingers around the steering wheel and prepare for Hannah Grace's response.

"A truck," she says and reaches for my hand now that we're back on the main road. "I've always been partial to pickups."

I lace my fingers with hers.

"I can check with Jared. He may still have my old pickup. I left it with him when I moved to LA."

"I have good memories of that truck," she tells me, smiling softly.

"So do I, Honey Girl. So do I."

Silence engulfs the car once more, and the drive is interspersed with music from the stations when they come in and random comments from one of us on our surroundings. But we don't talk about what just happened. It's not awkward, but companionable. It's what happens when two people are comfortable with each other.

The attraction still simmers between us, a tangible third passenger in the car, but I never doubted that was going anywhere. I'm painfully aware of every shift of Hannah Grace's hips against the seat, every deep breath that lifts her breasts, every facial expression.

We're just inside Nashville city limits when she turns in her seat, facing me as best she can. The move dislodges our hands from each other and my fingers immediately miss hers.

"This wasn't just a one-time thing," she says.

It's more a statement than a question.

"Not for me." I glance over, meeting her gaze briefly before turning my attention back on the road.

"Me neither." She sucks her lip between her teeth, nibbling on the lower one.

"What's on your mind, Honey Girl?" I ask.

"I…I don't have a plan for what happens next. I don't want to put any labels on this yet. A part of me thinks all of this—you being here, today, all of it—isn't real. That I'm having this crazy dream that is equal parts scary and amazing."

I exit the highway and stop at the light on the off-ramp. Reaching over, I snag one of her hands that is currently wrapped around the other.

"It is real. I am here. And I'm going to figure out who's scaring you. But then I'm not going anywhere."

"You live in LA."

"We'll figure it out. As for labels, I think I've made it clear what I want. I want to give this another go between us. But I can understand your hesitation. You can set the pace. Whatever you want to do, I'm here. I'm in it."

"What if I said I didn't want to pursue anything?"

Fuck.

"It would be hard. I'm not going to lie; I would try and convince you otherwise, but I will always respect whatever boundaries you set."

She falls silent again, wheels turning as she processes through what we've just said while I navigate the streets of Nashville to get us home.

"It's not that I don't want to pursue whatever this is," she says after several songs and a traffic report on the radio. "I do. But you can't keep shit from me anymore, Cole. If we're going to do this, we're going to do this as equals. I don't want you to hide stuff from me because you want to protect me. If you want this —if you want *us*—then I'm your equal partner. Capable of

197

making my own decisions. Of handling whatever life throws at us."

We pull onto her street and I wait until I've parked my car in her driveway to turn toward her. I need her to see exactly how much I want this. How willing I am to meet her condition.

"I swear to you, Hannah Grace. I won't hide anything else from you. Never again. I've wasted too many years because I made that mistake once. I'm not doing it again."

The lights above her garage catch the moisture in her eyes, making them sparkle like sapphires in the near dark around us. I lift a hand to her cheek, and she closes her eyes and leans against my palm. A tear slips out, tangling in the meeting of our skin.

"I promise," I repeat and wipe the bit of moisture away.

She leans forward, almost meeting my lips, but stopping just before.

"Don't break my heart, Cole."

"So long as you don't break mine."

Her eyes flutter open and she studies me.

"Honey Girl, you have no idea the amount of power you have over me. Do you?"

She shakes her head.

"It's always been you. Even when I thought what I was doing was right, it never stopped being you. I-I love you, Hannah Grace. From now until forever."

Her mouth finds mine, our tongues tangling as her fingers comb through my hair to hold me to her.

Like I'm going any-fucking-where.

Wrong. You're going inside so you can worship her properly. All night long.

"We should go inside," I murmur, breaking the kiss enough to say the words, my lips teasing hers.

"Let's go."

We both exit the car at the same time and I move fast to her side so I can reach for her hand again. I've gone years without her touch. Now that I have it again, I'm not giving it up anytime soon.

Our steps are slower than I would expect given how badly I want her. It's the knowledge that we have all night that allows me to keep our movements unhurried. But too many years keeping my head on a swivel mean that it's ingrained that I check out our surroundings as we move from the driveway to the front door.

"Wait." I stop at the bottom step to the front porch, tucking Hannah Grace behind me.

Metal pieces are strewn across the porch, the porch light glinting off the electronics carnage that stops our progression.

"What is it? What happened?"

Her nails dig into my biceps as she looks around my arm. Her gasp reinforces the scene in front of me. I move my attention from left to right and back again, lifting my gaze sector by sector until I find where the camera used to hang, and all that remains is the black disk screwed into the side of the house.

"Oh my God."

I hate the fear in her voice. I haven't heard it since the day with the flowers, and I could have gone the rest of my life without it echoing through my head again.

"Goddammit."

I spin around, moving her back to the car, all my senses on heightened alert. She doesn't argue, moving with me until I open the car door.

"I want to check things out, but you need to stay here. Lock the car door. I'll come back when I'm finished."

"But—"

"Honey Girl, I want you safe. And this is the safest place for you. Please."

She studies me for several heartbeats and I'm prepared for her to argue. Instead, she nods.

"Okay."

She sits in the driver's seat of the car and I pass over the keys.

"Lock the doors. If I'm not back in five minutes, I want you to drive to the nearest police station and tell them what's happened."

"Cole." She clutches my hand, her body trembling.

"I'll be okay. I'll be right back. Lock the doors," I remind her and lean down to find her lips with mine.

Closing the door, I wait for her to engage the locks before I move back to the porch. My feet crunch over the busted wires and innards of what was a high-end security camera. The door is still locked when I check it, and I breathe a sigh of relief and pull that key from my pocket, unlocking the door.

I regret not grabbing my gun out of the safe in the trunk of the car, but I'm already here. The light in the living room is still on from this morning and I move through each room of the house, making sure there are no signs of anything while still moving quickly enough to hit my five-minute time window with Hannah Grace. My final step is to check the camera on the back porch where I find the same as the front—a broken shell strewn across the concrete pad and some even glinting in the grass, but nothing else is disturbed.

"What the fuck?"

Jogging around the side of the house, I use the gate and approach the car from the opposite direction. Hannah Grace is facing toward the front door and jumps when I knock on the window, her scream audible through the glass.

I have to jump out of the way as she slams the door open and rushes into my arms.

"It's okay, Honey Girl. I'm fine. It's okay."

It isn't okay. Neither camera alerted with any motion.

Because you were keeping a close eye on your phone the whole *time you were gone?*

It's something I'll check once we're inside.

"D-d-did anyone…" Her teeth are chattering and I keep both arms wrapped around her as I lead her from the front of the car to the trunk to grab my gun out of the safe and finally back to the house.

"No one was in the house. It's both cameras. I want to clean them up in the morning when I can check for any other signs in the light. But for now, let's get inside."

She balks at the steps, unsure where to step, and I lift her off her feet and carry her through the threshold, locking the front door behind us before setting her on the couch.

"I'll be right back," I murmur, pressing a kiss to her temple.

She nods.

My next step is locking the back door since I'd gone out that way and grabbing both of us a glass of water.

"Here." I hand her the glass and sit close to her on the couch.

She curls into me and sighs.

"Why is someone doing this?"

I fucking hate this.

"I wish I knew. Let's check the cameras." I pull my phone from my pocket and pull up the app.

The cameras show as offline, but no missed alerts. Nothing to indicate at what point today they were both destroyed.

"Whoever did this knew how to approach the cameras to not set them off. And there's no sign of anything so we have no idea what time it happened today."

"Shit."

"Agreed."

I'm a mix of anger for not having a backup camera more hidden and relief that Hannah Grace had been with me all day.

"I'm so sorry this happened," I tell her, running my hand up and down her back.

It's reassurance for her and for me.

She's safe here. In my arms.

"You have nothing to apologize for. It's not like you broke the cameras. How could you predict something like this?"

"It's my job to stay one step ahead."

One I'm failing at.

"You can't always control what happens," she tells me.

"I can fucking try."

"Don't be too hard on yourself." She reaches over, grabbing my hand and weaving our fingers together.

"I need you safe."

More than I need anything else in this world, I need for her to be protected.

"I am." She snuggles into my arms as if to prove her point.

My arm tightens around her. After several moments in silence, she squirms free and stands.

"Where are you going?"

"To bed."

She takes a sip from her glass before disappearing into the kitchen.

"Are you coming?" she asks.

I blink, having been so lost in planning a secondary camera system and a full-on alarm system I don't remember her coming back into the room. Her hand is outstretched, waiting on my response.

She's safe in my arms.

What better way to assure myself that she stays that way than by holding her all night?

CHAPTER 16

HANNAH GRACE

"Hey, HG, Mom made me promise to bring you next time," Zach says as soon as I open my car door Monday morning.

He has a bright smile and a tray full of coffees. Three of them. For him. For me. And for Cole.

Now that Cole and I are on better terms, it makes me happy that Zach is going to accept him as well.

"Zach, hey! Guess I don't need to ask how your holiday was. Did you have fun?" I shoulder my bag from the passenger seat and close my door before wrapping Zach in a hug.

Cole is silent as he steps out of the driver's seat of my car. I'm sure Zach notices that not only are we in one car, but Cole is driving. But he doesn't say anything.

"It's family, so you know how that goes. But I feel like I got spoiled. Mom made all my favorites and sent me with enough leftovers for a week."

"Awww, that's so great." I squeeze his arm before I release him.

"You really would like them," he tells me. "And like I said,

Mom really wants to meet you. She hated that you were alone on Thanksgiving."

"I wasn't alone. I had Cole."

We had spent Thanksgiving morning cuddled on the couch watching the Thanksgiving Day parade and the afternoon alternating between football watching and making out before ordering Chinese food for dinner.

So far it was my favorite way to spend the holiday yet.

"Things seemed kind of…awkward…when I left on Tuesday. I wasn't sure how well that would go," he says and passes me my coffee.

"We—"

"Good morning, Zach. Welcome back." Cole walks around the car, aviators in place as he greets Zach with a handshake.

Walks is probably the wrong word.

Because he doesn't just walk.

Saunters? Strolls? Ambles?

This isn't the time for a thesaurus.

No, Cole doesn't just walk. He fucking swaggers.

Might have something to do with the morning shower you shared.

Heat fills my cheeks that I attempt to hide while taking a drink of my mocha.

Zach returns the handshake before handing Cole a cup.

"I wasn't sure what you drank. Black coffee okay?"

If Cole is surprised, his facial expression doesn't change. It's like the two of them are engaged in some sort of weird poker game, convinced that neither of them can show any sort of expression.

"This is great, thanks. I don't need a pound of sugar in my coffee like Hannah Grace," he says.

"Don't be talking about my mocha," I mumble and take another drink, nearly spitting it out when he pokes my side. "Hey!"

Zach studies the two of us. Cole and I have spent the last five days in a bubble made for two. But at some point we probably should have discussed how we were going to act when we were around other people. Cole's touching me is going to inspire questions. Questions I don't have answers for. Things are too new, too unpredictable, for me to want to be open about what's going on between us.

Even with Zach despite his best friend status.

I glare at Cole, hoping he understands before I start walking toward the school. Still engaged in their manly poker game of no expression, the two men follow me silently. I badge in, waiting next to the door until Zach badges as well and grabs the door. I've been lectured by both of them at different times in my life about opening my own door so let them work it out between them. Like some choreographed routine, it works out, and I find myself sandwiched between the two of them in the lobby.

An awkward sandwich since I need to talk to Cole, but without an audience.

"See you at lunch?" I ask Zach, aiming for nonchalant and coming across more as over-caffeinated goofball.

He eyes me like he doesn't quite understand my multiple brands of crazy before he nods. "You brought lunch today?"

Since Cole has been around he usually goes out close to lunch and brings something back for us. But today he has plans to talk to Sydney and Sawyer, so I packed two lunches. One for him and his meeting and the other for me.

"Yeah."

"Great. I'll see you later?"

"Eat in my classroom today?" I ask.

"Okay."

"See you at lunch." I wave with my coffee cup in hand, nearly slinging my mocha out of the lid.

He lifts his cup in a salute before turning to head to the gym.

"Thanks for the coffee," I call after him as he walks away.

I wait until he's in his office before I turn to go and nod my head in the direction of my classroom.

"We should talk," I say, closing the door.

"About what?" He leans against the bookshelf and takes a drink of his coffee.

"I…don't want anyone to know about this—us—just yet." It's hard to say, made more so by the look on Cole's face now that his aviators are off and I can see the hurt in his eyes.

Dammit, that was the last thing I wanted to do.

"Are you…having second thoughts?" he asks.

"What? No." I rush to him, wrapping my arms around his neck and tugging his head down for a kiss.

He takes control almost immediately, dipping his tongue to dance with mine while his hands grip my hips.

Slowly, I build the self-control I need to step back.

"We're at school," I tell him.

"So we can teach each other a few things," he says, waggling his brows.

"You're a nut."

I giggle and push against his chest.

"In all seriousness though, let me talk to Zach. I know he likes me. That he wants more. But—"

"I was wondering if you had picked up on that," he says.

"He's made it pretty clear that he'd be open to more if I was. But I've never felt that way about him. Not the same way he felt about me. He's my best friend. I don't want to hurt him and this will. So I have to figure out the best way to tell him. About you. About us."

His expression softens and he reaches out to cup my cheeks in his hands.

"I understand. As much as I want to shout from the rooftops about us, I love that you care enough about his feelings to talk to him about it. But I don't want to be your secret forever, Honey Girl. I want to be able to do this"—he drops his head and slides

his lips along mine in a kiss that's over far too soon for my liking
—"whenever I want."

I rub my lips together and capture the residual tingles, almost
wishing we could play hooky for the day.

"We probably need to set some ground rules for school."

"About what?" His thumbs skim a spot behind my ear.

One I want him to explore later. With his lips.

"Kissing."

One corner of his lips quirks into the signature panty-melting
smile that has gotten me into trouble more times than I can
count.

"Ms. Whittaker, are you talking about public displays of
affection?"

In high school, we'd been joined at the hip, holding hands,
sneaking kisses, and even finding out-of-the-way places if we
wanted more than just a quick kiss, but that was when we were
both students.

"We need to keep kissing to a minimum. And nothing during
school hours. I need to be professional."

He nods. "Which means I probably can't do this." His hands
drop to my waist before sliding back to my ass.

"Cole." I try to say his name as a warning, but the breathy
quality belies the tone I need to make it serious.

"How about a goodbye kiss? We didn't get one of those this
morning," he murmurs, backing us against a wall out of sight
from the door.

"You got a lot more than a kiss this morning."

"If I recall, so did you," he counters.

I open my mouth to retort, but am cut off by his lips as they
lay siege to mine. There's no warm-up, no preamble, but we've
never needed one. It's always been zero to sixty between us. And
time hasn't changed that.

He tilts his head, deepening the kiss, and I moan and lace my arms around his neck to pull him closer. His hands squeeze my ass and I gasp, breaking the kiss.

My core throbs, my breasts ache, and the hard ridge pressing against my stomach through his pants makes the throb worse. But we have to stop.

He groans and drops his forehead to my shoulder for a deep breath before stepping back.

"Okay, professional. We can do this."

I nod.

"We can."

"What time does school let out?" he asks.

"Umm, 3:07. Why?"

"Professional ends at 3:08."

"Cole!"

"Sorry. I just never thought making out in a classroom would be on my bucket list. But suddenly it is."

"Same here," I tell him with a wink. "But later."

"I'm going to hold you to that."

"I'm counting on it."

👑👑👑

"Okay, HG, spill the tea," Zach says, sitting at the spare chair in my classroom as we eat at the table I use for reading groups with the kids.

We've opted to eat in here—or it was my idea that he went along with anyway. This conversation is meant for Zach and me only. Not other people's ears.

Cole is in his car for his phone call so it's just the two of us.

"There's no tea," I tell him, my cheeks already heating to call me out as a liar.

"Uh-huh. Not only did you ride together, but you let him drive your car and that almost never happens. Plus your cheeks are as red as a fire engine. Why?"

"I...uh...it's warm in here."

He and I both recognize I'm lying, but he doesn't press. Instead he grabs a pack of carrot sticks from his lunch bag with a small container of ranch dressing.

"You're not going to push?" I ask.

He shrugs and snaps into the carrot, chewing as he considers a response.

"I figure you'll tell me when you're ready. You don't hide stuff from me. It's one of the reasons our friendship works."

"You really are the best friend I've ever had," I say, and wrap my arm around him in an awkward side hug.

It's true.

While Cole and I were friends as kids, the introduction of puberty—of teenage hormones and everything that came with them—made our friendship difficult. At least until we admitted we liked each other.

Zach covers my hand with his and squeezes.

"And you're mine."

Clearing my throat, I use the excuse of taking a drink of my water to extricate my hand which he releases right away.

"So when I left on Tuesday night, you weren't even acknowledging Cole. But this morning, you two seem more...comfortable is probably the best word...around each other."

The bite of sandwich I'm swallowing sticks like glue in my throat, and I take another drink of water.

"Y-yeah," I manage to croak out.

"So what happened?"

"We talked. About what happened."

"About why he broke up with you."

Zach has no idea about what happened with the first time Cole kissed me after we went bowling, so of course he's going to assume that was what we talked about.

"What did he say? Did he have an excuse for why he broke up with you like that?" he asks.

"Mm-hmm. This stays between us, Zach. Okay?"

"Who am I going to tell?" He pulls a piece of turkey from a sandwich bag and takes a bite.

"It was so sad. His last deployment, his unit met a little boy. Everyone thought of him like a little brother. Until he ambushed them one day. One of the guys in Cole's group was killed and a few more wounded. In the end, Cole…" Tears clog my throat and I try to swallow around the lump.

"Cole what?"

A tear I was fighting to hold back slips through and rolls down my cheek before I can wipe it away.

"Hannah Grace?"

Taking a deep breath, I wave away Zach's concern.

"Sorry."

"You don't have to apologize to me. Did he say something to you?" Tension radiates from his body.

I shake my head.

"No. Not at all. It's…I could feel his pain when he told me the story."

"You always were a softie," he teases.

"Hakeem was ten. But holding a gun and intent on killing them. I tried to explain to Cole that he had no choice but to shoot when Hakeem turned the gun toward him. But he still feels guilt."

"That's understandable," he says.

I take another deep breath and let it out, the lump releasing and making it easier to swallow again.

"Which part?"

"All of it. He didn't have a choice. But I can understand that guilt too."

"He didn't deal well with his grief. And he didn't think I was strong enough to help him work through it. So he broke up with me and tried to self-medicate with alcohol before his boss told him that he needed to make a different choice."

"And he never reached out afterward? This couldn't have been recent."

"No."

Would things have been different if he had? Maybe we wouldn't have lost so much time.

"Why not?"

The alarm goes off on my phone, a reminder that I need to go pick up the kids from the lunchroom.

We clean up quickly while Zach's question plays on repeat.

"He was afraid if he tried I would hate him. If not for breaking my heart then for what happened," I say as we leave my classroom.

He huffs a laugh.

"Sounds like that guy doesn't understand you very well, HG. Anyone who does knows you could never hate anyone."

"I did hate him for a while after we broke up."

But not really. Even then I didn't hate him. He broke my heart and I was pissed. But Zach is right; hate isn't in my nature.

So wouldn't the man who's known me longer realize that?

CHAPTER 17

COLE

"Nothing?" I ask.

I misunderstood Sydney. I must have.

"No shadows, no light plays, no nothing. One second the camera was working and the next it fuzzes out. But whatever caused that isn't visible in any of the frames, and I analyzed each one frame by frame for the five minutes before it stopped," Sydney explains again.

It doesn't sound better the second time around.

"Fuck." I hit the steering wheel with my fist.

Double fuck. This is Hannah Grace's car.

Luckily, I didn't do any damage. The bad news is that I'm no closer to figuring out what the hell happened with those cameras.

"Did you find anything with the actual cameras?" Sawyer asks.

"They were in enough pieces for it to be considered a jigsaw puzzle. Maybe if I could find all the pieces I could probably reassemble them. But I swear to God I'm missing shit. And I combed through the backyard and the porch to make sure I got them all."

That was before I called Detective O'Connell and told him about what happened. After he lectured me for contaminating evidence, he agreed to have the pieces checked for fingerprints and to send officers to talk to neighbors for the second time. This was starting to draw more attention than I wanted it to.

I shared with Hannah Grace that I thought pieces were missing, and she assumed they either went flying into the neighbors' yards or got tossed somewhere else. But we both knew that the cameras didn't destroy themselves.

"What about the security system?" Sawyer asks.

Over the weekend, I had finally convinced Hannah Grace to order the system he recommended.

"Back-ordered thanks to Black Friday. Who buys security systems on a shopping discount?"

"Me," Sawyer responds.

"Me too," Sydney adds.

"Fuck both of you. The soonest the installer can be here is two weeks because the parts are back-ordered that far out."

"But you got it for a good deal," Sydney says.

"I'd rather have gotten it sooner than cheaper." Even if Hannah Grace had made me swear she could pay me back.

That was never going to happen.

"Where are you at with all the background checks?" Sawyer asks.

"Well, first things first, I got ahold of pageant lady. Pervy Pete's real name is Peter Lawrence. According to her, he is no longer with the organization and hasn't been for several months."

"Was that his decision?" I ask.

She snorts.

"She didn't want to say. So I took it upon myself to find out. Peter was fired after multiple women came forward indicating that he used his position as an employee of the organization and judge of the preliminary rounds to sexually harass six different women over four different pageant years."

"Hannah Grace's year?" My stomach cramps as I voice the question.

BODYGUARD FOR THE BEAUTY QUEEN

"Two women. One was the runner-up and the other was top five."

"Where is he now?"

"Once I got a last name I was able to do a search. His address on record is less than a mile from Hannah Grace's. He lives in the same neighborhood."

Fuck. Way too close for my comfort level. But even danger on the same planet is too close for my liking.

"Anything else on Lawrence?"

"He's deactivated all his social media, but not deleted them. He's also subscribed to about a dozen OnlyFans accounts, and based on what he subscribes to, I can understand how he got the nickname Pervy Pete. I can't unsee that shit."

"I don't care what kind of porn he watches. He just better not cross my path."

Or Hannah Grace's.

"Sydney, keep an eye on Lawrence. What about the rest of the suspect list?" Sawyer asks, refocusing us on the task at hand.

"Michael Campbell, a.k.a. Grocery Guy, got arrested last year —had to have been after he followed Hannah Grace home—for violation of his parole. He—"

"What is he in jail for?"

"Was. What *was* he in jail for. He got out a month ago. Stalking and domestic violence."

"And they let him out?"

"Cole, you know just as well as we do that once someone serves their sentence, there isn't much more to do." I hate that Sawyer can be rational right now.

"He could be scaring Hannah Grace!"

"If he is, we'll find out. And we'll find him," Sawyer points out.

"And in the meantime we have to deal with someone terrorizing Hannah Grace?" I ask.

"What if it isn't him?" he argues.

"It might be."

"But it might not be too. Think, Cole. We still have several suspects. Including the second man who had a second date with Hannah Grace."

"Actually, he's clean." Sydney's words are even more frustrating, and I'm struggling with all the emotions bubbling up.

Fear for Hannah Grace.

The overwhelming need to protect her.

Every single sensation is lumped in a ball sitting in my throat, making it hard to breathe.

"What do you mean 'clean'?" Sawyer asks.

"Well, he may be an asshole, but that's not illegal. He took a job overseas after Hannah Grace got him booted from the dating app he was on. He lives in Qatar now."

"It sounds like Lawrence and Campbell are our two remaining suspects," Sawyer says.

"It could be someone else entirely. Someone new," Sydney suggests.

"The likelihood of that is small." I finally find my voice.

"Small but not impossible," she counters.

"We need to dig up more on both Lawrence and Campbell," Sawyer says.

"I can do some more digging." Sydney's reluctance is clear in her tone. "But I also want to keep looking and see if there's anything more I can find. Something about both of these guys isn't sitting right."

"You don't need my permission," Sawyer tells her.

"I'm open to any ideas you've got," I add.

Something. Anything to keep my girl safe.

Because that's what she is.

My girl.

"I also want to review everything from the beginning. I agree with Sydney. I feel like we're missing something," Sawyer says.

"We've gone over everything already." I hate to be the bearer of bad news.

But this is different. We haven't had this much personally tied up in a case since Evie's stalker.

Why is it the hardest jobs we have are for the ones we love?

I jolt, but I'm not sure why. I *do* love Hannah Grace. I never stopped. I've told her that. So why is it still surprising to me?

"I want to start brand-new files like we're getting this case for the first time. Sydney, I'll send you the original notes I took from my call with Ms. Smith Chabert."

But there's a difference from the original beginning to now.

Because your mind is too focused on Hannah Grace. And not on the professional part. On the being in love with her part.

"Cole." The tone of Sawyer's voice tells me it's not the first time he's said my name.

"Sorry, what?"

"Are you willing to go back through the original letters again? See if there's anything we're missing?"

"Of course. Whatever it takes."

"Text me as soon as you're done. Sydney, you know what you need to do?"

"On it." The clack of the keyboard is already moving in the background.

"Let's talk Wednesday if not before."

We end the phone call and I get out of the car, taking a deep breath as I tilt my head back. The sky is a fathomless baby blue, reminding me so much of Hannah Grace's eyes that I close mine. The sound of kids on the playground rides the wind, urging me to relax. To soak in the innocence.

But the world is not all innocence.

Am I too close to see something? Should I ask Sawyer to step in?

No!!

But the part of me pounding my chest and screaming no isn't rational. I need to think about the overall goal—keeping her safe.

Sawyer must have a direct connection to my brain since my phone vibrates with his name across the screen.

"I figured you would appreciate this conversation between the two of us," he says by way of greeting when I answer.

There's only one conversation I don't want to have with Sydney able to add her two cents.

"Am I too close?" I have to fight to say the question out loud.

"We've had close jobs before. She's your ex—"

"That's the thing. She's not my ex."

The silence on the other end of the phone is deafening.

"I take it you all have shared more than a kiss at this point?" Sawyer asks after several moments of awkward silence.

"Yeah." I lean against the car and tuck my free hand into the pocket of my pants.

Another long silence lasts long enough that I check the connection on my phone.

"You there?" I ask.

"Yes. I'm thinking."

"Thinking about replacing me?" I brace myself for the news.

"I'm going to make that your call, Cole."

"My call?" I'm not used to getting an option, and I'm not sure I like it.

"I've thought about what I would do if our situations were reversed. Fuck. What I *did* do with Evie."

It's not the first time we've compared the two situations, but usually it's me using that as my reason to stay.

"You said I was too close before."

"No, I voiced my concern that you were too close. More because I was concerned your physical attraction to Hannah Grace was going to blind you to everything else. But then I also thought about how every time I brought up my concern, you brought up Evie. You love her, don't you?"

I don't need to ask who he's talking about.

"I never fucking stopped," I choke out around the lump in my throat.

"Then I'd say you're perfect where you are. That love is going to drive you to solve this better than any other motivation I can give you. Long beyond the point where you would give up otherwise, you'll keep going. For her."

"What if I miss something?"

"That's what I'm here for. You're not in this alone. Even Sydney is all in on this one. She's reassigned the remainder of her workload to the rest of her department so she can focus on this. We will find who's doing this. Even if it means I spend Christmas with you."

I snort, his comment lightening the mood.

"I'm sure Evie would love that."

"We'll cross that bridge if we come to it. For now, let's see what we can find by going back to the beginning," he says.

"Thanks, Sawyer. Not just for this. But for everything."

"You'd do the same for me."

The line beeps in my ear. In typical Sawyer fashion, he hasn't said goodbye, not that I needed him to. Instead, I got something better.

His reassurance that I'm doing the right thing.

I'm not sure what happened at lunch, but something is different about Hannah Grace. Now that school is out and the kids are gone, she's quiet. Distracted. Not the same woman I kissed this morning and I haven't even had the chance to tell her about the lack of movement in the investigation, so I can't blame that.

"You alright?" I ask as we finish picking up baskets of crayons from the middle of each pod of desks.

"Fine." The word is quick, but her gaze stays fixed downward.

Until I stand in her way, using my fingers to lift her chin.

The doubts in the guarded expression of her eyes—the ones I thought we had worked on—swirl in the blue depths, making them more gray than the sapphire blue I'm used to.

"Honey Girl, what is it?"

She shakes her head, freeing my light grip on her chin.

"I've been thinking."

"About what?"

"You. Us." She tries to walk away but my hand on her wrist keeps her from going too far.

"The other day I promised not to hide stuff from you. To talk through things. Especially if we were going to give this a real chance. Don't I deserve the same courtesy?"

She sighs but doesn't say anything.

"Hannah Grace?"

"You do," she mumbles.

"What was that?" I press.

"You do!" Her voice echoes off the wall as she tugs her wrist free and stalks away.

"So why don't you clue me in to what's going on in that pretty head of yours?"

"You didn't come back."

Her words pull me up short.

"What do you mean?" I understand each word, but all together they make no sense.

Only they do.

"Before. You said you didn't come back, you didn't reach out to me because you were afraid I hated you."

"I thought you did," I tell her, closing the distance between us.

She glances up, lip caught between her teeth. She says a lot with that look, so much that tugs at my heartstrings that I want to reach up and rub at my chest. At the physical ache there.

Instead I reach out, tugging her against me and wrapping my arms around her.

I breathe a sigh of relief when hers wrap around me.

"What?" I ask. "I can't fix it if we don't talk about it."

"I'm not asking you to fix it."

"Then let's talk about it and see what we need to do next. Together." I brush my lips against her hair and try not to hold on to her too tightly.

"You know me really well," she says.

"I do. Better than anyone."

She looks up, arms still locked around me.

"If that's true, then why would you think I would hate you? I don't hate anyone. It's never been something I've done. And if you knew me as well as you say you do, you would understand that. Which makes me question, why didn't you come back after you were able to work through everything? Did you really not care enough? Did you not want to come back? If so, that's fine. But just tell me that. Be honest."

The vulnerability in her words, in her expression, is strong enough to cripple me.

Fuck.

"I...I never thought about it that way. I swear to God. I wanted to come back. The part of my brain—of my heart—that knew you couldn't hate didn't connect with the other part. The less rational part that feared something even worse."

"What?"

"Your pity. Hannah Grace, I'd love to be able to say that I could explain the decisions I made then. Maybe it was self-sabotage. Maybe it was thinking you deserved better."

"So what's different now?"

I need the doubts written in the lines between her eyebrows to go away. Permanently.

"I'm tired of torturing myself. Of depriving me of you in my life when you're already embedded here." I lift a hand to my chest. "I've loved you since I was fourteen years old, Honey Girl. And that shit hasn't gone away. It's not going to. Not now, not ever. And I don't need you to say it back—I don't want you to until you're one hundred percent sure. Until I've erased those doubts of yours. Until then, be with me. Be secure in the fact that I love you. And that that's never going to change."

"I..."

She wants to reciprocate the words. That's as clear as day.

"It's okay," I tell her and lift a finger to her lips. "When you're ready, I'll be here. I'm not going anywhere."

She stands on her tiptoes and slides her lips along mine. My arm anchors her in place, holding her up when she tries to drop to her feet again.

"Maybe we should go somewhere," she murmurs against my lips.

"Grab your bags. Let's go home."

"'Kay."

Only then do I release her. At least long enough for her to grab her stuff. Once we're walking out of her classroom, I lace my fingers with hers, squeezing gently.

"How did your call with Sawyer and Sydney go?" she asks.

"I'll tell you once we're in the car," I murmur.

There's no sign of Zach or his car when we leave, so nothing stops us from leaving the parking lot.

"We're in the car. Tell me," she demands, turning in my direction.

This time it's my turn to sigh.

"It's not great news."

"I didn't think it would be." Her words are so matter-of-fact, I can't help but turn my attention off the road and onto her for a moment.

"How are you so calm about it?"

She shrugs and I have no choice but to shift my attention back to the windshield.

"Good news would be you found whoever it is we're looking for. And something tells me you wouldn't have been able to hold that information until now. The only news that I don't want to hear is that you're leaving."

"I'm not going any-fucking-where," I growl, tightening my grip on the steering wheel.

"I *know*. I believe you. So what is the plan?"

"Well, first, tell me about Peter Lawrence."

"Peter? Pervy Pete? Is that his last name?"

"Yes. Did you know he lives a mile from you?"

She shudders. "Ew."

"Did he ever...try anything?" I manage to get the words out and hold my breath, waiting for her answer.

"Try anything? Like with me? No. I mean, he flirted. He told me I was pretty. Asked me out and I declined. But I caught him cornering Kelly at the last luncheon I went to. She's the one who won the year after I did."

"But he never made a move on you?" I ask.

"No way. I think he realized I was just as likely to punch him in the junk as all the other girls were to burst into tears. You and I both know I was never the true definition of what my mama considered the best-behaved beauty queen."

I can't fight the smile that lifts the corners of my lips. Because she's right. How many times had we heard the refrain from her mom about Hannah Grace's chances if she would only behave better?

"I don't like how close he lives, Honey Girl. So I'm going to need you to tell me if you so much as even think you see him."

She reaches over, lacing her fingers with mine and squeezing.

"I promise. Is he the only person you're still looking at?"

"No, but it's not like that pool is very big anymore. It's either him or that guy that bothered you at the grocery store. Apparently right after he followed you home, he ended up violating parole and was sent back to jail for stalking and domestic violence. He just got out right before all this shit started happening to you."

"You think it's him?"

I lift my shoulder and let it fall.

"We're not sure. Which is why Sawyer also wants us to go back to the beginning. Square one when we first got the call from the pageant person."

"Why?"

"It's not the first time we hit a wall trying to figure something out. Sawyer is convinced we're missing something. He wants Sydney to start all the background analysis again."

"Background analysis? Like on me?"

I nod. "You, the people closest to you, people you work with, anyone you have regular interactions with."

"You think it's someone I know?"

I coast to a stop at a red light and take the opportunity to shift my attention back to her.

"It might be."

She shakes her head so hard her hair creates a golden veil around her. "No way."

"Forty percent of stalking victims are stalked by a current or former significant other. Forty-two percent by an acquaintance."

Her eyes widen at the shocking statistic.

"Seriously?"

"Yeah."

"Do you think that's the case with me?"

"I wish I could tell you that, Honey Girl. Honestly, the last time we were this frustrated was when we were helping Sawyer's wife. Only she wasn't his wife then."

"And starting over helped?" she asks.

"We didn't do that in her case."

"What did you do for her?"

"In her case we knew who was trying to come after her. We ended up setting up a plan and leaking her location where she was with Sawyer. Only the bastard almost killed Sawyer and attacked Evie."

A shiver overtakes her body despite the warmth of the car, and I squeeze her hand.

"That situation was different," I say, trying to reassure her.

"I...did...what happened to the guy who attacked her?"

A car horn honks behind me and I realize the light turned green. Shit.

Pressing on the gas, I shift our joined hands to my thigh.

"He's in jail. Where he'll be for a long time."

"Oh."

"I'm not going to let anything happen to you," I say after several blocks of silence.

"I believe you. I...guess I never really thought about all of this as stalking. I just always figured someone wanted to scare me."

"Is there anyone who we should look at harder? Another teacher maybe? A parent? Anyone?"

"No one comes to mind," she says.

"So we go back to the beginning," I reply, pulling onto her street.

"How can I help?"

Pride at her strength, at the fact that she's mine, swells in my chest.

"You're pretty fucking amazing, you know that, right?"

I pull into her driveway, shifting the car into park so I can lean over and press a kiss to her cheek.

"I don't want to be a victim, Cole. If I can help, I'll do whatever I can."

"Sawyer wants me to go through the letters you got when you were Miss Tennessee. See if I can find any connection, any new clue that tells us who it was before to see if it's the same person."

"But it's been years between incidents."

"With Evie it was five years between events."

She takes a deep breath and squares her shoulders.

"So those letters," she says.

After reading them on the plane on the way out here, I never wanted to read them again. I damn sure didn't want her to have to relive them. But I promised not to hide anything from her.

Which means I need to trust in her strength as much as I am asking her to trust my ability to protect her.

"I hate that I'm asking you to help," I admit.

"You didn't ask. I volunteered." She opens her door before turning back to me. "So what are we waiting for? Sounds like we have a job to do."

Only now it's not a job. It never has been to be honest.

This is her life.

Her future.

With me.

CHAPTER 18

COLE

*D*espite it being the middle of the night, I'm awake, my mind sifting through pieces of information like scraps of confetti scattered on the wind.

"Noooo." Hannah Grace fidgets in her sleep, her body tense as she fights a nightmare.

Fuck. I should have seen this coming. We've been combing through the stack of letters I printed out every night for the last three nights.

Night number one had been her recapping her win as Miss Tennessee and going through the first few letters she had received from her pen pal, Eric.

Not that I believe that's likely his real name.

How do you know it's a him?

Yes, I had made that assumption. But something in my gut told me I was right.

For every letter we went through, Hannah Grace would provide an explanation of how she responded—what she remembered. The first few had large gaps because she hadn't thought anything more about it other than it being a piece of fan mail no different from the rest she had received after being crowned.

The only difference was that Eric had continued writing. Sometimes a letter a week, sometimes more. Once there was even a two-week gap between letters. But frequent or not, they continued.

And as we read them, as Hannah Grace explained her responses, I took notes on places, topics mentioned, dates.

Then came the letters from the second night. The same tone as those from the first night until we got to the last one. The one where Eric admitted how he felt.

You don't know what these letters have meant to me. How happy I am to see an envelope addressed to me with your pretty handwriting on it. These last few weeks, you've become someone I can't imagine not having in my life. I love you, Hannah Grace. And I imagine you telling me you feel the same. How could you not with everything we've talked about? Lately, all I can think about is walking up to you on campus at that coffee shop you study at—the one near your elementary education class. I tell you who I am and you smile at me the way you smiled on stage that night when they asked you your interview question. You'll be wearing a blue dress when we meet too. Not a ball gown, but something better. One that matches your eyes and highlights your breasts. Do you know how often I imagine them pressed against me? What they would feel like? What your lips taste like? But nothing will beat the real thing. When I come to you, you'll know me the same way that a soul recognizes its mate. We're meant to be.

I can't erase the image of Hannah Grace's face out of my mind as I had read that letter, stumbling over the words and trying not to fist the paper into my hand and throw it into the garbage. Her expression had shifted from curious and thoughtful to one of fear. Of shame.

Tonight's letters had been harder to process, and we weren't even through the last of them. But I kept stopping, trying to give Hannah Grace breaks, even when she denied needing them. I couldn't ignore how tightly she clung to me every time we put the letters to the side. How she refused to move from my lap as we read the last two for the night.

WHY DIDN'T YOU ANSWER ME, HANNAH GRACE? I HATE THAT YOU DIDN'T. I HATE WAITING FOR YOUR LETTER ONLY TO HAVE IT NOT COME. I COULDN'T HAVE SURPRISED YOU WITH MY CONFESSION. IT'S SO OBVIOUS HOW MUCH I LOVE YOU. HOW MUCH I WANT TO BE WITH YOU. DO YOU NEED THE WORDS IN PERSON? I CAN ALWAYS COME TO YOU. WHAT IF I CAME AND TOLD YOU IN PERSON HOW IN LOVE WITH YOU I AM? HOW MUCH I WANT TO BE WITH YOU? HOW I KNOW WE'LL BE TOGETHER FOREVER?

Another letter after Hannah Grace apparently hadn't responded.

WHAT THE FUCK? WHY ARE YOU IGNORING ME? YOU DON'T STRIKE ME AS THE KIND OF BITCH TO DO THAT. YOU'RE KIND. YOU LOVE ME. JUST AS MUCH AS I LOVE YOU. YOU HAVE TO. THERE'S NO OTHER CHOICE BUT FOR YOU TO BE WITH ME. HAVE YOU BEEN TOO BUSY WITH SCHOOL AND YOUR OBLIGATIONS? I'M TRYING TO BE PATIENT, HANNAH GRACE. BUT MY PATIENCE WILL ONLY LAST SO LONG.

She had been fucking shaking by the time we finished that one.

Each letter was always signed with "Sincerely, Eric." The return address was addressed as Eric Carle and an address in an apartment complex in Nashville that had been torn down two years ago. And it turns out Eric Carle wrote *The Very Hungry Caterpillar*, one of the books that Hannah Grace had been studying in her elementary education class. The one that "Eric" had mentioned in relation to the coffee shop where she liked to study.

Hannah Grace whimpers in her sleep, and I tighten my arm around her waist, pulling her back against my chest and pressing my lips against her bare shoulder. I don't want to go through any more letters. Not if they are going to cause this. And the remaining ones are the worst of the bunch.

"Cole." My name is a soft cry on her lips, her shoulders beginning to shake as the light I left on in the bathroom highlights the silver tracks of tears on her face.

"I'm here, Honey Girl. I'm right here," I whisper.

Fuck, I can't stand to witness this. But she has school tomorrow; she needs rest. Her brain needs the break from the darkness we've been reading.

Yeah, because she's absolutely getting a break right now.

The nightmare will fade.

Because it has so far? How long are you going to make her suffer?

Fuck.

"Han—"

"Noooo!" She bolts upright and her scream echoes through the bedroom.

"Baby, it's fine. I'm here. I'm right here. You're safe." I sit up, keeping my arm wrapped around her shoulders as sobs rack her body.

I continue to murmur the reassurances, moving my free hand up and down her back until her sobs slow to hiccups and even when she can take a deep breath. But the tension never leaves her.

"Honey Girl?"

She turns toward me, throwing her arms around me and flattening us both. I surround her with my arms, her cheek pillowed against my chest as my heart thumps against her ear.

"Do you want to talk about it?" I ask.

She shakes her head, her silky hair tickling my side.

"No."

"I don't think we should keep reading those letters."

"There's only a few left. We need to send the information to Sawyer and Sydney."

"*I* need to get the info to the two of them."

She lifts her head, her eyes sparkling even in the darkness.

"What are you saying?"

"Hannah Grace, these letters are hurting you. Whoever this guy Eric is, he's a fucking psycho. What he wrote is disgusting. You don't need to keep reading these. You don't need to relive this shit. I can't stand how much they're impacting you."

I lift my hand, tucking a stray strand of hair behind her ear and running my index finger along her jaw.

"You're reading them," she points out.

"And I'm ready to tear whoever wrote them limb from fucking limb. And I know the last few letters are the worst of the bunch."

"I can do it." Her fingers clench into fists against my ribs.

"I have no doubt you can, Honey Girl. But you don't have to."

"You listen to me, Cole Matthew Strickland. I *will* finish reading these letters. With or without you. Wouldn't you rather be next to me when I read them?"

"If I had my way, you wouldn't at all," I grit out through my clenched jaw.

The fact that she triple named me means I'm not winning this argument. But I at least have to try.

"That's not one of your choices," she tells me.

It's the same thing she tells her students when she gives them the options they have when things start to go sideways.

"Are you teachering me right now?"

"Teachering? Is that a word?" Her nose wrinkles as her lips stumble over the word.

"I have no idea. But I've heard you use that choice phrase in your class before."

Her lips twitch, and relief floods my limbs with the knowledge that she's at least a little distracted from the nightmare that woke her.

"What happens when I say that?"

"The kids make a choice," I grumble.

"What choice?" she presses.

"The one you want them to make."

She can't hide her smile anymore, and it stretches across her face.

"So what answer are you going to give me?"

I sigh, closing my eyes as my arms shift from the small of her back and my hands skate along her ass.

"I'm with you, Hannah Grace. Whatever you want to do. I may not like it. But it's your choice."

"Good boy," she crows and drops her lips to mine.

Her tongue teases the seam of my lips, and my fingers flex into the smooth skin of her hips until she moans, arching into me.

I try to ignore the heat of her pussy against my lower stomach and the way her nipples pebble against my chest. Now isn't the right time. She's scared, vulnerable. And I need to have more self-control than a randy goat.

But my good intentions fray as her tongue penetrates my lips, finding mine as she rolls her hips. I grip her hips tighter, stilling her movements, and she breaks the kiss.

"What's the matter?" she asks.

Her lips find my chin, tracing along my jaw, until her tongue can rim my ear.

Be strong, be strong, be—oh, who the fuck are you kidding?

I groan and lift my hips, grinding against her as my dick slides through her folds.

"We…should…stop." I have to fight to get the words out when they're the last thing I want to do.

Her fingernails scratch lightly through the hair on my chest.

"Why?" Her question should be innocent, but the way her hands and hips move against my body makes it anything but.

"I don't want to take advantage of you."

Fuck. It should not be this hard to string together a coherent sentence.

Then again, I've never had to think rationally when this woman is naked in my arms.

"You're not," she says, slipping a hand between us to wrap around my cock.

My eyes flutter closed, rolling back in my head as she runs her thumb over the tip.

My hips buck, unable to control themselves under her gentle, persistent touches.

"Honey Girl," I groan while praying for control.

She sits up, ass against my thighs, and uses both hands on my dick. Her breasts sway with her movement, highlighted by the light from the bathroom, and my mouth waters for a taste.

"You're killing me," I tell her, covering her hands with mine and stilling the torture.

Her fingers lace with mine and she drags our joined hands to her stomach.

"Cole," she whispers.

I drag my attention away from her pink-tipped breasts to meet her gaze.

"Make love to me." Every wall she's held, every hesitation and doubt that has existed every other time I've studied her, is gone. Eradicated.

The only thing that remains is...love.

Surging up, I bracket her face with my hands and bring my lips within millimeters of hers.

"I love you, Hannah Grace."

It's not the first time I've said those words since we've reconnected. And more often than not, she immediately kisses me, telling me without words that she feels the same.

"I..." She swallows, her tongue peeking out and slicking along her lips. "I love you, Cole."

The flavor of my name is still on her lips when mine close over them. Elation fizzes through my blood, rocketing me into the heavens. Our tongues circle one another, and I run my hands down her sides until they cup her ass and squeeze.

Breaking the kiss, I press a trail of hot, open-mouthed kisses down her neck and collarbone, using the leverage of where she rests against my legs to boost her until my lips can wrap around one of her nipples.

She mewls, arching against my mouth as her fingers tunnel through my hair.

"Tell me again," I say, shifting to her other breast and dragging that peak into my mouth.

"I...love...you," she pants.

"I love you." I kiss the tip of one breast. "I love you." Then the tip of the other. "I love you."

This time my lips find the spot above her heart.

"I love you." My gaze locks with hers as I repeat the words.

She lifts her hand, palm resting against my cheek, and I turn my head so I can brush a kiss against her hand.

"Show me," she whispers.

In a blur, I shift us until she's beneath me and I'm cradled between her thighs.

Using my lips, I brush kisses against her forehead, each of her eyelids, the tip of her nose, the right cheek followed by the left, one corner of her mouth before the other, finally settling my lips more fully against hers, allowing our tongues to glide together. Her hands grip my biceps, fingernails digging into my skin, and her legs wrap around my waist, tempting me to speed up. To go faster.

But I force the temptation aside, content to move at this unhurried pace.

She moans, the sound trapped in the merging of our mouths.

How is it possible that I got so lucky as to get a second chance with this woman? My lips continue their pilgrimage, finding spots along her neck, just below her earlobe and the pulse point at the base where I spend time learning the texture of the vibration of her pulse beneath my lips, the exact spot that makes her breath catch. Only then do I continue my exploration.

Her shoulders. The inside of her elbow, the pulse point of her wrist.

The entire line of her collarbone.

The valley between her breasts.

Her hips squirm against the bed, and my hands hold her in place.

"Please."

I trace a path up the slope of her breast, my tongue orbiting her nipple, before dragging the flat edge against the hard peak.

"Cole."

"I'm going to savor every inch of you, Honey Girl. Worship you with my lips." I press a kiss against the berry-colored tip. "My tongue." I shift my attention to her other breast and drag my tongue across the hard bud in the center. "My teeth."

Sucking her breast into my mouth, I close my teeth over her nipple, my cock jumping with her breathy cry. Despite the need I have to sink into her as fast as I can, to get us both there, I take my time. I learn the edge of her nipple with my tongue, the change in textures as it hardens further in my mouth. I spar with the tip, tapping it with my tongue before wrapping my lips around it, occasionally adding my teeth. While I map one breast with my mouth, I lift my hand to the other, molding the globe with my hand then dragging my fingers over the tip before I use my forefinger and thumb to pluck and twist.

Then I switch and start over again.

Her back arches, pressing her breasts forward as they continue to beg for my attention. Her husky cries grow louder, her fingernails scraping along my scalp as her hips shift against the bed. Finished memorizing the second breast, I switch back, nipping at one tip while my fingers twist the other. Her hips spasm.

"Oh my God, *Cole. Please.*"

She tries to lift her hips to make me move.

"*Please.*"

"I'm not done with your breasts, Honey Girl. I've missed too many years of tasting their sweetness to speed through this process."

Flattening my tongue, I lave first one nipple followed by the second. Her fingers tighten in my hair and she tugs, the sharp edge of pain something I enjoy.

"Are you close?" I ask before peppering the underside of one breast with kisses. My lips trace a line under her breasts.

"Yes. *Yes.*"

Her answer intensifies as I suck one breast back into my mouth while I trace one hand down her stomach. My finger slides easily through her folds and finds her clit, and her legs shake at the first pass of my thumb over the hard bundle of nerves.

"You're so wet for me. I fucking love it," I murmur against her rib cage and trail kisses to her navel. "Your pussy wants my mouth as much as your breasts do."

I dip my tongue into her navel and she squirms at the ticklish caress.

"More."

My lips continue south, stopping at the edge of her pubic bone.

"Cole."

"Patience, Honey Girl. Good things come to those who wait."

Shifting up, I lift one of her legs until my lips can find the arch of her foot. My dick weeps with my own need, but I push its demands to the side, focusing on the delicate curve of her ankle, the sensitive skin behind her knee. I graze my fingers along the sensitive skin of one thigh, circling higher until my fingers skim her slick folds.

Her fingers clench the sheets at her hips, her back bowing off the bed as pleasure continues to build. But I can build that flame hotter. For both of us. I reluctantly move my hand to her other thigh, retreating down the smooth skin while I lift that leg, tickling behind her knee with my lips before tracing the arch of her instep with my thumb.

"Cole."

I stay focused, sure that if I don't, I'm going to lose the little bit of control I have left.

"I need you. Please."

Her words, coupled with the way her hips move against me, are severing the leash of my control one thread at a time—and it was already frayed to begin with.

"Soon." I'm not sure who the promise is to—her or me.

But I settle between her thighs, lifting her legs onto my shoulders and pressing her thighs back farther with my hands. The moment stretches, the tension winding tighter and tighter, a rubber band ready to snap.

"Fuck," I whisper the word and close my eyes.

Patience. It's what I told Hannah Grace. But mine is wearing thin as I close the distance between my lips and her pussy and feather a soft breath against her.

"Cole—*ohhhh.*"

I snake my tongue along her slit, back to front. Her legs spasm against my hands and I increase my grip, doubling down as I turn my focus to her clit. I circle the hard bundle of nerves with my tongue before tapping a rhythm against it. Her hands slide through my hair, snagging on the strands to grip them tightly. As soon as her body figures out the rhythm of my tongue, I switch it up, circling her clit again before sucking it into my mouth. My cheeks hollow with the suction I apply, and she cries out as her breath breaks.

Using my shoulders to hold her legs open, I free one of my hands and slide my index finger through her folds to press it knuckle deep. Her muscles pull at the digit, pulsing around it as I continue to push. I add a second finger, scissoring the two of them before I bring them back together and withdraw them almost completely.

"I'm so close. Don't stop."

I flatten my tongue, swiping against her before I turn my head and nip at the inside of her thigh. She jumps and her hips lift and fall as she attempts to ride my fingers that rim her opening. I slide them back in, running my tongue over her clit again and again. I don't stop, only switch what I'm doing as I drive her higher, crooking my fingers until they find the spot that makes her legs lock against my back.

Her pussy clamps on my two fingers, and her whimper turns into a loud moan as her orgasm takes over, detonating her around my fingers. I take one last swipe against her with my tongue before I crawl up her body, lining myself up and sliding in as her orgasm still shakes through her.

"*Oh God.*"

"Fuck, Honey Girl. You're going to make me come." Her pussy milks my cock and I grit my teeth.

"Isn't that the idea?" The smile is clear in her question.

I open my eyes to confirm my suspicions before dropping my mouth to hers, tangling our tongues as I withdraw from her heat. She locks her legs around my waist and I snap my hips forward, bumping my pelvis against hers.

"Not until I make you come again," I whisper against her lips.

"Together."

"Together," I confirm.

I slide my hands to her hips, holding her as I roll us, and she settles her legs on either side of my waist. She meets my thrusts, rubbing her pelvis against mine, and it's like the first lightning strike in a storm that's building.

Fuck, I'm not going to last. Not the way her pussy grips me. Not the way her breath breaks on my name as her hands grip mine. She falls forward, her hair tickling my face. I take advantage, leaning up enough to tongue one of her nipples before sucking it into my mouth. Her rhythm falters and I release her hands to palm her ass, keeping her hips moving against mine as I piston my hips.

"C-C-Cole."

Releasing her breast with a pop, I increase my tempo as her pussy tightens further. The storm is picking up strength, almost on top of us, and I strain to hold on.

"I know, baby."

I use my mouth on her other breast, flexing my fingers against her ass as my tongue spars with her nipple. She meets each of my thrusts, each of her breaths accompanied by little sounds of pleasure that are wrenching my control from me. My orgasm races down my spine and I can't hold it back.

"Come with me, Honey Girl." I release her breast long enough to murmur the words before closing back over her nipple, sinking my teeth into the sensitive skin and tugging sharply. Her pussy clamps down like a vise and I'm done.

Lightning arcs from my balls and shatters my body into a million pieces of light as my orgasm overtakes me. I release her breast, wrapping my arms around her and drawing her to me, holding on to her as we come together.

"I love you, Cole. I love you."

If I thought my orgasm was powerful before, it's nothing compared to the music of those words moaned in my ear.

"Fuck, Honey Girl, I love you too."

After that, words are impossible as the pleasure finishes claiming us. Once it ebbs, she's sprawled on my chest as my hands trace nonsensical patterns along her back. She sighs and her breath tickles my chest as she shifts her hand next to her face, over my heart.

"I could stay like this all day," she murmurs, drawing a heart where mine beats beneath her fingers.

"Me too."

She lifts her head, and my gaze locks with hers.

"What is it?" I ask.

"I meant what I said. It wasn't an in-the-moment thing. I love you."

"I'm never going to get tired of those words on your lips, Honey Girl." Shifting us, I'm able to press a relatively chaste kiss against her lips. "I love you."

Our lips find each other's again and my dick twitches, readying for round two.

The blare of the alarm nixes that idea.

"Fuck." I sigh, dropping my head back against the pillow.

Her giggle is infectious as she stretches across me to turn it off.

"Time to get ready for school," she tells me, smacking a kiss to my lips.

"I don't wanna go to school," I whine and draw another giggle from her.

Fuck, I love that sound.

But I should have known, it wasn't going to last. Reality intrudes as we leave the house, her demeanor growing quiet. We're almost to school when she releases her abused lip and turns toward me.

"Can I ask you something?"

I squeeze her hand that's been laced with mine since we left the house.

"Of course."

"What happens if we don't find whoever is doing this?"

Not an option.

"We're going to find him."

Her sigh is one of weariness. Of losing hope.

"You can't promise that."

"I won't give up, Honey Girl. Not until I find this bastard."

"What if it's not a man? It's not like that's for sure."

Fuck. She's right. There's no certainty who this person is.

"You're right. But my gut is telling me it's a man. Although I hate using that word to describe him. A real man doesn't scare a woman."

"But what happens if rereading these letters, if starting from square one, doesn't help?"

"I-I'm not sure. We've never had that happen before," I admit. "It's always worked."

"But what if it doesn't?"

She pulls her hand away, turning toward the window and wrapping her arms around herself. I don't want to make empty promises. And given that we've never faced a situation where we weren't successful, anything I say right now would be exactly that. An empty promise.

We pull into the parking lot and Zach is already waiting. But Hannah Grace doesn't offer much of a greeting before she heads for the school, leaving the two of us behind.

"Did something else happen?" Zach asks as I lock Hannah Grace's car.

"Not a fucking thing," I growl.

He looks over at me, eyebrows raised.

"Sorry. We're just hitting a lot of dead ends. Hannah Grace is worried that we're not going to find whoever's doing this. She's now even questioning if it's a man."

"Really?" He badges into the school and grabs the door, holding it open until I grab it from him.

"Yeah. But my gut is telling me different. It's a man. But there's no connection anywhere. And nothing from the letters she got as Miss Tennessee. It's driving me fucking crazy."

We stop in front of the gym with no sign of Hannah Grace.

Fuck.

"So what's the plan now?"

"We still have two suspects left. A guy who used to work for the pageant who lives a mile from Hannah Grace and the grocery store guy. Thanks for that partial plate by the way. It seriously helped us find him."

"Yeah, no problem. Anything I can do to help keep Hannah Grace safe."

"My team is still exploring both to see what else we can find, but we're also going back to the beginning. Looking back through things in case we missed something. We've never had it happen that something didn't pop up. And Hannah Grace wants to know what comes next if it happens this time."

"Can I do anything to help?"

"Just...be there for her. She fucking needs you, man. And if you happen to notice anything weird, let me know?"

"Yeah, of course."

"Thanks."

"Absolutely. See you at lunch?" he asks.

I nod. "I was thinking I might run out and grab a pizza. You want?"

"Sounds good. Hannah Grace knows what to grab."

Reaching out, I shake his hand. This man is not my enemy. He wants to protect Hannah Grace as much as I do. Recognizing that is a big step for us. Hopefully it means that he'll accept Hannah Grace and me when she does tell him about us.

CHAPTER 19

HANNAH GRACE

LL

Hey, what are you doing?

*M*y sister's text comes through on a Monday morning on our way to school. Even over a week after we read the rest of the letters from Eric and sent information to Cole's team to see if they could make heads or tails of what little we could send them, there's been no progress on figuring out who could be scaring me.

Detective O'Connell also called to tell us the neighbors still haven't seen anything, and there was no evidence or fingerprints on the pieces of camera equipment.

At what point are they just going to give up and move on? And when they do, is Cole going to leave again?

"Laura Leigh," I tell Cole, lifting my phone to respond since he's driving.

We're almost to school.

> LL
>
> You guys aren't out yet?

Friday. We have a half day.

> LL
>
> That's what I was texting about.
>
> Would you be up for me visiting this weekend?
>
> I want to do Christmas shopping.

You can't Christmas shop in Knoxville?

> LL
>
> Ouch.
>
> What's the matter? Don't want baby sister hanging out with you this weekend?
>
> Did you and your hottie friend finally hook up?

With a sigh, I put my phone face down in my lap, leaning back against the headrest and closing my eyes.

"Everything okay?" Cole asks and squeezes my thigh where his hand has been resting.

"She wants to come Christmas shopping this weekend."

"You sound like she said you have to have a root canal. Why is it a bad thing she wants to come see you? I'd like to see her again."

"She doesn't know about you."

Guilt that I haven't told anyone, including Zach, gnaws at my stomach.

"And you don't think she'll approve." It's a statement, not a question, and the disappointment is clear in his voice.

"I—no. That's not what I was thinking." My teeth immediately find my lip as nervous energy floods my body.

"Honey Girl, are you completely unaware that your tell whenever you lie is that you chew on your lower lip?"

Busted. I immediately open my mouth to release the flesh between my teeth.

"It's not that I don't think she'll approve. She'll probably be ecstatic. She was at home when we broke up so she didn't..."

Awkward. This is so fucking awkward.

"Didn't?" he prompts.

"She didn't see how upset I was. I was at school when I got your last letter. I told people we broke up. Not that..."

"Not that I broke your heart," he finishes for me.

"Right."

"You understand that's not going to happen again, right?"

"I..."

A part of me wants to agree, but there's another part—a small one—that still doubts that he'll stick around.

He huffs a humorless laugh.

"Well, I guess that answers that question."

"No. It doesn't. I think right now you're not planning on leaving again."

"But?"

He turns into the school, and Zach is leaning against his car waiting for us.

"Can we talk about this later?" I ask, looking down at the way my fingers lace with each other.

"What more do I have to do, Hannah Grace? You told me you loved me—"

"I do!" I look up, studying the way his fingers clench on the steering wheel and a muscle tics in his jaw.

He glances at me as he pulls into the parking place several away from Zach instead of right next to him.

"Then stop hiding me like I'm some goddamned secret. I promised you I wasn't going anywhere. That I wasn't going to hide shit from you and I haven't. Instead, you're hiding me. If you don't want to be with me, then fucking tell me. But if you do, then I need to stop being your dirty little secret, Hannah Grace. I need you to tell your family. Or better yet, tell your best friend who you see every fucking day."

He's breathing heavily by the time he finishes, and the anguish in his eyes gives them a dull hue. I did this.

"Cole—"

There's a knock on the window and I jump, whirling around to find Zach waving at us.

Shit.

I hold up a finger and turn back to Cole.

"I will tell them. I don't want to hide you like my 'dirty little secret.' And I'm sorry if I made you feel that way."

"Zach is waiting for you," he tells me, voice flat.

"Cole."

"I understand you want to believe it, Hannah Grace. But just like you have doubts, so do I. We've been doing whatever it is we've been doing and you're no closer to telling Zach than you were when we first talked about it. Actions speak louder than words."

And his actions are definitely backing up what he's saying more than mine do for me.

He doesn't have to say it, but the look he gives me is loud and clear.

I need to do better.

Reaching behind us, he grabs my bags and lifts them as if they weigh nothing.

"Let's go inside," he says.

He's out of the car before I can say anything else and already walking toward the door by the time I get out and meet Zach at the back of my car.

"Cole's pretty upset," he says as we walk toward the building.

"Yeah."

"Is it still because you guys don't have any leads?"

"Huh?"

"He mentioned it to me the other day. How frustrated he was that you guys hadn't found anything."

I didn't realize he and Cole had ever had any conversations when I wasn't around, but I don't remember them talking about that.

"Oh. I-I think that's part of it."

"Maybe he's ready to go home," he says.

I freeze, my entire body locking as it rejects the idea. Cole is home.

Zach stops, turning back to me when he realizes I'm standing still. "You okay?"

"Yeah. Sorry. I...maybe." I stumble over the words as I start walking again.

Actions speaker louder than words, Hannah Grace.

I love Cole. So why is it so hard for me to tell my best friend?

Maybe I'll start with Laura Leigh. It'll be easier to start with someone who loved Cole to begin with.

Cole stays silent even after we're both alone in my classroom. Pulling out my phone, I send a text to my sister.

> No, Zach and I didn't hook up.

> And, yes, you can come stay this weekend.

LL

That's too bad, he's really cute.

I agree with her. Zach is cute. But no one holds a candle to Cole. And it's time I started proving that.

LL

My last final is Thursday so I'll leave Friday morning. Maybe I can meet you at the school?

> Why? So you can flirt with Zach?

Maybe I can play matchmaker for the two of them. Laura

Leigh has always had a crush on Zach. There's a small age difference, but it's not massive.

> LL
>
> It's like you know me or something.
>
> You wouldn't mind if I asked him out for a drink this weekend, right?

> You're not old enough to drink.

> LL
>
> We could get coffee. Maybe I can convince him to grab dinner instead.
>
> We already know I'm his type. You and I could be twins.

I can't help but laugh as I read her messages. It's true. Laura Leigh and I could basically pass for twins—I make a mental note to keep a lockdown on my driver's license while she's here—but the biggest difference is that she is the more audacious of the two of us.

> I'll see you Friday.

> LL
>
> Yay! See you then!

"My sister is coming Friday," I tell Cole who is as far away from me while being in the same room as he can get.

His grunt is not the response I hoped for.

I close the distance between us, cautiously wrapping my arms around him.

"I'm sorry."

He doesn't push me away like I was afraid he would do. Instead his arms wrap around me, holding me to him as if I'll blow away.

"I'm sorry too."

Leaning my head back, I rest my chin on his chest so I can study him.

"All you did was tell me how you feel. Which is what I asked you to do. You didn't do anything wrong. Why are you sorry?" I ask.

He sighs and drops his lips to the tip of my nose.

"I'm...sensitive when it comes to you. About our future. I spent too many years thinking that future was gone. And I want to believe in it again."

"Me too." I press my lips against the soft cotton of his shirt right over his heart.

We hold each other in silence for several breaths. He smells of whatever warm spicy cologne he wears—the bottle is familiar, since it now sits on my bathroom counter, but not the name—and something uniquely Cole. Something that reaches into my heart and puts back together several of the pieces that have been broken for the last four years.

"We just need to keep talking, Honey Girl."

He's talking about just the two of us, but it's time for me to do some talking too. Starting with Laura Leigh for practice, there's no more hiding what's between Cole and me. Not if I want to give us a real shot.

※ ※ ※

THE LAST WEEK of school passes in a blur. Zach doesn't mention anything about Monday morning and I don't tell him about Cole, but Cole seems content with my plan to start with Laura Leigh. Things between us have been different since Monday. He's there mentally, physically, emotionally, everything I need him to be, but it's like we're living parallel lives that don't intersect instead of the interwoven design we'd been creating over the last few weeks.

He sleeps next to me in bed, kisses me, and we snuggle on the couch, but we haven't made love since last weekend. But it's not like I've initiated anything either. We're in some strange balance that both of us are afraid to disrupt.

And it's driving me crazy.

"Brought you coffee," Cole says, setting a travel mug on the bathroom counter in front of me.

My hands are up in my hair as I finish curling the last piece, and he steals a kiss on my neck that creates gooseflesh along my spine.

"Thank you," I say, my voice husky as desire surges through my blood.

The Cole from a week ago would have continued the kisses along my neck, cupping my breasts with his hands while mine were stuck upright. This one doesn't do any of that.

"You're welcome, Honey Girl." He turns and leaves the bathroom before I can say anything else.

Further defining that something between us is…off. And I'm running out of time to press him about it, but I need to figure out what's going on before Laura Leigh gets here because she's going to see the tension between us from a mile away.

"Is everything okay?" I ask him a few minutes later as we're both getting into the car in my garage.

"Yeah. Fine. Why?"

"I… Cole, something has been different between us since Monday. I… you're upset with me. I've given you doubts about us. I hate it and I'm not sure how to fix it."

"I'm not upset with you. Not really. And I know you want to be with me. I've been racking my brain for how to talk to you about it. For how to focus on that at the same time we're trying to figure out who's been scaring you. I want to fix it. I want to just be us again." He stops the car partially backed out of the garage, throwing it into park and turning to look at me.

"I don't want things to be weird between us either. Not with my sister here for the weekend. I want her to see how happy you make me."

"You make me happy too, Honey Girl," he says and lifts a hand to cup my cheek.

I lift my hand to cover his and lean closer, my lips inches from his.

"Deliriously happy," I murmur.

"Enraptured," he whispers back and closes the distance.

Most people wouldn't be turned on by a word that sounds like it belongs more in a thesaurus than spoken in a regular conversation. But what we discovered in studying for the SATs is that we both considered the vocabulary lessons as foreplay.

And time hasn't dulled that belief.

The chemistry is back with a vengeance at the first brush of his mouth against mine, and I reach out, gripping his forearms as our tongues tangle together. His other hand comes up, and both hands hold my jaw like he's holding the most fragile piece of glass. Like I am precious to him.

Because I am.

He softens the kiss, turning it into teasing, nibbling caresses before pulling back.

"We're going to be late for school." One corner of his mouth lifts in a smile that will always be his signature look.

I can't help but smile back.

"Good thing we planned to go to school early."

"We get there early every day. Smart-ass." His finger taps the end of my nose.

Was it really as simple as that? A hot-as-fuck kiss and him tapping my nose?

He continues to back out the car and presses the remote control, lowering the garage door and staying put until it closes all the way. But he stops again when we reach the street, parallel to his rental car. We've talked about turning it in, but haven't gotten around to it yet.

"Do you want to take your car back to the rental car place this weekend?" I ask.

Cole puts the car in park and gets out.

"Cole?" I ask, opening my car door.

"Stay in the car, Hannah Grace." The tone of his voice has a shiver skating down my spine.

"Why? What's the matter..."

My attention shifts to the car and I suck in an audible breath. Sometime in the middle of the night it's been vandalized. No, not vandalized.

Destroyed.

The side windows are shattered out of the car, the windshield a spiderweb of cracks. Large scratches run the length of the car along the side. The tires on the side I can see have been slashed, and given that the car isn't leaning to one side, it's safe to say that the other two are in the same condition.

"Oh my God. Cole." I rush around the vehicle, wrapping my arms around him as he studies the destroyed car in front of us.

From this angle I can see the angry red spray paint across the hood of the silver paint.

Leave.

Cole is already pulling out his phone taking several pictures before starting a video. I follow him to the other side of the car and my hands fly to my mouth.

Or else.

"Cole," I murmur his name, reaching out and gripping his free hand.

He's silent but the way his fingers squeeze mine is proof that he's not as calm as he appears to be.

"Wh-who would do something like this?" I ask.

But I already have the answer.

"Seems like whoever is bothering you is tired of me hanging around."

He pockets his phone before walking me back to my car and stopping us in front of the driver's door.

"Honey Girl, you need to go to school. The kids are expecting you."

"B-b-but your car," I say, motioning to the destroyed piece of metal in front of us.

"I'm going to call the police and the rental car place. Your neighbors don't need to see this. Neither does your sister when she gets here later."

"You're going to send me to school by myself?" After this just happened, I don't want to be separated from Cole.

He nods and lifts a hand to my shoulder, squeezing gently.

"Zach is there. You'll be safe. As soon as I get this done—and I'm going to rush as fast as I can—I'll grab an Uber to the school."

"You'll be here by yourself. What if he comes back? What if he's still here?"

I try to swing my head around to look but Cole pulls me into his arms.

"I'll be okay. The police will be my first phone call. And I'm going to stay on Murphy until they find something. Whoever is doing this doesn't mind being out in the open now. And the message is pretty clear. Not like the roses in your bed."

I shiver at the combination of that memory and what's in front of us.

Burrowing closer, I squeeze Cole as hard as I can.

"Should I call Laura Leigh and cancel?"

"Have you told anybody in your family what's going on?"

"No. I didn't want them to worry."

He rolls his eyes and drops a kiss to my forehead.

"Someday we need to discuss your lack of communication with your family. But today is not that day. Don't cancel. Usually this piece of shit does something to scare you and disappears. This is just his latest scare tactic."

"You're sure?"

"I'm positive. Go to school. I'll be there soon."

I let him guide me into the driver's seat, then I readjust the position to reach the pedals.

"Please be careful," I say and reach out and grip his hand.

He leans down and brushes a gentle kiss against my lips.

"Always. I love you."

"Love you too."

He stands and shuts the door, tapping on the roof to send me on my way.

I keep my eyes on the rearview mirror, watching him until I'm forced to turn and head to the school when everything in me is telling me to turn around.

CHAPTER 20

COLE

I wait until Hannah Grace is no longer visible before I pull my phone out, shooting a text off to Sawyer and Sydney with images and video from the car followed by another text.

> Call you in a few minutes.

My next call is to the detective I've been working with at the Nashville Police Department who agrees to head over.

By the time I hang up with the rental company, I have five minutes before Detective O'Connell should be here, so I pull up Sawyer's contact and hit call.

"Are you okay?" Sawyer answers.

"I was inside when it happened. Probably in the middle of the night. This is why I wish I had that fucking security system already."

"How do we know they wouldn't have circumvented that system again? They destroyed the cameras," Sydney says.

"Cole, you're on speaker."

"Yeah, figured that out, King. Thanks."

"Where's Hannah Grace? Has she seen the car?" he asks.

Reaching back, I grip the back of my neck, rubbing at the tension building in my shoulders.

"We were on the way to school when I saw it. So yeah. I sent her to school while I dealt with the car. Her sister is due here this afternoon, and I don't want to freak her out. Plus this isn't something I want the neighbors seeing longer than necessary."

"The cameras were one thing, Cole. This is a completely different ball game. Whoever is doing this is escalating. But hopefully that means he made a mistake when he destroyed the car."

"That's what I'm hoping. Maybe this was the break we needed." I scan the car again looking for a clue.

The police department will process it on a more detailed level, but anything that sticks out, I want to see first.

"Break or not, this is getting out of hand. I'm flying out tomorrow," Sawyer says, interrupting my search of the car.

"What?" I'm not expecting Sawyer's announcement and nearly bobble my phone.

"I've already booked my flight," he says matter-of-factly.

"I can handle this." My defenses are rising and I want to argue.

"It's not about your ability to handle this, Cole. This is about finding this bastard before something worse happens."

"If it makes you feel any better, I'm not coming," Sydney adds.

"Thank God for small miracles," I mutter.

"I heard that!"

"If I didn't want you to hear it, I wouldn't have said it. Neither of you needs to be here. You're doing what you can."

If Sawyer shows up, is he going to find out that I screwed up this case because I was getting closer to Hannah Grace?

Were you?

The question is realized before I can stop it.

No. One hundred percent no. If anything, that closeness meant I was more concerned, more focused on figuring this out.

And Sawyer won't judge me. It wasn't that long ago that he was in my same position.

"I'm not coming to second-guess what you're doing. I'm coming to support you."

"I—"

A black sedan pulls up across the street.

"PD is here," I tell Sawyer and Sydney.

"We'll talk later. If not, I'll see you tomorrow," Sawyer says and the phone beeps over the speaker.

Detective Murphy O'Connell was assigned to the case when we first contacted NPD after the rose incident. While they documented it—and I had spoken to Detective O'Connell after that incident and met him after the camera issue when I took in the camera pieces, there hadn't been much for them to get involved with. And I wasn't looking for them to be involved before. I just wanted it documented that they had been contacted so once we did catch the bastard, they could prosecute him and limit his ability to get off on a technicality.

As he exits the vehicle, he whistles.

"Damn. When did this happen?"

I shrug and reach out a hand for a handshake when he gets close enough.

"I wish I knew. I got an email from the company I ordered the system from a few days ago apologizing for some 'unforeseen delays' that have now extended my delivery window. Security system is at least another week from being installed. The car was fine last night when we came home. When we went to leave this morning—this."

"You think it's related to everything else?"

"I think if it wasn't, this wouldn't be the only car destroyed, and the others parked on the street or in the driveways seem untouched."

He nods.

"Nothing between the cameras and this?" he asks, using his own phone to grab images of the car.

"Nope."

He glances up as he walks around the car.

"Nothing?"

"Not a damn thing. At least not yet. My team in California is going back through the data."

"Where is Ms. Whittaker?" he asks.

"I sent her ahead to school. I didn't want her to have to keep seeing this." I gesture to the car.

He nods.

"Wise choice. Someone really doesn't like you around." He points to the car.

"Nope. Too bad I don't scare easy."

Hakeem's face flashes through my brain, and the sharp edge of guilt slices through my stomach painfully. I suck in a breath, and Murphy's attention shifts back to me.

"Strickland, you okay?"

"Long story."

"I'm good with those."

"It's not related to the case. Nothing NPD or any other police department needs to look into." I try to keep it vague, but all it does is put Murphy on edge.

"Afraid I need a little more than that," he says, taking a more protective stance than a moment ago.

"I was Special Forces. Deployed twice."

Murphy relaxes immediately.

"Thank you for your service."

I nod.

"Have you already called your insurance company?" He changes the subject.

"It was a rental. I called the company after I called you."

"Yeah, they'll need our report for their insurance."

"I'm not looking forward to being anywhere around Sawyer when he gets the bill for this." I don't even want to imagine the cost for something like this.

"I want to have this towed to our lab. See if we can pull any fingerprints or DNA from it."

"Sawyer and I were just talking that maybe he finally slipped up."

"Let's hope so. If you give me the contact info for the rental company, I'll reach out. Keep them posted about what's going on."

"Can do. They didn't seem like they were in a rush to get this back after I explained what it looked like."

"I bet. Let me radio this in and request the truck. I also want to get a couple of officers out to canvas the neighbors again."

"You think it'll help? They haven't seen anything before."

Yet another dead end. How is it that Hannah Grace doesn't have at least one neighbor spying on the rest of the neighborhood?

"It can't hurt. From what I read from the previous attempts, most of the neighbors are gone during the day. It's a quiet neighborhood so they weren't looking for anything. I would bet most of them have video doorbells too."

I shrug.

"Maybe."

"Look, I'm aware this isn't the answer you want, but be patient. We'll figure it out."

"I have little patience when it comes to Hannah Grace's safety."

I try to ignore the statistics of the victims of stalkers that something actually happens to. But it's getting harder to ignore the more this situation drags out.

"Understood. First things first, let me start with getting everyone out here and we'll go from there."

"I'll grab the rental paperwork for the contact info," I say.

He walks to his car and I open the passenger side carefully since I don't feel like crawling over the glass scattered over the driver's seat. I meet Murphy by his car and hand him the contract.

"Here you go."

"Thanks. Dispatch said it could be a while on the tow truck. Morning rush hour accidents have most of our contracted trucks busy already."

"Fuck. How long?"

I glance at my phone. It's already been over an hour since Hannah Grace left for school.

"Earliest estimate is a couple of hours."

Fuck.

"Do I have to wait here with you and the car? I'd like to get to the school sooner rather than later."

I haven't heard from Hannah Grace since she left, and while I hadn't asked her to text me, I was hoping she would.

"I can request someone from our community services division to wait here." He reaches back in and grabs his radio, straightening as he calls for a community service officer on his portable radio.

I wait until he's done to ask my next question.

"You're sure only a few hours?"

He shrugs. "It should. Why?"

"Not only do I not like it being in front of Hannah Grace's house like a damn spotlight, but I don't want to risk any evidence being contaminated."

"Not gonna happen. I'll stay here until the CSO gets here. If there's evidence on the car, we will find it."

"Thanks, Murphy."

Pulling up my app, I order the closest Uber to my location.

"You sure you don't want to wait around? CSO is maybe fifteen minutes out. I can give you a lift to the school."

My body is on high alert being separated from Hannah Grace.

"Thanks, I appreciate it. But the Uber will be here in about two minutes."

He nods. "I'd do the same."

"Keep us posted on the car?"

"Will do."

"Oh, you need the keys." I fish the rental car keys out of my pocket and pass them over just as the car I ordered pulls up.

"Thanks."

"Thank you," I say, waving and getting into the car.

I'm anxious the whole way to the school, not taking a deep breath until Hannah Grace's car comes into view parked right next to Zach's.

She's here. She's safe.

But my heart still pounds and will until I can see that for myself.

You can't rush into the classroom. You'll scare the kids.

It's hard, but I manage to move at a brisk pace instead of the all-out run I want to make through the school. Zach has a class in the gym with him when I walk by, but I don't stop, intent on getting to Hannah Grace.

The room is dark, a movie playing on a portable cart and the kids eating snacks from plates on their desks. Hannah Grace's face brightens as soon as our eyes connect, and she meets me by the door, stepping into the hallway with me and wrapping her arms around me.

My arms tighten, holding her to me when I know I have to let her go based on where we are and who is watching. But that awareness doesn't loosen my hold on her.

Now.

Now I can breathe. My heart rate is finally returning to a normal rhythm.

"You're safe," she murmurs.

"I told you I would be. I was hoping you would text me when you got to the school."

"Sorry, I meant to. Zach asked where you were, and by the time I finished the story, the kids were already lining up. What did Detective O'Connell say?"

I shake my head.

"I'll tell you after the kids leave."

She squeezes me again, her eyes catching mine. If the kids weren't here, I'd drop my lips to hers. They're red, swollen, and I lift a finger to graze the skin there.

"I wish I could kiss you," she murmurs.

"In my head, I *am* kissing you," I tell her, enjoying her quick intake of breath and the pink that travels to her cheeks.

"I will kiss you once we're alone." Her words are a promise.

"I'm going to hold you to that, Honey Girl."

"I hope you do. Now, come on, we need to head back in there."

She pulls me into the classroom, keeping our fingers threaded until we both sit at her desk.

The half day means that the movie takes most of the day, leaving just enough time for the kids to clean up before it's time to walk them out.

"What time does your sister get here?" I ask once we're done with the kids and walking back to Hannah Grace's classroom.

"Let me text her."

I follow her into the classroom, and she grabs her cell phone from her bag, her fingers flying over the screen.

"She says she should be here in about thirty minutes. God, she must have left early."

"Don't college students generally sleep in?" I ask, making sure her door is locked before moving closer to her.

"Laura Leigh has always been an early riser, plus she gains an hour coming from Knoxville. What are you doing?" she asks.

Reaching out, I yank her into my arms. Her pupils dilate, her breaths becoming shallow as I search her gaze.

"The way I figure it, once Laura Leigh gets here, we won't really have much alone time." I circle her waist with my hands, brushing my fingers under the hem of her shirt.

She sucks in a breath.

"P-probably not."

"And you remember our conversation about making out in a classroom?"

I slide my hands back, filling them with her ass, as I squeeze.

"Mmm. Mm-hmm." Her eyes close and her lips part as she arches her lower half against me.

Lowering my head, I press a kiss against the side of her throat, nuzzling her hair aside so I can track upward.

"I hated not being with you this morning. My body felt like it was missing something," I whisper in her ear. "And it was. It was missing my heart."

Bright blue eyes pop open, twin flames of desire as her eyes clash with mine.

"Kiss me."

I don't need to be asked twice, slanting my lips against hers and tangling our tongues together. Her hands climb my chest to tunnel through my hair, and she presses her breasts against me. I curse the layers of fabric between us. Instead of touching her soft skin, my hands itch as they rub back and forth over the rough denim of her jeans. Her hips squirm against mine and my dick punches at my zipper. The need to prove how safe she is, to be as close to her as possible, is overriding my common sense.

She spins us, her hands dropping to my fly and releasing it.

"We don't have much time," she murmurs.

"What do you mean?"

She doesn't answer, at least not with words. Instead she pushes down my jeans and boxers, and my dick bounces into her waiting hand. My knees buckle, and it's a good thing her chair is behind me and catches my fall. Following me down, she sinks to her knees on the floor.

"Hannah *Grace*." Her name ends on a moan as she drags her tongue along my cock, and stars pop behind my vision.

"You locked the door?"

I open my eyes, her blonde hair mussed, lips swollen as she drags her tongue along the bottom one.

"Yes."

She leans forward again, another drag of her tongue from root to tip before she sucks me into her mouth. My hands find her hair as pleasure builds.

"Fuck." I try to hold my hips still, but she makes it nearly impossible, lowering herself onto my cock until I bump the back of her throat.

Using her knees, she shifts back and forth, almost releasing me before sliding back down. Her hands grip my thighs as she hollows her cheeks with the suction and runs her tongue along the underside of my dick.

"Honey Girl."

This isn't something we've done before, and it's probably a good thing given how quickly the leash I have on my control is snapping. She slides back down again and hums. The vibration is all it takes to sever the last thread. I'm done. With a growl, I yank her off the floor and into my lap, slamming my tongue into her mouth and tasting a combination of her and me and groaning as she sucks at my tongue almost as well as she sucked my dick.

Reaching my hands up her shirt, I unclasp her bra, pushing it and her shirt out of the way and latching on to one of her breasts, nipping at the stiff peak before dragging my tongue.

"*Cole*." She grinds against my dick, and my orgasm settles in my balls.

I'm not some inexperienced teenager, but I'm about to embarrass myself like one.

"I need to be inside you right the fuck now," I growl against her breast.

She moans, pushing herself against my mouth.

"Yes. Hurry. We don't have much time."

My arms grip her waist as I surge from the chair, trying to identify a flat surface while continuing to kiss any skin I can reach with my lips. Her desk is clear enough, and I slide her down my body only long enough to unbutton her jeans and slide them and her panties around her ankles before I boost her back onto the wood surface. Shoving things out of the way, I push her until she's prone. Her shirt is pushed up, jeans and panties around her ankles, and the image she makes with her bare breasts and pink nipples, her pussy waiting for me, has my dick weeping.

"Cole." She opens her arms.

I shake my head.

"Not yet, Honey Girl."

Lifting her legs, I dive under her jeans until I can slide my tongue along her pussy. She cries out, covering her mouth with her hands to stifle the sound as I find her clit, running my tongue around the hard bundle of nerves while my fingers find the tip of her breast, tugging on the nipple while I focus my attention on building her orgasm.

Her hips lift against my mouth, and I use my other hand to keep her still, making it impossible for her to do anything other than feel the pleasure I know is racking her body.

"I'm...going...to...*Cole*."

Recognizing how close she is, I untangle us enough to line myself up at her entrance, pressing into her until my hips tap against hers. Her pussy is already spasming, milking my orgasm to the surface.

My hands grip her hips and I piston against her, speeding up as her hands lift to her mouth again, her cries becoming louder as the orgasm builds higher and higher. She lifts against me,

BREANNA LYNN

meeting thrust for thrust as I increase our rhythm, yanking her against me as my fingers flex into her hips.

"Fuck, Honey Girl, I'm so close," I grit out, fighting to keep the orgasm at bay until she comes.

"Me…too," she pants.

One of her hands leaves her mouth and trails to her breast, her fingers plucking at the tight bud, and the image is gasoline to the fire that rages.

"Fuck. I need you to come, baby. I need you to come right the fuck now. Come on my cock."

Between my cock, her fingers, and my words, she detonates around me, sinking her teeth into her hand as her pussy locks around me. Her vise-like grip on my dick is all it takes and I unleash, losing the rhythm as I piston into her, locking my own shout behind my teeth as I grind my molars together while light explodes behind my eyelids, shattering into a star-filled universe where Hannah Grace is the center.

"Holy shit," she murmurs, sitting up while we're still joined together.

Her arms circle my neck and her hard nipples brush against the cotton of my shirt.

"Holy shit indeed," I say and claim another, more chaste kiss.

"We may need to make some alone time when Laura Leigh is here," I tell her when we break the kiss.

I step back, tugging up my boxers and jeans, and help Hannah Grace straighten her own clothing.

"I'm trying to convince Zach to go for coffee with her."

"Isn't he a little old for her?"

She shrugs. "Seven years isn't that much of a difference."

She has to slide her bra out of her shirt to redo it, her breasts swaying beneath her shirt, hard nipples poking through the fabric.

"Not that much of an age difference," I echo, ready for round two.

"We'll find time for us," she says and finishes fixing her bra before closing the distance and lifting on her tiptoes to graze my lips with a kiss.

"I'm holding you to that," I tell her, locking my arm around her waist.

"Feels like you're holding me to a lot more than that."

Her giggle is infectious and I bark out a laugh.

"Always, Honey Girl."

"I think I just proved I'm good for it," she teases.

"That you did. And I'm going to keep that memory fresh until round two," I tell her.

"Promises, promises," she says and dances away to grab some supplies to clean up after us.

"How much longer until Laura Leigh gets here?" I ask, stepping behind her and caging her against the counter above her supply cabinet.

"Mmm." She grinds her ass against my cock.

I'm ready to say the hell with it and engage in round two when she speaks again.

"Let me check."

I release her and she grabs her phone.

"Oh, she texted me ten minutes ago. She's here. Let me go grab her."

"I'll finish cleaning up here if you want to drop your bags off at the car when you grab her," I offer.

She nods.

"Then we can start our Christmas break too."

I help her load up her bags and drop a kiss to her lips.

"I love you. In case I don't have the chance to say it much while Laura Leigh is here."

"You better say it a bunch when she's here," she tells me, poking a finger into my chest. "Love you too. We'll be back in a minute."

"I'll meet you guys up front. This won't take long."

She blows me a kiss, and I turn my attention to straightening her desk, the image of her still sprawled on top of it fresh in my head.

Fuck, I love that woman.

"I'm going to marry her." I say the words out loud, getting used to them again.

All I have to do is ask her.

CHAPTER 21

HANNAH GRACE

J really want a shower, but that will have to wait as I rush to the front of the school. I expect to find Laura Leigh lounging on one of the benches just outside the entrance, but she's not there.

Her car is parked next to mine, and I walk up to it, smiling as I look for her. But no sign of her. A duffel bag is in the back along with a backpack and several already wrapped packages. The passenger seat is a wreck of snack food trash, an empty diet soda can, and a sweatshirt tossed on the floor.

"Jesus, Laura Leigh," I mutter.

How can she stand the mess?

"She better not think I'm riding with her," I tell myself as I drop my bags in my much-cleaner car and pull my phone free.

> Hey, sorry, I just saw your text and came out front.

> Where are you?

With no immediate response in the form of the three

bouncing dots, I head back toward the school and meet Cole at the entrance.

"Where's Laura Leigh?" he asks, tossing his arm around my shoulders.

"I'm not sure. When I got here she wasn't here but her car is. I just texted her. Do you think someone let her in the school and she's waiting inside?"

"We can check."

"Ohhh. Maybe she's with Zach," I say, excited for my sister after her admission.

Damn girl, way to already put your plan in place.

Cole's lips flatten.

"I'm still not sure how I feel about a seven-year age difference."

"Stop. You act like he's not my best friend." I push at his chest, giggling at his overprotective big brother nature.

But he doesn't have anything to worry about since there's no sign of Zach even though the gym is still lit up and his office door is still open. We're almost to the office to check for Laura Leigh when my phone buzzes with a text.

> LL
>
> Sorry! I ran into Zach and he and I went to grab lunch.
>
> Wish me luck.

> Don't do anything I wouldn't do.

> LL
>
> What exactly does that entail?

> Laura Leigh!

> LL
>
> J/K. I'll have Zach drop me off at my car after lunch and meet you at your place?

K. See you later.

I show the text exchange to Cole who grunts.

"Maybe I should have a talk with Zach," he says.

"No, no, no. You don't need to have a talk with Zach. He's fine. And if he and Laura Leigh hit it off, even better."

"You're pretty cute when you play matchmaker," he says and squeezes my shoulders.

"I know."

His fingers graze my side and I squeal, the sound echoing off the empty hallways of the school.

"Jeez, that's almost louder than—"

My hands cover Cole's mouth, stopping the words, and my attention fixes on the red mark below my thumb where I had to bite my hand earlier to avoid crying out with my orgasm.

"You're terrible," I tell him and roll my eyes.

He waggles his eyebrows at me and I release his mouth.

"That's not what you said earlier," he murmurs for my ears only.

"Cole!" I stop and rather than letting my lack of movement stop him, he lifts me with one arm and carries me toward the entrance.

"I'd say I'm sorry, but I'm not," he tells me and steps through the entrance, moving to the car with me still in tow.

"I can walk."

His grip doesn't lessen.

"I know that." He's not even breathing heavily despite carrying me.

"Are you going to put me down?" I ask.

And he does, but not until we're next to the passenger door of my car.

"Here you go," he says.

"Show-off."

"You love it," he teases and smacks a kiss to my cheek.

I giggle.

"I love *you*," I correct.

"Let's go home." He closes the door softly and walks around, sliding into the driver seat.

"Hoping for a round two?" I ask, my thighs already tingling.

He groans. "Think we have time?"

"We may have to combine round two with a shower."

"You naked and wet? Say less."

My phone buzzes again when we pull into the driveway.

> LL
>
> Still hanging out with Zach. We're going to his place.

> Ok. ::smile emoji::

> LL
>
> He's super sweet, Hannah Grace. And sexy as hell.

> I'll vouch for the sweetness.

> LL
>
> You're not mad are you?

> No. Have fun!

"Looks like we have more time than I anticipated. Laura Leigh is going to go hang at Zach's place for a little while."

Cole's nostrils flare, and I'm concerned for the state of the garage door as he presses on the gas, accelerating and parking the car as fast as possible before closing the garage door. In a blur, he's at my door, lifting me out of the car and over his shoulder.

"Cole!"

His hand comes up and slaps my ass.

"Hang on tight, Honey Girl."

Since it's exactly what I want to do, I don't argue.

Not only do Cole and I have time for round two and round

three in the shower, but we also spend the afternoon watching holiday movies. Between movies, Cole catches me up on what Detective O'Connell had to say when he came to look at the car.

"Have you heard from him since?" I ask, wiggling my feet in his lap while I lean against the side of the couch.

"Nothing yet."

"I'm glad the car was gone by the time we got home," I say and fight the shiver that wants to slide down my spine.

"Me too. It looked like they even cleaned up the broken glass in the street. I had planned on doing that when we got home."

I really like how he refers to my house as "home." A smile curls my lips, and he lifts a finger to trace the line.

"You're happy."

"I am. I love that you call this home. Would you—do you think you'd ever move back to Tennessee?"

"I'm thinking that's a definite possibility. Are you saying you want to stay here?"

"My family is here. And Zach. My job."

"There are teaching jobs in California too. Sawyer's brother-in-law is a teacher in LA. If you wanted another option."

"Maybe. I've never considered living anywhere else. This has always been home."

"I understand that. And my home is wherever you are, Hannah Grace. If you want to stay here, I'll figure it out with Sawyer."

"You will?"

He nods and I lean up, throwing my arms around his neck in a tight hug.

The doorbell rings and I release him reluctantly.

"It's probably Laura Leigh. Finally."

I bounce up and open the door to find Detective O'Connell on the other side of the door.

"Evening, Ms. Whittaker. Is Cole here?"

Cole comes up behind me, his warmth a welcome sensation.

"Murphy, what's going on? I figured you'd call me when you had something."

"I figured this type of news warranted an in-person conversation."

"What news?" Cole asks and we step aside and allow Murphy inside.

"Can we sit?"

Nerves swamp my belly as I grip Cole's hand where we sit on the couch while Murphy takes the chair.

"After our last canvas of your neighbors, seems like everyone decided to turn on the recording feature at night. When officers spoke to your neighbor diagonal from you, they had also increased their distance that would turn on the camera. They found this."

Murphy presses a few things on his phone and hands Cole the camera.

"This was taken at around three this morning," Murphy explains.

There's nothing on the screen, until it flashes on, the porch illuminated brightly by the light. But on the sidewalk, just outside the light, is a shadow figure dressed in a black hoodie and black pants carrying a silver baseball bat and a dark backpack.

The figure approaches Cole's car and drops the backpack, lifting the bat overhead and bringing it down twice on the windshield before moving to the lights. They then move to each window, shattering them with sickening intensity.

"W-what's he using on the door?" I ask, watching the shadowy figure walk the length of the car, a deep gouge appearing behind him.

"Too much shadow to confirm," Detective O'Connell says.

"Screwdriver?" Cole suggests.

Murphy shrugs. "Could be. Our forensics guys were, and I quote, 'excited' to figure out what did it."

"Does he ever show his face?" Cole asks, eyes still on the video where now the shadowy figure dips back into the backpack and pulls something out to hold it in his hand.

Based on how he positions over the hood and on the side of the car, it's not hard to figure out it's the can of red spray paint. A few more minutes and he tosses the can back into the backpack and shoulders it before grabbing the bat, walking back by the camera calmly. Like he didn't just destroy a car.

"No."

"Goddammit."

"But in case you didn't realize, about halfway through the video, he makes a mistake. He touches the side of the car when he leans down to slash the tire. My guys are pulling prints now, and if they're in the system, I'll know soon."

"How soon?" Cole asks.

"Couple hours." Murphy meets Cole's eyes in some sort of nonverbal communication.

I wish I spoke whatever language they're using.

"But only if he's in the system," I add and both men look at me. "If the person has fingerprints in the system. If they don't…"

We're back to square one.

Again.

"Let's cross that bridge when we come to it. Something tells me with the violence he exhibits that he's in the system."

I shudder. Because he's right. Whoever did that to Cole's car was incredibly violent. And he's been close enough to me to be in my house.

Cole rubs his thumb over my knuckles in a soothing gesture.

"Can I get a copy of that to send to Sawyer?" Cole asks.

"Yeah, of course." With a few swipes of his phone, he looks back up at Cole. "Sent. I'm heading back to the lab to see if I can help with anything, but I'll call as soon as I learn more."

Murphy stands and heads for the door.

"Thanks, Murphy," Cole says, standing and shaking hands with the detective before he leaves.

After he leaves, Cole relocks the front door.

"I'm going to use our room to call Sawyer in case Laura Leigh gets here while I'm on the phone."

"Okay."

He squats in front of me, his hands skimming my thighs.

"Are you going to be okay?"

"I…yeah. I hope so. That video was…"

Cole nods. "It was."

"What if—"

"No 'what-ifs,' Honey Girl. The bastard screwed up. We are going to find him. And you're going to be safe. I'll just be down the hall." He stands, pressing a kiss against my forehead.

Alone with my thoughts, I turn on the TV to try to distract myself, leaving the channel on the Hallmark movie that's on while I pick up my phone and shoot a text to Laura Leigh.

> Okay, I think you've kept Zach to yourself enough.

> Do you want to bring Zach over for dinner? We can watch Christmas movies.

LL

Are you alone?

It's a strange question. Laura Leigh doesn't know about Cole. Not unless Zach told her.

> Yeah.

The next text from Laura Leigh makes bile rise to my throat. She's lying on a dirty mattress, hands and feet tied together, a gag in her mouth. Her eyes are closed, but I can see where tears have streaked silver tracks down her face. I stand, ready to run to Cole when another text comes through.

LL

Tell Cole and little sister pays the price.

Tell ANYONE and I make it hurt.

Oh my God. What do I do?
Whoever is after me somehow got my little sister.

Please don't hurt her.

LL

Good girl, Hannah Grace.

What do you want?

Tears are clouding my vision as they fall and I stand, closing myself in the bathroom and turning on the water. Cole can't find out. Laura Leigh depends on my ability to hide this.

LL

I want what I've always wanted.

You.

Grabbing the hand towel, I muffle my sob as memories of the violence on the video overwhelm me.

Please don't hurt her.

You can have me.

LL

Glad you're finally coming around.

Meet me at this address.

An address pops through next. One I'm not familiar with.

I'm not sure where that is.

LL

Google it.

Meet me there in 30 minutes.

What if it takes longer?

LL

It's only 20 minutes from your house. I'm giving you 10 minutes extra.

Don't be late. Otherwise I may decide to have some fun with your sister.

Please. Don't. I'm coming.

LL

Come alone. If anyone shows up with you, you'll be burying your baby sister.

Oh God.

Wiping my eyes with the towel, I splash water on my face before turning it off.

Cole is still in our bedroom when I open the door, and I grab my car keys, sneaking into the garage and taking a deep breath. As soon as I open the door, Cole will know I'm leaving.

Come alone.

Figure this out, Hannah Grace.

I don't have time. Laura Leigh depends on it.

I can't open the garage door, but I can make sure Cole doesn't come after me.

"I'm sorry," I murmur and tuck the keys into the glove compartment before sneaking out the door on the side of the garage.

I move fast, pulling up the Uber app while I walk several blocks in the direction of the address. I order the closest Uber, checking over my shoulder for Cole at least a dozen times. But he's not there. While I wait for the car, I keep walking and pull up Zach's contact.

"Hello?"

"Zach, i-is Laura Leigh with you?"

Please let the other texts be a hoax.

"No, I dropped her back at her car a couple of hours ago. Why? What's going on?"

Oh God.

This monster has had my baby sister for a few hours. The Uber pulls up next to me.

"I gotta go."

"Wait, HG, what's going—"

I hang up on his question, focusing instead on what I have to do next.

"Ma'am, are you sure you have the right address?" the driver asks me.

I swallow around the lump in my throat.

"I'm sure."

We're halfway through the drive when my phone rings.

Cole.

I ignore the phone call and it starts ringing again. This time when I ignore it, a text pops through.

COLE

What the fuck is going on? I got out of the bedroom and you're gone.

I got news about Peter. It's not him. There's more evidence that points to Michael.

Cole sends another text. Ironically, it's close to the address I'm currently heading to.

COLE

That's his address and his phone was pinged close to your house last night.

> Where are you?
>
> Answer your phone.

I'm sorry.

I want to tell him, but I can't risk him finding out. At least not yet. I have to show up alone. But that doesn't mean Cole can't still show up after I do.

Swiping into my text message settings, I share my location, hoping Cole gets the hint.

I don't turn off my phone completely—something tells me not to—but I set the phone on do not disturb. My phone burns between my fingers, begging me to break and to text Cole, to forward him the address, to tell him what's going on.

But Laura Leigh is counting on me.

We pull up to an old, abandoned house. Most of the windows are boarded up, the weeds tangling around the rusted chain link and growing over the pavement that leads to the front door.

"Th-thank you," I say and open the back door.

"Ma'am, are you okay?"

I nod despite being anything but.

"Thanks for the ride." I close the door, waiting for the car to drive off which it eventually does.

"Hang on, Laura Leigh, I'm coming."

My heart pounds as I push at the rusted gate, the hinges groaning as it opens under a push that has me falling to my knees on the sidewalk. I bite my lip to keep from crying out and stand, dusting off my knees while the warm trickle of blood runs down my leg. I have a rip in one of the knees of my leggings, the scrape the source of the blood, and I swipe at it before continuing to move forward. My palms are clammy, my heartbeat thundering in my ears as my steps echo off the rotted porch. I avoid a particularly bad board, and the plank I move to groans under my weight.

The last thing I need is for it to give way, so I'm more ginger stepping the remainder along the boards. When I reach the door, I knock and wait.

A dog barks somewhere close by and there's yelling from somewhere in the neighborhood, but despite how I strain, I can't hear anything on the other side of the door. I knock again.

"Try the doorknob, dummy," I tell myself.

I doubt whoever kidnapped my sister is concerned about my manners. Lifting a shaky hand to the door, I try the knob, not surprised to find it unlocked. The house is covered in dirt and dust, graffiti adorning the walls. Cobwebs hang in the corners, and the smell of mold and decay fills my lungs with each breath.

"Laura Leigh?" I whisper.

The only light comes from the back of the house, and I tiptoe in that direction. The hallway is dark, and I don't want to imagine what I would find if I could see.

Focus on Laura Leigh.

The darkness recedes to shadows as I reach the end of the hallway and turn left. The light is blinding after the darkness, and it takes my eyes a few minutes to adjust to the sudden brightness. I blink several times, and the scene in front of me is just as bad as it was in the text.

"Laura Leigh!" I rush toward her, dropping down and removing the gag before I wipe the remnants of tears from her face.

Her eyes don't open and I check for a pulse, feeling it thrum under my shaky fingers.

She's alive.

Her feet and wrists are bound with zip ties and no matter how hard I tug, they won't budge.

"Maybe there's something I can use in the kitchen," I mutter to myself.

I stand and run from the room, slamming into a hard wall of muscle and immediately starting to struggle.

"HG, it's me. It's Zach. Ouch."

My foot connects to his knee and he nearly goes down.

"Zach, what are you doing here?"

"After you hung up, I used Find My Friends."

I'm trying to think if I've ever granted him permission to see my location, but my adrenaline is pumping too hard.

"Shhh!" I whisper-yell.

"What are you doing here? And why are we whispering?" he asks.

I wrap my arms around Zach's body and squeeze, thanking God that my best friend is here too. He can help with Laura Leigh.

"Laura Leigh is in the next room. Cole figured out who it was. It's the grocery store guy. He took her once you dropped her off. I don't know where he is, but he told me to meet him here. We need to hurry. Help me get her out of here."

"I have a Swiss Army knife in my pocket; lead the way," he says.

"You're a lifesaver, Zach. Literally."

Once we're back in the light, I drop back to the mattress behind Laura Leigh and motion for him to do the same.

"We have to hurry," I tell him.

"Where's Cole?" he asks.

Dropping next to me, he tugs the knife out of his pants and flicks open the blade.

Lie. Don't tell Zach you shared your location with Cole.

Something is screaming at me to not tell Zach the truth. But can I make him believe me?

"I…ummm…I snuck out of the house. He has no idea where I am. Can we talk about this later? We need to get Laura Leigh untied and get out of here."

She moans and I wrap my arm around her in an awkward side hug.

"Hang on, Laura Leigh. I'm here. Zach's here. We're going to rescue you."

I shift my attention back to Zach who hasn't moved, and his attention shifts from me to Laura Leigh and back to me.

"You guys could be twins. I saw it earlier, but it's uncanny now that you're next to each other."

"Zach, come on, we need to hurry."

He reaches in front of me and grabs Laura Leigh's hands, but doesn't make a move to cut the zip tie holding them.

"You really are a terrible liar, Hannah Grace. Only for some reason you think I've forgotten that about you. Because you've done nothing but lie to me for weeks."

He extends his index finger, running it along the plastic binding Laura Leigh's wrists, and my attention focuses on his hands where flecks of red dot the back of his hand and travel up his wrist.

"W-why are your fingers red?" I ask.

You already know the answer.

"And now baby sister has to pay the price for your lies."

My hand freezes where I was reaching for his arm. My entire body may as well be in Antarctica for the chill that racks me.

"Zach?"

"I tried to clean it all off," he whispers.

"Z-z-zach?" I try to put myself between Zach and Laura Leigh, protecting her.

"Give me your phone, Hannah Grace."

"I—"

"Now!" he shouts, his voice ringing off the empty walls.

He doesn't wait for me to give it to him, grabbing it from my back pocket and hurling it against the wall where it shatters into a million pieces. It's the only move he makes, seemingly out of place with my best friend.

He turns back, looking at me expectantly, like he didn't just destroy my cell phone in a fit of rage.

I've been an idiot.
Zach isn't here to help me rescue my sister.
He's the one who took her.

CHAPTER 22

COLE

> What the fuck is going on? I got out of the bedroom and you're gone.

> I got news about Peter. It's not him. There's more evidence that points to Michael.

I wait for several agonizing heartbeats and still don't hear anything back. Fuck. Where is she?

> Where are you?

> Answer your phone.

I'm pacing back and forth in the living room, waiting for Hannah Grace to either call me back or text me. What the fuck? Why did she leave without telling me?

There's still no response and I call Sawyer.

"She's gone," I say as soon as he answers the phone.

"Hannah Grace?"

"I came out of the bedroom after talking to you and Sydney and she's gone. The car is in the garage but she's not answering

285

her phone and not responding to the texts I sent. I'm freaking the fuck out and have no idea what to do."

"Did you have her share her location with you when you got there?"

"Huh?

"That answers that question," he mumbles.

"Sawyer, I'm scared. Fuck, if anything happens to her…"

A lump forms in my throat, making it hard to breathe.

"We'll find her. First, check your phone. Open your text thread with her."

I put him on speaker, opening the text app and clicking on my thread with her.

Below the four text messages I sent her is a new message from the app.

Hannah Grace is now sharing her location.

"Holy shit."

"What?" Sawyer asks.

"She just shared her location with me."

"Good. Click on the info icon at the top. From there you can scroll down and check her location."

I do as instructed and see her about twenty minutes away. She's headed straight for the address I just texted her.

"What the fuck is she doing there?" I murmur, more to myself, but Sawyer answers.

"Where is she?" he asks.

"She's headed straight for Campbell's address, but she's almost there and I only texted her that a few minutes ago."

"Call O'Connell. Give him the address and meet him there. I can only think of a few reasons why she would go somewhere and not have you with her. And none of them are good."

"Fuck." I drag a hand through my hair, the same reasons pinging through my thoughts like a pinball bonus game.

"Keep me posted," Sawyer says and the phone beeps in my hand.

Pulling up Murphy's number, I press the call button and he answers on the first ring.

"That was spooky. I was just getting ready to call you," he says.

The phone is still on speaker, and I scan the hook by the garage door looking for Hannah Grace's keys and come up empty.

"Hannah Grace is gone."

"Gone? What do you mean gone?"

"After you left, I called my team in LA to discuss the video. By the time I got back to the living room, there was no sign of her. She's not answering her calls or her texts, but she shared her location with me, and she's headed for an address my team found for Michael Campbell."

I rattle off the address.

"Campbell isn't there. He's in our morgue. Someone slit his throat and dumped his body in a dumpster downtown."

Numbness overtakes my body followed by a wave of fear. If Michael Campbell is dead, where is Hannah Grace going?

"I'm leaving now." Murphy's words echo like they're being spoken through a tunnel, but it's enough to bring me back to what I need to do right now.

Hannah Grace needs me.

I eye her purse, loathe to riffle through her personal belongings. But this can't be helped. Upending the bag on the kitchen table, I scan the contents for what I'm looking for. But still no fucking keys.

"Shit. How far away are you?" I ask.

"I'm at the lab. It's about ten minutes from you guys. Actually, I'm about halfway between you and the address you just gave me."

Thank God for Google that allows me to pull up the location and tells me it's a thirty-minute walk. We'll see about that.

"I'm leaving the house now and heading your direction. Can you pick me up?"

"Yeah."

I'm already out the door and pick my pace up to a jog as soon as I confirm the door is locked.

"I can't find Hannah Grace's keys. Anything off the rental?"

"That's what I was calling you for. Right after I left your place I asked my guys at the lab to do a rush job on those prints. They were in the system."

"Tell me," I say, moving from a jog to a run.

"They're not in the criminal database. They're in the database for people who need to be fingerprinted for employment. Do you know Zach Nolan?"

The name settles in my stomach like a rock.

"Yeah. That's Hannah Grace's best friend. They work together at Meadow Ridge."

The amount of information both Hannah Grace and I have shared with Zach is staggering—he never crossed my mind as a threat. Well, maybe at first, but I knew how much he cared about her.

"The prints are registered to him," Murphy says.

Wrong. And now every interaction I had with Zach, every look I witnessed from him when Hannah Grace wasn't paying attention, takes on a different light.

"Are you picking him up?" I puff into the phone, following the turn I need to make.

"I have two officers on the way to his address to question him," he says.

Only something tells me we'll have better odds of finding him where we find Hannah Grace.

"I don't think he's there," I say.

"Where do you think he is? Wait, is this you?" A car moving in my direction flashes its headlights.

"Yeah." I slow down, crossing the street, and drop into the passenger side of the car.

We're already moving before I can buckle my seat belt.

"Damn, you move fast."

My lungs are burning, my heart pounding. But I refuse to let any of that stop me.

I grunt, too focused on trying to control my breathing.

"Where do you think he is?" Murphy asks, glancing at me as we speed in the direction of the address.

"Can you call backup for the address I gave you?" I ask.

"You think he's there?"

I nod. "I do."

He lifts his portable radio from the cup holder, calling in the request.

Belatedly I realize I don't have my gun, having locked it in the house earlier.

"You think he's dangerous?" he asks, squealing his tires as he takes a turn.

"I think any cornered animal is dangerous. Plus, you saw the video."

The car jumps forward as he presses on the gas and lifts the radio, relaying the additional information to his dispatcher.

Potential hostage situation. Dangerous.

Fuck.

It's been more than thirty minutes since Hannah Grace left the house. Twenty since I texted her. While Murphy is speeding faster through town than I could, I can't help but worry that we'll be too late.

That Zach is going to hurt Hannah Grace. Or worse.

Hold on, Honey Girl. We're coming.

CHAPTER 23

HANNAH GRACE

"Why are you looking at me like that?" Zach asks.

From the deep furrow in his brows, his confusion is genuine. But I have to be cautious with what I say. Based on how quick he was to smash my phone, it's obvious to me that the person in front of me is a stranger.

Cole, please be on your way.

"Looking at you like what?" I ask and try to slowly push Laura Leigh farther away from Zach.

"Like you don't recognize me. Like you didn't know it was me all along." He reaches out a hand and I flinch. "You don't need to be scared of me, HG."

His finger moves to Laura Leigh's hand, and he runs his thumb over the plastic zip tie.

"I didn't want to do this," he says.

"Why did you?" I ask, continuing to push myself between Zach and my sister.

"Stop! You act like I'm some fucking creep. I already told you you didn't have to be afraid of me! I'm not going to hurt you!" he screams, surging up from the bed and moving to the window.

"Of course I'm scared of you. You broke into my house. You

destroyed Cole's car. You kidnapped my sister, Zach. Or what-ever your name is."

"My name is Zach. And I've loved you since I saw you crowned Miss Tennessee. The moment I saw you, I knew you were meant for me. That's why I started writing you. So I could tell you. But when I did, you stopped responding. And I-I couldn't think straight. I couldn't imagine my life without you."

A different piece of the puzzle clicks into place.

"Eric?" I whisper.

One side of his mouth quirks up in a half smile.

"I thought you'd appreciate the name. I picked it after that book you were studying. *The Very Hungry Caterpillar.*"

Tension fills Laura Leigh's body. She's waking up. I squeeze her shoulder, hoping she can hear me and not react.

"H-how did you even find out about that? All that informa-tion was private."

"You didn't try so hard to hide who you were, Hannah Grace Whittaker. From Mistletoe Creek, Tennessee. I love that town at Christmastime by the way. I've spent a lot of time there learning who you were, where you got accepted to college. A little more effort and I figured out where you lived. Followed you to your classes. Fuck, I audited all of them, so it wasn't too hard to fake the credentials I needed for my job as a gym teacher. But it all started with that class. I sat staring at you while that boring-as-fuck professor droned on about that stupid book. I still get hard every time I think about it."

Bile churns in my stomach.

"It was so easy to predict what you were going to do. Which school you wanted a job at. Of course, I had to get rid of the previous gym teacher—"

"What?!"

"Aww, don't worry, HG. I didn't kill him. But it's hard to teach gym when your leg is broken. So I became the substitute. And made sure he didn't want to come back."

Keep him talking; buy time for Cole to get here.

"Y-you didn't have to do any of that."

"Yes, I did!" He yanks his hands through his hair as he paces from the window to the bed. "You stopped fucking responding to my letters, you fucking bitch. You acted like you were better than me, so I had no choice than to try to be your friend. To make you see that we were meant to be."

Shivers rack my body as his mood goes from explosive to calm again.

"So I became your best friend. Watching all those stupid movies, doing all the bullshit to be your best friend, scaring off anyone else who tried to befriend you, just to have you ignore me anytime I brought up anything resembling a date. Do you know how hard it was to hear all about those dates from those apps? How badly I wanted to find those guys and slit their throats? Do you know there's a weird sort of sound someone makes when you do that?"

His eyes take on an excited glow, and I don't want to ask how he knows that.

"I—"

"I figured, what better way to convince you how perfect I was than to rescue you from your boogeyman? The purse perfume was easy. I grabbed it from your bag one day at school and snuck into your house while you were still there and dropped it in your bedroom. Just something little. Something to make you run to me. Instead *he* showed up. *He* was the one who got to rescue you, not me. But he could never feel the way I felt about you. So I had to show you how incompetent he was."

"The flowers."

He nods, his eyes glowing brighter.

"Again, I thought you'd come running, but you ran in the opposite fucking direction. To him."

"You broke the cameras too," I say.

293

"I did. After watching him fuck you on his car, he's lucky I didn't break him like that."

"H-h-how…you were in Ohio."

His laugh contains no humor and sends another cold chill down my spine.

"How fucking naïve are you? I didn't go anywhere. I don't have family in Ohio, HG. I aged out of a group home when I turned eighteen. There's no 'Nolan Family Holiday.' Not unless me eating a frozen Thanksgiving dinner counts. No, instead I sat in my apartment, watching your phone as it started to move."

"I never gave you access to Find My Phone." It was strange when he had mentioned it earlier, but I hadn't caught it.

A small part of me had known though. Just not enough to keep my guard completely up. I trusted the enemy and this is what I got.

"Tsk tsk. You think that's the only way I could track it? So much for big, bad security guard."

"He's not a security guard," I argue.

"But he's not smart enough to check your phone for apps that track you? I figured out where you were going, but I couldn't figure out why. It was easy enough to drive the same direction. And what an eyeful I got when I hiked to that overlook. I didn't take you for such a slut, Hannah Grace. But there you were spread-eagled on his fucking car." His gaze drops to my breasts, his tongue slicking along his lips. When his hand drops to adjust himself in his track pants, I cringe.

"He's lucky I didn't end him right there. All I saw was red. But if I ended him, you wouldn't end up with me. You'd mourn him."

"Is that why you destroyed his car?"

"No, the car was because you guys seemed to be getting too comfortable and I knew I had to make another move. The cameras got the brunt of my rage the day I saw the two of you."

After watching the video where he destroyed the car, I can only imagine how much violence he took out on the cameras.

"But no matter what I did, you didn't choose me. You kept choosing him—a fucking murderer—over me, your best friend."

"He's not a murderer," I say.

"You still don't want to see it! He has you fucking brain-washed!" He reaches down, yanking on my wrist and pulling me upright.

I squeal, looking over my shoulder at Laura Leigh. She hasn't moved.

"What did you do to her?"

I struggle against his grip and it tightens painfully.

"Stop fighting me. I don't want to hurt you."

"What did you do to my sister?" I ask again and try to hold still.

His grip lessens but he doesn't let me go.

"She's fine."

"She's not fine." Tears stream down my cheeks, and I start to struggle against his grip again. "What did you do to her, you fucking psycho?"

If I thought his grip was painful before, it's nothing compared to what it is now as he picks me up and slams me against the wall behind me. My head cracks against the drywall, stars popping in my vision.

"Had you been more concerned about her when she got to the school today than on getting eaten out on your desk, this wouldn't have happened to her."

I gasp and his smile is downright evil.

"That's right, HG. I came down to your classroom after school to see if you'd tell me anything about the car and tried the handle. It was locked, but it wasn't too hard to look in the window in the doorway. You really seem to have a thing for sex in public places. We could have some fun with that."

The glint in his eyes has bile building in my throat.

"She could need help, Zach. I need to know what you did to

her. What if she needs to go to the hospital? You think I'd want to be with you if you killed my sister?"

"It's just a little Ambien in her wine. Just enough to knock her out to get her here. Quit being so fucking dramatic." He's so matter-of-fact about what he did. Like he doesn't believe he did anything wrong.

Does he?

"You fucking drugged her?"

"I had to get you here, didn't I? Although I considered letting things play out between us beforehand. Just enough to fuck her. It wouldn't have been hard; she was practically begging for it. But then I realized that she might look like you but she wasn't you. I didn't want a copy of the original. I was saving myself for the real thing. For you."

"I'm not going to be with you like that, Zach. I don't love you." I try to keep my voice calm, but under the exterior, I'm shaking.

What the hell did I get myself into?

"You do love me. You told me so yourself. And it wasn't a lie." His voice pitches at the end, becoming almost a screech. It's like driving a needle into my temple, and I struggle not to show how much pain his voice is creating.

"Not like that, Zach. You were my best friend. That was it. That's all that was ever going to be between us."

"No! You're going to learn to love me. If you let yourself. If you forget about him."

His ranting shows how unhinged he is.

I shake my head. "No."

His grip on my biceps is bruising where he still holds me against the wall.

"You'll either choose to be with me, HG, or I'll make it so you wished you had made a different choice." His voice is a calm kind of seriousness, more terrifying than any of his outbursts so far, and he turns his attention to my sister.

"W-w-what do you mean? Don't hurt her."

"There are worse things than me hurting her physically, HG. What about the pain she would feel when her beloved older sister disappears? How would she feel if she never saw you again?"

"You wouldn't kill me," I say with more belief than I feel.

"You're right, I wouldn't." My relief is short-lived as he keeps talking. "But I would kill for you to be mine. Indefinitely. I already have. I may not have family in Ohio, but I do have a house similar to this one there. I've been getting it ready for a while now. One just for us. It will be just you and me when I come to see you. But I'll have to split my time. I'll need to be there for Laura Leigh as she misses her sister, mourns her loss. And every time I come see you, I'll bring you every detail of how I make her fall in love with me. Every detail of what I do to her to make her call my name when I fuck her. Every way I imagine it's you as I slam inside her pussy. Every moment I count down until it's you and me in the same positions. Maybe we should start right now." He frees one of his hands and pulls more zip ties from his pocket. "I could use these on you and have you watch while I convince her that we're at my apartment. That I'm feeling everything she is."

He knocks my feet out from under me and my head hits the wall again, stunning me. The tie is around my ankles before I can fight back, my hands zip-tied in front of me.

"Don't," I whisper.

"You're giving me no choice," he says and presses a kiss to my temple, a gesture meant to comfort.

Maybe in his mind he is.

He moves away from me and toward Laura Leigh.

"Stop. Zach!" I struggle to sit up, leaning against the wall as a headache throbs in my skull.

"Shhh. Or I'll gag you too," he warns and leans down to Laura Leigh's ear, nuzzling it much the same way Cole has woken me up a time or two. "Laura Leigh, sweetheart, you fell asleep."

She murmurs and stretches against the bands, struggling

against their grip. He brushes a kiss against her cheek and continues to murmur in her ear. Words I can't hear, but I have to stop. I can't let him do this to her.

"Zach!" I hiss and he looks up. "I…um…I changed my mind. I-I'll be with you. Please. Just leave my sister alone."

The smile is so much like the ones we've shared hundreds of times before, my heart shatters, discolored by the knowledge that he's been playing me all along.

"How can I be sure you're telling the truth? Maybe you need more incentive," he says and slides his hand under the front of Laura Leigh's shirt, pulling it up and exposing her stomach and the underside of her bra.

"No! Th-there has to be something else. Please. I'll do anything else. We can leave here tonight and I'll be with you. I'll stay with you. But you have to leave my sister alone."

"You'll do anything?" He moves closer to me, and I breathe a sigh of relief even as I struggle to hold still as his hand reaches out to me.

"Yes." I keep my gaze steady on his, needing him to see the truth.

"You're not lying." It's more a statement than a question.

"No."

I am willing to do anything he says if it means Laura Leigh is safe.

"Prove it," he says.

"H-how?"

"Kiss me." He raises an eyebrow, almost like he's waiting for me to refuse.

Swallowing around the lump in my throat, I hold out my wrists.

"Cut me free, please?"

He reaches over, snagging the knife off the dirty mattress, and slices through the ties on my wrist and my feet.

"What are you waiting for?" His question is issued more like a challenge, and I realize my time is up.

Using the wall for its steadying support, I stand up and try to ignore the way the room spins around me.

You can do this. You have *to do this.*

I press my fingers into the wall behind me, pushing off and lifting them up and around his neck. He tugs me flush against him, and I resist the urge to gag at the bulge he rubs against my stomach.

"I love you, HG," he says, licking his lips.

It's my cue.

This is for Laura Leigh. This is for me.

Closing the distance, I hold my lips against his and my entire body rebels. I have to force myself to stand still. To not yank myself out of his arms. But just like I knew he would, he takes over the kiss as soon as our lips connect, stabbing his tongue down my throat. My stomach heaves and I have to fight the recoil that builds. His hands move from my hips to my ass and he squeezes roughly.

This is wrong. Everything is wrong. The urge to vomit is so strong, I swallow the bitter taste, and my stomach knots on itself, cramping with how hard I'm fighting my body's natural revulsion to Zach's kiss.

Pretend you're kissing Cole.

I try, but Zach isn't Cole. He doesn't smell right. He doesn't feel right. He isn't Cole.

I have to make this convincing though. I need him distracted.

So I scrape my nails through his hair, moaning enough that he doubles his efforts. With my free hand, I move down, dragging an index finger down his chest to the waistband of his track pants before shifting to the front pocket of my jeans, my fingers closing over the small cylinder I stashed before I left the house. A little travel-size stocking stuffer I've had for years that has stayed tucked in the glove compartment of my car. I'd almost forgotten about it, my fingers only grazing it when I tossed my keys into the compartment earlier to hide them from Cole.

I palm the canister and pull my hand free as Zach breaks the kiss.

"That was better than I imagined," he murmurs, squeezing my ass again and rubbing me on his erection.

I don't say anything, but I doubt he needs me to. What I have to say would ruin whatever fantasy he's woven in his head.

"Now for your second thing you need to do to save your sister. You're going to call him and tell him you ran away from him because you don't want to be with him."

"Him?"

Why can't Zach say Cole's name?

"Your boyfriend."

"Cole?"

I test my theory and am rewarded by a vein that pops on Zach's forehead as his entire face turns bright red.

"Are you fucking more than one man?" he asks.

I flinch. I've never heard Zach talk like this, and I'm still trying to reconcile who he is with who I knew him to be.

"No."

"Then you know who I mean."

"I don't have my phone." I point in the direction where the electronic device lies scattered on the floor.

"Use mine." He pulls his phone from his pocket. "Put it on speakerphone."

"What do I tell him?"

"Fuck, do I have to think of everything?!" he screams again and my head throbs.

"I-I don't know what to tell him that'll make him back off. He's...stubborn."

And he is. Nothing I say—even what Zach wants me to tell him—is going to make him stop.

"Tell him...tell him that you're tired of pretending with him.

That you don't see a future with him because he's not who you need him to be. He couldn't even figure out who was harassing you. And rather than be a man and find out, he came and whined to me about it. Me." Zach laughs again, the laughter verging on the maniacal. "God, that was such a fucking high. And he had no idea."

"You want me to tell him it was you?" I ask.

"Fuck, you really are a dumb bitch. No. I want you to tell him that you realized today that you love me. That you want to be with me. Calling him from my phone will clinch the deal."

I stare at the phone, using the passcode he's had me use when we've been out and I used his phone.

The irony that I know his passcode but not the real him is not lost on me.

"His number is in my contacts. Under Murderer," he says.

I suck in a breath, fighting the sob that wants to break free. I gave Zach that ammunition over Cole. It was my fault. Mine for trusting Zach when he was the bad guy all along. Pulling up the contacts, I scroll until I do find one titled *Murderer* and click on it.

"Speakerphone," Zach reminds me.

I click the icon and wait. But I don't have to wait long.

"Zach, hey, man, what's up?"

Zach nods at me.

"C-cole, it's me."

"Hannah Grace, I've been looking for you. Where are you?" His voice is calm, like he didn't frantically text me after I ran out of the house.

I glance up at Zach. He points at the phone and then at Laura Leigh. Closing my eyes, I take a deep breath, praying for strength.

"I'm with Zach. Cole, this...this isn't working for me anymore."

"This?" Cole asks.

"Us. I realized today that the two of us aren't meant to be

together. You're my past. I l-love Zach and I want to be with him. I want you to leave my house and go home. Go back to LA." Tears blur my vision as they run unchecked down my face and drop onto the carpet at my feet.

"What about whoever is after you?" he asks.

"You should have found him by now. The fact that you can't means he's not meant to be found. It's time I accepted that and moved on. Zach will keep an eye on me. He'll help me."

"Hannah Grace—"

"I'm sorry, Cole. Goodbye."

I hang up the phone, a sob breaking free as Zach snatches the phone out of my hand.

"Quit your fucking blubbering. I'm doing you a favor. You don't want to be with someone as stupid as he is." Zach closes the distance between us, grabbing my hair and yanking it back so that I look up into his eyes. "Now kiss me again."

I fight the grip on my hair, struggling with the throbbing pain in my head, as I shake it.

"No."

"No?" He tugs harder and I bite my lip as the throb intensifies.

"F-first you have to do something for me. Cut Laura Leigh free. Let her go."

"You have nothing to negotiate with, HG. Give me another kiss—a real one this time—and then maybe I'll consider cutting Laura Leigh free," he says.

I sigh, squeezing the canister still hidden in my hand.

"Fine."

But he doesn't release the grip on my hair, and I have to fight through the black that hovers at my vision as I lift to my tiptoes. He moves closer, releasing the grip on my hair, and I lift my hands like I did earlier. Only while one wraps around his neck, the other lifts in front of his face and I depress the can of pepper spray. This close, it hits his eyes, nose, and mouth and bounces back at me, stinging my eyes.

"Fuck!" he screams, pushing me away as he lifts his hands to his eyes.

I fall close to Laura Leigh, landing on my hip in a way that shoots pain through my toes as my head throbs from the jarring fall, but I fight through it, grabbing the knife he drops and ripping through the zip ties at Laura Leigh's wrists and feet.

Zach is still screaming as he staggers blindly around, and my own eyes water.

"Leigh, you have to wake up. We have to go." As I'm shaking her awake, her eyes open groggily for a moment before they widen at Zach's screams.

"What's going on?"

"We need to go. We need to run." She staggers up and we race for the front door while Zach continues to shout behind us.

The door bursts open in front of us and I tuck Laura Leigh behind me, lifting the knife still in my hand.

"Honey Girl, it's me. Murphy's with me."

"Cole." I race forward, launching myself at him.

He catches me, holding me close to him and reaching out a hand for Laura Leigh.

"Cole?" she asks.

I don't blame her for being confused. I haven't even told her about Cole yet. Before he can respond, Murphy rushes past us, gun drawn while he charges down the hall in the direction of Zach's voice.

"He's the one...it was him all along," I stutter out.

"We know. Come on. Let's get out of here and I'll tell you about it," he whispers and brushes a kiss against my temple.

"Please," I say and blink to clear the burning sensation in my eyes. "Laura Leigh?"

I lift my head from Cole's chest to find my sister looking at me, eyes wide.

"I'm here. Can we get out of here though? This place is giving me a major case of the icks."

I take a step, the throbbing in my head growing tenfold and the burning sensation of my eyes overwhelming me.

My next step makes me feel like my leg weighs two hundred pounds.

"Hannah Grace?" Laura Leigh's voice is warped, and I try to turn my head to find her.

"Honey Girl!"

That voice follows me into the darkness, but I know I'm safe. Because he's here.

CHAPTER 24

COLE

*H*annah Grace starts to crumple to the ground in front of me and I reach out, catching her before she can hit the ground.

"Hannah Grace!" Laura Leigh cries out and rushes to Hannah Grace's other side.

"Honey Girl!"

I lift her up into my arms and make my way back out to the street where Murphy parked his car and another squad car sits idling next to it.

"Sir?" One of the officers steps out of the car and questions my rushing toward them with Hannah Grace still in my arms.

I'm glad Murphy took the extra time to introduce me to the backup, otherwise I'm sure I'd be facing an entirely different situation.

"She fainted. We need at least one ambulance. Maybe two," I say, taking in the way Laura Leigh wobbles next to me.

The officer nods and drops back into the car.

"I'm okay," she says. "Help Hannah Grace."

"Do you remember what happened?" I ask her.

"No, I'm sorry. One minute I was talking to Zach at his apartment and the next Hannah Grace was waking me up here. What happened?"

I shake my head.

"Your sister's going to have to fill in a lot of the details."

A siren grows closer as Zach's screaming becomes clearer. Glancing up from Hannah Grace's face, I look up just in time to witness Murphy hauling Zach out in handcuffs. I tense and Laura Leigh shrinks closer.

The ambulance pulls up and the EMTs rush to pull the gurney out, and I lay Hannah Grace on it.

Zach's screams grow louder the closer they get, and without Hannah Grace in my arms, I want to close the distance and knock his ass out.

"That fucking bitch. I'm going to kill her. I'm fucking blind!" he screams, running his hands over his streaming eyes.

"What'd she get him with?" I yell the question to Murphy.

The corner of his lips lifting is visible in the flashing blue and red lights.

"Pepper spray."

That's my girl.

At least now I understand why Murphy cuffed him with his hands in front. A small mercy, but until he gets some water to wash the oil out of his eyes, nothing will help.

"Sir, do you know what happened?" one of the EMTs asks me as they check Hannah Grace's vitals.

"No. She was walking and talking okay and then she folded to the ground. I caught her before she could hit," I tell her.

She nods.

"And that guy got pepper sprayed?"

"Yeah."

"That could be why the skin around her eyes is red and irritated. Any idea how close they were when he got it?"

I shake my head again, feeling useless. Fuck, do I hate this sensation.

"I don't."

She gives me a sympathetic smile and turns to Laura Leigh.

"Miss, are you okay?"

I shift my attention to Laura Leigh whose whole body is shivering. The other EMT is still checking over Hannah Grace, so the one we've been talking to reaches in and pulls out a trauma blanket. I reach for it, unfolding it to wrap around Laura Leigh's shoulders.

"Thank you. What are you doing here? The last time I saw you..."

I nod.

"Yeah. You were twelve. Your sister has a lot of explaining to do. But first we need her to wake up."

Zach's screams grow quieter again as he gets put into the back of the squad car. Murphy walks over to the EMT we've been talking to.

"Do y'all have any saline solution?" he asks.

"Let him burn," I mutter.

The asshole is lucky it wasn't me who found him.

"I'd love to, but I don't want him to claim that we didn't help him and use that as a technicality. I can explain leaving him there versus having him checked out over here," Murphy says, thumbing toward the patrol car.

The EMT tosses him a bottle, and Murphy walks it over to the squad car.

The other EMT who has spent the entire time checking over Hannah Grace finishes his original exam. She still hasn't woken up.

Come on, Honey Girl, open those pretty blue eyes for me.

"Pupils are sluggish, but heart rate and oxygen are good. Ready to transport?"

Our EMT nods.

"We're going to take her to Forest View Med Center. We've got enough room for one of you."

Everything in me wants to tell them I'll ride with her. I don't want to let her out of my sight. But I know what choice Hannah Grace would make, and I have to make sure her sister is okay too.

"Take Laura Leigh so she can get checked out too. We'll follow behind."

The EMTs load Hannah Grace in first and then assist Laura Leigh into the open seat.

"You guys rolling to Forest View?" Murphy asks, walking back up as the squad car takes off.

"They are," I say.

The driver closes the doors, securing them, and Murphy lifts a hand to my shoulder.

"Let's head that direction. I'll stick around to get her statement and take Laura Leigh's official statement."

He leads me to his car.

"She doesn't remember much," I say as he starts the engine.

"Probably for the best. Hannah Grace wake up?"

"No."

We're following the ambulance, and every fiber of my being wants to be in the back with her.

"She'll be okay," he says, and we pull into the hospital parking lot as the ambulance continues to the emergency entrance.

It's a mantra I've been echoing the entire drive.

She will be okay.

I just need her to wake up.

I need you to wake up, Honey Girl. Do you hear me?

I have no idea who I'm talking to. The Universe. God. Whoever listens.

Please wake up.

CHAPTER 25

HANNAH GRACE

The first thing to penetrate the darkness is a steady beep, followed by pain that radiates from my toes to my head where it sits throbbing in time to the noise from somewhere nearby. Bright lights tease my eyelids and make it hard to stay asleep despite the siren's song it uses. A grip tightens on my arm and I groan as the sound changes, my upper arm protesting against the restricting cuff.

"Honey Girl?" Cole's hand is in mine, his lips close to my ear as he whispers my name.

My head throbs as I shift it in his direction, and I have to fight to open my eyes even a sliver. It takes a moment to adjust to the brightness, but when I do, Cole's face becomes clear—eyebrows knit in concern over brown eyes that focus on mine as he squeezes my hand.

"Cole?" I croak out.

My throat is dry, and I force a swallow before I cough in an attempt to clear the sensation. My head protests at the violent movement, and I close my eyes again as the pain takes over everything.

"Here," he whispers.

A straw brushes my lips and I part them, sucking at the cool liquid.

"Better?"

"Mmm." Maybe if I don't talk, my head won't pound so hard.

But Cole has a different idea.

"Do you remember what happened?" His question is hesitant.

Sifting through the layers of darkness, I suck in a breath as the memories rush back—a tsunami of fear and sadness mixed with relief.

It's over. All those years of not knowing who wrote me those letters, the events of the last month—it's all over. But I've also lost my best friend.

"Laura Leigh!" I sit up, fighting the pain in my head as I struggle to stand.

The staccato of the beeping machine increases, an alarm ringing as an IV pulls at my arm.

He moves fast, resting his hands against my chest.

"It's okay, she's safe. She's here. The doctors checked her out and she's talking to Murphy right now. Giving her statement."

My body relaxes as his words sink in.

She's safe. I'm safe.

"What do you remember?" he asks, his thumb skating over my fingers.

"Most of it." A shudder works its way down my spine. "But not how I got here."

"Do you know where here is?"

"I'm assuming a hospital." The glare I shoot his direction at the stupidity of his question only backfires, making my head hurt worse.

He nods.

"We were at the front door of that house when you started to faint."

"I remember a fuzzy black ring around my vision and then... nothing," I say.

"Once you fainted, we called an ambulance. They checked you out and brought you here."

"Laura Leigh?"

"Traces of Ambien in her system and a scratch on her wrists from the plastic zip tie, but otherwise she's fine. I'm more worried about you."

"W-where's Zach?" My lips want to refuse to wrap around his name, and the pang in my chest is almost instantaneous.

Will it always be like this from now on?

Cole's mouth flattens, a muscle ticking in his jaw.

"The last time I saw that fucker he was screaming about being blind in the back of a squad car," he grits out.

"Blind? Ohhh…the pepper spray."

"You must have been too close." He lifts a finger and runs it along the side of my eye, the sensation the same as a light breeze, but I still wince.

"Yeah." My teeth capture my lip.

"What is it?"

I keep my gaze focused on my hands that twist in the light blanket that covers my stomach.

"I kissed him. I didn't want to, but—"

"Honey Girl." He uses a thumb and index finger to lift my chin until he can look me in the eye. "Nothing you did was done willingly. You were doing whatever you could to survive. I wish you hadn't put yourself in that position—"

"I sent you my location."

"I know you did, but you put yourself in danger. And while I'd love to lecture you right now, you being in a hospital bed is keeping me quiet on the subject. For now. But don't let my silence fool you. As soon as we're home and you're feeling better, we're going to talk about your decision-making skills."

"Laura Leigh was in danger." The panic is still very real in the pounding of my heart, and my hands grow clammy.

"I'm aware. And I know you think you were doing the right

thing, but putting yourself in danger is never the right decision. You should have told me."

"I—"

"I don't want to argue with you right now," he says.

If he thinks I'm going to just sit back and be lectured, he doesn't know me that well. But I don't want to argue with my head still pulsing. Once that disappears, different story.

"Headache?" he asks and reaches out a hand to graze my temple.

"Mmm." I close my eyes again and try to get comfortable against the hard mattress.

"Hopefully the doctor will be in soon and they can give you something for it."

"How long have we been here?" I ask and peek my eyes open.

He glances at a clock hanging on a wall.

"Little over an hour."

The door opens and I tense, unable to stop myself.

"Hannah Grace!" Laura Leigh rushes forward, folding herself on top of me with her hug.

I wince, trying to push away the pain, and concentrate on my sister.

"It's okay, Laura Leigh. I'm okay," I murmur.

Murphy steps in behind Laura Leigh, and he and Cole have a private conversation that based on Cole's body language isn't going his way. Finally he nods and they both turn in my direction.

"Hannah Grace, do you think you're up for providing a statement? Otherwise, we'll need you to come down to the station when you're released," Murphy explains.

Oh. Now I understand Cole's grizzly bear impression.

I shift my attention from Murphy to Laura Leigh. I don't want her to have to listen to what Zach told me when she was asleep. But she beats me to the punch.

"No. I'm not a kid anymore. I was there and I don't remember anything. I want to know what that psycho did," she says, crossing her arms and staring at me.

Cole is no help when I look at him.

He shrugs.

"She has a point, Honey Girl," he says.

Taking a deep breath, I blow it out, the heart rate monitor betraying my appearance of calm.

"Okay."

Murphy moves across the room, dropping his notebook to the counter by the sink.

"Let's start at the beginning. Tell me what happened tonight," he says.

I start with the texts I got from Laura Leigh's phone. The pictures, the demands, my running from the house, and sharing my location with Cole. It's harder once I reach the point of everything Zach said, and when I get to what he said about killing for me already—something that doesn't seem to surprise either Murphy or Cole—and his threat about me being gone permanently and what he was going to do with Laura Leigh, she starts to cry. The tears are silent, but each one is a powerful punch. She drops to the chair in the room, and I stumble to a halt.

"That's enough," Cole says, closing the distance between us and squeezing my hand.

I shake my head.

"Let me get the rest of this out," I tell him.

"Honey Girl." The name is a whisper meant only for my ears.

"I don't want to have to keep living this over and over again."

There's so much in the look we share, and I pull from the strength of Cole's grip and clear my throat, continuing the story. The kiss, the phone call to Cole that happened just before he and Murphy rushed to the door of the house, the pocket-sized pepper spray that helped tonight turn out the way it did.

Murphy's lips twitch when I describe the small canister and the knowledge that I would only have one chance.

"I'm going to have to remember that for my sisters at Christmas," he says.

"You know what happened next," Cole tells Murphy.

Tension radiates through his body, but his grip on my hand remains soft.

Murphy nods, closing his notebook.

"I do. I may have more questions about your relationship with Zach and those letters."

"I figured as much," I sigh.

"But not tonight," Cole says.

"No, not tonight," Murphy agrees.

There's a knock on the door and the doctor enters the room, eyes widening in surprise at Murphy's presence. Granted, how often is a detective in the room with a patient, gun in plain sight?

"Murphy?" The familiarity as she says his name is clear.

So maybe it had nothing to do with *a* detective and everything to do with it being Murphy.

"Kristy." He nods at her before looking at Cole. "I'll be in touch."

He leaves and the doctor blinks, turning her attention to me and clearing her throat.

"Sorry about that. I'm Dr. Roberts. Let's see what's going on, shall we?"

Three hours and a concussion diagnosis later, Murphy is dropping Cole, Laura Leigh, and me off at my house. The porch light casts a welcoming glow, and between my sister and Cole, I'm not sure which of their hovering is going to get on my nerves first.

"I'm fine," I tell them both as they crowd either side of me on the walk to the front door.

"The doctor told you to take it easy," Laura Leigh says.

"I can walk," I grumble.

Although even this short walk has my head pounding again. According to the doctor, that will fade with time. It's mostly a dull, peripheral sensation, but has moments of migraine-like intensity where I just want to hide in a dark room.

All the lights are on in the house, the same way we left them earlier.

"I'm going to get Laura Leigh pajamas so we can all go to bed," I say.

Laura Leigh yawns before she smiles sheepishly.

"Sorry."

"No need to apologize. It's late," I tell her.

"I think you mean early," Cole corrects.

"What time is it?" I ask, not used to being without my phone.

"About one thirty. I'll let you do that, but before you do, where are your keys? I don't want them out in the open, and I couldn't find them earlier."

Heat travels up my neck and settles in my cheeks.

"I hid them in the glove compartment of the car," I admit.

His expression is a combination of exasperation and awe.

"I'll be right back," he says and presses a kiss to my temple.

"We definitely need to talk about that. When did all this happen?" Laura Leigh asks, following me to my room.

"Tomorrow. I'll tell you almost anything you want tomorrow," I tell her and pull out a pair of pajama pants and T-shirt for her.

"Almost anything?"

"There are some things that even a sister doesn't need to know."

She smiles, reaching out and wrapping me into a hug.

"You're more than my sister. You're my hero. Thank you for... tonight." Her voice grows tight and when she pulls away, tears line her lashes.

Not like mine are dry either.

"Of course. You're sure you're going to be okay by yourself in the guest room? We can kick Cole over to that room and you can sleep here with me." I'm not sure how Cole will feel about that, but I doubt he would protest too loudly.

"Honestly, I slept through most of it. I think I'll be okay. But I'll let you know."

"You better," I tell her.

"Promise."

Another hug and she leaves, hugging Cole on her way to the guest room. He's smiling as he walks in the room and closes the door.

"That's the first time I've seen you smile all night," I say.

He grunts. "You were in the hospital, Honey Girl. Not much to smile about."

"What has you smiling now?"

"Your sister demanded I keep an eye on you," he says and shrugs out of his T-shirt.

My lips curve.

"Does she know who she's talking to?" I ask.

I grab a second pair of pajamas and start to change, struggling with stiff muscles. I drop my pants and his breath hisses.

"Fuck," he says, reaching out a hand and pausing before his fingers brush my hip.

"What?"

I glance down, the dark blue bruise taking up most of my hip.

"It looks worse than it feels," I say, reminding him of what I told the doctor when we first noticed it.

"I fucking hate that you got hurt tonight," he whispers, closing the distance between us until he can wrap his arms around me.

I wrap mine around his waist, finding his heartbeat with my cheek.

"If it were up to you, you would wrap me in Bubble Wrap."

He huffs a laugh.

"You think you're joking," he says, and his arms tighten slightly before he releases me.

I groan as I slide under the covers, my body relaxing into the soft mattress.

"This feels amazing." I run my cheek along my pillow.

He finishes changing into pajama bottoms and slides into bed as well, pulling me into his arms.

"This is better," he says.

"Mm-hmm." Puckering my lips, I press a kiss against the spot where his heart beats steadily.

"Good night, Honey Girl," he whispers, his fingers drawing nonsensical patterns against my back and shoulder.

"'Night."

"I love you," he says.

"I love you too," I tell him, snuggling against his chest.

Matching his breathing, I'm having a hard time staying awake, but I don't have to.

"Sleep, Honey Girl." His voice is a whisper.

I want to reply, but instead I drift off with Cole's heartbeat in my ear.

CHAPTER 26

HANNAH GRACE

*T*he light tapping on my door is so quiet I could have imagined it, if I hadn't been staring at the door waiting for it.

I don't have to say anything, the door opening as small as it can to fit Cole through the crack.

"It took you long enough," I tease him, lying back against the pillows.

"Shhh. I'd rather not have your dad finding out I'm sneaking into your room after I was specifically told to stay on the couch," he says and makes his way through the darkness to the bed.

The day after I came home from the hospital, Mom and Dad had driven up, staying for several days to make sure that Laura Leigh and I were both okay before heading home with Laura Leigh for Christmas break. The only reason they didn't take me was my promise to spend Christmas Eve and Christmas Day at home.

I giggle remembering the stern look Dad had leveled at me and then at Cole with the explicit instruction that Cole was to stay on the couch regardless of what we did in my house.

"I didn't think your dad was ever going to go to bed," he grumbles, sliding under the covers.

"You're here now," I say and lean against him.

His hands glide along the bare skin of my stomach while his lips find my shoulder.

"I see someone already unwrapped my Christmas present," he murmurs.

"I didn't think you would mind." Reaching behind me, my fingers brush his already hard cock. "Now who's unwrapping whose present? I doubt you walked from the living room to my bedroom naked."

He palms my breasts, his mouth moving to my neck.

"You're right, I didn't. And I'll be dressed and on the couch when your dad wakes up tomorrow. But for now, I want to enjoy my present."

He wedges one thigh between mine, his fingers plucking at the tips of my breasts. I mewl, rubbing my hips against him as a throb begins to build in my core.

"We're going to have to be quiet, Honey Girl. Very, very quiet." The words are growled against my skin, and one of his hands slides down from my breasts to between my thighs. His finger moves easily through my folds, finding the spot where I ache the most and circling the hard bundle of nerves.

I press my mouth against my pillow, letting it absorb my moan as I grind against his finger. He slides another finger inside, and the pleasure intensifies.

"That's it, Honey Girl. Ride my finger."

He runs the digit along a spot that has me seeing stars, and my hips buck, the orgasm lapping at my toes as it builds. The other hand shifts to my hip, and he rolls us until his lips can wrap around my nipple. I whimper but there's nothing to muffle the sound and he stops.

"Shhh," he whispers and drags his tongue over the hard peak.

"It's hard."

"That's what she said."

I giggle and the sound bounces through the room.

"Honey Girl, you have to be quiet." He withdraws his hand and lines his dick up at my entrance and pushes in inch by inch until his pelvis bumps mine.

"Please. Move." I cup my hands against his ass to pull him closer.

He thrusts against me, his lips claiming mine at the last minute to swallow the mewl.

"Quiet," he reminds me before sealing his mouth to mine again.

Only then does he do what I asked, pistoning his hips against mine, his pelvis rubbing along my clit. The orgasm fizzes through my blood, speeding through as pleasure continues to center in my core. I can't make a sound that Cole doesn't take, the limitation somehow making this experience hotter.

No wonder Cole was never allowed to be in my room in high school.

He speeds up, and the lights behind my eyelids burn brighter. My fingers flex into his ass and he grunts, losing his rhythm for a heartbeat before finding it again. His hands tunnel under my ass, holding me in place as he pistons against me, my own hips lifting to meet each one of his thrusts.

Our tongues tangle together and my hands slip. I wrap my legs around his waist and lift my hands to his biceps. The pleasure is almost overwhelming, building higher and higher, and I focus on the sensation, giving in to it as it takes over, the orgasm working through me, driving me into the heavens, my only tether the man who freezes as his own release takes over. I roam my hands along his back as we both drift down, our breaths sawing in and out as our chests move in unison.

"Your dad is going to kill me," he whispers, his breath tickling my breast.

"My dad isn't going to find out."

He lifts his head, his eyebrows raised as he studies me.

"How do you figure when you can't be quiet?" he hisses the words.

I can't fight the smile that stretches my cheeks.

"It's not my fault. Maybe you're too good at what you do so I can't be quiet," I tell him.

"You can use that on my tombstone, Honey Girl. Too good at sex and it killed him." His fingers tickle as they skate along my side.

"Stop." I giggle, squirming away. "I thought you said you didn't want to wake up my dad."

He stops, his face growing serious as he looks back at the door.

"I should probably head back to the couch. What if he decides to come check on me?" He tries to lift himself off, and I lock my legs around his waist again.

"Not yet," I tell him.

"I don't want to go either," he says and drops his lips to mine again before rolling to the side and tucking me against him.

I sigh and my body relaxes.

"Merry Christmas, Honey Girl," he whispers against my hair.

"Merry Christmas, Cole. I love you."

"Love you."

His arm tightens around me.

Best Christmas ever.

It's my last thought before I drift.

⁂

"Hannah Grace, wake up, it's Christmas!"

I jolt awake to Laura Leigh's announcement as she bursts into my room. I yank the covers over me just in time, my arm reaching out and looking for Cole.

I breathe a sigh of relief when he's not there.

Laura Leigh bounces onto the bed with her knees, shaking me under the blankets.

"Laura Leigh!" I groan, trying to hold the blankets in place before I give her an eyeful.

"Oh my God, are you...naked?" Her voice drops to a shocked whisper and she stops bouncing.

"Shhh," I hiss.

I have no idea what time Cole left last night. I just know that I stayed asleep and didn't wake up and put on my pajamas like I planned.

We both glance at the open door.

"Girls." Mom's voice echoes up the stairs, the first tread creaking under her weight.

"Crap," I say and reach for my pajamas that are still on the nightstand next to my bed.

"I'll go distract her." Laura Leigh scrambles from the bed.

"Thank you."

The door closes behind her.

"Merry Christmas, Mama." Her voice is muffled, but the creaking of the stair treads stops.

I release the breath I'm holding and rush to throw on my pajamas and finger comb my hair. When I make my way downstairs, everyone is sitting in the living room, a second cup of coffee in front of Cole. The pale color of the liquid is exactly how I like it. Grabbing the cup, I take the seat next to him.

"Okay, Daddy, we're all here. Let's get started," Laura Leigh directs from her regular spot on the floor.

I snuggle into Cole, his arm wrapping around me.

Dad studies Cole and me for several moments, his attention shifting to where Cole's hand rests against my hip and mine rests on his knee.

"Either of you have anything you want to confess?" he asks.

Cole tenses.

I shake my head. "No."

"Jake."

Mom takes a sip of her coffee and my parents have a nonverbal conversation before Dad sighs. He stands, grabbing the stockings from the mantel before passing out the presents. The tradition is stockings first, followed by presents but only after Santa's helper (a.k.a. Dad) has divvied the stack from under the tree to the various recipients.

"Did you make it in time?" I murmur to Cole while we wait for Dad to finish.

He snorts. "Barely. I ended up falling asleep too."

"Sorry." I squeeze his thigh and his hand flexes against my hip.

"Don't be. I'm not. I got to cross something off my teenage bucket list last night."

We share a smile and he waggles his eyebrows.

Dad clears his throat and puts the last present in front of me.

"Stockings," he says and takes his seat.

Everyone has one, including Mom and Dad, and Laura Leigh has already started pulling items from hers. Cole and I reach into ours and each pull out a lump of coal.

"Daddy!" I fight the heat that fills my cheeks.

He shrugs.

"Santa knows, Hannah Grace."

He plays Santa every year during the Christmas Eve breakfast, so I'm not sure if he's talking about himself or the general warning every kid gets when they still believe in Santa.

"It's okay, Honey Girl, we have more fun on the naughty list," Cole murmurs in my ear, and the heat flares hotter.

I dip my hand back into the stocking, the coal not the only thing. I find my favorite candies and other stocking stuffers, then my fingers brush a small canister at the bottom. I pull it out, the small can familiar and needed since I just used my other one.

"Pepper spray," I say and glance up to witness Dad and Cole share a nod.

A lump forms in my throat, grief over the loss of my best friend taking a little bit of joy from the day.

"I didn't mean to make you cry," Cole whispers in my ear.

I wipe at the moisture on my cheek.

"I know." I turn my head, pressing a kiss against his jawline. "Thank you for the pepper spray."

"Honey Girl," he murmurs and uses his thumb to wipe away more tears.

"It's okay. I just…I miss my best friend. Does that make me crazy?"

"No, it doesn't."

"It would probably be better if he had actually died," I say.

Cole shakes his head.

"It wouldn't change your grief, Hannah Grace. But don't let him ruin today."

I turn my attention back to my family who have tried to give Cole and me some privacy. Laura Leigh is already partway through her stack of presents.

"What time are we expected at Cole's parents' house for dinner?" Mom asks.

We may be staying with Mom and Dad, but Cole's parents have offered to host Christmas dinner.

"Mama said three o'clock," Cole replies.

"Plenty of time for cinnamon rolls then. But first the two of you better open your presents so I can get them started," she says.

Cole hands me a present.

"Is this from you?" I ask.

He shakes his head and picks up a present for himself, and we both unwrap the stacks in front of us until everything is unwrapped. Mom and Dad head into the kitchen to start breakfast, and Laura Leigh starts taking her presents to her room, leaving Cole and me by ourselves.

"I feel like this was a setup," I say and eye Cole warily.

"Maybe," he replies and stands, going to the tree and pulling out a rectangular present left under the branches.

He holds it out to me.

"Wait," I tell him, standing and reaching for the present I tucked into the branches yesterday.

We exchange presents and I motion for him to go first.

He unwraps the box and pulls out the watch I found for him last week when he was complaining his watch face was scratched.

"It's engraved," I say and help him flip it over.

"'Love is the truest destiny,'" he reads.

"It brought you back," I say, and he presses a chaste kiss to my lips.

"You brought me back, Honey Girl." His lips brush mine with his words.

He pulls back, gesturing to the present in my lap, and I open it to find a scrapbook nestled in paper.

"What's this?"

"Open it."

The first page is different pictures of us growing up—two friends enjoying ice cream, playing in a sprinkler, present at different town events. The next two pages are us as a couple, one so worn that the edges of the picture are frayed. It's me and Cole on the back of his truck after a harvest parade.

"Where'd you get this one?" I ask, fingering one of the edges.

"Mama. I asked her to send it to me the first time I was deployed."

"Cole." I lean my head against him and sift through other pictures, other memories he's included. Homecoming, prom, even the picture we took the day before he left for basic training.

Heat suffuses my body at the memory of what came next.

"Keep going," Cole murmurs.

Another page turn and it's the first letter he sent me from basic training, followed by my letter back to him. Page after page of our letters and my body tenses as I near the one that broke my heart.

"I-I didn't include that one, Honey Girl. It may be part of our past, but it's not one I think either of us wants to remember."

So the last letter in the book isn't the one that broke my heart, but is one dated the day after I got out of the hospital.

"When?" I lift my gaze to his.

"I woke up early that morning. Read it."

> Hannah Grace,
>
> After last night, I don't know if my heart will ever be the same. I've lain awake for over an hour holding you, watching you sleep, and thanking God and every other universal power for bringing you back to me. For keeping you safe.
>
> I have loved you most of my life. But I gave you my heart when we were fourteen and I was never the same. Even when I thought you would be better off without me, my heart remained yours. I just needed a reminder that you were strong enough to make decisions about your own life. And that what I knew wasn't always best.

A giggle escapes me and he smiles.

> If it takes a lifetime to make up for my stupidity, I'll spend my life reminding you how much I love you. How I cannot imagine my life without you in it. Seven years ago, I made you a promise. One I broke, but never forgot. One I want

to renew. Honey Girl, I promise to love you with all that I am for as long as I draw breath and beyond. Forever is a start for us, not an end. And I will spend every hour of every day proving that to you for as long as you'll let me.

This letter is my promise to you. To love you. To protect you—with your knowledge and consent. To never stop.

All my love,
Cole

I glance up, leaning over to claim his lips with mine in a kiss that is less chaste than the one he gave me.

"It's not a proposal, Honey Girl. Not yet," he says against my lips.

"No and that's okay," I tell him.

And as much as I love him, I'm okay with that.

"I want time to prove to you that I mean every word in that letter."

"Time to be us without the adrenaline. Maybe we'll get bored," I tease.

He laughs and threads his fingers through my hair.

"Honey Girl, one thing I can promise with one hundred percent accuracy. We'll never be bored."

His lips claim mine, his tongue finding mine as every ounce of love pours between us.

Forever is a start for us, not an end.

And it looks like we're only beginning.

EPILOGUE

COLE

6 MONTHS LATER

"*J*thought we were going to Justin's house for a barbecue?" Hannah Grace asks as we pass the outer limits of town and head up into the mountains.

"Nope." I drop one hand from the steering wheel of my truck and wrap it around her where she's curled against my side.

"So what are we doing?" she asks, resting her head on my shoulder as the country station picks up the remnants of George Birge's "Cowboy Songs."

"Spending some time just the two of us," I tell her.

"You say that like we're not staying at The Glass Slipper all week." She smiles and shakes her head.

I opted for the bed-and-breakfast route when we planned to spend the week of my parents' fortieth wedding anniversary and Fourth of July in our hometown.

"I have no interest in being caught by your dad again. Once was enough." I shudder at the memory of the look I received when he walked into the living room Christmas morning.

He knew. And I knew he knew. And *he* knew that I knew he knew.

"He didn't catch us doing anything," she argues much the same way she has for the last almost seven months.

"He still knows I snuck into your room that night. Now we don't have to worry about it for the week that we're here." I take the turnoff and we bump along the trail until it flattens out into the clearing that overlooks the town. Maneuvering the truck, I back it up so that we can enjoy our picnic looking out over the view.

"Are you sure you have to leave again next week?"

I've been splitting my time since last December commuting between LA and Nashville. I hated when I was away from Hannah Grace, but my job was in LA. But missing her just made coming home all the sweeter.

"Just for a few days. Then I'm coming back to help you finish getting the house packed for our move to LA."

"Do you think they're going to like me?" she asks.

"The teachers at your new school?"

"Yeah." Her fingers twist in the cotton of my T-shirt.

Thumb and forefinger beneath her chin, I lift her gaze to mine.

"They're going to love you."

"At least there, none of them know about…"

Zach. She trails off before she can say his name out loud, but his presence is still in the cab with us.

It was the biggest reason she had decided to move to LA rather than me moving back to Tennessee. Everything at her old school as she finished the school year reminded her of the man that had kidnapped her sister and attempted to kidnap her. And the teachers had been so conditioned by him to avoid Hannah Grace, that even without his physical presence in the school, no one approached her.

I'd hated to witness her light dim these last few months.

When Sawyer's brother-in-law West had offered to put in a good word with the school system he worked for, Hannah Grace had jumped at the chance.

"You met a few of them at your interview, right?"

She had flown out for an interview just after school ended here for the summer.

She nods.

"Yeah. Catherine is another kindergarten teacher and Daisy teaches third grade."

"And?"

"And they seemed really nice."

"But?" I prompt.

"How did you know there's a but coming?"

"Because I know you almost as well as I know myself."

She pushes against my chest, but the small smile on her lips is what I was aiming for.

It fades as her gaze focuses on mine again.

"Look what happened the last time I thought someone was nice. He ended up being a psychopath."

A psychopath who was spending at least the next fifty years in a Tennessee state correctional institution after he was sentenced a few weeks ago.

"Honey Girl, I promise I won't let that happen to you again," I say and wrap my arms around her now that we're parked.

"I know. And I trust you. I'm just feeling anxious."

"You still want to move to California, right? If not—"

Her lips cut me off before I can explain that she can tell me.

Her tongue slides along the seam of my lips and I open, tangling mine with hers as I lift my hands to slide through her hair, cupping her face to hold her to me.

My dick punches at the zipper on my shorts.

"Does that answer your question?" Her words are all but a purr, her nipples poking through her thin tank top, and I struggle to remember what we were talking about.

"Yes?"

She giggles and more blood moves back into my brain.

"Let's just relax and enjoy the sunset," I tell her.

Her teeth capture her swollen lower lip and I want to kiss her again. But I hold back.

"What?" I ask.

"Well, I thought we were going to a barbecue and I'm hungry." As if on cue, her stomach growls loudly.

"Good thing I came prepared then. Wait there. And no peeking."

I get out of the driver's door and move to the back only to find her watching me with a grin that's impossible not to return.

"Hannah Grace." My smile softens my warning tone, and it takes a moment for her to realize I'm not moving to do anything else until she turns back around and faces front.

Only when I'm one hundred percent sure that she's not going to cheat do I pull the tarp off the blankets, arranging them and the pillows I brought and putting the picnic basket within reach. Thank God for Elle at The Glass Slipper who was able to pull it together while I kept Hannah Grace distracted.

Satisfied with how everything is in place, I walk around the back to the passenger door, opening it and holding out my hand.

"Ms. Whittaker?" I ask.

She giggles and shakes her head.

"You're such a goofball," she tells me and hops down, allowing me to lead her to the back of the truck bed. "What's all this?"

"I thought we could enjoy a sunset picnic," I say and boost her into the truck, letting my hands linger on her hips before sliding down the curve of her ass.

Her breath hisses out and she sits suddenly, almost falling against the pillows.

We've been here as kids, with nothing more than bikes and sneakers. We've been here as teenagers with nothing more than my truck and hormones. But tonight? This is special. Tonight, I have everything I ever wanted, right here next to me as I climb in and settle next to her.

She already has the picnic basket open, pulling out two sandwiches, a bottle of wine, and two plastic cups.

I use the included corkscrew—thank you, Elle—and open the bottle, pouring us each a cup, and she hands me a ham-and-swiss sandwich and takes a bite of her own.

"Do you hear that?" I ask her and take a drink of my wine.

"What?" she asks.

"Nothing. It's quiet." LA is never quiet, and even in Nashville, there's always some small sound near our house.

But right now it's just her and me and a few sounds of nature surrounding us.

She leans against me and sighs.

"It's perfect," she says.

"Perfect," I agree and brush my lips against her hair.

We sit in the silence, the sun providing a technicolor glow to the world as it sinks down behind the horizon, the shadows of dusk sprinkling the periwinkle-blue sky with flecks of silver.

"Sunset to stargazing and everything in between," I murmur.

"Hmm?" She lifts her head from where it leans against my shoulder.

"Every moment," I tell her and press a kiss against her lips. "You know, this spot has been ours for as long as I can remember. Even as kids, it always felt like we were the only two in the world up here alone. But to be honest, whenever we were together, you were the only person in the world for me, Hannah Grace. Even when I didn't think you were in the picture again, even when I was thousands of miles away, it was only ever you."

"Almost eight years ago now, I brought you up here and made you a promise. I promised I would love you forever. And together or apart, I held on to that promise like a talisman. My mantra. But I lied." She sucks in a breath and I have to fight the twitch of my lips. "Forever isn't long enough, Honey Girl. Forget about me trying to find the words that tell you how I feel. They haven't been invented yet. Enchanted. Adore. Cherish. All of these and so many more. Every day that feeling grows stronger until I can't hold it back. I don't want to. I love you. So fucking much. And those words seem inadequate when I'm asking you to marry me, but—"

"What?"

"What?" I stop, studying her.

"You're asking me to marry you?" Her blue eyes—those big, beautiful windows to her soul—are wide as they search mine.

Fuck. I hadn't meant for that to slip out that way.

"I–yeah." Reaching into my pillowcase, I pull out the small bag I stashed when I packed the truck and turn it over into my palm.

The sparkle of the diamond catches the last of the light around us, glinting like another star in the twilight.

"Hannah Grace, I promise to love you until the day after forever. And maybe then even after that. Would you do me the honor of marrying me? I want a forever with you claiming my last name. Of babies and watching you walk down that aisle to me in a white wedding dress. Marry me."

I've now asked the question three times, but if it bothers her, she doesn't show it. Tears line her lashes, turning them to an oceanic blue.

"Yes. Yes, I'll marry you."

She lifts her hands to my head, pulling me down in a tangle of lips and tongues. To whispered words of love and forever as our breaths mingle under a star-filled sky.

Breaking the kiss, I slide the ring onto her finger, squeezing her hand when it slides on in the perfect fit.

"I think you had another idea for these pillows and blankets," she tells me with a sly smile.

"What's that?"

She shifts, sliding into a straddle position against my hips.

"This." She yanks off her tank top and her breasts bounce free.

"I like the way you think," I tell her, skimming the tight tips with my knuckles.

My lips capture her laughter, and I spend the night worshipping her body with the stars as witnesses.

‽‽‽

The bell on the Mistletoe Creek Cafe jangles the next morning as we step inside.

"It hasn't changed at all," she whispers to me.

She's right. The place looks the same, but the people have changed.

I gesture toward the *"Seat Yourself"* sign and lead her to a clean booth on one side.

"Maybe we should have stopped for a shower before getting breakfast," she says, sliding into the booth and lifting her hands to finger comb her hair.

I reach across the booth, tugging her hands free of her hair and interlacing our fingers.

My finger grazes her new ring, and I lift one set of our joined hands, pressing my lips to where the ring rests around her finger.

"You look beautiful," I tell her.

"You have to say that. You're my fiancé. Fiancé. We're engaged."

The smile that lights her face takes my breath away.

"We are." I run my thumb over her knuckles.

"How do you want to tell everyone?" she asks me.

"What can I get you?" A server stops by our table before I can answer.

"Oh. Sorry, we didn't even look at the menu yet. Coffee?" I ask.

"Two, please," Cole adds.

"Cream and sugar?" The server scribbles on her pad without glancing up.

"Please."

"Be right back." She's gone as suddenly as she appeared.

"We should probably look at the menu." She hands me one from behind the napkin holder and takes one for herself.

"Hannah Grace? Cole?" An elderly woman with light-pink hair stops as she passes our table, reversing direction until she's directly in front of us. "Goodness gracious, I didn't expect to see the two of you here this morning. Especially together. What are y'all doing here?"

Flora is one of three women who runs everything in this town. I consider it lucky that she's by herself. They'd never leave if the three of them were together.

"Miss Flora, it's—" Hannah Grace is interrupted by Flora's gasp as she reaches for Hannah Grace's hand—her left hand.

"Oh my, is that what I think it is?"

"Yes, we're—"

"I'm so happy for the two of you! I always knew you two were going to find each other again. And now that you're engaged we'll be seeing you a lot more. And Cole, I bet your parents loved having you back here for their anniversary party over the weekend. And they must be over the moon for both of you."

I had forgotten that speaking to one of these three women meant not getting a word in edgewise.

"Yes, ma'am."

"Just wait until I tell Fawn and Merry I saw the two of you this morning."

An alarm sounds out of Flora's purse and she pouts.

"Drat. That's my alarm for my karate class."

I choke on the breath I take.

"Karate?" I manage to choke out.

"Mmm. I'm a green belt now."

I share a smile with Hannah Grace as Flora tucks her phone back in her purse.

"It was so wonderful to see the two of you. And Hannah

Grace, I can't wait to see you next summer in your wedding dress."

"Miss Flora, we haven't set a date yet," Hannah Grace says.

"Didn't you?" She winks at the two of us and leaves just as the server comes back with coffee.

"Did Miss Flora just set a wedding date for us?" Hannah Grace asks, reaching for one of the two cups placed in front of us.

"Did you expect anything else?" I ask and grab my own.

Dorothy was right.

There's no place like home.

THE END

Thank you so much for reading!

CURIOUS ABOUT SAWYER AND EVIE? You can binge their happily ever after in book 1 of the SAFE Haven series, SOLDIER FOR THE STARLING, available in KU or keep reading for a sneak peek of their story!

ARE WEDDING BELLS RINGING FOR COLE AND HANNAH GRACE? Was Flora right about the wedding date? Turn the page to find out!

BONUS EPILOGUE

HANNAH GRACE

1 YEAR LATER (BECAUSE FLORA IS ALWAYS RIGHT)

"*A*nd, here we go," Mom says as she slides the comb from my veil into my updo. "Oh, Hannah Grace."

I glance up from where I'm fingering the lace at my waist. Her eyes, similar to mine in color, are lined with tears, and my nose burns as moisture builds in my own.

"No crying," I say and blink rapidly.

She lifts a tissue to each, drying the moisture before it can ruin her makeup.

"You look beautiful, baby. Both of you." She steps to the side, and Laura Leigh moves closer in her dusty-rose satin bridesmaid's dress.

The full-length mirror in the bridal suite of the civic building in Mistletoe Creek reflects the three of us—blonde hair and blue-eyed. Our only difference is our dress styles. Laura Leigh is in her bridesmaid's dress, Mom is in her mother-of-the-bride dress, and I'm in my wedding dress.

In some ways it feels that this day has been a long time coming, and in others it feels like no time has passed since Cole and I got engaged regardless of everything that's happened.

The joy of telling our families.

The exhaustion of moving to California.

The anxiety of starting a new job.

Finding a routine as we settled into our life together. Working with Mom and Laura Leigh to plan the wedding remotely since it made more sense to get married in Mistletoe Creek than trying to fly everyone to LA. The only thing not planned in Tennessee was the dress I just finished getting zipped into. They'd flown out for a weekend after Christmas, and we'd found my dress in a small boutique halfway through the day.

The A-line dress is a soft white and covered with lace appliqués along the bodice and down the front of the skirt. The cut of the liner is sexy, made more demure as the appliqués cover my collarbone and shoulders before the lace creates three-quarter length sleeves. I've worn more evening gowns than I can count. Fancier than this one. Beaded and shiny, a rainbow of colors. But this dress tops them all. Or maybe it's the reason for the dress.

Because today is the day I marry the man I gave my heart to.

"Thanks, Mama," I tell her, spinning to give her a hug and motioning for Laura Leigh to join us.

"Group hug," she says and wraps her arms around both of us.

We spend several moments in our hug, sniffling and blinking to avoid ruining any of the makeup before a knock raps against the door.

"Knock, knock, I have your bouquet and we're ready to go," Judy, the wedding planner, singsongs as she walks into the room.

To match the mix of light pink and dusty rose for my wedding colors, my bouquet is a cascade of silk flowers—roses of multiple shades of pink, white camellias, gardenias, and green eucalyptus leaves. I take the proffered bouquet, standing with Mom and

Laura Leigh as the photographer snaps more pictures before turning back for one last glance in the mirror.

Everything is perfect.

I follow Mom and Laura Leigh into the hallway, my eyes landing on the groom's suite where Cole has been all morning. But everyone made sure that we couldn't see each other.

"I have your bouquet!" Sydney comes bounding up the stairs, tossing the bouquet at Laura Leigh.

The two of them have become good friends since Laura Leigh came out for wedding dress shopping, much to Cole's chagrin after demanding that couldn't happen. He didn't need Laura Leigh teaming up with Sydney to give him a hard time.

But the two of them enjoyed it.

"Wow, Cole is going to swallow his tongue," Sydney says and wolf whistles.

Sydney's direct—borderline abrasive—style of communication has taken me a little bit of time to get used to. What I had to learn was that she has a heart of gold and loves my soon-to-be husband and their boss, Sawyer, like the older brothers she never had.

"Thanks, I think," I tell her.

Judy finishes fluffing my train and eyes Sydney and Mom.

"Ladies, we're ready to start." The words are spoken softly, but with enough steel in the undercurrent that both Sydney and Mom rush to do their bidding.

Sydney heads downstairs first, and Mom gives me a hug before descending next.

"Laura Leigh—" Judy points at her.

"Leigh," she interrupts.

It's so hard to think of my baby sister as anyone else except Laura Leigh, but when Cole and I arrived earlier this week for the wedding, she informed us both that she wanted us to call her Leigh from now on.

"Leigh, you're next. Where is your father?"

"Here, I'm here." Dad rushes from down the hall, his white beard trimmed and in place for the occasion.

He freezes just before he reaches us, his eyes softening.

"You're not allowed to be this grown up," he tells me, his eyes suspiciously bright.

"Thank you, Daddy."

"Okay, Dad, you ready?" Judy asks, ushering us both toward the top of the staircase.

Leigh is about halfway down the polished mahogany stairs.

"No. But we can go anyway," he grumbles.

I laugh and slide my arm through his.

The music changes, Pachelbel's "Canon in D" floating up the staircase.

"And here we go," Judy whispers.

Our movement down the stairs is measured, slow, and I keep my eyes trained on the floor to avoid tripping over my dress. It isn't until we're at the bottom that I shift my attention and my gaze finds Cole's.

A giddiness fizzes through my blood at the expression on his face, everyone else fading until it's the two of us as I make my way closer, mesmerized by the heat and adoration that make his brown eyes glow almost amber.

"Who gives this woman to this man?" Pastor Jack asks.

Dad huffs a laugh.

"They've belonged to each other for as long as any of us can remember. But her mother and I give our blessing."

The urge to cry mixes with the need to laugh, and I give in to the laughter. As does Cole.

Truer words have probably never been spoken.

Pastor Jack smiles and nods at Dad.

"Very well. Friends, please be seated," he says.

There's a murmur as everyone sits, but I can't take my eyes off my handsome fiancé. He's wearing a light-tan linen suit, a dusty rose tie knotted at his neck. He reaches out a hand, weaving our fingers together, and reels me closer until our chests are millimeters apart.

"That's far enough, son," Dad warns, and more laughter echoes through the group.

Cole grins, but he doesn't apologize.

"You look beautiful, Honey Girl," he murmurs and squeezes my hand.

"You're not so bad yourself, handsome."

Pastor Jack clears his throat.

"If we're ready to begin," he tells us with a pointed look.

"Almost," Cole answers and leans forward, brushing a chaste kiss against my lips before straightening. "Okay, I'm ready."

"Thank you. As I was about to say, friends, we come together today to share in the joy of the union between Hannah Grace Whittaker and Cole Matthew Strickland. I've had the pleasure to have known the two of them since they were babies in their mothers' arms and have had the privilege to watch them grow up, secure in their friendship, before love found them."

Memories surface at Pastor Jack's words.

Birthday parties with superhero themes.

Class spelling bees and field trips.

Our first kiss shared behind the bleachers at the high school football field when we were fourteen. Homecomings. Proms.

Our first time.

Our proposal.

Sunset to stargazing and every moment in between and every memory since.

"I do," Cole says, pulling me back to the present.

"Will you, Hannah Grace, choose this man from this day forward to be your wedded husband, your best friend, and your only love? To live together, play together, and laugh together? To work by his side and dream in his arms? To fill his heart and feed his soul? To always seek out the best in him, always loving him with all your heart, until the end of your forever? If so, say, 'I do.'"

"I do," I say and Cole tightens his grip around my fingers.

"Do you have the rings?" Pastor Jack asks Cole.

He nods and turns to Sawyer who hands him our wedding bands. Cole hands both to Pastor Jack.

"These rings are a physical representation of the promises you have made to each other. The wedding ring is a symbol of eternity, no beginning and no end. Cole, please take Hannah Grace's ring and place it on her finger, repeating after me. I choose you now and always. Let this ring be a symbol of our marriage, for the promise I make today and tomorrow, and for all the days yet to come. In all times, in all places, and in all ways. Forever."

Cole locks his gaze with mine, his voice ringing out as he repeats the words.

The ring slides on and rests next to my engagement ring, and gooseflesh ripples down my spine.

My turn. Pastor Jack turns to me and gives me the words to say. As if I could forget them. I swallow, butterflies exploding in my stomach as each word takes flight.

"I choose you now and always. Let this ring be a symbol of our marriage, for the promise I make today and tomorrow, and for all the days yet to come. In all times, in all places, and in all ways. Forever."

Cole's smile lights up the world—or at least mine—and he reaches out and interlaces our fingers together.

"Hannah Grace and Cole, you have come here today before your family and friends who have witnessed your love and affection through the joining of hands, and the promises you have made to each other, sealing those promises with the giving and receiving of the rings. Therefore it is my privilege as a minister and by the authority given to me by the State of Tennessee that I now pronounce that you are husband and wife. Cole, you may kiss your bride."

Cole closes the distance, yanking me into his arms as his lips claim mine while our friends and family cheer and applaud. He dips me back, and his brothers cheer louder until he finally sets me back on my feet and we turn toward everyone.

"Friends, it is my privilege to introduce to you for the first time Mr. And Mrs. Cole and Hannah Grace Strickland."

Cole turns back toward me, sweeping me into another toe-curling kiss.

"I couldn't resist kissing my wife," he murmurs against my lips.

"I don't mind if my husband kisses me again," I tell him and weave my fingers through his hair, kissing him back until I moan against his lips.

"Do we have to go to the reception?" he asks and we straighten.

Heat suffuses my cheeks at the whistles and catcalls of our friends and family.

"Yes," I tell him although I wouldn't mind skipping it either, but if I tell him that, he won't hesitate to throw me over his shoulder and make a run for it.

"I love you, Hannah Grace Strickland," he says, lifting his hand to cup my cheek.

"I love you too."

He groans, closing his eyes and running his thumb over my lips as he leans close enough to my ear for words meant only for me.

"I'm counting the hours until we can be alone," he murmurs.

"Me too. Maybe we should start this party so we can get to the happy ever after," I tell him.

He grins, taking a step down the aisle and pulling me with him until the end. The photographer flits around us, capturing every angle for us to look back on later.

Like I could forget.

After all, this is the beginning of our forever.

And I intend to enjoy every moment with the man who owns my heart—yesterday, today, and all of our tomorrows still to come.

———————

Want to go back where it all began?

Read on for a sneak peek of SOLDIER FOR THE STARLING!

SOLDIER FOR THE STARLING

EVIE

The baby's belly laugh carries across the reception room and tugs at my ovaries. Or maybe it's the brawny man inspiring the sound. When my boss, Mia, insisted I tag along to her best friend Michaela's wedding after filming wrapped, I should have declined. I should have gone home.

But I didn't want to give up the chance to ogle Michaela's older brother Sawyer—even if it's from a distance. Because as much as I love to admire him, he knows too much about me. About my past.

Deep blue eyes meet mine, and warmth floods my cheeks. I've been caught staring. I glance away from Sawyer and his nephew quickly, focusing instead on the couples swaying on the dance floor—Michaela and her new husband, West, are there, and so are Mia and her husband, Garrett.

Seven years ago, I dreamed of being part of one of those kinds of couples. Happy, in love. I'd be famous, with a handful of chart-topping albums, and my husband would be supportive and kind. But reality crushed that dream and stomped on it for good measure.

Stop wishing for something that will never happen.

Standing, I grab my small purse and turn my back on the vision, then make my way quickly to the restroom. Two years ago, after I ran away from Brad, I made the decision. I can't let anyone get close enough to ask questions.

Because there would be questions. Ones I had no desire to answer.

At least now, when I look in the mirror, I see a little of myself in the nondescript brown hair and the baggier clothes. I'm... content with being Mia's assistant. She's my friend. And when I'm not at her house or on location with her, I'm at home in my cheerful apartment. I don't venture out except for errands and the occasional trip to a coffee shop she and I found.

My life is predictable. I've curated it that way. Except when Sawyer is close.

"No," I tell my reflection. "There are no feelings there. There can't be."

Taking a deep breath, I wash my hands and stand a little straighter. I'll find Mia and let her know I'm headed back to my room.

Only the first person I see when I open the bathroom door is the one person I was hoping to avoid.

Sawyer King.

Looking sexier than he should in the remnants of his tuxedo —dress pants, white shirt with the top button undone, and a loose bowtie.

"W-what are you doing here?" I swallow to steel the tremor in my voice.

"Looking for you."

"Oh," I breathe out, caught off guard. Immediately, fear settles in my stomach.

I don't want to talk about my history. Especially here. And there's no other reason he'd want to talk to me.

"Why?" I croak out.

"Mia asked me to come find you and let you know she and Garrett were heading back to their room."

I barely hold back a groan. Of course my matchmaking boss would ask the hunky single guy to deliver her message. She could have texted me since my phone is in my bag. But her tactics no longer surprise me. She tried to set me up with Garrett before she realized she was in love with him.

I. Am. Not. Interested. In. Dating.

It may be time to remind her of that. Even if she doesn't understand why.

"Thank you. For letting me know."

I turn and head for the exit, shuffling as quickly as I can in heels.

"You're going to need a ride back to your hotel."

I freeze and spin around. He knows where I'm staying? "H-how—"

"I know where everyone is staying. Curse of the job." He shrugs like that explains it all.

I guess it should, given that he owns a security company.

"Can I give you a lift?" he asks.

My choices are to walk back to the hotel in the dark, grab an Uber or Lyft, driven by a stranger, of course—are there even ride share options available here?—or confine myself in a small space with the only man I've found attractive in years.

Dammit. Is there really a choice?

"Um, okay."

"Are you ready?" His question is a murmur as he steps closer.

Why does the low timbre of his voice affect me the way it does?

"Y-yeah. Yes."

He reaches out to guide me toward the exit, and I shift out of the way. His hand drops, and he puts some additional distance between us.

"My car is this way."

The leather and vanilla scent that clings to him is even stronger in the small space of his rental as he pulls out of the parking lot. The hum of the road is the only sound. No small talk, and no radio.

I brace myself for his questions, dreading the moment he brings up my past.

Only he doesn't.

He drives the car like he does everything else—confidently. With his left hand, he grips the steering wheel easily, while his right arm is propped on the console between us. He doesn't take his eyes off the road, and he doesn't try to fill the silence, like he's content to ride in absolute quiet. I envy that quiet confidence. That assuredness of who he is and the space he inhabits.

Meanwhile, I'm constantly fixated on where I am and who I'm with. Like right now. I've got my attention trained on what's ahead, but when the fingers on his right hand stretch forward, I can feel them. And he's not even touching me. This desire to be closer buffets me like waves crashing on the shore.

The hotel isn't far from the venue, but for my sanity, the ride can't be over soon enough.

"Thank you," I tell him as we pull into the hotel's lot, my fingers already gripping the door handle.

"Can I walk you to your room?"

A small part of me knows I should decline, but the bigger part wins before I can harness my response.

"Okay."

Why did you do that?

Though I hate to admit it, his presence calms all the anxiety that normally filters through my blood. I'm attracted to him, but there's something more. Something I'm afraid to think about too much but loathe to distance myself from the way I normally would.

Without giving me time to rescind my response, he rounds

the car, each of his strides precise and purposeful, and opens my door.

Inside, the lobby lights are dim, and the sound of a TV comes from the office, but we're alone as we make our way to the elevator. The silence continues as I press the button for the third floor. The chime sounds, and then the elevators open to the empty floor.

I don't look at him again until I'm in front of my door and have swiped my key and gripped the handle. All the lights I left on still blaze brightly, and I breathe a sigh of relief. I don't like the dark.

"Thank you." I meet his gaze, then quickly drop my focus to the shiny button near his throat.

"You're welcome."

"Good night, Sawyer." I take a step back to retreat to my room.

"Evie?"

The way he says my name—like he can't help himself—pulls my attention back to his face. Only this time, I can't look away. The deep blue of his irises is magnetic, the color like light filtering through the ocean. And just like the ocean, I could so easily drown in them.

"Evie." This time my name is a whisper on his lips. He lifts his index finger and drags it along my jaw.

For the first time in years, I don't pull away from physical contact—I can't. I want that light touch too much.

"Hmm?"

"You looked beautiful today," he murmurs.

Mia begged me to let her pick my dress, so it's more fitted than usual but still loose around my curves.

"I did?"

"Mm-hmm."

"Thank you."

It's hard to get my words out. My lips tingle with curiosity, almost silencing them. What would it be like to kiss Sawyer? I've kissed guys before. Before Brad. High school boys who had no idea what they were doing. But something tells me Sawyer knows exactly what to do.

We've gone silent again, and his finger continues to drag back and forth along my jaw. The sensation is hypnotic, sending that question—what would it be like to kiss a man like Sawyer?—pulsing through my body until all the anxiety is gone. All the walls I've kept in place are down.

Just once.

Standing on my tiptoes, I cup the back of his neck and tug him down until our lips meet. He sucks in a surprised breath, but it doesn't take him long to take masterful control of the kiss. It's a slow slide of his mouth over mine, small kisses pressed from one side to the other, then he settles them fully into place.

He licks along the seam, requesting entry, and I open for his tongue to tangle with mine. Cupping my face, he brushes his thumb over my cheekbone, as if I'm the most precious thing in his universe.

My fingers flex against his shoulders. I want more than anything to take this further. To be worthy of him. To leave my past behind and stay lost in his kiss.

I allow myself one more heartbeat, then I break the kiss. His eyes flutter open, and the desire in them is nearly crippling. I step back again, shivering at the cool air that rushes between us.

"Evie?" The desire in his eyes turns to confusion, and a frown mars his handsome face.

"Good night, Sawyer." I retreat fully and close the door quickly.

"Good night." His voice is clear on the other side of the door.

Lifting my fingers to my swollen lips, I try to memorize the way his mouth felt pressed against mine.

It's the closest thing to normal I'll ever allow myself to have.

Because Brad is still out there, and my baggage is heavy. I'd never allow myself to burden someone else with it. I may dream about that shared kiss with Sawyer, but my reality is haunted by a very real boogeyman.

THIS ISN'T THE END FOR EVIE AND SAWYER...WANT MORE? You can binge their forced proximity happily ever after, SOLDIER FOR THE STARLING, in KU by scanning the QR code!

ARE YOU READY FOR DETECTIVE FOR THE DEBUTANTE?

He swore he'd never fall in love…until she became the only thing worth falling for…

Coming September 30, 2025

Scan the QR code to pre-order this first responder, age gap, romantic suspense happily ever after on Amazon!

PLAYLIST

The playlist for *Bodyguard for the Beauty Queen* is a mix of music like Taylor Swift's "I Can Do It With a Broken Heart" and "New Rules" by Dua Lipa that best describe Hannah Grace and some great ballads with a country tone like "Spin You Around" by Morgan Wallen and "Cowboy Songs" by George Birge…and everything in between.

In short it's a lot of me in a playlist and such a great representation of the chemistry between both Cole and Hannah Grace.

Want to listen to the music that inspired *Bodyguard for the Beauty Queen*? Check out the playlist on Spotify by searching for the "Bodyguard for the Beauty Queen" playlist or scan the QR code below.

 You can both the playlist and the bonus tracks on my website:
https://www.breannalynnauthor.com

ACKNOWLEDGMENTS

To you. Yes, you. The one who just read Cole and Hannah Grace's story! Thank you for taking the chance on the two of them. When I wrote Cole into *Soldier*, I knew he was going to have an amazing love story. And he didn't disappoint!

To Dennis—for two years of our crazy shenanigans!

To the Twinx—maybe someday you'll read this and maybe you won't. But if you do, know how much I love you.

Claire and Alina—I have always felt that the reason I am where I am today is because of you two. Thank you for being my cheerleaders!

To Tonya—thank you for the early feedback on *Bodyguard for the Beauty Queen* and all your help in getting Cole and Hannah Grace's love story prepped!

To my Alpha Readers, my Betas, and my ARC team—your excitement as you anticipated reading Cole and Hannah Grace's story kept the words flowing! Thank you for being patient! I hope you enjoyed *Bodyguard for the Beauty Queen*!

I can't imagine this journey without any of you! XOXO

ALSO BY BREANNA LYNN

Heart Beats Series

Written in the Beat

In The Beat of the Moment

Keeping the Beat

Betting on the Beat

Embracing the Beat

Falling for the Beat

SAFE Haven Security

Soldier for the Starling

Bodyguard for the Beauty Queen

Detective for the Debutante

Stand alone novellas

Rockin' Around the Christmas Tree

Midnight in Mistletoe

Hating Mr. Write

One Weekend in Vegas

She's rebuilding her life. He's fighting to save his career. Falling for each other was never part of the plan.

Charlie has spent the past year piecing her life back together after an injury nearly shattered her dream of dancing forever. She's focused, determined—and not looking for distractions.

Jax Bryant has burned through headlines, patience, and second chances. With his rockstar image spiraling out of control, his label gives him one last shot to clean up his act. Love? That's not on the schedule.

But then he meets Charlie. She's everything he didn't know he needed—and exactly what he can't afford to lose.

When the label delivers an ultimatum that could cost him everything, Jax has to choose: the career he's built or the woman who's changed everything.

See where it all began. Keep reading for a sneak peek of WRITTEN IN THE BEAT!

ABOUT THE AUTHOR

Breanna Lynn lives in Colorado with her two sets of twins (affectionately referred to as the Twinx), her boyfriend, his son, their two dogs, and three cats. A classy connoisseur of all things coffee, Breanna spends her free time keeping the Twinx from taking over the world. When not coordinating chaos, Breanna can be found binge reading, listening to music, or watching rom-coms with a giant bowl of popcorn.

Want to follow Breanna? Scan the QR code for all the ways to stay caught up!